ZOMBIE
APOCALYPSE! ENDGAME

SHOCK XPRESS

INSIDE:

WIN GRAVE MISDEMEANOURS AND BRAIN DEAD ON VIDEO!
INTERVIEWS WITH NIGHT OF THE LIVING DEAD'S
GEORGE A. ROMERO! TALKING ITALIAN ZOMBIES WITH
LUCIO FULCI, ANDREA BIANCHI, CLAUDIO FRAGASSO,
DAVID WARBECK AND LUCIANO PIGOZZI!
RAMSEY CAMPBELL'S NEW COLUMN LOOKS AT THE
FILM CAREER OF THOMAS MOREBY!
REVIEWS OF RE-ANIMATOR 2 . . . THE DEAD NEXT DOOR
. . . BEVERLEY HILLS BODY SNATCHERS . . . SPIRIT VS.
ZOMBI . . . THE DEAD PIT . . . AND MANY MORE!
BELA LUGOSI IN WHITE ZOMBIE!
VIDEOS CONSUMED! LETTERS DIGESTED!
BRAINS! BLOOD! BABES!

Vol.3 Issue 2. £1.75

Winter 1989

GEORGE A. ROMERO
LUCIO FULCI

ANDREA BIANCHI
RAMSEY'S RUMINATIONS

ZOMBIE APOCALYPSE! ENDGAME

Created by Stephen Jones

With

Peter Atkins
Randy Broecker
Ramsey Campbell
Les Edwards
Brian Hodge
Nancy Kilpatrick
Paul McAuley
Lou Morgan
Kim Newman
John Llewellyn Probert
Michael Marshall Smith

Stephen Baxter
Pat Cadigan
Peter Crowther
Jo Fletcher
Paul Kane
Alison Littlewood
Gary McMahon
Lisa Morton
Thana Niveau
Angela Slatter
Conrad Williams

ROBINSON

RUNNING PRESS
PHILADELPHIA · LONDON

ROBINSON

First published in Great Britain in 2014 by Robinson

Zombie Apocalypse! Endgame
© Stephen Jones, 2014

"Zombie Apocalypse!" and "ZA!"
© Stephen Jones. All rights reserved.

The moral right of the author has been asserted.

A CIP catalogue record for this book
is available from the British Library.

ISBN 978-1-47210-642-1 (paperback)
ISBN 978-1-47210-643-8 (ebook)

Design by Basement Press, Glaisdale
Printed and bound by CPI Group (UK) Ltd, Croydon, CR0 4YY

Robinson
is an imprint of
Constable & Robinson Ltd
100 Victoria Embankment
London EC4Y 0DY

An Hachette UK Company
www.hachette.co.uk

www.constablerobinson.com

First published in the United States in 2014 by Running Press Book Publishers,
A Member of the Perseus Books Group

Books published by Running Press are available at special discounts for bulk purchases in the
United States by corporations, institutions, and other organizations. For more information, please
contact the Special Markets Department at the Perseus Books Group, 2300 Chestnut Street, Suite
200, Philadelphia, PA 19103, or call (800) 810-4145, ext. 5000, or email
special.markets@perseusbooks.com.

US ISBN: 978-0-7624-5465-5
US Library of Congress Control Number: 2014936269

9 8 7 6 5 4 3 2 1
Digit on the right indicates the number of this printing

Running Press Book Publishers
2300 Chestnut Street
Philadelphia, PA 19103-4371

Visit us on the web!
www.runningpress.com

I want to go ahead of Father Time
with a scythe of my own.

H. G. Wells

MOREBY IN THE MEDIA

By Ramsey Campbell

Who's the occultist who shows up most often in the media? I imagine we'd all say Aleister Crowley. Most people who know would point out that Karswell in 'Casting the Runes' and *Night of the Demon* is based on him, and he's the model for Oscar Clinton in 'He Cometh and He Passeth By', not to mention Mocata in *The Devil Rides Out* and Rowley Thorne, John Thunstone's adversary in Manly Wellman's series of tales. He's even on the cover of *Sgt. Pepper's Lonely Hearts Club Band* (though we'll come back to that), and looms in Led Zeppelin's background. Several of Kenneth Anger's films are based on his magic. He's the man who gets all the pub-

licity, but he has nothing on Thomas Moreby, whom nearly all of us may never have heard of.

He was a pupil of Nicholas Hawksmoor (although he isn't mentioned by name in Peter Ackroyd's novel). He helped build several of Hawksmoor's final churches and was responsible for a later one, All Hallows in Blackheath. There's disagreement over whether he picked up his interest in the occult from Hawksmoor or taught it to his master, but it's clear that they both incorporated magical elements in the churches they constructed. Moreby went on to design country houses, concealing occult secrets in the process. When Sir Francis Dashwood

(founder of the Hellfire Club) employed him to redesign Medmenham Abbey, Moreby provided the motto above the front door, 'Do what thou wilt' (which Crowley made famous, but he confided to his associates that he had learned much from studying Moreby's life). It was also Moreby's idea to extend the caves (renamed the Hellfire Caves) beneath the abbey, where he had located a pre-Christian altar. This rediscovery prompted Dashwood to have Moreby restore the local St. Lawrence Church as an openly pre-Christian edifice. While Dashwood never identified the ancient cult he sought to revive, it was rumoured to be the Well of Seven, an occult society so sinister that he may even have used the Hellfire Club as a device to distract attention from it. Supposedly the famous St. Lawrence church tower – topped with a golden ball that contains six seats "from which all creation may be viewed" – signifies this association, and so do the six bells in the tower. This may explain an obscure pronouncement by John Wilkes, a leading member of the Hellfire Club: "Seven is the number of the resonance; the globe resounds with the six-fold peal of those who mount within" – apparently one of the few recorded examples of what's called the Wisdom of the Well.

We'll come back to the Well of Seven. Moreby is said to have lived until 1803, when he was over a hundred years old. He may have been killed in a riot or died in Bedlam. While his occult leanings weren't known to many in his lifetime, they were rediscovered by various interested parties after his death. The Ghost Club began to investigate his work until one of the founders, E.W. Benson (father of E.F., R.H. and A.C. – a dynasty of supernatural authors – and later to become Archbishop of Canterbury) forbade all research into Moreby's life and practices. This earned him notoriety among writers – Dickens and Conan Doyle were both members of the Ghost Club – and perhaps that's one reason why M.R. James based Count Magnus on him.

James appears to have regretted this as well as referring to the Black Pilgrimage, an occult excursion Moreby had made to the accursed city of Chorazin. In May 1904

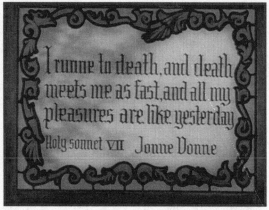

James wrote to his illustrator James McBryde "On further reflection I do not think I care to see Magnus illustrated at all – that is, the Count himself. I think it best to ensure by this means that even an accidental resemblance to the historical model T— M— is avoided. If my publishers were not so insistent on having a book I might well prefer to suppress the tale, for it has been giving me some horrid visions in the night lately." Less than a month later McBryde died young, from complications after an appendix operation that should have been routine. He left two illustrations for 'Count Magnus' uncompleted, but his sister apparently told James that the artist had destroyed a third.

Lovecraft borrowed Moreby too. In January 1927 he wrote to Donald Wandrei "My return to my beloved Providence has inspired me to renewed endeavours. I am at work on a new short story, based in part upon material brought to my attention by my favourite

adopted grandson, the ebullient & erudite Belknapius *(author Frank Belknap Long. S.J.)* In some shadowed bookstore in a New York alley where few human feet have trod, he found a mouldering tome which whispered of one Thomas Moreby, occult architect & seeker of dread secrets which history prefers to veil. It appears that he believed the 'essential saltes' of corpses could be used to reconstitute the dead, by some method I am now at pains to imagine. Alas, Belknap lacked the lucre for an immediate purchase, & when he returned some days later, the bookseller denied that the volume had ever been in the shop. From his quick perusal Belknap also brought away an impression that Moreby, already said to be over a century old, might have survived far longer. What a boon his like may be to my tale! Indeed, the tome (the name of which my forgetful grandson sadly cannot bring to mind) apparently suggested that the Shelleys were wont to dally near Moreby's grave, which exerted a sufficient influence on Mary's dreams to inspire *Frankenstein*. Might this obscure scribbler from Providence be similarly possessed to pen a masterwork?"

In fact, Lovecraft based Charles Dexter Ward's evil ancestor Joseph Curwen on Moreby – at the time he was writing it he thought *The Case of Charles Dexter Ward* would be a short story, much as Stephen King found *The Mist* outgrowing his original notion of it. Lovecraft also wrote in his Commonplace Book of notes for stories: "Moreby's resurrection by employment of 'essential saltes'. Hideous marriage of necromancer & wife he has summoned from grave. Unholy ceremony conducted by corpses. What offspring may this union produce?" This was presumably Lovecraft's inspiration rather than actual material from the book Frank Belknap Long mentioned to him, and I used it in my early story 'The Horror from the Bridge'.

The use of "essential saltes" appears to have been Moreby's contribution to the Well of Seven, whose central aim was physical immortality. Some members of the cult may have been buried in Hob's Lane in Deptford, an area that subsequently became known for inexplicable disturbances. Nigel Kneale is said to have based *Quatermass and the Pit* on these rumours, and in his studies of British witchcraft Gerald Gardner identified the horned apparition in the last episode of the television serial with Anarchon, Lord of Fleas, a demon apparently regarded by the Well of Seven as their occult patron. Gardner also claimed that William Blake's monstrous painting *The Ghost of a Flea* (based on a vision Blake had during a séance) was both a version of Anarchon and a reference to the fleas the demon brings (fleas Blake described as "inhabited by the souls of such men as were by nature blood thirsty to excess", but regarded by the cult as somehow conferring immortality). According to Gardner, the cult's secret sign – four fingers of the left hand fully extended at the same time as three of the right, while both thumbs and the remaining finger are pressed against the palms (not as easy as it sounds: try it yourself) – is concealed in many paintings, including religious images. Sometimes it's signified by the right hand of one figure and the left hand of its neighbour (in the Bayeux Tapestry, for instance) or by these hands in the two panels of a diptych, even occasionally the outer panels of a triptych (see works by Bosch, Rubens, Lippi, Brueghel the Elder and others). Gardner apparently believed some of these images were meant as warning messages to the well-informed viewer, but others may reveal that the painter was involved with the Well of Seven.

An engineer at EMI claims he overheard John Lennon proposing Moreby for inclusion in the collage on the *Sgt. Pepper* cover. An image of Crowley was used instead, whether since he would be more recognisable by the public or because other members of the band objected (as they did to Lennon's other unused suggestions, Christ and Hitler) isn't clear. Or could pressure have been brought to bear by the cult itself? That certainly seems to have been the case with the Val Lewton film *The Seventh Victim*.

This wasn't the first film to include references to Moreby and the Well. A 1915 silent serial, *The Seven Wizards*, apparently began the trend. The film was written by Charles W. Goddard (best known for *The Perils of Pauline* and *The Ghost Breakers*) and made by Wharton Incorporated in Ithaca, New York. Like the Whartons' other overtly occult serial *The Mysteries of Myra* (1916), which is said to have alluded to the Well under the name of the Black Order, the 1915 serial appears to be completely lost – in fact, some film histories suggest both films were deliberately destroyed. A review of *The Seven Wizards* in *Variety* questioned whether resurrection was a subject for entertainment. The reviewer also advised the makers to take more care with their intertitles; in some episodes the leader of the cult is called Moseby, in others Morley. Perhaps this was intended to suggest that neither was the real name.

White Zombie (1932) offers several details to the knowing audience. Murder Legendre (Bela Lugosi) is constantly attended by six zombies – in other words, a band of seven – and the six remove the heroine in her coffin from the vault, again adding up to seven undead. We're told that voodoo and the revival of the dead were "old when Egypt was young", and other lines of dialogue suggest that the practices are based on ancient magic. Beaumont, the plantation owner who turns to Legendre for help in winning the heroine, reacts with horror when the zombie master whispers her fate in his ear. Even before the Hays Code came into play, the film mutes Legendre's original line (obviously based on Moreby's notion of occult marriage) that the planter would be marrying the dead. The film also stops short of showing the sign of the Seven, instead concealing it within the gesture Legendre makes to control the zombies. However, several shots show Beaumont making it in the midst of his convulsions once Legendre has drugged him. The film's director Victor Halperin also alluded to the Seven in *Supernatural*, his 1933 film about the resurrection of a serial killer, and particularly in *Revolt of the Zombies* (1936). However, he subsequently denied all interest in horror and expressed regret for making these films. It has been suggested that he'd been made to regret referring to the Well.

The most detailed Hollywood treatment of the Seven would have been *The Seventh Victim*. Val Lewton had already referred obliquely to them in *I Walked with a Zombie*, where the zombie who guards the path to magic is called Carrefour after Moreby's zombie servant. Later *Bedlam* would recall Moreby by having Karloff play Sims, the apothecary general of the asylum where Moreby is rumoured to have been an inmate. Just as *Cat People* was originally to have been based on Algernon Blackwood's 'Ancient Sorceries', *The Seventh Victim* would have dealt with a young woman's search for her sister, who had fallen under the influence of the Well of Seven. The younger sister was to rescue her, only to discover that she is already a zombie, who is recaptured in the final reel by a private eye employed in the search, now himself undead. Very little of this remains in the film that was made, but *The Seventh Victim* is full of hints of the secret it had to keep.

Mary Gibson still tries to find her elder sister Jacqueline, who has joined a cult. In some prints, particularly of the European release, the stained-glass windows over the stairs at the school Mary attends display the sign of the Seven. The room Jacqueline has rented above an Italian restaurant proves to contain just a chair and above it a noose. The restaurant is called Dante's, no doubt to remind us of the number of deadly sins and virtues in the poet's epic, and the room is – yes – number seven. The legend above the entrance to a morgue Mary visits in her search is "He calleth all his children by their name", a motto Moreby added to Francis Dashwood's church during the restoration. (While it sounds scriptural, it isn't to be found in the Bible, and may have a more occult significance.) Irving August, the private eye who helps Mary in her search, is murdered when he enters a locked room at La Sagesse, the cosmetic firm Jacqueline signed over to the cult. The name of the firm clearly refers to the Wisdom of the Well, and the door of the locked room is the seventh one we see at La Sagesse (although the firm may also recall Maison Desti, the cosmetics company owned by Preston Sturges' mother, who practised magic with Crowley and manufactured the scarf that strangled her friend Isadora Duncan). After the murder Mary flees to the subway but seems to be trapped on the train; she keeps passing 14th Street (twice seven, of course). She consults Louis Judd, Jacqueline's psychiatrist, who is one of the film's clearest references to the revival of the dead practised by the Seven; he has already been killed in an earlier Lewton production, *Cat People*. Later Jacqueline refers to "coming back to life", a line left over from her undead character in the original draft of the screenplay. The La Sagesse trademark is also the sigil of the cult in the film, a triangle inside a parallelogram – seven points, in other words. Mary finds herself a teaching job and leads a kindergarten class in singing 'Oranges and Lemons' – which, in the version printed in *Songs Every Child Can Sing Well* (1803), names several Moreby churches. As the cultists attempt to persuade Jacqueline to do away with herself for betraying them, one of them plays sevenths on a piano. The assassin who pursues Jacqueline through the streets is played by an actor chosen to resemble the murdered private eye – not quite a resurrection but suggestive of one. In the final scene Jacqueline's dying neighbour goes out for a night on the town, and we hear the chair fall in Jacqueline's room, recalling Judd's enigmatic line in the original screenplay – "No resurrection without sacrifice" – that apparently refers to a tenet of the Wisdom of the Seven.

Two final points about *The Seventh Victim* – Lewton's wittiest details. In the film the Seven are replaced by the Palladists, a Satanic cult so genteel that we never see a ritual or even a magical device. This is Lewton's way of signifying that they're not just a substitution but an attempt to tone down the reality to placate the actual cult. The Palladists did exist – or rather, they're a matter of historical record, but in fact they were fabricated in the 1890s by the anticlerical French journalist Léo Taxil as a hoax at the expense of the Catholic church. Lewton presumably hoped some of his audience would recognise that the cult in the film was so thoroughly fictitious that it must disguise something else. Undoubtedly he meant informed viewers to notice the betraying detail in the quotation from John Donne that opens the film ("I run to death, and death meets me as fast, And all my pleasures are like yesterday.") The quote is accurate, but it comes from Donne's first holy sonnet. In his subtlest touch Lewton misattributes it on-screen to the seventh sonnet, which contains the formula "Arise, arise from death".

Since then the cinema appears to have been wary of referring to the Seven – perhaps the pressure exerted on Lewton was enough to deter others, and the film industry may have included members of the cult – although Mike Raven is said to have concealed allusions in his horror films and later in his paintings, which were first exhibited in the crypt of a Hawksmoor church (St. George's, Bloomsbury). The Seven have kept their secrets well enough that little else is known about them. Their name is supposed to refer to Beersheba, the Biblical name that has been translated as "well of the oath" besides "well of the seven". Their oath is meant to be the Oath of the Abyss, which Jack Parsons – rocket scientist at Caltech and leading member of Crowley's occult organisa-tion – took when he made the Black Pilgrimage to Chorazin. A crater on the dark side of the moon is named after him.

So there we have it: a mass of strange glimpses that may fit together in ways we can't quite see. Perhaps we never will. Since the Seven seem hardly to have been heard of since they leaned on Lewton, they may have faded into history. No harm in keeping our eyes open, though, and I'll be happy to report sightings in a future issue. It will take more than an obscure occult society to silence *Shock Xpress*.

LAST AND FIRST MEN

A STORY OF THE NEAR AND FAR FUTURE

BY

W. OLAF STAPLEDON

SECOND EDITION

METHUEN & CO. LTD.
36 ESSEX STREET W.C.
LONDON

SIMON'S FIELD,
CALDY,
WEST KIRBY,
WIRRAL,
HOYLAKE 1154

13th February 1946

My Dear H.G.,

I was motivated to write to you again, having read (and admired, but not much enjoyed!) your latest.[1] Indeed I was moved to look again at a copy I kept of my very first correspondence with you -- perhaps you remember it, a gushing note I sent on publication of my own first romance[2] -- about a chap not recording his debt to the air he breathes, and so on and so forth.

You know that I admire you, that you dominate the landscape of my mind, as your Time Traveller's Sphinx dominated the England of the year 802,701 A.D. And yet I do not follow you, H.G., not without question.

And I cannot follow you now, into the vale of gloom which you so eloquently explore in your latest.

Of course I agree with you that it is hard to be optimistic about the state of mankind, given the horrors which we have seen exposed as the Nazi tyranny has unravelled since August last, like a bandage drawn back from a suppurating wound -- and you may recall that with my service as an ambulance driver in the last lot I saw enough of that. The industrialisation of pain, the

organisation of death! And all in pursuit of a theory of
the perfectibility of blood and race . . .

(Incidentally, and oddly enough, you and I share a grisly
connection with the camps of death, though you will not
welcome knowing it. On the publication of my *Last & First
Men* in '30 I was contacted by a fellow called Tomas Moerbitz,
a German "chemist„ as he called himself -- a prominent and
wealthy industrialist as it turned out, and later a
significant supplier to the Nazi machine -- a ghastly one-
eyed fellow judging³ by recent photographs.

(Moerbitz claimed to have sought you out in London after
your *Time Machine*, with suggestions on human evolution and
perfectibility in stark disagreement with the content of
your novel -- as well as arguments with your portrayal of
time travel⁴-- and claimed too that as a consequence of
that meeting he had been the inspiration for the Moreau of
your novel. If so it must have been a memorable but
unpleasant encounter for you, H.G., which would rather
satisfy the fellow I think. The name's the thing --
Moerbitz, Moreau -- a plasticity of names, and "the
plasticity of living forms„, to quote your own words back at
you, was his subject matter, his fascination.

(He also had the gall to praise my own *Last & First* for
showing whole human species created and raised up by the
appliance of eugenic science in the deep future. A prophet
of the blood and the scalpel, he called me. Described my
book as an inspirational vision! Well, in the war, as well
as stocking the death camps with poison gas, it seems
Moerbitz bloodied his own hands with practical experiments
of that sort.

(And now, according to sources I shall not trouble you
with naming, he has escaped the justice of the trials by
attaching himself to the Peenemunde rocket group who have
fled to the bosom of America. Ugh -- enough of him!)

No, H.G., in spite of it all, I cannot agree with you that even the horrors of the recent war presage the end of things -- that as the latest war recedes into the past, "extinction is coming to man„. Who can say what our ultimate destiny is? But we shan't be extinguished in the near future at least. We need only watch our own ragged children, happily playing amid the rosebay willow herb that flourishes in the bomb sites of our scarred cities, to be assured of that. I myself am determined to throw my remaining energies into a quest for global peace, and trust that you, my model, my inspiration, will yet find it in your heart to forgive the rest of us for our faults, and rejoin me in hope.

Yours very truly as ever,

W. Olaf Stapledon

1/ H.G. Wells, Mind at the End of its Tether, Heinemann, 1945

2/ Olaf Stapledon, Last and First Men, Methuen, 1930.

3/ H.G. Wells, The Time Machine, Heinemann, 1895.

4/ H.G. Wells, The Island of Doctor Moreau, Heinemann, 1896.

Tomas Moerbitz (d.o.b. unknown) was the principal shareholder in Todt Chemie-AG, a chemical company specialising in the manufacture of industrial gases. Founded in the late 19th century by another Tomas Moerbitz, in 1925 Todt joined with several other German chemical companies to form the conglomerate IG Farben.

At the time the largest chemical company in the world, IG Farben was involved in numerous war crimes in World War II. IG Farben was seized by the allies in 1945, and liquidated in 1952.

Among the surviving successor companies are BASF, Bayer and Hoechst. Todt did not survive, and indeed its contribution to IG Farben is poorly documented. Moerbitz, however, went on to found the U.S. corporation New World Pharmaceuticals Group, it is rumoured with funds smuggled out of IG Farben through Swiss bank accounts during the closing stages of the war. But despite the strenuous efforts of those who objected to the presence of such men as Wernher von Braun and Moerbitz in American public life, this was never proved.

OUR WORLD IN *THEIR* HANDS?

PHARMACEUTICAL COMPANY'S SECRET BID TO RULE THE WORLD UNCOVERED!

A *HARD NEWS* EXCLUSIVE
by Janet Ramsey,
Head of Current Affairs

A DECADE AGO, almost no one had ever heard of New World Pharmaceuticals Group – but today this secretive organisation ranks alongside Pfizer, Johnson & Johnson, Roche and Glaxo-SmithKline as one of the top five drug research companies in the world.

And if they have their way, within the next few years they will be double the size of all those companies put together – thanks to a mysterious family dynasty which has run the company ever since its modest start-up almost five decades ago.

NWP was originally founded by wealthy German industrialist Tomas Moerbitz, who fled to America after World War II. However, despite being linked by a number of Death Camp survivors to the Holocaust, he is reputed to have escaped the Nuremberg Trials through his wealth and influence. After working on the fledgling U.S. space programme for several years with such fellow émigrés as Wernher von Braun, he went on to create the pharmaceuticals company in an attempt to develop cures for smallpox and typhus.

Since control of the company passed to Moerbitz's son, T. J., a few years ago, this giant in medical research and development has grown into an $85 billion dollar (in excess of £56 billion) corporation, comfortably topping even Johnson & Johnson, which turns over $60 billion a year.

Last week's shock announcement that New World Pharmaceuticals Group has toppled American giant Johnson & Johnson from the top of the table was followed by rumours that it is making a hostile take-over bid for Novartis Vaccines and Diagnostics – specifically to get its hands on Novartis' innovative work using reverse genetics to manufacture vaccines for avian flu.

But in Britain, the Competition Commission – known as the Monopolies and Mergers Commission until last year – is already considering last week's surprise offer for German company Chemie Grünenthal, the family firm responsible for releasing the deformed babies drug thalidomide into 46 countries and continuing to sell the so-called "wonder drug" for months after Australian doctor William McBride had linked thalidomide to the sudden rash of deaths and hideously deformed births in 1961.

The unspecified but "generous" offer was initially withdrawn when the commission put forward its concerns about NWP linking itself with the company which was responsible for 100,000 miscarriages and thousands of serious deformities to the babies who survived, but the offer was re-presented after a public statement from NWP accused its rivals of trying to derail a deal which would be excellent for employees and shareholders of both companies alike.

Speaking for the NWP board from their offices just outside Baltimore, Mr Bill Pogany said, "Ill-informed scuttlebutt has done untold damage to a well-respected and venerable firm which has contributed greatly to the world of medical research. Chemie Grünenthal has always been known as the home of innovation and excellence, and as such will be a welcome addition to the NWP family."

And from the UK headquarters Dr M. T. Déesharné said, "Many companies have moments in their history that they would wish never happened, but every company, like every person, is the sum of its experiences, and there is no doubt that Grünenthal's experiences have resulted in some exciting developments the medical world has been watching with anticipation.

"New World believes that with our backing and funds, the company will be better able to fulfil its potential, which will be of enormous benefit to this country and indeed the world. Our aim has always been to make life better."

But our source has revealed that NWP has little interest in the painkilling drugs for which Grünenthal is now known; instead, the reclusive businessman who now heads the board is desperate to get his hands on the work of brilliant Nazi chemists Otto Ambros and Heinrich Mückter (see sidebar) – especially their experiments on controlling the deadly disease typhus.

But NWP CEO T. J. Moerbitz has denied there are any sinister reasons for the sudden expansion of the company. Through a press officer he agreed to speak to *Hard News* from the multi-national company's British headquarters, a state-of-the-art laboratory believed to be somewhere in the West Country.

"The word will soon know our name"

In his first public interview for several years, Mr Moerbitz told me, "Our motto – I believe you would call it a 'Mission Statement' – is 'Your World in Our Hands' and you must believe me when I tell you that is something we take very seriously indeed.

"Today the New World Pharmaceuticals Group comprises a number of researchers and businessmen who have severed our ties with pharmaceutical companies with whom we have enjoyed many years of fruitful relationships to come together to serve the common good.

"Thanks to the work of NWP I can assure you that Britain is now at the forefront of disease research. We have great plans for the future, and when our acquisitions of Grünenthal and Novartis have been satisfactorily concluded, I believe this country will quickly see the benefit. We already have some of the most brilliant men – and women – in the world working within the NWP family, and the whole world will soon come to know our name."

But not everyone in the New World Pharmaceuticals Group family believes in Mr Moerbitz's benevolent plan.

One researcher told us, "We have a whole department doing DNA sequencing on old bones and teeth dug from cemeteries and even plague pits, and another studying radical deviations in disease pandemics. It feels like we're preparing for something major – but anyone who is heard asking the big questions seems to leave the company soon after.

"A mate at Novatis told me NWP is trying to get its hands on the Influenza Genome Sequencing Project, even though it's a multi-company project – everyone knows how ambitious Mr Moerbitz is. I wouldn't put it past him."

But T. J. Moerbitz is an enigma even within his company. One chemist told us, "No one's ever even seen this Mr Moerbitz – when I worked for my last company our CEO used to walk the floor regularly – I do believe he knew every employee by name, even though we had more than 2,000 people on the books."

And another source close to the CEO's office told us, "Here – well, there's no doubt the labs are the most modern I've ever seen, and no expense is spared in R&D – we don't have any limits on what we can spend on Mr Moerbitz's pet projects – but no one really knows what they are: everyone knows their own job, and anyone caught discussing anything with a different department immediately gets a final written warning – it's really scary, sometimes. I feel like I'm constantly being watched.

"And you should see our consent forms! I've never seen one like that – once you've signed, that's it: you're ours for life, no matter what! And even if your body gets reanimated – what's that about? If people really understood what NWP were going to do with them they'd run a million miles rather than sign."

Protecting Patents? Or Planning for Disaster?

Mr Moerbitz was quick to deny anything underhand was going on. "Consent forms must look scary to everyone the first time they read one," he said. "I defy anyone to find anything illegal in what we are doing.

"As for our insistence on confidentiality: in the pharmaceutical industry there is, I regret to say, an enormous amount of industrial espionage. Of course we trust each and every one of our employees implicitly, but we would be fools to make it easy for anyone to divulge company secrets. The R&D to secure a successful patent is not inconsiderable, and obviously one protects one's upcoming drugs: they are, in effect, the company's crown jewels."

When we asked Mr Moerbitz about the company's readiness for a global pandemic, he was more open. "Of course we, like every other responsible member of the pharmaceutical trade, are preparing for the worst while hoping it never happens. I would be the first to beg the Almighty to ensure avian flu remains a nightmare rather than reality.

"But planning for a secret pandemic? Do you really think her Britannic Majesty's Government would not know if that were the case?"

Department of Health spokesman Euan Chambers denied any such knowledge. "We are always researching changing diseases, but there is no new pandemic surfacing that we know of," he said. "We have enough on our hands dealing with the influenza virus, which mutates every year."

Turn to page 7 for our exposé:
The Flu That Kills!

MOERBITZ – RECLUSIVE PHILANTHROPIST OR RELATED TO ZOMBIE KING?

MR T. J. MOERBITZ, the mysterious figure who heads global drug company New World Pharmaceuticals, is a well-spoken and obviously highly educated man – but *Hard News* could find no trace of him dating back more than a decade. This is not unusual for a moneyed man who wishes to hide past misdeeds, but it is highly unusual in the pharmaceutical industry, where birth, educational and social background can have strong influences on future relationships.

Despite his family name and connections, he appeared in Debrett's *People of Today* last year for the first time, where details are few and he is described only as "a reclusive genius and philanthropist". His place of residence is given as the company's UK registered headquarters. His only listed hobby is "architecture" – which led our sister paper, the *London Sketch*, to speculate that because of the similarity in their names, NWP's T.J. Moerbitz might in fact be distantly related to the 18th-century architect Thomas Moreby. Known as "the Zombie King", Moreby was once apprenticed to Nicholas Hawksmoor, who was himself nicknamed "the black magician" after designing a "Devil Worship power-matrix" of six churches and two obelisks in London.

The infamous architect was fascinated with the idea of rebirth, and those within the drugs industry claim our own Mr Moerbitz shared that fascination.

However, Moerbitz shrugged off the allegations, saying, "Who isn't interested in eternal life? But I fear I am too busy with more mundane concerns to devote much time to fantasy these days."

We will watch New World Pharmaceuticals Group's new patents with interest.

EVIL NAZI PAST OF "BRILLIANT CHEMIST"

THE SURPRISE BID by New World Pharmaceuticals Group for Chemie Grünenthal, a little-known German company which generates most of its income from pain medication, shocked the pharmaceutical word and took the Stock Exchange by surprise, judging by the sudden rise in share prices on Friday. NWP announced its specific interest in Grünenthal's R&D into typhus – but our investigations department has uncovered the evil truth behind that knowledge: it came from the Nazi death camps!

The now-defunct *Daily Beast* revealed the full extent of Grünenthal's murderous research in their groundbreaking work *The Nazis and Thalidomide: The Worst Drug Scandal of All Time*. Not only was the company responsible for inflicting thalidomide on an unsuspecting world, but Nazi scientist Otto Ambros, Hitler's advisor on chemical warfare, was one of the four inventors of the lethal sarin gas, and later was believed to have used his own experiences to cover up the trail that led from the production of thalidomide back to any origins it may have had in Hitler's death camps.

Fellow scientist and head of research Heinrich Mückter used death-camp inmates to further his anti-typhus work. The disease was rife in the army, and he was determined to find a vaccine – his ingenious solution was keeping the culture alive by injecting it into prisoners in camps like Auschwitz, Buchenwald, Grodno and Kraków. He was reportedly responsible for the deaths of hundreds of prisoners, not just by infecting them, but by then using them as guinea pigs to test his prototype vaccines.

After the Nuremberg trials both Mückter and Ambros were released and welcomed into the United States where, like their colleague Tomas Moerbitz – the father of NWP's current CEO – they were tasked with working on anti-Cold War measures like . . .

(cont. p. 17)

STOP PRESS

Police are appealing for witnesses after the mutilated body of Jessica Vannhelssin was found in a remote beauty spot in Pembrokeshire early this morning. Jessica, 29, was last seen leaving The Consort's Arms in St Bride's Bay at 9:00 p.m. last night.

Detective Sergeant Simon Norwich of Pembrokeshire CID said, "We are trying to establish the exact circumstances that led up to this crime. Anyone who might have seen Ms Vannhelssin is asked to get in touch."

Jessica, a personal assistant for a multi-national company, was a blue-eyed brunette, cut in a short bob. She stood 5ft 5in tall and weighed around 8 stone. The last time she was seen she was wearing distressed denim Guess jeans and a pale blue T-shirt with a Swarovski crystal star on the front.

Call Pembrokeshire Police on 909 quoting serial 731 of 07/7 or the independent charity Crimehalt anonymously on 0845 666 11.

MISSING BOY FOUND; FRIEND MISSING, PRESUMED DEAD

Hunt called off after two teenage boys vanished from a "haunted" churchyard

AUGUST 20, 1993: The identity of the amnesiac teenage boy discovered in the graveyard of All Hallows Church last night is now confirmed as Andy Jarvis, 13, who disappeared a week ago with his best friend, Roderick "Roddy" Chu.

There is still no sign of Roddy, also 13, and police say that budget cuts mean they have no choice but to now scale down the hunt.

Brown-haired, brown-eyed Andy was still wearing his favourite black T-shirt with the *Tombstone* logo when he was found wandering through the graveyard a few minutes before midnight.

His father Rip Jarvis said, "We checked that church a million times or more – God knows where my boy was. But we're just relieved to have him back."

A spokesman for University Hospital Lewisham confirmed Andy was suffering from shock, but was otherwise unharmed. "At this point in time he has little memory of the events after he left his school at midday on Friday 13 August," said hospital press officer Ransy Rumbole. "We are obviously hoping that he will remember enough to help us find his friend Roderick, who is still missing. The police are investigating the church crypt again, following an interview with young Andy. It may be that his fears of "shadowy figures" are simply nightmares spawned by his dreadful experiences.

"Obviously our thoughts go out to Roderick's family at this time."

A Met spokesman described Roddy Chu as being of "Asian appearance, black hair and brown eyes, around five feet eight inches tall". He was wearing a blue sweatshirt, denim jeans and Nike "Air Max" trainers.

DEVIL WORSHIPPERS – KIDNAPPERS?

LOCALS claimed the boys, who vanished on Friday 13 August, exactly a week ago, had been taken by "devil worshippers" who are alleged to "worship" at the condemned church in Blackheath Road, SE.

Their disappearance, which was reported by science teacher Ms Sara Barker after they failed to turn up for the end-of-week chemistry test at the Tower of Moab Secondary School in South London, sparked a frantic city-wide search.

A police informant who wishes to remain anonymous said that they had found possible bloodstains inside the church, and strange markings sprayed across the tombs set into the church floor and on the walls of the undercroft, as well as a pile of old bones, which were later confirmed to be the remains of rats.

The two Year 8 boys were described by local newsagent Mr Kenneth Boxall as "typical teenage tearaways". In an exclusive interview with our reporter he told us,

"Andy and Roddy were always late for their paper rounds, always bunking off school. They used to nick fags when they thought I wasn't looking – if I had my way I'd have taken a slipper to them. That was how we dealt with this sort of thing in my day, none of this molly-coddling 'sharing feelings' stuff.

"I knew they were up to no good. They used to talk about breaking into the old church – all the kids did. Everyone knows it's a drug den these days."

The missing children charity Find-a-Kid has logged more than three hundred phone calls and e-mails from witnesses and other parents whose children have gone missing in the same area over the years.

Roderick Chu and Andy Jarvis, who live next door to each other in Cold Bath Street, London, SE, were last seen leaving the Tower of Moab Secondary School at midday on Friday 13. That evening police activated the Child Rescue Alert system, which is used for abduction and kidnap cases and supported by all police forces across the UK, and locals joined in a search across the area.

Detectives discovered the wire fence surrounding All Hallows Church, on the edge of Eliot Park, had been broken in one area, and a schoolbook with Andy's name on it was found beside a broken gravestone.

cont. p3

ALL HALLOWS CHURCH: DEVIL-WORSHIPPING CENTRE OF LONDON

ALL Hallows Church, a grand old example of 18th-century church architecture, sits on the edge of Eliot Park and is believed to be designed by the apprentice of the great baroque architect Nicholas Hawksmoor: Thomas Moreby, the so-called "Zombie King".

The church has had an unfortunate history, including a mysterious blaze that nearly destroyed the whole building in 1850.

It was claimed by devil-worshippers right from the start, after they discovered Hawksmoor's own churches had been sited and built to form a power matrix which attracted evil.

Local vicar and Hawksmoor expert the Rev Paula Biller said, "The myths surrounding Moreby and Hawksmoor are just superstitions; the only devil-worshippers to be found in late 20th-century Britain are those who appear in the latest video nasties."

But local police chief Detective Inspector Simon Wisden said, "Rev Biller can think what she likes; she's not the one who has to investigate the dozens of animal deaths, the missing persons, the graffiti in the churchyards . . . all I'm saying is we in the Met are not laughing it off."

In a further bizarre twist, the school attended by the two boys, Tower of Moab, was built in the early 1960s on the site of an unfinished structure reputedly commissioned by an obscure American religious sect.

According to experts, it shared certain architectural similarities to some of the more outré works later credited to Thomas Moreby.

. . . Our obituary of screenwriter Barry Pound (10 May) contained an incorrect assertion about the reasons for the rejection of a storyline proposed by Pound for the BBC's long-running *Z Cars* television drama series.

As we described, Pound would have seemed well-suited to contribute to *Z Cars*, with credits in such BBC crime shows as *Dixon of Dock Green* and, later, the *Z Cars* spin-off *Softly Softly*. Furthermore the storyline of his proposed scripts, a serial-killer story with working title "The Blob Murders", was based on research into a real-life crime case. However, according to records preserved by Mr Ben Quinn of Formby, Merseyside, an amateur archivist of the show, the proposal was turned down by the *Z Cars* script editor, not as we claimed because it was too fanciful for the show's format or for a lack of plausibility, but in fact for its over-authenticity.

In Pound's story, PCs Jock Weir and Fancy Smith would have tackled a serial killer known as "Blob" working the streets of Newtown. According to the correspondence between Pound and the BBC preserved by Mr Quinn, the script editor protested that Pound's story adhered too closely to the reality, as reported in police files, of a long-running series of cases concerning a killer, or killers, known – not as "Blob" as in Pound's storyline – but as "Amoeba". These murders had been recorded by forces across the country as far back as the 1830s, though the record is fragmentary; over the years many police files, like other public records, have been lost through wartime bomb damage and other mishaps. The Amoeba murders, presumably committed by several copycat perpetrators over such a long period, featured the same *modus operandi*: slayings in city or town centres, with each solitary victim's brain and other organs wholly or partially removed, and the flesh of the back marked with a distinctive twisted-band knife carving. All these elements would have featured in Pound's script. Witness sightings and descriptions are fragmentary and inconsistent, the only common element being that suspects are generally described as being one-eyed, or wearing an eye patch; again this would have featured in Pound's story.

There was concern expressed within the Corporation that such a storyline could encourage further copycat killings. Mr Quinn, however, was of the opinion that the storyline may actually have been suppressed because of pressure on the staff involved from another source – possibly even threats from the killer(s). But this cannot be substantiated.

According to our news department, similar slayings have indeed been sporadically reported in other British towns and cities (and, it is reported, in some American cities), even after Pound's failed *Z Cars* pitch in the 1960s. Mr Quinn, apparently following leads developed from his interest in *Z Cars*, also began researching the Amoeba killings, including instances both before and after 1965.

Our correspondent concerning this correction has been Mrs Thelma Ferris, daughter of Mr Quinn, who has been studying her father's records since he, too, by what is presumably extraordinary coincidence, fell victim to a slaying of the "Amoeba" type in 2003.

We apologise for any misrepresentation.

Barrington Arthur Pound, screenwriter, born 5 December 1927; died 1 May 2005.

Extract No.1, dated May 30, 1849.

It hardly seems right to put pen to paper.

My hands, the hands of an old man, should be laden with the mourning rings to mark the deaths of my poor babes – as are the softer hands of my young wife Jessie – not scratching with pen and ink. Yet I want to record the events of the last days in their full destitution and horror, while they are fresh in my mind and heart and memory, before the shining light of the countenance of our one surviving little girl obliterates the darkness, and the stain of blood on my soul.

It began a week ago. Only a week! And how extraordinary it seems that such a figure as August Ferdinand Möbius the mathematician should have been present in our lives throughout all of this trauma of illness and death – and how much more extraordinary it is, and I can admit it only in the privacy of these journal pages, that he was in fact responsible for some or all of that trauma.

It was illness that drove us to the village of B—, in Kent, a small, unprepossessing place that yet has family connections for my dear Jessie; when she was a child the Martins frequently stayed here with relatives, and the memory remains precious in her heart. The relatives are now long gone, but there is a cottage outside the village still owned by the family.

Illness, yes, it was the whooping cough that had caught our bairns – all five of them. And I myself was nursing something more subtle, darker, a pain in my stomach and chest, a kind of pressure on the ribs: perhaps it was a muscle pull or a rib break, perhaps something more serious, and I kept that internal burden a secret from my Jessie. At just twenty four years old the children were enough of a worry, without her having to take into account obscure conditions of my own fifty-three-year-old body. Oh, we were quite a crew in that five-hour-long stagecoach ride along the turnpikes, coming down from our home in London, five sickly poppets, myself grimly clamping down on my own discomfort, and Jessie finding strength she did not know she possessed, yet should not have needed to discover.

But the destination, as we reached it, was scarcely balm to the soul, at first sight.

I had not visited that country before. Between the Medway and the Thames, the world is flat as a board, the endless horizontals of land and sea broken only by few verticals, sailors' beacons, windmills, the spires of the churches of scattered villages. In one place we saw a gibbet. Much of the terrain is marsh, and is a maze of dykes and mounds and gates. You must watch your step, though there are stones to make paths across some of the worst of it. The month was May but the sky was obscure, the air damp and cold. We had come to this place in the hope of finding cleaner air than London's pall, but I could not help but wonder how such an environ could be beneficial to the health of our poor bairns.

Then, from a scrap of higher ground, we saw the river itself, wide and grey, and the misty forms of great hulls on the water. "Look, Mummy!" said our eldest, in a phase of feverish brightness. "Ships! Ships on the river!"

So they were ships, but, mastless and dark, there was no romance about them; I knew they were hulks, prison ships, and I stared at their grey silhouettes, imagining the misery and deprivation that must be contained within.

When we got to the village it was a pretty enough place, set amid alder trees. I spotted a church, a blacksmith's shop, a public house.

There waiting to meet us at the hackney-carriage stand outside the apothecary's were two figures. One was the village doctor, for I had written ahead to ask him to be ready to greet our family of invalids.

And the other was the noted mathematician, August Ferdinand Möbius, of Saxony.

As we clambered down from the stage coach, as the doctor called up hackneys, and our luggage and our little ones were transferred for the short ride to our cottage, I shook the hand of Möbius with all the vigour I could muster – though the pain in my chest made me wince, and I thought he noticed. "I am honoured you have come so far to meet me, sir."

"The honour is mine, Herr Bonomi, to meet such a noted Egyptologist and the illustrator of Burton's *Excerpta hieroglyphica*. And it is no trouble. For you are far more important to my own purposes than you may imagine . . ."

These rather enigmatic words were oddly troubling. Graciously enough I hope, I introduced my exhausted young wife. But the children, those who were awake, were staring at Möbius with what seemed an instinctive mistrust.

I had expected a visit from Möbius. We had corresponded; Möbius and I were considering collaborating on a book on the mathematical proportions of the human body. We had discussed his visiting London to meet me, and others, but he had agreed to be diverted to visit during our necessary sojourn in Kent. Yet I could scarce believe my eyes that such a man was standing here, a figure of world renown in such a place as this.

Certainly he was not what I had expected. I had known the man was in his late fifties, and his shock of white hair fit that age – yet the relative smoothness of his skin, and the general robustness of his physique, belied it. With a kind of hard vigour about him, he did not look very scholarly! And, most surprising of all, he wore a patch over his left eye socket. Once I saw this displaced; the socket beneath was empty and, frankly, stank of corruption. I had had no idea Möbius had suffered such an injury.

Here is my honest first reaction, dear reader: *suspicion*. It was as if this was an impostor, who had somehow, for some purpose, taken the place of the real Möbius, as if he had eaten his life from the inside out – and now was here, a strange and uncomfortable presence in our fragile lives. Absurd it may seem, that was how it felt – and you might feel the same if confronted by such a figure, in such a circumstance.

But, it soon turned out, he knew his mathematics. That was proven in those first moments. The children, you see, were staring at him; the young gazed in fascinated horror at that patch over the eye, but our eldest inspected a kind of brooch he wore on the lapel of his heavy greatcoat. Made of what looked like fine silver, it was a strip with a single twist, and the eye was compelled to follow it, travelling around and around, seeking an end, but there was no border between the two sides.

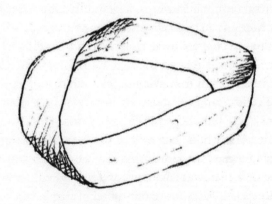

Möbius bent down, smiling; my children recoiled. He said in lightly accented English, "My achievements in mathematics are manifold. Perhaps it is my pioneering introduction of homogeneous co-ordinates into projective geometry that will be my lasting legacy, and some day your father may tell you all about that . . . but what the common people know me for is this little toy – a two-dimensional surface with only one side, thanks to a twist in the third dimension. Look . . ." He ran his finger around and around the little brooch; from one side his finger tracked around the twist to the other side, and then back again, without ever leaving the surface. Of course the toy was familiar to me, and a well-known curiosity in my own circles.

The children stared, simultaneously fascinated and repelled; later I wondered if their childish senses detected something about the man that still evaded Jessie and I.

For now he said only, "This toy, this 'Möbius strip', may be trivial, but I am rather pleased to have my name attached to such a spark for the imagination. Just think, children: how curious it would be, would it not, if a human life was distorted in such a way. One day after another in this three-dimensional world of ours – and then, thanks to a twist in some fourth dimension, a kind of reliving, all over again!"

I, at that time, had no idea what he meant, and even now in retrospect I am unsure if I truly understand. It was a strange business, that life of Möbius! As you will discover.

But then our second youngest coughed; and, bending in concern, I winced at the sharp pain in my own chest. I fancied the doctor noticed – and now I was certain that Möbius did, for he grinned, as if sharing a secret with me . . .

Our cottage was small, stoutly built of stone, and was damp and cold, a pocket of autumn in a late spring day. Seeing our dismay at the accommodation, the doctor, Möbius, and to his credit even the driver of the hackney, helped us move our brood of fragile chicks into their grey nest. The doctor administered tar water to the children, while I opened windows and shook out dusty curtains, and strove to light a fire in the grate. The small parlour was dominated by a huge, clumsy Dutch clock, a relic of Jessie's family. Yet, in retrospect, that dismal arrival was the high point of the evening.

Our visitors left us – including Möbius, who turned down an offer of a ride in the hackney, and stomped off on foot in the direction of the river.

And as the night wore on the tide of our lives began to recede. The children, coughing and crying, were unable to sleep, as was I, nursing my own egg of pain in my chest, my own secret.

And in the deepest dark our second youngest breathed her last.

In the dawn, again Jessie showed a strength she, and I, had never suspected she contained, while I at first could barely function. As she settled our remaining children as best she could, she despatched me in the grey light to the nearest neighbours' home. They were a kindly but impoverished couple who scraped a living somehow from the marshes – they called it "the meshes" – the husband set off in his cart to fetch the doctor, while the wife came back with me.

When we returned to the cottage – it was still not long past dawn – I could not bear to go back inside that sarcophagus-like building. What had possessed us to come to this place? As the woman went in, and I heard Jessie's tremulous voice, weak from the weeping, I walked off, alone, in the dismal grey light, the dampness filling my head, that pain in my chest burning like my conscience.

And here came Möbius.

The light was indistinct, the mist over the marsh thick. Yet I could swear I saw him *running*, running along the dykes and over the stepping stones, running like an athlete – no, more determined than that, like a warrior leading the charge into battle, or perhaps *animal-like*, almost wolf-like, not human at all.

And yet when he reached me he came walking out of the mist, scarcely breathing deep, wearing the same heavy coat as the day before, only a few mud splashes on his trousers to betray his exertions. "Herr Bonomi," he growled at me. "Your loss – how sorry I am. Our encounter has been so brief, and yet already disfigured by the death of a babe . . ."

This may strike you, dear reader, as an innocent enough remark, and yet I, in my confusion and distress, was distracted by what might seem an inconsequential, given the moment. I looked back the way Möbius had come; that was in the direction of the river, and I knew there was no habitation that way save the prison hulks on the water. "Where have you been staying, sir? The village is that way," and I pointed.

"Please do not concern yourself. I will not say I have slept well, but I have fed well – indeed eaten my fill, for now at least . . ." He grinned, and I thought I saw traces of blood around his teeth. "It is your plight that concerns me more, Herr Bonomi. Please, allow me—" He dug into his pocket, held out his hand.

Automatically – distracted by his bloody teeth! – I took the gift. They were mourning rings, a matching pair.

"Only Britannia metal," he said. "I know that you and Jessie are not inclined to ostentation. But they are hallmarked and dated, and inscribed with the name of your lost little one."

I said reflexively, "Thank you." I closed my fist on the unwelcome gift. But then a corner of my mind began to function, as if slowly waking. "But, Herr Möbius – how did you know of our loss? It happened only hours ago." I tried to think. "I suppose our neighbour took the news to the village; we called the doctor. But you are not staying in the village."

"I know many things."

I opened my fist and stared at the rings. "And how could you have these made up in such a short time? Inscribed with the name—"

"I have capabilities beyond your understanding, Herr Bonomi." His one eye was a pit of darkness.

I began to feel afraid, and angry. "See here, Möbius – if that is who you are – you have come into our lives because of our correspondences over matters of mathematics and anatomy..." I scarcely knew to what I was objecting, what I feared. "We have never met before yesterday. And yet here you are tangling yourself up in the lives of our children."

"And their deaths," he said bleakly.

I started at that. Remember, reader, at that time only one of my precious poppets had died. "*Deaths*? Why do you say deaths?"

He grinned, and a fouler grimace could not have crossed the visage of Satan himself. Again he dug into his pocket. This time he produced a whole series of rings.

I took them unwillingly, inspected them even more reluctantly. There were four more pairs, I saw, one ring for me and one for my wife in each set, and inscribed, as I somehow already suspected, with the names of each of our surviving children.

And then one more ring, alone, without a partner. It was inscribed – I could scarcely force myself to look – with my own name.

Möbius said evilly, "A present for Jessie. You may give it to her yourself if you wish. Unorthodox, I know, but efficient."

How is one to react at such a moment? Would you have thrown the rings down in the dirt, assaulted the man? I, in shock still from the death of my second youngest, horrified by this ugly, predictive gift, fell into analysis. "What do you know, Möbius? The other four are ill, but not yet dead."

"They need not die."

"And I am not ill at all—"

"Liar. You may lie to your wife, your children, your doctor, even yourself." He leaned forward and tapped my chest. "But you may not lie to me. What assails you is not a bruise or a sprain or a cracked rib, Herr Bonomi. It is a tumour, a growth." He glanced over me, appraising. "We corresponded on the mathematical proportions of the body, did we not? I can tell at a glance that the arithmetic of your own body is all awry, Herr Bonomi. There's nothing you have done wrong, by the way; it is merely your own divine misfortune. But it is eating you from the inside out. And it will kill you within months."

I imagine I blanched; I felt faint, standing there, clutching the rings. "The doctors in London—"

"Can do nothing save kill you quicker."

I took a breath of the foul air of the marsh, and I imagined I smelled corruption coming from the man. "Jessie – my poor babies – without me—"

Möbius snorted. "Spare me the self pity, man. The fact is, *you need not die either*." He grinned again. "In fact it is important, it is vital, that you must not die, not here, not now."

"Vital? For Jessie, the children? For my own work?"

"No, Herr Bonomi. For me. Only for me. Well, and my ultimate victory. Now, you have a choice, Herr Bonomi. If you wish to live, *give me back your ring*. It will be a token of your acquiescence, you see."

I could not understand what kind of arrangement was being offered here, but I sensed fully the power of this man – if indeed he was a man – the power of life and death, over me and my children. I needed more information; I must draw him out. As if bargaining, I said, "How could I live if my children die?"

"You will have more by that tasty young wife of yours," he said dismissively. "Twelve in all, you dog."

"*Are you August Möbius?*"

"Yes. Well, I am now. If you mean the original – no. He had a place in society I coveted. And so I took it." He smiled. "Also his name, which pleased me for its aptness.

"I need to hide, you see, Herr Bonomi. In a sense I must hide *from myself*. Perhaps you imagine that is some obscure philosophical posture; not in my case. You are of a scientific turn of mind; perhaps you can grasp it better than some.

"*I am not of this time*, Herr Bonomi. At this moment I, or an earlier copy of me, lies imprisoned in a crypt in London. That is me – that *was* me. I escaped from the crypt in the future, in an age you cannot imagine, and then I was given up to a mechanism that can bend time itself – I was hurled back again, back beyond this year, back into the past . . . I have a mission, you see, Herr Bonomi. A mission to fulfil in that distant future. Oh, I will fulfil it. And part of that mission concerns you." He clenched one fist, an almost subtle gesture. "And more. I will take revenge on he who thrust me into the past, and take his place . . . In the meantime I must get back to the future the long way round. Year by weary year, like any common mortal. Sometimes I think I should join my imprisoned self in his crypt! But, failing that, I must hide. In my arrogance I rather enjoy hiding in plain sight, you know. And I hide my name in the names of others. *Möbius . . . Moreby* . . . As I suggested to your innocents, my life itself is a kind of Möbius strip in time, is it not? How apt the name is. And of course I must feed, I must feed..."

I transcribe this rambling as best I remember it; I do not claim a full understanding. I clung to the details that concerned me. "And the original Möbius, the man with whom I corresponded—"

"I can fill his boots. I remember his later results – what he would have produced had he not died; it is not hard to churn them out as my own. And his brain was very fine." And he *licked his lips.*

All of this overwhelmed me, the ambiguous horror of these statements, the mortal peril into which I and my family had suddenly been plunged. I could only repeat, "How could I live if my children die?"

He sighed, theatrically. "Oh, call me a sentimental old fool," he said now in his clumsy German accent, "but I will give you one back." He held out his hand. "Give me one pair of rings. One name. One child to live, of the four survivors. Your choice."

"I could not choose—"

"One, or none," he snapped. "Choose!"

And, to my eternal shame, I plucked out one pair – I tried to be random, tried not to read the inscribed name, of course I failed, I *knew who I had chosen* – I thrust the rings at him. Then I could bear no more. Sobbing, I turned away and started the walk back towards the cottage.

"The same time tomorrow!" Möbius called after me. "Be here! I will bring your cure! Be here, Herr Bonomi. You have sold your soul. You may as well collect the fee!"

Of the twenty-four agonising hours that followed, I need say little. What I remember of that awful day is fragmented, like pieces of an ugly dream.

The doctor and the apothecary attended us for most of the day. Our surviving children suffered, and their conditions worsened – but none died, during that day; none died.

I went into the village to arrange transport back to London, out of this terrible place. There would not be a coach for some days; I paid excessively to ensure our seats, although the doctor had warned me the children might not be well enough to travel; I was determined we would go from here come what may.

I did not show my wife the mourning rings, not then.

And I told her nothing of my strange encounter with Möbius on the marsh. Distracted by the children, exhausted, she did not ask after Möbius, or notice anything odd about my own condition on my return from that encounter – nor indeed did she notice my own mounting distress over the lump in my chest that burned now, like a coal.

When I sat at last at the end of the afternoon, spent, exhausted, eating soup and bread provided for us by the kindly neighbour, I found my mind wandering back to earlier days – times long before my young wife had even been born. I had travelled extensively, primarily in Egypt and the Holy Land. I had had plans to use my declining years to publish my findings, perhaps to indulge in some architectural experiments reflecting those experiences, following in the footsteps of my own father. Now, even as my children lay ill and dying all around me, a selfish, craven, unworthy part of me reflected that if Möbius did have the gift of life for me, if he could save me from the assassin in my chest, I would have time to pursue such ambitions.

Möbius! How he dominated my thoughts all that day, much as he has ever since. In my travels I had been imaginatively drawn to the culture of the pharaohs, their tremendous monuments to death – their obsession with the afterlife. That was a place where Möbius – whatever his true name – might have fitted, I thought; he was a creature of death rather than life.

When the children, and Jessie, were sleeping in early evening, I took a solitary walk. And I heard cannon fire, booming across the flats.

I went across the marsh towards the river, and I gazed upon the hulks, the prison ships. I knew that the cannon was a signal of alarm aboard, but from this distance I could see nothing but stillness, the huge forms in the dying light. I wondered what their names had been, what action these vessels had seen; perhaps these ships had served

Nelson and Collingwood as they fended off Napoleon's navies, in the heroic encounters I remembered from my own boyhood. Now, shorn of their masts, they were locked in place by heavy, rusty chains, like evil Noah's Arks permanently tethered in this flooded land.

When the wind turned, I thought I heard noises coming from within the hulks: laughter and screams, and cries of alarm.

And I thought I saw a running figure, almost wolf-like, running from one hulk to another, pursued by slower, heavier forms, guards perhaps, or Constables, even soldiers.

Was that Möbius?

What was his business on the hulks?

I remembered the blood on his teeth.

Horrified by nameless, inchoate images, I turned away and hurried back to the cottage.

And where one more horrific detail awaited me, before I could sleep.

The vicar of the small village church stood by the door, wringing his hands, with the doctor standing by, grave. A Constable had been called, I was told. The body of my daughter, lying out in a side-chapel of the church, had been "tampered with". That was the phrase the vicar used.

We hurried in a chaise to the village, my senses overloaded, my mind too full even to register this fresh horror, the pain in my chest ever more like a troubled conscience – the mourning rings in my pocket like lead weights.

At the church, the doctor talked me through what had been done, but I, with my knowledge of Egyptology, could recognise it for myself. As if my daughter had been a young pharaoh, or his queen, laid out for the mummification, *her brain had been removed*, extracted with a hooked device through the nose.

My wife Jessie knew nothing of this; the doctor and vicar, grave, good men both, if overwhelmed, promised me that. And she never will know, for I will have this journal sealed until after both our deaths.

I knew who had done this. Möbius! And I had a gruesome presentiment of why.

The next dawn I was waiting for him on the marsh.

He came running again, from the direction of the prison hulks. I put aside that aspect of his activities, as if closing a drawer in my mind.

He stood facing me, panting this time, like a dog come in from the hunt.

"I should kill you," I said.

He shrugged. "You could not if you tried. And even if you could, you would condemn yourself and your child." I noted he used the singular. "And remember, it was not I who inflicted you with the tumour, Herr Bonomi. Not I who brought down the cough on your *kinder*."

"But it is you who are here and now, you who are manipulating my pain."

"I have the potion," he said now, carelessly. He drew a small glass flask from his pocket, shook it; its crimson contents bubbled. "It looks like a fine claret! But it is not. The main ingredients are water, some drops of my own rather unique blood, and—"

"Do not tell me."

He eyed me. "Very well. *But you know*, do you not? You will become Cronus, the Titan—"

I held up my hand. Cronus, who devoured his own children as they were born. I did not need a lecture in mythology from this monster.

He handed over the vial, and a brown envelope, sealed. "A teaspoon per patient will suffice – including yourself, Herr Bonomi. You may apply it to your children as you will. *But only one will survive.* The rings, remember? That was the deal."

"A pact with the Devil!"

"Oh, I am no devil, Herr Bonomi. I am giving you life where you embraced only death, you and your children. Where is the devilry in that?" He took a step back, and another, soon becoming indistinct in the mist. "You will see me again, but not for some years, not until the time is due."

"What time?"

"The time of your death, of course. And of course it is written down, in that envelope I gave you – you will have guessed that much."

Another step; his voice began to grow faint. "Do not bother to try to trace me. Do not correspond with Möbius – ha! He is gone, as you deduced. But the shell of his life will suit me for some years yet. Hurry back to your nest now, Herr Bonomi. And take care not to spill the medication . . .!

"Oh, and Herr Bonomi. *Your own death is necessary*, you know. Suffice it to say I will be there with you. The place is irrelevant. But the time, Herr Bonomi, the time is all!"

I fled, stopping my ears to shut out his foul rant.

I hastened back to the cottage. When Jessie was out of the room, I spooned the foul medication into the mouths of all my little ones – of course, would you not? And, yes, I took a spoonful myself.

I destroyed Möbius' Britannia-metal rings. I hid the envelope.

In the end, it was as Möbius had promised. Of the four remaining children, only one survived.

Aye, and myself!

IN MEMORY OF
FOUR CHILDREN WHO WERE CALLED OUT OF THIS LIFE
INTO A BETTER IN THE EASTER WEEK OF 1852

JOSEPH MENES BONOMI ON APRIL 11 AGED
CAUTLEY FREDERICK
JESSIE
JOHN IGNATIUS

THE LORD GAVE AND THE LORD HATH TAKEN AWAY
BLESSED BE THE NAME OF THE LORD

GRANDMOTHER
WIDOW OF JOHN MARTIN BORN JULY 27 1780 DIED DEC 20 1858

MOTHER
BONOMI BORN APRIL 6 1825 DIED SEP 10 1859

THEIR FATHER
JOSEPH BONOMI
SCULPTOR TRAVELLER AND ARCHEOLOGIST
BORN 9TH OCTOBER 1796
APPOINTED CURATOR OF SIR JOHN SOANE'S MUSEUM 1861
DIED 3RD MARCH 1878

▼ [Extracts from the private journals of Joseph Bonomi the Younger, unsealed on March 3, 1978, the centenary of his death, and published as *Joseph Bonomi, My Ancestor: England, Egypt and Beyond* by Grape Press Ltd., ed. Wayne Bonomi, 2004.]

Extract No. 4, dated March 2, 1878.

. . . I knew he would come for me, yesterday, today, or tomorrow. For I had opened the envelope. Of course I did. Would you not?

I went to my club by hackney, one last time. I had the driver take me along the river, and I watched the traffic pass along that great artery, the steamers bound for Rotterdam, Hamburg, Glasgow, Aberdeen. At the club, as I climbed out, I stiffened my posture, ignoring the Pain as I have aspired to do for most of my life – the corset I wear now helps with that concealment – and I looked on the grand architecture of Pall Mall, blackened by the magnificent sooty fog of London. Then into the entrance hall with its parquet floor, and to the gallery with its circular cupola and its porphyry pillars, and to the smoking room, where I sat for much of the day with my glass of wine spiced with cinnamon, and the company of such fellows as showed themselves, and I read through the papers of the day: *The Times*, the *Morning Chronicle*, the *Standard*, the *Daily Telegraph*, the *Illustrated London News*. Immersed myself for one last day in the affairs of Britain, the Empire and the world.

I watched for him, of course, though I did not expect him to confront me there. He would haunt my home, as he had haunted that wretched cottage in Kent where poor Jessie and I had watched our babies die – and where I should have died too, for better or worse. I did wonder if I would recognise him, after all these years, and with my own eyesight failing; I am eighty-two years old. But I had confidence the fellow would show himself to me.

And after tea I took a hackney home, leaving the life of London behind, the noise and debauchery of the oyster rooms already starting though the sun had not yet gone down – home to my house in Wimbledon. I checked for mail, but there was none. My affairs are wound up now, by my own hand, and there was none from the family.

Jessie and I had more children – twelve in all, just as *he* prophesied, and in later years a clutch of grandchildren. But my offspring have always been cold to me. It is hard to accept the reluctance of a small child when one approaches to play, simply to talk. And the smaller they are the more suspicious; even babes would wriggle restless in my arms. I always thought they sensed something wrong about me. Something of *him*. As if, like him, I deserve no place in this world – as if I should have died in Kent, on that ghastly beach, and the thing that lives on, that is *me*, is unnaturally alive. All this children sense better than adults, under the words.

My children recoiled from me as they had from Möbius.

Thus, no mail.

I repaired to my parlour, where I sat then as I sit now to complete this final account, in this comfortable room with its overstuffed divan and chairs, the ornately carved uprights, and a glimpse of the mahogany dining table through the door. There's little of a woman's touch here, a keen observer would no doubt conclude, and indeed the only trace of Jessie is the big ugly Dutch clock we had brought here from the Kent cottage, a relic of her childhood, and a souvenir of the bairns we lost to the cough.

Here I sat, in the light of the gas mantles, until the electric doorbell rang, and I heard the steady tread of my man as he answered.

It was *he*, of course, changed – younger, lighter, more handsome perhaps – but still with that ugly patch over the missing eye. Changed but unmistakably *he*, my nightmare incarnate once more.

I did not rise. Why should I rise for him? And I dismissed my man, who had fussed over offering tea.

When *he* spoke there was not a trace of a German accent. I wondered what guise he wore now – what identity he had donned, as one wears a suit of clothes appropriate for a function, no doubt leaving more blood in his wake, more curtailed lives, so that he could continue to "hide in plain sight". I did not ask him; I did not care.

"I have come," he said.

I shrugged, ignoring the Pain as I moved, glad of the support of the corset. "You said you would."

"I did. It will be tomorrow morning, by the way. Your man will find you in your bed; you will not wake. If that is any comfort."

"I reject your comfort."

"As you wish. You opened the envelope, did you not?"

"As you knew I would."

"And so you expected me." He grinned, oddly almost boyish – a boy gleefully intent on dissecting a live frog, perhaps. "You must admit I added spice to your life, Bonomi! Gave it a frame, perhaps, a shape – an author must know the end of his story in order to draft the middle passages. I have known a few authors, you know, or met them. Like to shock them, and see how the horror works out in their fictions. Have you heard of Poe?"

"Of course I've heard of Poe."

"What he took from me was rather abstract: that is, my notion of hiding in plain sight. His 'Purloined Letter' ought to have been dedicated to me—"

I had no patience with his bragging. "Have you killed me? Is that the true meaning of the potion I drank, all those years ago?"

"Not at all. It is more a question of timing. I told you then. The medication has kept you alive, until now – until tomorrow. It was the opposite of lethal, it was life-giving."

"Because you needed me to die tomorrow, March 3rd."

"That is it, exactly."

"So the potion preserved me. But, Möbius – if that's your name—"

"There is only us here. It will do."

"I refuse to believe you are omnipotent. What of an accident? If I had fallen under the wheels of a train twenty years ago—"

"You should be glad you were spared such calamities. Because, whatever the damage, however much pain you suffered, *you would have lived on*, Herr Bonomi. No matter how grotesque the relic."

I managed to laugh. That "Herr" – a relic of his old imposture! "I count myself lucky, then. Tell me what this is about. Why has it been so important, why has it been necessary to plot for decades, to have me preserved to this date? Why am I so special?"

He shook his head. "Ah, Herr Bonomi – such an intelligent man, yet such a poor listener. It was never about you, you fool! *You* are irrelevant. Despite your association with my proselyte Mrs. Courtoy – ah, I can see from your expression that you were unaware of our affiliation – all that matters now about you is the date of your death . . . as it will be inscribed on your tombstone. 'Died 3rd March 1878' – that message, and the hieroglyph that will sit below it, have been the sole purpose of my project."

I genuinely did not understand, not yet. "What message? It is a date, not a message."

"You will never comprehend it – a mayfly like you! Herr Bonomi, in a time very remote from this gaslit fog of yours – more than a century hence – that date will indeed act as a message, a kind of code, if you will. A guide for a traveller, leading him from one haven to the next."

And I remembered the strange, garbled tale he had told me on the marsh, of a man locked in a crypt, erupting into the London of some remote future, and being hurled back into history once more. Was my own memorial stone to play some part in that Möbius-strip of a biography?

But my glimmer of understanding was overwhelmed by a sense of outrage, of humiliation. "That is all you want of me? To leave a stone? All I have achieved, all my life, my loves, my work and family – all for that, a date and an inscription on a stone?" And I tried to rise from my chair, but the Pain stabbed at me.

He regarded me, amused. "Sit down, you old fool. Oh, and do not bother to conceal your distress. I know about your inner agony."

"It never went away. The tumour – cured evidently, absorbed. But the Pain remained. A part of the misery and pointlessness of my later life."

"A life *I* gave you – you would not have lived to see 1850 if I had not—"

"Pointless! A life of pain. My wife dead at thirty-four, my children estranged. My work a muddle – I had always aspired to curate a museum, as a retirement project . . ." A plan that had been achieved after a fashion, but only after years of bitter personal struggle and criticism. It had been a battleground for elderly men, for myself and my rivals; it had brought me no pleasure.

I ran out of energy. I slumped back.

He took a step forward, impossibly young, that patch of black satin over his eye gleaming in the gaslight of my parlour. "It is all up for you, Herr Bonomi. But not for me . . . Just think, though. You will be remembered. For about five seconds, in the year two thousand and thirteen. *Then*, you will be remembered again. Is that a comfort?" He studied me with a kind of passionless curiosity.

Then he turned, walked out of the parlour, and out into the street; I heard the door close. I do not expect to see him again.

And nor do I expect to see the sun rise.

Now I retire to my bed. I have left instructions in my will that this volume should be sealed until a century after my death. I pray that my descendants and those around them, in the wisdom and maturity of a better age than this, will be better able to deal with the monster that called himself Möbius than I ever was.

To my wife and children – I loved you always, even though I could not save you.

We will meet again in the arms of the risen Saviour.

Signed this day,
　　JOSEPH BONOMI, Esq.

...M BORN APRIL 6 1825 DIED SE...

FATHER

Joseph Bonomi

OR TRAVELLER AND ARCHEO...

BORN 9TH OCTOBER 1796

URATOR OF SIR JOHN SOANES M...

DIED 3RD MARCH 1878

COLONEL ... ... C.B....

THE WORLD'S GREATEST MYSTERIES! NO.17

By Janet Ramsey
(Published by HardNews Press, £12.99)

Reviewed by
Gerry Brown

This venerable paperback series has been running since the late 1980s, and if like me you're a sucker for the unexplained and inexplicable, you'll be rushing to your nearest bookstore to pick up this latest dose of the weird, the wonderful and the frankly unbelievable. As always, Ms Ramsey has selected a dozen topics of varying verisimilitude and dug deeply enough in some cases to get through to the Antipodes! It's hard to pick favourites in this cornucopia of delights, but I do have to single out Ming the Mollusc – I kid you not! – a dapper little bivalve that turns out to be a staggering 507 years old,

which makes it the world's oldest living creature by a long shot. (Well, that's if Ming hasn't been fished out and ended up on someone's plate by now.)

I've always had a soft spot for the Brompton Cemetery, so I was particularly interested in Ms Ramsey's chapter on the Brompton Time Machine: that imposing twenty-foot-tall trapezoid of dark polished granite decorated with carved hieroglyphics that supposedly inspired H.G. Wells' famous novella. Some of her wilder revelations had even this old hack reeling a little.

We all know that the imposing mausoleum decorated with elaborate Egyptian figures was built to house the highly eccentric (if they hadn't been so wealthy they'd have been called crazies!) Courtoy spinsters – an unmarried mother and her two daughters – who are reputed to be buried inside. So far, so yawn . . . but then, living up to her hard-won reputation as one of Britain's more tenacious hackettes, Ms Ramsey leads us unerringly on to the good stuff. Here's the first weirdness: unlike every other building in Brompton Cemetery there is *no paperwork* for the Courtoy Mausoleum. From the very start the directors of Brompton Cemetery have always required plans, blueprints and schematics before any tomb or monument is approved. She points out far wealthier Irish peer Francis Jack Needham, the second Earl Kilmorey, gave up throwing money at the directors when his attempts to build a magnificent Egyptian-style mausoleum for his mistress, Priscilla Hoste, were continually frustrated by persistent bureaucratic red tape, that in the end Needham moved it (and the remains of his mistress) to the grounds of his house at Chertsey Park in Weybridge – his architects obviously didn't have the same pull as the Courtoys'. And the second weird thing according to Ms Ramsey: we can only *assume* the women are buried inside as the tomb wasn't completed until five years after the death of Hannah Courtney, the mother, and the key's missing so the huge bronze door hasn't been opened in more than a (cont. p23) . . .

READ ON! For an exclusive extract from *The World's Greatest Mysteries!* No.17 by Janet Ramsey.

BROMPTON CEMETERY AND THE TIME MACHINE

BROMPTON CEMETERY – then the West of London and Westminster Cemetery – was established in 1836 and opened four years later, in 1840, on the cusp of the Georgian and Victorian eras. It was to be one of "The Magnificent Seven", a ring of suburban garden cemeteries opened between 1833 and 1841. However, right from the beginning the ambitious scheme was mired in controversy, for its founder, the architect, inventor and entrepreneur Stephen Geary (1797–1854), who had previously created the cemeteries at Highgate and Nunhead, was forced off his own board when the directors discarded his own plans for those of a different architect, Benjamin Baud.

A "Committee of Taste" led by Sir Jeffry Wyatville (1766–1840) – King William IV's "Surveyor of the Fabric" – had been brought in to judge an "open" competition for the cemetery design. When Wyatville, himself a highly distinguished architect, chose a design by Baud (c.1807–1875), one of his own assis-

tants, whose design was strongly reminiscent of his boss's own work, Stephen Geary felt he had no choice but to resign from the board*.

The original 39-acre site, a half-mile-long flat stretch of land between Old Brompton and Fulham Roads, was purchased from Lord Kensington, though the directors later found themselves entangled in litigation when it turned out Lord Kensington might not have had the rights to the land in the first place; that expensive dispute was finally settled in favour of the cemetery in 1854.

Baud's original estimate of £30,000 was very quickly spent and by the time the consecration of Brompton Cemetery was due, in 1940, not only was it still not finished, but the directors had had to borrow considerable sums from the builder, Philip Nowell. With the high-class and wealthy middle-class dead piling up with nowhere to bury them, the company, desperate to open the site, agreed that part of the northeast lodge should be converted into a temporary chapel.

Charles James Blomfield, the Bishop of London, consecrated the site in June 1840, and the first burial took place a few days later.

However, business was slow and the management began to notice structural defects, for which Nowell the builder and Baud the architect blamed one another. The directors owed so much to Nowell that they took his side; Baud was dismissed, and later tried – unsuccessfully, like his predecessor – to sue the Company. The smaller shareholders – who held a lot of the power through weight of numbers – insisted the directors sell to the government when they made a tentative bid under the Metropolitan Interments Act of 1850, which prohibited burial in congested urban churchyards and crypts, and gave the state powers of compulsory purchase over commercial cemeteries such as Brompton. Whilst the act was repealed two years later, the sale went ahead – though the shareholders netted only £75,000 instead of the £170,000 they had been expecting.

As a result, Brompton Cemetery became the only private cemetery purchased under the 1850 Act, and also the first ever to be nationalised. It is still Britain's only Crown cemetery, held for the last 154 years in the care of successive government ministries, the most recent being The Royal Parks Agency.

Today the site still embodies Baud's vision of the cemetery as an open-air cathedral, with the tree-lined Central Avenue as its nave, and the domed Chapel (based on St Peter's Basilica in Rome), in honey-coloured Bath stone, as its high altar. The Chapel, colonnades and imposing North Gatehouse on Old Brompton Road, which was built to look like a triumphal arch and represents the "great west door", are all now Grade II* listed.

The symmetrical layout of the smaller paths creates two pairs of "aisles" running parallel to the central "nave". The North Gatehouse was faced with stone from the Aislaby Quarry near Whitby, which also provided blocks for Whitby, Margate and Ramsgate Harbours, as well as the Strand Bridge (later renamed Waterloo Bridge). It had to be rebuilt after Nazi bombs nearly destroyed it in World War II. Cast-iron doors lead into the catacombs which run directly under the colonnades flanking the Central Avenue and Great Circle above-ground; originally supposed to be an extra way to make money, the coffin-niches on either side remain empty to this day. Matching bell towers were planned for either side of the arcades, but again, lack of funds meant only the western one was built.

Brompton Cemetery today has hosted more than 200,000 burials, amongst them epidemiologist Dr John Snow, suffragette Emmeline Pankhurst, composer Constant Lambert, actor Ernest Thesiger and Egyptologist Joseph Bonomi. There are some 35,000 monuments, ranging in intricacy and importance from simple headstones to private mausolea; twenty-seven of them are , and one — the Leyland tomb by Edward Burne-Jones – is Grade II* – deemed to be of special interest, and warranting every effort to preserve it. The cemetery embraces all, from large plots for family mausolea to common graves, as well as a small columbarium.

And every one of those 35,000 monuments has paperwork – plans, blueprints and schematics – attached to it, with *one* exception: the Courtnoy Mausoleum, also known as the Brompton Cemetery Time Machine. The exceedingly wealthy Irish peer Francis Jack Needham, the second Earl Kilmorey and former Viscount Newry, had scandalised society when he abandoned his wife at the age of 56 and eloped with his twenty-year-old ward, Priscilla Hoste, the daughter of Admiral Sire William Hoste and Lady Harriet Walpole. When Priscilla died ten years later, he commissioned an Egyptian-style tomb for her – but despite throwing money at it, the bureaucracy of Brompton Cemetery overcame him and the mausoleum – in which he himself was later interred beside his beloved mistress – ended up in the grounds of his Weybridge home, Chertsey Park.

But – and this is where things get weird – no such red tape got in the way of the eventual tomb of the Courtoy spinsters, Hannah, and her two daughters, Mary Anne and Elizabeth, believed to be the daughters of John Courtoy, Hannah's lover. Courtoy was a French-born wigmaker who changed his name from Nicholas Jacquinet when he moved to England from Jussey in Franche-Compté; Hannah Peters took her lover's English name for convenience.

On his death, Courtoy's much younger mistress became extremely rich: he was one of the hundred wealthiest people in Britain when he left her his fortune, which today would be some £16 million. As a result, the Courtoy women's eccentricities were widely regarded by Victorian society as "interesting" rather than crazy – and at that time they were far from alone in their fascination with the subject of time travel; the belief that the ancient Egyptians had uncovered the secret of time travel was widespread.

Hannah, like many in her circle, firmly believed that having theorised time travel, Leonardo da Vinci had also put it to use, only to find himself stuck in the 15th century, where his only comfort was to draw the things he would never see again, including submarines, aeroplanes, parachutes, helicopters and other devices so far ahead of his time as to seem almost magical, even to the entrepreneurial Victorians.

Whilst visiting an exhibition and talk on da Vinci at the British Museum, she fell into conversation with sculptor, artist and Egyptologist Joseph Bonomi the Younger, son of Italian architect Joseph Bonomi the Elder. The younger Bonomi had long been fascinated with the ancient Egyptians, and in 1824 he accompanied Robert Hay on the first of what would be several expeditions to Egypt, forming part of the team who first deciphered the hieroglyphic texts found on papyri in the Valley of the Kings. A few years later, in Cairo, he was commissioned to illustrate James Burton's *Excerpta hieroglyphica*.

It was his particular expertise with hieroglyphics that fascinated Hannah, as well as his experiences in Egypt, and she is believed to have financed his expeditions specifically to hunt for proof that time travel existed, and subsequently commissioned him to design a mausoleum along Egyptian lines for her and her daughters.

After the death of her much older lover, Hannah had allegedly become a Royal mistress, but her heart remained untouched and she continued her investigations into time travel, which had begun to obsess her.

Bonomi was not himself an architect, though he had studied under his father, so Hannah Courtoy sought advice from several sources, including an unnamed apprentice of the infamous architect Thomas Moreby. Moreby was himself an apprentice of the great baroque architect Nicholas Hawksmoor, and he had been a specialist in grottoes, follies, mausolea and vaulted subterranean chambers. During the time he spent working on Sir Francis Dashwood's Medmenham Abbey he is said to have been inculcated into darker secrets; it was that knowledge Hannah was eager to learn from his apprentice.

It was the apprentice who suggested eccentric maverick inventor Samuel Warner be included in the team. Warner had been in discussion with the Duke of Wellington about his latest inventions – a long-range torpedo and a sea-mine the size of a sea-urchin – and was eager to put several of his own theories into practice.

Hannah insisted on being included at all stages of the design, and there is some evidence that after meeting the mysterious "apprentice" she started to obsess not just about time travel but she also began investigating the possibility of life after death. She had commenced a study of the buildings of Thomas Moreby, and the writings and teachings of Moreby's infamous inner circle, known as "The Well of Seven", believed to be buried somewhere in the grounds of St Pancras Old Church, near King's Cross in London.

The site for the mausoleum was chosen at her explicit instruction, and careful study of London's hidden rivers suggests that it lies immediately over where Counters Creek once ran before it was briefly diverted into the short-lived Kensington Canal that once formed a boundary of the cemetery. In mediaeval times that part of Counters Creek was called Billingswell – and there is some evidence to suggest it once formed part of an intricate system of wells linked by long-forgotten rivers that run deep beneath the city.

Between Bonomi, Warner and the apprentice, they designed an imposing mausoleum, a twenty-foot-tall trapezoid of dark polished granite with pyramidal roof and a huge copper door. The edifice was decorated with narrow bands of carved hieroglyphics, built not only according to formulae Bonomi discovered in Egypt, but also drawing on some of da Vinci's more obscure sketches which Bonomi and Hannah believed to indicate a way to twist time into a dimension through which one could travel safely.

The location of Brompton Cemetery was a canny decision, according to current cemetery employee James Mackay, who recently told Reuters journalist Howard Webster, "His choice of the cemetery was a shrewd and appropriate one . . . it was one of the few places where one could work unobserved and where even the most eccentric of structures could be explained away. A cemetery where the wealthy and famous are buried is also a location that one could say with great certainty is unlikely to be the subject of redevelopment over time . . . like Egyptian tombs, where structures could remain intact over centuries."

Hannah Courtoy died in 1848, but her mausoleum was not finished until 1853 – the same year Samuel Warner died in mysterious circumstances. Immediately after his death was discovered, government spokesmen started claiming Warner was a fraud, that his inventions would never have worked, but others believe the prototypes to be entirely functional, and that he was murdered by someone who stole the designs from his dead body.

There is no trace of the mysterious apprentice; whatever happened to him is not recorded, and the only clue to his identity is a description attributed years later to one of Hannah Courtoy's housemaids, who spoke of "a frightening-looking gentleman with a black eye-patch over one eye".

When Bonomi died in 1878, he too was buried in Brompton Cemetery, some sixty feet away from his crowning achievement. Similar hieroglyphic carvings appear on his headstone, and Anubis, the jackal-headed Egyptian god of the dead, is sitting on a replica of the Courtoy mausoleum and facing towards the actual structure, which, in Egyptian mythology, represents a soul lost out of time.

As rumours of the magical properties of the mausoleum grew, so people tried to discover the truth – either to debunk the myth, or to prove its truth – but the key to the great bronze door was found to be missing, and the lock quite impervious to even the cleverest of lock-picks. The hieroglyphics have also proved difficult to decipher, although some of the best Egyptologists in the world have tried to rise to the challenge.

Whilst he was never formally identified and no charges were brought, mystery and adventure writer H.G. Wells was believed to be one of a group of gentlemen who attempted to break into the Courtoy Mausoleum, hoping to find out, once and for all, the truth behind the enigmatic structure. Although he failed to get into the building, it continued to play upon Wells' imagination, and in 1895 he published *The Time Machine*, reigniting the Victorian fascination with time travel. Wells himself said, "We all have our time machines, don't we. Those that take us back are memories . . . And those that carry us forward, are dreams." But many of his contemporaries believed he never stopped searching for the real thing.

The story of the Brompton Cemetery Time Machine continues to grow. More recent attempts to decrypt the hieroglyphics have partially succeeded, following the discovery of the personal diaries of renowned Egyptologist F.W. Green, and the band on the southern side is now believed to read:

Nehes, nehes, nehes, Nehes em hotep.

This is the start of the ancient Egyptian Prayer of the Dead to Isis, exhorting her to awaken: *Awake, awake, awake! Awake in peace!* But thereafter it diverges from the more normal prayers, and one hundred and fifty years later, scholars are still trying to understand what – or who – Bonomi and Warner were trying to achieve.

If the Courtoy women did indeed want to cheat death and travel in time, perhaps they felt no one would suspect a building in an isolated corner of a graveyard. But whatever the truth, there is no doubt that after their deaths, they vanished as surely from the face of the world as if they had stepped into another era. Despite their enormous wealth there is barely a trace of their existence. What is also undeniable is that the body of the architect Thomas Moreby is no longer believed to be where it is buried . . .

Mr Webster, the Reuters journalist who spent months investigating the Brompton Cemetery Time Machine, was not the first to suggest the graves of Samuel Warner and Joseph Bonomi are also empty, and that all three men are alive and travelling with the Courtoy spinsters through time in his machine.

Many believe it was the inspiration for the fictional Doctor Who's time-travelling machine the TARDIS, which stands for Time and Relative Dimension in Space, first introduced in 1963, and it came to the forefront of public consciousness again a few years ago when the mausoleum was used as the cover picture for the elec-tronic album *Musick That Destroys Itself* by Mount Vernon Astral Temple. The album's title was considered to be a premonition, because not long after it was released the mausoleum apparently began to self-destruct as chunks of granite fell from its surface and cracks appeared in the lintels above the doors.

So has the mausoleum finally started to fall apart because of its constant journeying through time and space? Or is it simply an old building in need of some renovation?

The jury's still out . . .

To whom it may concern,

I'm nervous – so very dreadfully nervous – as I type this. I can hear sirens outside. Voices: people running and shouting. The television is on, there's a news report about yet another disturbance near All Hallows church. That fucking New Festival of Britain, it's caused more problems than anyone could have imagined.

But enough of that . . . I have something to tell you, whoever *you* are who finds this document.

Blood.

There's blood on the computer screen. Shall I wipe it off, or just leave it there to remind myself of what I've done, what I have become? Like Edgar Allan Poe's 'Tell-tale Heart', it's a constant reminder of the sin I've committed.

I spent fifteen minutes just staring at the red smear. It's drying now. It looks like I've been using a red pen and it leaked. There's red down there, too, behind that door, in the cellar. A lot of it – so much more than this measly little mark on the monitor. So much red you could swim in it.

A lake of red. An ocean of red.

But perhaps I should begin now . . . I need to start telling my story before it's too late, or before I lose my mind. You fancy me mad. Madmen know nothing . . . Ha! Sorry, couldn't resist another Poe reference. That's the writer in me, I suppose. I can never allow a good literary reference to go to waste.

Now, let me begin . . .

I'm aware of how foolish – and how pointless – it might seem, writing everything down like this. Nobody will ever see this note and, if they do, they won't care. My sad little account will be just another story lost among so many others, not even as much as a footnote in the short history of the end of the world.

I've always needed to write things down. Even as a child, I never felt that anything had really happened until I'd written about it, put it down on paper. Call it evidence. Call it a form of OCD. Call it whatever the fuck you like, I don't care. I don't care about anything anymore. Not after this . . . not since *it* happened.

But I'm getting ahead of myself. Let me backtrack and fill in some details.

I was born into a poor working-class family in Yorkshire. I attended state schools, got average grades, hated sport but loved art and literature. This last thing alone turned me into an outsider from an early age. I was accused of being gay, beaten up in the playground, and generally treated like shit because my interests fell outside of what was socially acceptable within the circles I moved.

My parents died when I was a teenager, both taken by cancer. They were not missed. I went to live with an aunt whom I hated and, as soon as I was able, I left her hovel to attend university in London, where I was to study English literature. I left the North behind, and have never looked back since.

University life opened up a lot of options for me. It made me realise that I was not strange, and there were other people from my background who shared the same cultural tastes.

I met the woman who would become my wife in my second year of study.

Tanya was beautiful. She came from a well-off background. She wore expensive clothes, always had people around her, and seemed to float through life, as if everything caught up in her orbit would simply bend and adapt to make her passage that little bit easier. Even now, I have no idea what she ever saw in me. I've asked her on several occasions, and even back when we still communicated in a civil manner, she was vague about the reasons why she was first drawn to me.

I was as happy as a pig in shit. My grades improved, I got a part-time job in a bar, and I had a girlfriend – my first one. I was a virgin before I met Tanya. She wasn't, of course, and she had to teach me how to go on. But I was a fast learner.

I started taking my writing seriously after she began to encourage me. She found a bunch of short stories I'd written and sent them off to an agent without telling me. The agent liked what he saw, and contacted Tanya to speak about taking me on as a client. The deal was done before I was even let in on the details. This soon became an established pattern in our lives together: I rarely had any say in my own affairs, and Tanya took over the organisation of everything.

We graduated. Tanya went to work for her father's company and I sold my first novel to a major publisher. We moved into this nice big house in Blackheath, South London. Everything looked rosy. We were married. It was an expensive affair. Then, one morning some years later, I awoke to the realisation that Tanya did not really love me.

I had found a letter from her lover – one of them, at least. It was a man who'd been at our wedding. I subsequently found out that they'd fucked just before the ceremony. At the time, I wondered why her dress was so creased, and noted a tear in her stocking.

That man – he was simply one of many. When I confronted her about it, she laughed in my face. She didn't want a divorce; she thought it best that we stay together. Her job took her away from home more and more in those days, and she would sometimes spend weeks in hotels around the world, having meetings, developing client contacts, fucking strangers in the service elevator.

When she calmed down, she became a little softer, more sympathetic. She said that she did love me when we met, but over the years it had weakened. She blamed me: she said I never gave her enough. "Bits and pieces," she said. "You only ever gave me bits and pieces of yourself, like fragments of a story. I never got to see the full person, only those fucking bits and pieces."

I suppose, in a way, she was right. I spent so much of my life trying to hide my true self that it became my default position. Nobody ever got to see me in my entirety, just small parts, or reflections of the whole.

It was then that the truth really hit me. All I was – all I'd ever been – to Tanya was a caretaker. She needed someone to look after the big old house and the dogs while she was away, and with me working from home, it made me the ideal candidate.

My novels were no longer selling. My name faded from the bestseller lists. That's how it happens: you don't slip, or fall away. You fade, like bad ink on a page.

So there you have it. Some background material, a potted history of my pathetic marriage. An explanation, if you will, of how I got from there to here. The excuse I'm using for becoming a murderer.

How neat that word looks when it's written down: MURDERER.

I remember reading a horror novel where the word appeared backwards: *redrum*. It always made me think of the racehorse. We own a couple of racehorses – well, Tanya does. She owns a lot of expensive toys, and some cheap ones, too. I'm probably the cheapest, the one she discarded but kept around out of duty, and because I still had a minor function to serve.

The television news is still on – it's an extended report. There have been incidents at All Hallows. I think some people are dead. It's confusing. The police and the army have been mobilised. I hope they don't come here, not until I've finished my confession – because that's exactly what this is: I am confessing to something, and I need to get it down before I run out of energy, before I break down and sink into a black abyss of my own making.

We had an argument. It was about that damn festival – the New Festival of Britain – and all the problems the preparations have been causing. Demolition, building new structures, roads closed off, streets and footpaths dug up. It's more trouble than it's worth, an empty political gesture. But Tanya didn't agree with me on that one (she rarely agreed with me about anything these days). She thought it was a *good* idea, something to galvanise people and reinforce everything that's great about "Great" Britain.

I struggled with that one, I'll admit it. What on earth is so great about this country? Is it the failing infrastructures of our cities, the antiquated transport systems, or the depressed, discouraged inhabitants of this Sceptic Isle?

"You're shallow," she said to me.

"How do you mean?"

She smiled, but there was no affection in the expression. It was sly, almost obscene. "You never see to the centre of things, you only ever skirt around the edges. Like your writing – all those silly little crime novels set in a world that doesn't exist except on the page. Why don't you ever just face reality?"

I didn't know what to say.

I'd been waiting for her to come home, running through the plan in my head. It had taken me a long time to summon the courage, and tonight was the night I was going to act. I'd had enough of this woman; she was no longer the person I'd married. She was an adulteress, a vile, venal insect of a woman who thought more about money than she did of people.

So today – yes, today – I was going to kill her.

The cellar door had been broken for ages. I kept promising to get someone in to fix it, and had even gone as far as getting a couple of estimates for the work. That door . . . it was lethal –

especially now, since I'd taken my screwdriver to the hinges and loosened them off even more. The steps behind the door – the ones leading down into the vast, dark cellar beneath the house – were old, made of stone, and often quite slippery.

Especially now, today . . . since I'd poured some greasy water over them.

She was standing there, beside the door. All it needed was a little shove and she would go down, smashing her spine, or her skull, on those steep, greasy steps.

"I'm not shallow," I said.

"Oh, *fuck off*," she countered. "I need some wine."

That was when it happened. Serendipity arrived and took care of everything. I need not have planned: I'd wasted countless hours worrying about whether or not I could do it – push her against the door.

She turned, reached out for the door handle, and not realising the door was already open, she pitched forward, toppled, lurched heavily against the door-frame, and fell through. I saw her drop, as if a hole had opened up beneath her. The sound she made as she went down the steps was ghastly – like a sack of broken sticks bouncing off each stone tread.

"Tanya?"

She hadn't stopped tumbling.

Then, at last, all was silent.

I just stared at the door, realizing that I was unable to even approach it. I'd not really believed that I could go through with it, so hadn't visualised what I might do next, once she was down there, lying shattered on the cellar floor. It was the same as usual: I'd only focused on bits and pieces of the proposed event. My planning had, in fact, been shallow, just as Tanya had accused me of being. I'd never really had any intention of really killing her . . . but now there she was, hopefully as dead as could be at the bottom of the steps.

"I . . . I'm sorry." God, I was so weak, such a puny excuse for a man. I couldn't even fully commit to murder. Redrum. Race horses. My mind was reeling . . . I felt like I was going insane.

Hesitantly, I stepped forward and reached out, my fingers brushing against the cellar door. It swung inwards, letting out the darkness. I leaned through the doorframe and flicked the light switch. Illumination seeped up the stairwell. It wasn't much – the bulbs are a low wattage, and I'd screwed one of them out of its socket in preparation for this dark deed – but it was more than enough to guide me down beneath the ground.

"Tanya?" I needed to be sure she was dead. I hoped she was, I really did. I wasn't up to finishing her off, like a wounded bird. When I was ten years old I'd found a crow with a broken wing in a field near the old railway line. I was too afraid to do anything, so I just sat there and watched it die.

I didn't want to do the same with Tanya.

I began to descend the steps. The old stone was still wet and slippery. I grabbed onto the wall-mounted handrail and moved slowly, mentally chastising myself for not thinking this through properly. If she had slipped on the steps, then there was a good chance I might do the same. Why the hell had I not thought of that?

"Idiot." My voice fell flat against the solid walls and floor. The acoustics were weird down there.

I got halfway down the flight of stone steps before I saw her body. Not her whole body, just her legs. They were clearly visible, the left one turned so far around at the knee that the lower half looked as if it was facing backwards. She must have hit the ground with some force. Surely it had killed her.

I became aware of a dark shadow in the far corner of the cellar, near the wine racks. It was about six or seven yards from the bottom of the stairwell, and unlike the other shadows down there, it was moving. Twitching. I thought it looked like a swarm of insects – flies, perhaps, or gnats – gathered around the old coal chute. As I neared the bottom of the stairwell, I heard a low buzzing sound.

I didn't like this at all. The whole situation was very strange. Not just because my wife was lying dead at the bottom of the steps, but due to the presence of those insects. Did I recall that insects had something to do with the commotion at All Hallows church?

Then my gaze was snagged by another movement, this one more pronounced. One of Tanya's legs had twitched, as if she'd jerked on the cellar floor.

"Tanya . . . are you okay down there?"

The leg twitched again, I was certain this time – there could be no mistake. She was *still alive*. She was alive, and I would have to take care of her. I remembered again the crow, the way it had taken over an hour to die. I cried all the while, watching it writhe in agony, but still wasn't brave enough to help it on its way.

I reached the bottom of the steps, but I was unable to let go of the handrail. My fingers wouldn't budge; the fist refused to unclench.

With great difficulty, I managed to prise my hand off the wooden rail, and then I moved sideways, heading towards the centre of the room. The buzzing sound had stopped. I glanced towards the wall, where the insects had gathered, but they were no longer there.

Now I could see the rest of Tanya's body. Her head had been wrenched around one-hundred-and-eighty degrees, so it was facing backwards over her shoulders. Her dyed-blonde hair was caked in blood; the skin of her cheeks was as pale as the cheap paper I used to print out my novels. One of her blue eyes had a grey film across it, making it look like that of a vulture. I stared at that eye, even though I knew it couldn't see me. Her mouth was twisted. It almost looked as if she was smiling.

As I drew closer, I saw the little nub of spinal column sticking out of the nape of her neck, which was now just below her chin because of the way her head had twisted around.

"Oh, God . . . oh, Tanya. What have I done?"

I know it seems self-serving, that I could be lying when I say that I regretted what had happened, but I did. I was filled with remorse when I looked into that vulture eye. The other eye was closed. I was terrified in case it suddenly flickered open to return my gaze.

I couldn't leave her to die slowly, like the crow from my youth. I needed to "man up", as she was wont to say to me whenever she required me to take a stand, or even voice an honest opinion. I had to be merciful, despite the evidence that I was clearly anything but.

There was a garden shovel at the bottom of the steps, propped up against the brick wall. I kept all my tools down there; they were scattered around the cellar in no particular arrangement. I walked over to the shovel, grabbed the handle, and held it close. Tanya's leg twitched again, but this time the movement was less violent. Perhaps she was fading away, slipping into death? But the next twitch was twice as energetic as the first, so I knew that I was simply trying to convince myself that I could leave her and she wouldn't take long to perish after I returned upstairs.

"Man up, you coward." My voice sounded odd in the subterranean space, as if it were being suppressed.

I walked over to Tanya and stood over her, tears in my eyes, sweat on my brow, hands shaking as they gripped the shovel handle. I raised the tool like a weapon above my head, closed my eyes, and brought it down without giving myself time to think about what I was doing. The impact sent a jolt along my arm, which carried through into my shoulders. When I opened my eyes, I stared down at her ruined face. Her mouth hung open. The grey-filmed eye was bulging.

She was dead.

I hoped the police would assume that the injuries had occurred during her fall. It was only now – after I'd done it – that I wondered if smashing the hell out of her face was the best way to go. Perhaps I should have smothered her with one of the plastic refuse bags I kept down there, or just leaned on her chest with my knees, allowing my bodyweight to crush her lungs?

I hadn't thought about any of this. I was simply reacting.

I desperately needed a drink. Hastily, I put the shovel back in its place, and turned away, starting to climb the steps. Then I heard a rustling sound, as if Tanya's body was moving again. I refused to look back. I reached the top of the steps, firmly shut the door, and held tightly on to the handle. I didn't want to go down there again, but I knew I would have to. There was still work to be done. But first I needed to decide how to proceed. My original plan had been to call an ambulance, tell them that she had fallen. But now that I'd been stupid enough to finish her off with a gardening implement, that no longer seemed like the bright thing to do.

So what *was* I going to do?

I poured myself a double whisky, and then topped it up to a treble. I barely tasted the warm liquor as I gulped it down in two mouthfuls. I left the kitchen and walked into my study, where the television was still on. There had been deaths at the Blackheath church, and a killer – or perhaps killers – was running wild. I heard sirens outside. This was good. It meant that the authorities would be busy – even if I did call in an accident, I'd be low down on their list of priorities.

I wondered again what the trouble was at the church. I'd once researched a little about the building, for a book I ended up not writing. The place had an odd history.

The man who'd designed the place was some kind of occultist or alchemist, depending on which source you believed. Thomas Moreby. He was an interesting character, from what little I could fathom. He reputedly sealed up the dead bodies of plague victims in the crypt under the church, and told anyone who'd listen that those corpses would be reanimated, bringing forth some kind of vengeance upon London, then the rest of the world. He claimed that he knew the secret of eternal life.

What utter nonsense. It was like something out of a Hammer horror film – crazy, creepy, utterly insane.

But who was I to judge what was sane or otherwise, after what I'd just done?

I put down my empty glass and walked back into the kitchen. I opened the cellar door. I still had no idea what I was going to do, but I had to do *something*. The rustling noise I'd heard before was still going on – something was still moving down there. I took a step over the threshold and peered down into the gloom.

Tanya was climbing up the steps, on her back, wriggling and writhing because she couldn't get up on to her feet. Her backwards-facing head was pointed right at me; that filmy, unblinking eye judging me for what I'd done from an inverted position. I watched in horror as she slowly made her way towards me, hands grasping the sides of the stone steps, broken backbone rustling as it bent and folded to accommodate her obscene movements. One of her shoes fell off as I stared, bouncing down the steps to the bottom. Her head twitched. Her good eye blinked.

"No . . . please, no." I could hardly believe what I was seeing, but I couldn't dispute the reality of the scene. She was dead – surely she was – but still she kept coming, moving up the steps like some hideous creature from the depths of Hell.

I backed away, raising my hands. Gibbering, I stumbled and fell backwards into the kitchen, desperately grabbing for the door handle in an effort to close it. But the door wouldn't stay shut. It was broken, of course; I'd tampered with it to help carry out my plan, my ill-thought-out crime.

I started to laugh but managed to pull back from the brink. Tanya's twitching, inverted face appeared around the doorframe, followed by her shuffling, disjointed body. She was moving like an enormous crab: her chest was facing upwards, towards the ceiling, and her arms and legs were bent in several places due to fractures. She began to scuttle – slowly, but it was still a scuttle. She moved from side to side as she advanced, again reminding me of a crab. Her upended head, dangling on her shattered neck, hung down to almost touch the tiled floor. Her mouth opened; she hissed. Bloody spittle sprayed between her blue-tinted lips.

I scrambled to my feet, slammed into the dishwasher as I attempted to run, and somehow managed to pull open the door. There were still dirty dishes in there – pots, pans, plates, cutlery . . . a few sharp knives. I grabbed the biggest knife I could see and turned around. Tanya was only a few feet away from me, trying to gain her footing. She kept flopping over as she tried to stand. It gave me enough time to move in, slashing with the blade.

She wasn't very strong, but she kept trying to bite me – her teeth snapped noisily and emptily. I brought down the knife, cutting into her flesh. I was frenzied, like a madman, and felt stronger than ever before in my life. I stabbed and slashed, cut and sawed, and when her arm came away from the joint and flopped to the floor, I was filled with even greater vigour. I worked hard to cut off the other arm, and then I stepped back to survey my handiwork.

Tanya was still moving, but only barely. She couldn't do much without her arms.

Blood pumped, thickly and slowly, covering the kitchen floor. I had no idea what to do next, so I started kicking at her, moving her inch by inch towards the half-open cellar door. I grabbed a broom and used it to shove her at arm's length. Before long, I'd reached the opening. I gave her a couple of final almighty kicks, and she tumbled through and down the steps. She didn't make as much sound as the first time, but it was somehow even more unpleasant. She sounded somehow boneless.

I dragged the door shut and sat against the frame, breathing hard. I knew I was losing my mind, but right now that didn't seem like such a bad option. I could still hear her down there, behind the door, in the dimness at the bottom of the steps. She was moving around, trying to adjust to having two fewer limbs. I glanced to my right, at the small hand-axe we used for cutting firewood propped up against the AGA cooker.

The next thing I knew, I was standing at the open door looking down the steps. I had no memory of grabbing the axe, but I was holding it in my hand. My breathing was steady. I no longer felt so afraid. Tanya had always accused me of only ever showing her bits and pieces of myself, and it seemed ironic that she would now end up that way herself – *literally*. I tried not to laugh, but I allowed myself a quiet snigger.

"I'm coming down," I said. My voice was steady. I had never felt so together in my life. I laughed again at that last thought; the unconscious imagery amused me.

I heard her broken nails scratching on the stone floor. She hissed again, as if trying to communicate with me. I looked at my hand, my fingers gripping the axe handle. There was blood on my wrist. It was mine: she had scratched or bitten me in the struggle. There was no pain, just a curious sort of warmth at the centre of the wound, and a soft pulse, like a tiny heartbeat.

"Get ready for me, darling."

I used to love her. Maybe I still did. After all this time, all the hurt we had given each other, there might still be a chance to save our relationship. I'd only ever given her small pieces of myself rather than the whole man, but now it was her turn. I wondered if those parts could be rearranged, and made into something more palatable.

I'm not sure how much time has passed, but it feels like hours since I last saw Tanya. It's now dark outside. I've bandaged my wrist as best I can, but I can't seem to stop the bleeding. It still doesn't hurt, but I'm worried about what's happening under the wrappings. My flesh is pulsing. It feels like its changing shape, or tying itself up in knots.

I can still hear Tanya behind the door – or some of her, I'm not entirely sure which parts.

I used some old timbers from the kitchen storeroom to nail shut the door, but I didn't hammer the nails all the way in. I need to go back down there. I'll do so as soon as I have finish typing up this rambling account of what happened. I'm sorry about that – my novels lacked focus, too, or so the critics always claimed.

I don't expect anyone to believe me – if the television reports are correct about what's going on out there, nobody will even care.

What does it matter anymore about the distinction between truth and lies, fact and fiction? There is always truth in the heart.

Believe what you will. I will dissemble no more. I did the deed, and now I'm off to join my wife, so that we might be together again at the end, when everything – including me – falls apart. It'll be just like old times; she'll take me in her arms, wherever they are, and hold me tight. Perhaps her legs will even join us.

I'm not so sure about the rest of her though – it got pretty messy last time I was down there, frolicking with her in the dark.

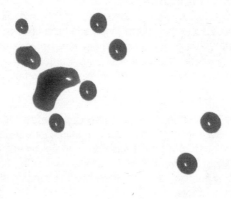

WethaZ

Formerly "WethaCrowd"
Copyright © MeteoStudio/Reflavored by ZApps

APP DESCRIPTION

Can't take much credit for this one, friends. Was originally a crowd-sourced weather app, the idea being people out there in the world clicked buttons to upload real-time intel about the actual weather where they were — like, was it raining, cloudy, windy, freakin' cold — to be more accurate for on-the-ground conditions than the lame-ass predictions on the news.

But the weather these days ... who *gives* a shit, right? Now that *we're* the food, ain't no such thing as a good day for barbecuing.

So I repurp-ed the app, switched a few things around, and now there are buttons for:

- Single zombie sighted
- Zombie hoard sighted
- Secured location

Clicks are uploaded and collated, and updates to the map in the app happen in real time, and will do until the facility where the server's housed falls.

NOTE: Use this app at your own risk, okay? Fact a location was tagged as "Secured" this morning doesn't mean it will be tomorrow, yo. Or even this evening. Or right now.

NOTE 2: Goes without saying that if you deliberately put up fake "Secured location" logs, you're going straight to Hell.

Even faster than the rest of us.

VERSION HISTORY
1.0 - First public release
1.1 - Won't be one. We're done.

Zeke @ ZApps

Wednesday, May 15

I don't need anybody else to tell me that I really should have another go at this journaling thing. Now, of all times. I did it once and then fell out of the habit, probably to my detriment, because even if I've managed to dodge an official diagnosis, I can't dispute the observations that I really do manage better with routines.

Although even if Gerri understands that, she doesn't quite understand why I still insist on having that morning walk of mine. Which, to me, is non-negotiable. It sets the day right.

Gerri: "What's it take to get you to rethink a thing like that? Because obviously it takes more than the end of the world to get enough leverage on you."

You'd think she'd never seen one of those KEEP CALM AND CARRY ON posters.

Gerri again: "Routines may help, but they can get you killed, too, you know."

Then she told me about something she'd seen on the telly once, something about Mexico, where they were having a lot of kidnappings. The first thing the bodyguards got their clients to do was start varying their routines, so the bad guys wouldn't expect them to show up at a certain place at a certain time by a particular route.

I don't know. Varying your routine sounds like an oxymoron to me. Once you start varying it, it's not really a routine anymore, is it?

I don't see why this has to be such an issue. The dead aren't especially fast and they're most assuredly not bright. All you have to do is keep your eyes open and keep moving.

Or maybe they just don't want me.

After all, wasn't it my father who once called me an acquired taste?

Thursday, May 16

We watched them take down another one today, from the window. A pensioner, by the look of him, only marginally faster than the biters who were after him. If it had been a race, on a track, in a straight line, he would probably have got away, but of course it's not set up like that at all. There's no starting line when the starting line is everywhere.

Gerri: "And to see it happen again like that, right in front of your eyes, that doesn't make you stop and think at all? About what could happen to you out there?"

Me: "There wasn't even all that many of them. He was just slow, that's all. He's like the zebra with a broken leg and they're the lions. It was the natural order of things."

Gerri: "Poor old bear. I wonder what he was doing out like that in the first place."

Me: "Maybe it was Alzheimer's. He went wandering."

These are the kinds of conversations we have now. Like we're used to this already, and the awfulness of it doesn't register anymore. Just stuck up here in our flat, four floors above everything, waiting for some sign that somebody's going to come in and turn this mess around, only nobody ever does.

Now and again we hear another promise to that effect on the radio, and we fall for it every time, because, I suppose, we're primed to. So it's easier to have our hopes dashed here, where we still have the safety of our own roof and a good stout door and a stockpile of food that should last us the better part of a month, than it would be to have them dashed out there somewhere, left with a minute or two on some unfamiliar roadside to wonder why we'd not chosen a different route, and come to terms with why our best-laid plans had still led us straight to slaughter.

So we wait another day, and then another. We've not been to our jobs for over a week, because our jobs stopped mattering. Within a matter of days, we became obsolete. There's no need for an assistant bank manager to go in, not when the banks are on permanent holiday. Gerri doesn't know if money's even good anymore. And myself, what is there for a draughtsman to do when all the engineering projects have gone on hold? I'm having a hard time of it imagining anything being built ever again.

Before long, the pensioner was just a slick on the pavement. And it wasn't like it happened right in front of our eyes, the way Gerri said, not really. When your flat's on the fourth floor, you're well above the street. Things don't look the same when you're looking down on them instead of straight at them. We couldn't hear him, either. That makes a difference. It happened in a kind of slow motion, the whole staggering knot of them kind of tumbling to the street all at once. They could've been playing. It could've been a joyous reunion, like dogs in the park.

Until the end, of course, when they all dispersed, all but the pensioner, and you could see the stains of what had really been going on.

I'm not without empathy. I'm really not.

I'm glad it's spring, for one thing. I'm glad for the rains. They help wash things clean.

Friday, May 17

Still watching them from the windows. What else are we going to do? It started with us waiting and watching for an evacuation that didn't come, and now that we've finally admitted it's never going to, we're so used to doing it that the habit doesn't seem worth breaking. And after a while, there's only so much you can go at each other in bed, if only to pass the time. It just doesn't seem right, not with the world falling apart, and anyway, we're not really wired that way to begin with.

Today's observations:

Gerri: "I wonder what it would be like to be one of them."

Me: "A bit basic, existence-wise. Walk, eat. That looks to be about it."

Gerri: "They have a kind of solidarity, don't they? They're all on the same page. They don't care what anyone else looks like. There's no such thing as too fat, too skinny. No such things as bad hair, bad skin. They don't point and laugh when one of them trips or falls over."

Me: "They don't seem to stop and help each other up, either."

Gerri: "Like how we went down and helped the old man?"

She was right about that. But it's six flights of stairs to street level. All it takes is one bite. He'd have already been a goner by the time we got there. It's only logical.

Gerri: "If you don't come back some morning, after one of those stupid walks of yours, you'll be killing us both, you know. Because I'll give it another day or two, just to be sure, and then I'm going down there to join them. I'll let them have me."

I told her she shouldn't do that. It's what you tell people when they say such things. Even I figured that out a long time ago. I don't know how convincingly I said it, but I told her so anyway, because it was the right thing to do. I have empathy. I really do.

Gerri: "Well, there comes a point when there's just *no* point. I'm not so sure we aren't there already."

Sunday, May 19

I may have found us a way forward. The best possible outcome, if we've got the stomach for it.

Gerri's got me wondering if I don't have a death wish myself, and that it's really what pushes me out the door each morning. If it was just about the walking, I could make do with the stairs and hallways of our building. It's almost entirely empty now. Some of the neighbours fled. Others nipped out and never came back and that's just the way it happened. One of the flats still has a live occupant — Mr. Popplethwaite, who's never wanted anything to do with anyone else even in the best of times. And there's another where you can hear some bumping around at all hours that doesn't sound quite right. All in all, safer than outside.

Yet out I go, regardless, and always come back, although luck seems to cover it only so far. To which I've only been able to conclude that they genuinely don't want me.

But today . . . maybe fate's got a hand in this.

My usual wake-up route gelled so long ago I don't even recall it happening. It seems now that I've always done it: a loop that drops south-west a few blocks, until I hit the entrance to King's Cross Underground station. I used to get a coffee, then turn around and head for home. Now I just turn around. It was a brisk twenty minutes, give or take, before this business with the dead; faster now, with no coffee queue or traffic. Whatever dead are out, I give them a wide berth, and detour around the messes they've left.

Lately I've taken to wondering if they don't want me because I've become a fixture as familiar as a landmark, and they no longer recognize me as prey. Or if, in doing the same thing, repeating the same patterns, I've simply become another version of them, from before there even *was* such a thing as them. And now that they're here, they know their own. Overall, my fit with the living has never been a particularly comfortable one for either of us.

Which brings us to today.

When I first saw her, I thought she was merely another casualty, a victim either of the dead themselves or of the unfathomable process that has stirred them up again. She was the only thing different this morning about the entrance to the Underground, a body that wasn't there yesterday, sitting propped against the square pillar that stands between the stairs and the lift.

From a distance she seemed entirely lifeless . . . obviously not living, but also devoid even of that dull, instinct-driven spark of the revivified dead. She seemed to me an anomaly, and whilst there's been no end to the corpses I've seen since this began, there was something I couldn't explain at first that compelled me to look at this one.

It was, I soon realized, the feeling of being watched.

From what I've witnessed so far, there's nothing behind the eyes of the dead, even less than what we might credit to an animal. No thought, just blind obedience to the force that moves them. I couldn't understand what it was about this one that made her so different . . . not just watching my wary approach, but seeming to command it.

Until finally, of all things, she spoke: "Help me . . . would you be so kind as to help me?"

It took several moments before I could answer: "How? You can't still be alive."

Which I said, I think, to convince myself. The look of death about her was blatant: the ghastly pallor, the sunken cheeks, the bones seemingly propping up the withered skin. And if her right leg wasn't tucked beneath her, it was gone at the knee.

"And who, sir, says that I am?"

"But you're talking."

"Obviously. What of it?"

"You don't talk. The dead, I mean. None of them do."

She appeared to have a retort to that, which she quickly thought better of, and held it back. If anything, this news seemed to be something she had to assimilate, and she slumped in what I could only read as disappointment.

Mind now, to refer to that reedy croak she made as talking was being generous, but still, it was nothing I should've heard at all. She wasn't merely dead, but appeared to have been dead for a long time. Decades, at least. The remnants of her clothing looked drab and archaic. The only colourful thing about her was the red of her hair, but it was in such disarray that it seemed to match the rest. There had been no rain the night before, but she appeared to have been thoroughly soaked, and was only midway to drying. The concrete beneath her was dark with dampness.

It was only then that I noticed the streaks of drying mud that led to the stairs down to the Tube.

Her: "Then, sir, why have you not run from me? Why have you not sought to kill me again?"

Fair questions. But not all questions have answers. At least none you want to give. It takes long enough just to think of them and write them down later.

Could it be that I actually enjoyed talking with her? She didn't speak quickly. I don't think she could. Everything was an effort. It gave me time to think, pauses that I never had with other strangers once we got away from the safe things I could repeat because I'd heard them all before, excruciating exchanges about weather and the like. It gave me time to feel I didn't have to worry about saying something wrong.

Her: "Where are the other six?"

Me: "Other six what?"

Her: "You would know them if you saw them."

She pointed towards the stairs without looking at them and told me she would be grateful if I checked. But of course I didn't move. Anything could be down there, in the Underground.

Her: "I have seen no more of your world, sir, than what I can see from here, but even I know that it has fallen and will never right itself again. Not as it was before. It will be something very different. This is precisely as it was meant to be. I was privy to the plans by the great architect that made them."

Whatever had happened to us all, I'd never once thought it was by design.

Her: "You would not suspect me capable of it, to look at my wretched state in this present moment, but I offer you the greatest possible gift. I offer you a choice. So decide, sir, what you would rather be in this world to come. Would you rather be a respectable part of it? Or would you rather be a small and inconsequential smear of the dust and ash and dung on which it is built?"

So I went down the Tube for a look. Just a look wouldn't hurt. Even if I didn't find any of whoever or whatever it was she was hoping to find, I must confess, I was curious how she'd got down below to begin with.

Daylight reached only so far along the ticket hall to the platform below, but whilst the escalators were stilled, a few of the overhead lights still burned and flickered, so I could see where to step and, more importantly, where not to. Signs of death and massacre were everywhere, and none of it looked unique.

But the train track, that was the strange part. The rails were submerged beneath a shallow, muddy creek flowing south along the bottom of the Tube. The water was calm now, but must've first surged through with great violence. I could see the marks where it had climbed up the grimy tile walls, and a mucky debris line had been flung as high as the platform.

The tracks themselves were intact, so whatever had happened to flood the tunnel hadn't happened here. I can only surmise that the River Fleet broke through somewhere to the north. I've heard it gets close to the Piccadilly line somewhere near the old defunct York Road station, so if it carved itself a new path and broke through the walls, well, here was the result, although it must also have carried away part of a cemetery and brought it along too.

How else to explain the remnants of a coffin, bashed apart and scattered around the platform? The wood looked old and spongy, and some of the fragments were bound together with tatters of silk or velvet. One of the larger chunks caught my eye: a rotten slab with the nameplate still bolted to it. It looked to be made of brass, crusted green with corrosion, but I could still read the lettering carved into it in an ornate script:

Cecilia Fowler
Died May 9, 1814
Aged 37 Years, 2 Months
"Fear not death; fear never having died"

There were no others anywhere to be seen. If six more graves had been washed out along with hers, the coffins could already have come to rest upstream somewhere. Or they could've continued south, towards Russell Square and Holborn. They could be anywhere.

Although I did find Cecilia's lower leg. I only knew what it was because of the shoe. I don't know why I took it back up to her. It just seemed the thing to do, like it was supposed to be consolation for the bad news, but really, it was just one more thing I didn't have enough time to think about. So I can't really blame her for reacting the way she did . . . looking at it for a moment, then flinging it away with what I found to be surprising strength.

Until then, I thought this was all she meant by needing my help. But it wasn't even the beginning.

I still don't know if I can go through with the rest. Especially now that I know who she is.

Fowler, Lady Cecilia (1777–1814)

Best known as a member of the Well of Seven, the inner circle of architect and occult guru Thomas Moreby. Only daughter of Lord Humphrey Langdon, of Twickenham, to have survived to adulthood. Married at age eighteen to Lord Benjamin Fowler, a notoriously weak-willed Member of Parliament reputed to have spent his entire tenure under the thumb of various shadowy cabals intent on wielding influence and furthering their agendas from behind the scenes.

Whispers of the Lady Cecilia's scandalous disposition began on a purely carnal note. Her husband was widely rumoured to have a predilection for being cuckolded, with which she apparently complied with considerable enthusiasm, even going so far as to conduct her arduous and noisy trysts in the room adjacent to where Benjamin bedded down alone.

She was, by all contemporary accounts, remarkable for her loveliness. An oil portrait confirmed as painted by Lemuel Francis Abbott reveals its subject to have been a young woman of cold, remote beauty – no small feat, perhaps, given the red of her hair – with a manner and bearing that were the antithesis of modesty.

In an interesting, although perhaps entirely coincidental, side-note, this portrait of her as a twenty-one year old has been dated to 1798, making it one of the last, if not *the* last, commissions that Abbott fulfilled before he was declared insane and put under the care of Dr. Thomas Munro, chief physician of Bethlem Hospital (a.k.a. Bedlam), until the artist's death in 1802.

Although Cecilia was no stranger to the scandal sheets of the day, and no doubt the focus of numerous juicy gossip sessions in salon gatherings across the county, no particular malevolence seems to have been ascribed to her until she was revealed as one of the key participants in the Hob's Lane Horror incident. On October 7, 1803, under ritual circumstances that can only be described as Satanic,

Thomas Moreby and his Well of Seven assembled in the basement of a popular Deptford bordello run by a madame named Moll Hackett. Here they ritually sacrificed Moreby's new wife, the former Anna Whitby, whom he appears to have married just weeks earlier for the sole purpose of guiding her towards this spectacularly grisly demise.

As the overseer of this gruesome tableau, Thomas Moreby was seized by the mob assembled by Anna's father – who had too late begun to fear for her safety – and entombed alive in a crypt at the nearby All Hallows Church. Ironically, All Hallows was an edifice of his own design, built in the late 1730s, making Moreby, at the time of his death, a man of uncommonly advanced years, and all the more remarkable for his apparent vigour. This may well have played a factor in the church itself being subject to longstanding rumours of blasphemy, witchcraft and devilry, even before the Hob's Lane incident.

Lady Cecilia, along with the rest of the Seven, fared better than Moreby. Although some of them were beaten and bloodied on the spot, none of them ever faced prosecution for their participation in this episode of human sacrifice, and Cecilia herself seems to have slipped away into the night unscathed.

However, her reputation, already a tattered thing, only worsened. For years, newspapers attributed to her an array of crimes and debaucheries that seem, at least to a point, to suspiciously echo the histories of such notorious figures as the Countess Elizabeth Báthory and Gilles de Rais. However, no evidence is known to have ever supported allegations that she, for instance, bathed in the blood of virgin girls or sacrificed an endless stream of children that somehow were supposed to have made their way to her door.

However, in her day she was unquestionably the most reviled woman in Great Britain. Rather than attempt to salvage her reputation, Cecilia appears to have decided to revel in it and encourage the rumours, no matter how salacious, unsavoury or fantastical . . . perhaps in the belief that fear would protect her as much or more than money and position would.

The Lady Cecilia and the rest of the Well of Seven – so named for their habit of meeting beside an actual well located on the grounds of St. Pancras Old Church, in South Camden, which was replenished by the waters of the subterranean River Fleet – continued to gather for years after the loss of their leader. They appear to have been undaunted in their wish to carry on Moreby's work, a mélange of beliefs unusual even by occult standards, involving the cultivation of fleas as an instrument of regeneration and immortality, and the summoning of the demon Anarchon, whose ascension to power would herald a new age of triumph over death.

While obvious failures in this endeavour, they nonetheless were successful in ensuring a long life to Moreby's legacy of terror. For decades to come, the Hob's Lane area remained an epicentre for reports of all manner of hauntings, apparitions and other bizarre occurrences. No less a notable figure than James Boswell was not immune to its influence, as evidenced by an unpublished 1782 fragment of his *Life of Dr. Johnson*, in which he appears to lend credence to "much talk of the dead gnawing at each other's bones beneath the ground".

Lady Cecilia Fowler died in 1814 of some unspecified fever at the age of 37, possibly as a result of a deliberate exposure to fleabites intended as a kind of primitive inoculation against plague. All her fellow members of the Well of Seven died within a two-year period, under what appear to have been similar circumstances. The possibility exists that this was planned before Thomas Moreby's death, as neither Lady Cecilia nor the rest of the Seven were buried with their families. Instead, they lie interred together, their seven graves arranged beside the well where they met in life, spending eternity in one another's company because, as the sour joke went at the time, nobody else would have them.

Monday, May 20

I suppose it was the kind of conversation that neurotypicals would say they save for the end, when there's no alternative left but to get into the hardest things they've ever had to talk about. But for me it hasn't been like that at all. Everything is real and true, and it feels good to finally say it.

What are Gerri and I, really, besides doomed? We've always liked order and predictability. At the bank, her greatest triumph was making sure the sheets balanced. And I liked the precision of lines, 2-D drawings that reflected perfect analogues in the 3-D world. You could look at one and immediately see in it the other.

That's gone forever.

I thought I already knew how much I didn't like change.

We're doomed if we do nothing. Our food will run out and then we'll have to forage, and everything nearby will run out too, and we'll have to keep foraging farther and farther away. Nothing will last. I don't know how much longer the power can even stay on. Sooner or later, we'll encounter somebody or something we shouldn't, and that will be the end of us. So we're doomed if we leave, too. We're not made for this.

It's the having no control of how and where we die that bothers us the most.

Me: "You said you'd go out there and give yourself over to them if I didn't come back one morning. But suppose they only leave half of you. Where will you be then? You wouldn't be able to get around. You'd just crawl."

Gerri didn't like the sound of that. It's like she'd been thinking she could go out and reason with them, the same way she could calm down an irate customer at the bank.

Gerri: "And she'll only take one bite?"

Me: "It's what she said."

Gerri: "One bite's not so bad."

This way, at least, we'll have control.

Gerri: "How long will it take?"

Me: "Didn't someone on BBC 2 say that it takes a few hours? But maybe it's not as long if you're not fighting it. Maybe it's faster if you welcome it."

Gerri: "Would we get to stay together? I've never been with anyone else but you."

I never thought of it that way. As many hours as we've spent watching them out the windows, not once have I ever seen anything that's looked like couples. They may work together, but beyond that, they all come off like independent contractors.

But maybe staying a couple isn't what Gerri means. Maybe it's that she still just wants to start the day with a familiar face, no matter how much this face of mine may change.

I understand now why aspects of this whole paradigm shift haven't fazed us as much as they have other people. We've been afraid for a lot longer than since this mess started. We recognized early what there was to be afraid of from other people, simply because we weren't just like them. We got used to that, and learnt to cope. We've never known what it's like to truly fit in, and there's something appealing about seeing how little it would take to finally be able to, for a change.

The sun is rising, and we really should be off.

And I guess we're down to all the last things now. It doesn't seem real to think that what's left in this cup is the last tea I'll ever have. I'll never see these walls again. And this new journal is a lot shorter than I expected it would be, now that I know I'll never write another word in it. I'll not likely write another word anywhere, ever.

So I leave it to the future to sort out what it means in the grand scheme. If it means anything other than dust, ash and dung.

The sun is rising and our path is clear.

I can't figure out why Cecilia wants me to bring a sharp knife, though.

Monday, May 20 (continued)

I believed her. I believed what she told me was going to happen would be what actually happened. I believed it. Except none of it was the truth, and I'm now alone again, even though I'm not. Even with the dead, it's just the same old lies and duplicity.

Gerri and I got to King's Cross a few minutes past dawn. We drove. Took my Vauxhall because Gerri wasn't any too keen on walking for blocks, out in the open. Maybe she was right to be. Maybe the biters would still want her, if not me.

Cecilia was where I had left her the day before. We walked up and made our hellos, and whilst I'd had time to get accustomed to the idea of one of them talking and thinking, it was still something Gerri had to get used to before she wanted to get close. There's been something different about her from the very beginning, this Lady Cecilia, and even though I didn't understand it, and still don't, it's obvious, and it's more than just the power of speech. It was in the way she sat and the tilt of her head and the way she looked at me with what was left of her eyes.

From the first moments I saw her yesterday morning, it wasn't only that I knew something more was there. It was the realization that she was perhaps the best chance I could hope for that we would end up as something better than the rest of the rabble.

Cecilia, for her part, looked almost exclusively at Gerri, as if inspecting her. When we finally got up close, I thought I saw the faintest flicker of distaste cross her features. I didn't know how in her state – wizened and dried, like battered leather – she could even register something so subtle. Had to be my imagination, right?

Now I know better . . . that perhaps Cecilia remembered what it was like to be beautiful, and maybe even still thought of herself that way, and found Gerri lacking by her standards.

She's an evil thing, but all I have now.

She wanted to turn Gerri first, and Gerri wondered why the rush, why she couldn't go second. Cecilia's reason seemed logical at the time: "I sense you're not as committed to this as he is. Better we leave you with as little opportunity to change your mind as we can."

I thought she would bite us one after the other, but her plans were more involved.

Cecilia: "What is that manner of cage over there?"

She was referring to a newsagent's stand.

Cecilia: "They keep them in cages now? After all the vile things they printed about me in my time, I believe a cage is a most suitable place for them."

I had to tell her it wasn't like that, that it was just a shop with a type of metal grill that rolled down over the opening, so people wouldn't loot it whilst the fellow who worked in it was away, and he didn't have any control over what got printed, although there was a newsman named Rupert Murdoch that a lot of people thought belonged locked inside a cage just the same.

Cecilia asked me if I could open it up.

It was secured with a padlock, but amongst the flood debris down below in the Tube, I found a long, thin shank of iron that served as a crowbar, and used that to peel the hasp off the door.

Cecilia then asked if I would carry her inside, since, missing half a leg, she couldn't walk, and refused to crawl any more. She felt as light as a child, and though she'd had time to air-dry from the deluge that had swept her here, she still smelt of wet earth and rot. There was just enough room to set her down on the bare concrete, between stacks and shelves full of newspapers with headlines that had lost the plot and magazines no one would ever read. There was even less room for Gerri, but somehow they managed to fit. In truth, Cecilia didn't take up much room.

Cecilia: "The knife. Leave it."

I have to imagine now that Gerri was looking at me as I stepped outside, wanting one last moment between us, except I don't much like eye contact, and now I wish I'd forced myself to endure it because it was the last time I could've had to see her just as herself, nothing but Gerri, and instead I let it go and pulled the metal grill back down behind me.

If she was only going to change one of us, for god's sake, why couldn't she have changed me?

After another minute or two Gerri gave a loud wailing cry. I ran to the cage to make sure things hadn't gone wrong, because it all seemed wrong now, but the deed was done and Cecilia wasn't being greedy. One bite was all she'd taken, and not even a deep one. Gerri was bleeding from the shoulder – bare, as she'd worn a tank top to make it easy – and had her face in her hands as she dissolved into sobs.

She cried for a long time. She cried until she wore herself out. Or maybe it was that she cried until she couldn't, because she was getting too sick, curled up on her side, and getting sicker.

We knew this would take a long time. Hours at least. There just wasn't any way of preparing for how long it actually felt, waiting for it to be over.

I should explain at this point why Cecilia wanted to do it in the newsagent's shop. She said it was because Gerri would be a long time in between states: bitten and dying, but not yet dead, and certainly not yet returned. Cecilia didn't want her lying out exposed, where the scavengers who had preceded us could come along and feed on her.

It seemed sensible to me at the time.

But as I waited, sometimes up top, sometimes down in the cool of the Tube platform, I started to recall that none of them actually ever seemed to come near us. Not yesterday, not today. They were about. They were always about. They might look our way, might even take a few steps in our direction. But then they would always find a reason to steer themselves elsewhere.

It was so slow that I didn't even think of it as a reaction. It seemed a natural part of their aimlessness. And I thought it was just me, again. Their disinterest in me.

Now, though: now I'm forced to wonder if it wasn't that Cecilia was somehow controlling them. Is this any more impossible than the fact of her speaking?

It was a very long day. By some point, I'd forgot about the knife.

Deep into afternoon, I began to hear sounds from the newsagent's. Stirring and bumping and a cascade of papers knocked to the ground. I'd been hoping all day that Gerri would revive conversant, articulate, still more like the old Gerri than not, but with a more predatory nature. A survivor, finally.

These were not those sort of sounds. These were much more base.

I didn't want to see her. Not until I was like her.

For all that, Cecilia, with her wheezing croak of a voice, still sounded content with the way things were going: "That's a good girl. That's my girl . . ."

I really didn't want to see her. Yet how was I to make my own transition if I didn't take Gerri's place, or get Cecilia out? Given what I was hearing now, with Gerri sounding no better than the mindless hordes who'd been shuffling through the streets for weeks, I now thought that perhaps Cecilia had done it this way to protect me, to keep Gerri from being the one to turn me. That perhaps it would take time for us to become like Cecilia.

Release her . . . that was my idea. Roll up the grill and let her out, use the shop for cover, then slip in and secure the grill from inside.

But first I needed to know how close to the front of the shop Gerri was. Even though I didn't want to see her. Not until she would know me as one of her own again.

Would we get to stay together? I've never been with anyone else but you . . . I can't stop hearing her say that. It echoes.

When I stepped up to look through the metal lattice, I saw how wrong I'd been. About everything. Even if I didn't understand at this stage what was actually going on.

She'd begun with her ruined leg, Cecilia had. Nothing was left of that by now but the last clinging scraps of flesh and her thighbone, scored by the kind of crude butchering marks our Cro-Magnon ancestors left on the animal bones in their midden heaps. She'd moved on to the other leg, starting low, above the ankle, and working her way up. This must've been going on a while. Most of that leg was gone too.

I assume she felt no pain. Cecilia seemed quite pleased to be doing this. But it was just the idea, the horrible idea of it, no matter how much of a ruined state you were in: carving away chunks of yourself to feed them to someone else.

But to hear it, they could've been mother and child in there.

"That's my girl. That's my good girl . . ."

Cecilia noticed me staring, unable to move, and told me she'd be with me soon. As for Gerri . . . there was almost nothing left to recognize. I imagine it must be like this when someone confronts a sleepwalker in the family, and the part that would recognize them is somewhere far away. Except there was no way to wake her up, and she was so very hungry.

She reached for me, with a grunt and a lurch as if to get up – I can't stop hearing that either, now – but Cecilia caught her by the wrist and stuffed her mouth with

I can't even say it. I just can't.

The best I recall, I backed away from the newsagent's and dropped to the ground, and didn't move because there was nowhere left to go. Whatever was going on in the shop, it went on a good while longer before it was finished. I only knew it was done when the grill began to rattle. I was trying to decide whether or not to open it and face whatever was to come next when it stopped. Whoever was trying to get out gave up.

Then a few moments later the metal lattice rattled again and scrolled up out of the way, as if the world had gone back to normal and the place was opening for business. Then she crawled out and swung around on to the concrete with a sense of co-ordination I'd witnessed on exactly none of them.

Gerri crawled out.

Except it wasn't really Gerri. Not anymore. Yet, this time, there was so obviously a soul again behind her eyes. Amazing how we know it when we see it, once we've seen what the utter absence of it looks like. She'd even made an effort to clean herself up.

She took a couple of steps forward, tentative, like someone trying on strange new shoes. Or strange new feet, strange new legs.

She pinched at her fleshy midriff and scowled. She poked at each breast and seemed to find them wanting. She squeezed one thigh and found it too chubby. She ran her fingers through the bobbed blonde hair and found it too short, too fine. I'm sure she already knew just how red it wasn't.

Not-Gerri: "I wish I could say there was even one thing I like about this body. But I cannot. She was the best you could do, this one, was she?"

How could she say such a thing? Gerri wasn't beautiful? I'd thought she was. Once I'd got to know her.

New-Cecilia: "Well, it will have to suffice for now."

I found it in myself to get up off the ground and look inside the newsagent's. Below the waist, it was mostly bone that was left, and from what I'd seen of the damage these things could sustain and still keep moving, Cecilia's body should've been "alive" in its fashion, but now it was well and truly dead. The deadest thing I've ever seen. She'd cast it off like an old tattered coat, now that I'd brought her a new one.

As I said, they could've been mother and child in there. More than ever now, seeing as how mothers sometimes try too hard to live through their daughters.

As for Gerri, the real Gerri, I've no idea where she's been pushed to. If there's anything of her left in there, trying to get out.

I already knew Cecilia wasn't like the others. I just had no idea how *much* she wasn't like them. But that's not entirely true, is it? There's one of the first things she said when I found her, when she asked where the other six were.

The Well of Seven, going by the entry on her in that book I downloaded. They're all like this, all like her?

I brought her home because I didn't know what else to do. And because it was kind of implied. When I asked if she wasn't going to make me over to be one of them, she only laughed, and said in time, all in good time, but for now she had better uses for me.

She found Gerri's closet as if she already knew the way, and made a few scathing remarks about what passed for women's fashion now, then resigned herself to accepting that this was what she would have to work with.

So that was today. I end it as I began it . . . as myself, and wishing for better.

Sunday, May 26

Back again. I lost myself for a while.

There's a part of me over the past week that's been thinking I should kill her again and be done with it. There are moments when I look at her and see something that shouldn't exist wearing Gerri like an elaborate disguise.

But there are moments when she looks at me and *I know that expression*, so purely Gerri that I expect her to say something I alone would get, a private joke or recollection. Is it even possible? I've read about transplant patients who exhibit new characteristics – new likes, dislikes, habits and the like – that turned out to be traits of the person whose organ they received. So perhaps there's something to it after all.

It is her power over me, her hold.

Or maybe I'm just not the murder-suicide type.

She's spent the days learning about the world, how it's changed since her time. She can't believe how big London has grown, and her speech is changing, becoming less formal. She also took down Mr. Popplethwaite, but I can't begrudge her dinner.

The rest of the time she's been trying to figure out what to do next. It's as if she's listening for something that only she can hear. She's lost and she knows it, and the fact that she's got six friends out there doesn't mean much if she can't find them.

I can't bear to see her hurting because it's Gerri's face that shows it. Then I remind myself what kind of people her friends are.

Who's really the lost one here?

Monday, May 27

Today Cecilia decided she wanted me to take her to that old church, All Hallows. At first I thought the name was only familiar because I read it in that encyclopedia entry I found on her, as the place where the leader of her group – cult? coven? I have no idea what to call them – had been walled up alive.

But it's where all this began around May Day, too. Ground Zero.

On the drive there, I got to see more of the city than I'd seen since then, and it's the same as the blocks around our flat, only scaled outward for as far as we travelled. I'd got used to the idea of a few city blocks having fallen. But this is everything, an entire city tipped into lawlessness and chaos. The ruin will come soon enough. I could see where they'd set up army checkpoints and barricades, but these were all deserted. The dead roam the streets and sidewalks and parks in idle packs. They're like the wild animals that moved into ancient Rome once the people had all gone.

As we rolled through, the dead watched us pass, and at first I thought it was just because we were something moving, the way predators instinctually home in on their prey. But in time I realized they never seemed to be seeing me. It was always Cecilia they were looking at.

They too know something is different about her. They know it before she even gets to them, when she's still half a block away. They know it in a way that makes them like flocks of birds that all turn at once.

Gerri said it first: They have a kind of solidarity about them.

All Hallows isn't what I was expecting. It looks more like a construction site than a church now. Which I suppose I would've known had I followed these things on the news better. Oddly enough, whereas I was thinking the place may have been holy ground to Cecilia, the sight of it seemed to bother her.

Cecilia: "They threw him into the crypt and walled him up inside still very much alive. No trial, nothing. He was like a lion brought down by rats. All of them, happy to let him die slowly in the dark, with 'praise God' on their lips."

Thomas Moreby, she would've been talking about.

Me: "Didn't the lot of you butcher his wife?"

Cecilia: "I'm sure that must have been what it looked like to ignorant people."

Me: "The results were the same."

Cecilia: "The results would have meant a different world if they'd only had the chance to come to fruition. But she was spoiled for us, the simpering little ninny. Her maidenhead . . . she had surrendered it already."

Me: "So I'm not wrong. In the end, all you did was butcher her."

Cecilia: "Not everyone who achieves something great does it willingly, or by their own choosing. Not every great achievement is free of pain. She was born and groomed to be a doorway. It is her own fault she failed in that."

Me: "And what is it I'm being groomed to be?"

Cecilia: "A survivor?" For the first time, conversation with me seemed to amuse her. "But you do not need to worry about doorways now. As you can see, the door to our new world has already been kicked wide open."

That she left me in the car then, alone, as she ventured into All Hallows' crypt, I can only regard as a test. Would I leave? Would I stay? I stayed, of course, but I've no idea what test I passed or who I failed.

I only know that in the car I was speaking with Cecilia, and that from behind, I was watching Gerri.

When she came back out, I expected her to be carrying

something, maybe, but she wasn't. She had to get back in the car before I understood that it was still an errand to fetch something. It was just too small to see until she was next to me again.

That's another point between them that couldn't be more different. Gerri, of course, would never have stood for fleas. Especially big reddish ones that aren't much smaller than common flies. They hopped and crawled around on her for a few moments after she returned to the car, then scuttled out of sight. Maybe they found a place to hide on her. Or in her.

I spent the drive home thinking I could feel them on me, too.

Tuesday, June 4

London is behind us now.

I was already expecting it, that Cecilia would insist on leaving. After all, what was left to do there? Whatever her plans are, and I believe she has some now, they don't involve London. Just the same, I never thought I'd actually leave the place.

My Vauxhall Corsa was no good for her, though, for reasons I haven't been able to get out of her. Maybe she doesn't like sitting as close to me as we were in the Corsa. Or maybe she wants a higher vantage point. Nothing would do for her but that we get a truck. You'd think any car would be good enough for her, since, back when she was alive, the best she could hope for was a horse-drawn carriage.

But she's a quick study, and there are times when, even though I know Gerri is no longer in there, Cecilia seems to be raiding her memories, assimilating them and making them her own. To a point. Although she understands the concept of cars, she's none too eager to try driving one herself.

Of course she needs me.

And so she wanted a truck, and knew just what kind: no open flatbed, but one with an enclosed cargo area. It's a thieves' paradise – vehicles are there for the taking everywhere you look, the keys right in them. Although I had to find a vehicle that even I could handle, without having to fuss about with changing gears. But there were people in the process of moving when all this began, and never got a chance to get to their new homes. I felt a bit bad about tossing their belongings out into the street, but if they were still there to be tossed, the owners must've had worse things to worry about, if they could even worry at all.

It was slow going at first. Slower than slow. All the abandoned traffic, all the rubble of countless calamities left scattered where it fell. In my nimble old Corsa, I could've steered around it. Now I just grind through and slowly bash things out of the way. The further we get out of the city, the more it thins.

I ask her where we're going.

Liverpool, she says.

What's in Liverpool?

Better you ask what *was* Liverpool.

But when I do, she doesn't say anything more. And I don't really know how to answer it for myself. Where the Beatles came from? It has to be more than that.

Some foolish part of me keeps expecting to drive out of the world's end, but the edge of that border always seems to leapfrog us and stay a mile or two ahead. Even so, there are spots so peaceful and seemingly untouched, you can get to feeling that the worst is behind, and you've come to a normal zone.

Until another military jet screams overhead, or a helicopter the size of a bus, or you happen across another checkpoint that's still manned by living troops who look a day or two away from turning their guns on themselves.

Then there's no more pretending. You remember there's no end to it.

It was the first of the manned checkpoints that scared me more than anything has since the whole mess began. We rolled up on it on the M40 outside of Uxbridge, before I could stop to think that it could turn disastrous. Four jumpy soldiers who looked as if they'd been dropped there days before, with no idea what they were supposed to do or when they might be relieved – what could go wrong?

They peered into the truck's cab, and one of them hopped up on the running board, and I thought that's it, they'll shoot her on sight, and me with her.

But then they waved us through.

She passes for living, Cecilia does. She speaks, she moves normally, and she reasons. At worst, she looks like a woman who's not had a good night's sleep in a while. Which no doubt describes every other poor sod they've been seeing on the roads.

Although I wonder how differently it would've turned out if they'd been close enough to see the fleas.

Thursday, June 6

The calendars may say it's early June, and the rains feel like spring and the green is in full force, but to my eyes it's autumn that's descended on us. The land has turned itself inside-out with death and change, the desolate silence of the cluttered motorways the most obvious sign of the hibernation we've plunged into.

There are more refugees out than I thought there would be. I thought they'd all be like Gerri and I were, before Cecilia . . . holed up waiting for someone to get this thing in hand. But they've already hit the point I was worried about before. They've already exhausted their supplies and are on the move for more. In just weeks, they've gone from salaried cogs in civilization's machine to hollow-eyed nomads propelled by a delusion that there's something better out there to be found.

They find me when I'm siphoning a little more petrol for the truck, or sifting through wreckage for food and water, and they look at me with hope and interest. They ask what I know, what I've heard.

Cecilia studies them whilst I tell them I haven't heard a thing.

It's why I've actually come to like her. She's the only one who acts as though she has any idea of what comes next.

Friday, June 7

I didn't see *that* coming.

Late this morning I was trying to pick our way around a barricade south of Coventry, and cursing Cecilia's insistence on travelling in something the size of this truck, when the sky flickered with light. Just once. If you blinked, you would've missed it.

Within a minute or two, the wind picked up behind us, fiercer and fiercer, seeming to build with no end to it, howling up from the south-east. Trees swayed with it, and rubbish tumbled along the ground ahead of it, or flurried through the air. I still didn't get it, not until the sound of the faraway roar caught up with us, and the cloud started to climb from the distant horizon like a pillar reaching for Heaven.

London. It could only be London.

I didn't think the dead had it in them to still feel true fear. Or awe. Or whatever it is in that football-shaped part of the Venn diagram where they overlap.

Cecilia: "What . . . is . . . that?"

So I had to tell her about nuclear bombs. I can't grasp how unbelievable it must sound to someone who has no context for understanding them or why you would want to stockpile them. Me, I've never known a world without them. So it was harder for her to fathom that most of London was gone than it was for me. She couldn't tear her eyes from the sight.

"They would actually use a thing like that?"

She kept asking that. Asking what they would hope to get out of it when there's nothing left.

Me: "Leaving nothing . . . that's kind of the point."

And she didn't even have to say it: that she and her kind – all of them, the stupid ones and the ones who could still think and reason, and the ones she'd come from, the Well of Seven, who'd planned for this more than 200 years ago – were by our definition monsters, but even they don't believe in utter nothingness. They don't believe in annihilation, or in extermination. They don't believe in acceptable levels of collateral damage. They believe in transformation.

Cecilia took a step closer to me as the cloud grew, and another, until I could put my arm around her, and because she didn't stop me, or pull away, for a while it just felt like Gerri.

I don't know how long we stood there. A thing like that, you don't worry about the time. But a bit later, once calm had settled over the land again, I noticed that the wind was once again blowing from the north. Good. Let it carry the bomb's fallout across the Channel. Let the French deal with it.

Saturday, June 8

I'm starting to think she's taken me to Hell, and Hell is driving.

Motoring distance between London and Liverpool is only a bit over 200 miles. Before, you could start after lunch and be there for teatime. Even under the current conditions, it's still not a journey you'd expect to take as long as it's taking.

But she's had us going on detours, keeping to the smaller towns and villages, away from the insanity of wherever there's more people, the living and dead alike, because wherever there's more dead, the greater the risk there's going to be a convoy of troops mounting an offensive, and that's not a thing we want to be caught up in.

Plus, now that they've nuked London, who's to say they won't take out Birmingham next? Or that we'll see another mushroom cloud, ahead of us this time, and there goes Manchester.

Cecilia seems to be making this up as she goes. She gets off by herself where things are quietest and plays with those ungodly big fleas and it's as if they whisper to her, laying secrets in her ears. Which sounds absurd, and it *is* absurd, but I'm already playing *Driving Miss Daisy* with a living corpse inhabited by a different soul, and if you open the door to one absurd thing, you have to consider letting in the rest.

What she's got us hunting out here is wooden crates. Actually, what she's really got in mind is coffins, but her idea of what people get buried in remains outdated, rooted in her own times.

Coffins are harder to get your hands on than you'd think. We've found a few mortuaries, but they're not easy to break into. Presumably because there used to be people keen on violating the dead, before it all got turned around. Anyway, we can forget about those big bulky things they use now, all polished up like stainless steel refrigerators, because guess who it is that's going to be lugging them around, getting them in the truck? There's no way I can lift one of those by myself, and we're short on pallbearers.

That's why I've been thinking crates, but these days not much seems to ship in wooden crates the size of coffins. Cardboard boxes, I can find those all over the place, but they're not sturdy enough. Not when Cecilia says that we can't have their occupants clawing their way out before it's time.

So even though I have a good idea of what's going to go in them, I can't fathom why. The entire world is a coffin now.

Sunday, June 9

What I want to know is this: what kind of person sees the fall of the world and decides that it's what they've been waiting for all their lives? That they've finally got the chance to live the way they've always wanted, now that even martial law has lost its grip?

We were stopped in a supermarket in a town called Lilleshall so we could replenish my stock of bottled water when from up the road came a rumble that sounded like something big on its way, even bigger than our mover's truck.

I got to the shop-front's window in time to see a big flatbed lorry rolling past, the kind Cecilia *didn't* want, except this one was built up on the sides with slats of wood topped with barbed wire. A rolling pen is what it was. It looked full, too, except those weren't dead people in there. It was mostly women and girls, and a few men who looked like they wouldn't put up much of a fight.

You could say I recognized the type.

There was a gigantic bearded fellow sitting above them in an iron frame that appeared to be welded to the roof of the lorry's cab. He had a rifle or a shotgun, and looked just like a guard in a tower. There were two more in the cab, and a dog.

Nobody was being protected here. None of them in the back wanted to be there. I've never seen anything more obvious. I'm not without empathy. I'm not. It was all tears and clinging to each other back there, and the numb acceptance of defeat, and the stark paralyzing terror of wondering how much worse a situation could get.

All that in a few moments, then they were past, and I had no idea where they were going. Someplace deep in the farmlands, I guess, where no one would disturb the ones who chose to be there, or find the ones who didn't.

How can I see a thing like that and not conclude I've made the right choice in who I've ended up siding with.

Monday, June 10

So it's caskets after all.

I didn't even know they still make them this way, but I guess it's the kind of thing you shouldn't be surprised would come out of a monastery in the countryside, where the times don't change. If you're a Cistercian monk and not keen on brewing ale to keep the abbey in funds, well, might as well build coffins. People always need coffins. Or used to.

I'd never heard of the place. It was something Cecilia remembered.

We've had to do some serious backtracking, though. We've dropped way down into the Cotswolds. The last name I recognized was Gloucester, and the place is tucked in ten or fifteen miles south-east of there, but it seemed even farther than miles, like going back in time. All stone and trees, with the lawns starting to get overgrown. Whilst Cecilia wandered off to play with her fleas, I explored the grounds, and finally got drawn around the back of the abbey by a banging sound, fast and sharp and even. The sound of work.

By the time I found the woodshop, the monk had stopped hammering and was using a plane to smooth a length of pine. At least I assume he was one of the monks. He was a shorthaired man, seventy if a day, and in his shirtsleeves looked like any other carpenter. He wasn't wearing a robe, but I have to think robes aren't very practical in a woodshop.

I've never in my life seen so many coffins as there were along the far wall. And almost never in my life, except for Gerri, have I seen someone so glad to see me. Maybe he was the last monk left.

I told him I needed coffins. Seven, eight, nine. However many he could spare. Call it eight. Cecilia hadn't been specific, but I was thinking of how many I could fit in the truck without stacking.

Him: "You can take as many as you like. It's what we do here."

Me: "I'm sorry. I can't pay."

He seemed to find that amusing, and I finally laughed with him, because I thought I got the joke, but really, I hadn't. Not yet.

Him: "You'll be doing me a favour. I was almost done here. But if you take eight, that'll keep me busy a while longer. It's good to keep busy."

It was somewhere in here that I noticed one of the hammers on his workbench, the business end stained red and clotted with hair and worse, and he caught me noticing it.

Him: "You didn't go in the chapel, did you? Before you found your way back here?"

I told him I hadn't.

Him: "Good. See that you don't."

So I backed the truck around and he even helped me load them. Without me having to ask, he gave me a hammer and a box of nails, too. Said he couldn't stand the thought of me needing them and realizing too late I didn't have them.

I picked up Cecilia again along the drive back out to the main road.

The strange part isn't that she remembered this place after spending over 200 years in the ground, or that it was still here, doing what it did after all this time. The strange part is that she couldn't have remembered it at all.

I didn't notice it on the abbey's sign near the road when we first drove in, only when we drove out: ESTABLISHED 1887. The order hadn't even existed in her lifetime; hadn't been founded until more than 70 years after she was dead.

Me: "How did you know? How could you?"

Cecilia, in a hazy kind of way: "I read about them . . . in *Artisan Britain*."

Gerri had loved *Artisan Britain*. Never missed an issue.

She rises inside at the most unexpected times, like a fish in a pond coming to nibble at the surface, then plunging deep again. I find myself wishing she'd either stay for good, or go for good.

Tuesday, June 11

My theory was that she wanted the coffins for her friends, the rest of the Well of Seven. And maybe a spare or two. That somehow they'd made their way to Liverpool, but hadn't been as lucky as she was in finding a newer body to inhabit, and needed to be safely transported somewhere before they did.

I couldn't have been more wrong.

We'd headed north again after getting the load of coffins, not quite out of the Cotswolds yet and passing through some village whose name I hadn't caught when Cecilia said to stop. Right there in the middle of the main road. Open up the truck, she told me, set up the ramp in the back, and she'd take care of the rest. Oh, and take the lids off the coffins.

She was gone for a while then. She told me not to follow. Stay in the truck's cab, out of sight, because she didn't want me drawing attention or getting attacked when she wasn't around. I told her they don't want me. To which she said *she* wanted me, and that was what counted.

I'm still puzzling over how she meant that.

When she came back, she was leading a group of eight of them, all recently dead by their appearance, all men with rangy builds, with the look of men of the land who were as tough as leather. She led them single-file down a row of houses of tan stone and slate roofs, and they followed as surely as if she'd been leading them by a leash, like a row of slaves shackled along a chain.

After I could no longer see them, I heard them clomping up the ramp. After some noisy shuffling about in the back of the truck, she called out for me to come join her. The dead men had laid themselves out one to a coffin, neat as you please, staring up with their milky eyes, waiting for me to put the lids over them and bang them shut with a few nails.

Cecilia: "They used to breed them strong and hearty out here, as I remember. Let's hope that still holds true."

The bad ones seemed to not even know I was there. They only had eyes for the roof. The worse ones noticed, their eyes following my every move until I got the lid rattled into place. And all of them were hopping with a handful of fleas that looked to have been scattered across them like seeds.

Thursday, June 13

The whole zigzagging trip, I was never able to solve her riddle: better you ask what *was* Liverpool. Now it all makes sense. What Liverpool was was a seaport. Not just any seaport, but the greatest one we had.

I was never there before, but I imagine the place was always busy as a beehive. The docks are an eerie place now, mostly silent except for the screeching of gulls and the surging of the water, and full of ghost ships that will never sail again, creaking at their moorings. There's a heap of scorched wreckage about 100 metres out from where we rendezvoused where something went wrong – too many people trying to flee at once, maybe.

I've always admired ships. Freighters, passenger liners, tankers . . . all kinds, really. They're engineering marvels. Seeing them all there, knowing that one by one they'll rust out and sink where they sit until the harbour is a giant's graveyard of old metal hulks . . . I think I felt the impending loss of them more than I have the loss of humanity. Because I keep being reminded of humanity at its worst, but ships . . . they show what we can really do.

At least the one I'm on now is still in use, and away from the clutches of land.

Liverpool wasn't just a destination. It was a departure point, and not for us alone. Cecilia's people were here already, the rest of the Seven, and had apparently spent days putting together the pieces and logistics of this voyage. I suppose we were so far behind the rest because Cecilia had had a harder time of it in the aftermath of the flood that had freed them.

The remaining Seven consist of two other women and four men. Looking at them together, it's not hard to see how they might be perceived by the lesser dead as gods, or at least a kind of royalty.

They're proud and disdainful, even in death. Maybe they have a right to be – they've triumphed over the one thing everyone fears. They've all found new bodies that serve them well, and carry themselves just like you'd expect Colonial-era nobles would. There on the docks, they greeted Cecilia like a long-lost sister, even as they jeered at the body she was in. Gerri's body.

It never gets easier, hearing the insults.

When they first set eyes on me, they lit up, seeming to take me for a treat she'd brought them, and at first I really thought I'd served my purpose and was ready to be discarded, but Cecilia shut them down quickly, telling them that I was useful, and full of potential.

And I was only too happy to prove this, when they wanted our payload moved to the deck of the small cargo ship they were set up beside. There was no unloading first. They wanted it truck and all, and so I drove it across a ramp set up from dock to deck, where it joined three other vehicles there already. Clearly the cargo has some more travelling ahead of it once it gets where we're going.

I wonder who the other drivers were?

That we're bound for the U.S. seems obvious, although I can't fathom the grandiosity in why, given the size and type of the ship, and that there's just the one.

I heard one of the Seven say they're going to take back the Colonies.

Ireland is before us and the sun is setting now and we seem to be heading straight into the dull, glowing fire of it. I'm living a legend now – a mortal man trapped aboard a ship crewed by the dead.

. . . Captain Wonnacott, forgive this use of unofficial channels. This is rather an "unofficial" time, isn't it? I do need to make this note, as long as my phone keeps working, if the satellite signal keeps up – if this blessed Chinook holds just a little more steadily in the air and my trembling fingers can work the screen, or if I don't drop the instrument out the open door!

But I must not be churlish. Our American allies are risking their own personnel and equipment to retrieve as many of our national treasures as can be saved from such sites as the burned-out wreck of the British Museum below me now, before either (a) the living dead swarm overwhelms the last holdouts of civilisation or (b) the rumoured final solution is imposed on the capital by the Government in exile – rumoured to be planned for as early as tomorrow, as you'll know, sir. Yes, "Operation Bargain Hunt" is in full swing! The Yanks have even agreed to ship the treasures to Canada rather than into their own vaults in Area 51, so there's an outside chance we Brits might actually get to see them again some day without having to pay fifty bucks for the privilege . . .

No, Kate! Be gracious. It is as if we are rescuing the wisdom of antiquity from the burning library of Alexandria. When one is saving civilization, one becomes civilized by proxy . . .

No again, Kate! If ever there was a time to put aside one's rather overheated private education it is now – good preparation though Roedean might have been for a career as a junior officer in the British Army. No more cute classical references. This is not Alexandria; it is London burning below, and the reason our pilots wrestle with their controls is because our Chinook bobbles on the blisters of rising heat from that colossal wreck, like a paper model of a Leonardo da Vinci spiral helicopter above a roaring hearth.

And it is of da Vinci that I must speak – a man five centuries dead, as the still older city below me prepares to die in its turn.

In these last days we, in our improvised fortress in the basement of the Museum, bundling up treasures for the scheduled shipments out, have been busily scanning as many documents and pieces of artwork as we could manage. It is an extra layer of security, you see; whatever was left behind when the cut-off time ended the physical transfer, at least a digital ghost of those treasures might survive the city, and ourselves.

And it was my poignant privilege to scan in the Codex Ulaanbaatar, the relatively recently discovered da Vinci manuscript that wound up in the collection of a shale-oil oligarch in Mongolia – hence the clumsy moniker – a manuscript on loan to the British Museum when the "The Death" broke out. There I was in that dingy, overheated basement, in full battle dress, handling the precious parchments as if they were of no more consequence than a pile of old *Beano* comics, and marvelling at Leonardo's precise, perceptive diagramming of the wing bones of birds and bats – and, indeed, what looked like a sketch of a pterosaur wing, an antique flying lizard, or at least a prescient guess at how such a structure might look, made long before such animals were reconstructed from the fossils. All of this crowded by Leonardo's notes in his strange, cramped, mirror-image style.

But it was not Leonardo's work that was consuming my attention, but what lay beneath it.

The document pages turned out to be palimpsests: that is, with the Leonardo content written over an older set of writings, scraped off but with the indentations made by the pen still surviving on the parchment. But our crude, or perhaps over-sensitive, scanning technology picked up the underlying indentations as well as the over-writing, and could not distinguish one set of markings from another. It took some hasty coding to devise a routine to separate the two – and, as Leonardo's work and the underlying scribbles were slowly peeled apart, my attention was increasingly drawn away from da Vinci and the bird bones, to the extraordinary story hidden beneath.

One preliminary professional note: a quick check shows that the account herein does seem to accord with known details of Leonardo's biography, from the sodomy charge he faced as a young man to the fact that he had legal access to cadavers for dissection only after the events described here. The world is (or *was*) full of Leonardo experts who will be able to analyse all this better than I could.

But the point of it is, sir, the startling relevance of the found text to the events of our own time, the here and now.

God only knows if I'll get out of here. God only knows if the transmissions I've made so far have survived. But, even in this moment of extreme peril, and with the death throes of my home city below me, I feel impelled to leave some record of what I must call, after the author, the "Testament of Giovanni". I'm going to download the original imagery of the palimpsest, together with an OCR rendering of the text, and a rough first translation from medieval Italian into English – *if* I get the chance . . .

The name by which you will know me is Giovanni. That alone; I would not shame my family with a connection to this affair.

The date as I write is April 15 in the Year of Our Lord Fifteen Hundred and Thirty Six; the events of which I write transpired in April and May in the Year of Our Lord Fifteen Hundred and Four [note: old-style Julian calendar dates. K.S.].

If you read this, you will understand how I have laboured to create and preserve this record. Nobody knows Giovanni or cares for his name, but all the world knows the name of my Master, Leonardo di ser Piero da Vinci, and always will know it. And so I hide my humble words beneath his great utterings — I will scrape clean these parchments and offer them to my Master for his own work, trusting to God to preserve and reveal their true message in due course.

Herewith, my Testament.

I was at my Master's side at the beginning of the affair.

We were in one of his studios, a villa in the heart of Florence. It was a sunny morning, and the light slanting through the windows caught in the air that was full of dust and flakes of dried paint. I remember well the various projects on which we were engaged. We had already sketched details for a mural we had under commission to complete that quarter; my Master was engaged in a complicated correspondence concerning the relocation of Michelangelo's "David", much against that great man's wishes; a more agreeable chore for me had been to write to the Guild of St. Luke, the guild of artists, which it had been my Master's pleasure to rejoin on his return to Florence - not his native city, but as the world knows his home town of Vinci is in that region. And I recall vividly that I was preparing a fresh canvas. Following the normal course of preparation the surface was to be sized, primed with oil, glue and lead white, and left to stand for twenty days before it would be ready for use. It was pleasing, engrossing work.

I was then seventeen years old. I believe my Master had engaged me in the first place for my looks; he had used me as a model, and I had more than once shared his bed. But when he discovered my facility with the pen, and my reasonable mastery of Latin and French - greater facilities than the artistry to which I originally aspired - he had begun to employ me more as an *amanuensis*. Trusted with such work I had learned to keep out of the way of the Big Beasts who stalked his household, Salai and

Pacioli and the Este sisters and others, long-term companions and servants, many of whom believed they were great figures in their own right, and great in jealousy at least they certainly were.

You must picture the scene, then, the room cluttered with my Master's gadgets — the clocks for one thing, mechanical or driven by water or sand, and a shelf full of animal skulls, each neatly labelled in his mirror writing, and tables and easels laden with books, and half-formed lumps of clay that were sketches for sculptures, and heaps of parchment scribbled and drawn over, and a few half-finished paintings — and, more enigmatically, for me at any rate, a tangle of pipes and tubes and glass vessels in which water stood, and over which my Master would work for hours on end, skipping sleep and food in his customary way, studying aspects of the flow of water that were mysteries only to his active mind. And in the midst of it all my Master himself, patiently working, as if the studio itself were an expansion of his own mind.

That was when *he* walked in, entirely unannounced, and it was as if a cloud had crossed the Florentine sun.

"Leonardo! I heard you were back. How long did you have to trail around the country with Borgia, pretending to care about gun placements and city walls? . . ."

He was a big man, a heavy man, and I immediately felt disquieted by his presence. For one thing I could not place his age. He wore cape, doublet, laced shirt, hose, all in bright colours, the uniform of a young man. His face, too, was symmetrical enough, with wide eyes, a high brow, straight nose - in fact it was like the face of a hefty woman, or a somewhat delicate man. Yet there was no sense of delicacy about him, but of power, strength. And despite the lack of lines on that smooth face there was no sense of youth about him, but of cobwebby age. That was my very first impression — that everything about his appearance was artifice, a lie. I tried to imagine how I would capture his character in a charcoal sketch, but failed to conjure it.

My Master rose from his stool. He was then fifty-two years old, but with bald pate and flowing beard he looked considerably older. His face, though, was keen, with that long, handsome nose, those piercing eyes. He faced the intruder. "Morbi. It is you. I do not recall receiving your note—"

"Oh, need old friends stand on ceremony, Leo?" He turned to me. "And will you not introduce me to your latest bum boy? Though he looks a little on the delicate side for your taste."

With a massive hand he grabbed at my left buttock, pushing his fingers crudely in the cleft; I endured this intrusion and bit my tongue to stay silent.

"He generally likes them big, your Master, big chunky boys for him to plough . . . My name is Tomas da Morbi, boy. And you?"

I stammered out my name.

He walked around the studio, flicking through our work with casual contempt. "All this endless study, the sketches and the notes, scribble scribble scribble. Do you not ever *finish* anything, man? For I have no reason to believe it is *all* nonsense, yet will be forgotten after your death if you do not seek to communicate it . . ."

Aware of my Master's growing unease at this criticism, I dared to venture, "I have not heard of Morbi, sir."

"A town in India. Far from here. My deeper ancestry is English, as you might tell from my coarse accent. I use the *Italianate* form for the name I prefer. Of course I was not born in Morbi . . ." He winked at my Master. "Eh, Leonardo? We all have secrets. What is a name but another layer of lies?

"Giovanni, I will tell you what your Master called me when we first met. 'Buttocks Like Boulders'. That was his name for me, oh, thirty years ago, when he and two of his chums spent the night ploughing a male tart, and then spent a more uncomfortable few nights on a sodomy charge - only for that ploughed furrow to rise up and acquit them of any wrong behaviour - yes, Giovanni, that tart was me, that was how we met, and it was not your keen artist's eye you turned on me from the start but another of your organs entirely, was it not, Leonardo?"

"What is it you want, Morbi?"

"Oh, we will get to that. But as a preamble it never does any harm to remind you of the debt you already owe me." He winked at me, and that repulsive mixture of age and androgynous smoothness made me recoil. "You see, Giovanni, decades after the rental of my bumhole — your Master, you know, has always had a fascination for the human body, and that is aside from the anal passages of fourteen-year-old boys. A fascination in particular for its inner workings. But how is one to study those workings, how to scribble one's sketches of the engineering of heart and lung and bowel, without access to the interior of such a body — warm or cold? Eh, Leonardo?

For to acquire either would be against the law of God and man. And so, Giovanni, more than once I have procured for your Master—"

"Enough, Tomas!" my Master snapped now, almost regally — but then he has consorted with Borgias and Medicis, with kings and popes and the sons of popes, and knows how to command. "Every few years you come back to me, like the orbiting of some baleful moon. Must you haunt my life?"

Morbi smiled enigmatically, a smile of secret knowledge and control. "Oh, you would not have it any other way. Life would be so dull without me, do you not think?"

"What do you want? If it is that you would have me join your cabal, your gang of Seven—"

"A place could be found for you if you assented. Your God must know I have tried hard enough to persuade you." He glanced at me. "Your Master, you see, Giovanni, is one of the least stupid human beings I have ever met. And coming from me that is quite a compliment, for I have known very many human beings." Daringly — or so it seemed to me — he reached forward and rapped his knuckles, gently enough, on my Master's bare cranium. "What a pity that such a brain is wasted in a mortal body. But we could fix that. Could we not, Leonardo?"

My Master drew himself up. "I immerse my soul in life — the life of the body, the vitality of the good Earth. You, sir, are death incarnate, a blot of darkness on the face of the sun — you stand for the opposite of all I hold dear."

Morbi sneered. "Pah! You are more pompous and pious than those priests you look down upon. And as hypocritical. You are a Gnostic seeking salvation through knowledge, not faith. You are a closet heretic, one of that strange breed that dotes on John the Baptist, and I can tell you from personal experience *he* was nothing but a chancer. And yet you grovel for commissions for art on religious subjects from the popes themselves—"

My Master thundered, "Say what it is you want of me, man, or get out!"

Again this monstrous man winked at me. "And I have not even been offered a cup of his cheap Tuscan wine. Oh, very well." He reached into his doublet, and for a heartbeat I tensed, for he had the manner of a man seeking to draw a weapon. But he pulled out only a leather satchel. He cleared a table of manuscripts with a rough swipe of his arm, and he tipped out of his satchel two items: a small muslin bag, and a sketch on what looked like leather.

My Master and I were drawn by the innate curiosity that, if nothing else, united us. My Master cautiously opened the bag. It

contained some kind of herb that released a
dazzling aroma as soon as the bag's tie was
loosened, and my Master recoiled.

And I picked up the leather and studied
it. It was covered in sketches of what
appeared to be an inscribed monolith, and
the centre was dominated by a geometrical
drawing that I reproduce here, as best I
remember it. After staring at this for some
interval, with my awareness drawn in and
out of the scribbled-on surface as the
shape seemed to flip over in my head, I too
recoiled from Morbi's gift.

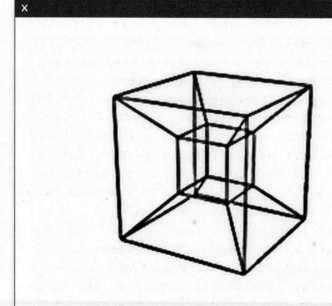

The feel of the skin itself in my hands was unusual, however, unfamiliar. Tremulously I asked Morbi, "What sort of leather is this?"

"Not a leather at all." He smiled at me, and I saw how his teeth gleamed, perfect as a row of children's tombstones. "Unless you count *this* as a base for leather." And he pinched the skin of his own arm.

Human skin. Now I saw it. This was a tattoo, inscribed on a piece of skin flayed from the body. I dropped the scrap, recoiling anew.

My Master glared at Morbi. "What is it you have brought us here, man? Do you mean to addle our brains?"

He grinned. "As to the second — yes, if necessary. As to the first — I bring you treasure, Leonardo, treasure from the east, treasure far more precious than the gold and savages returned by that buffoon Cristofero Colombo from the New World . . ."

And, sitting at his ease on the stool so recently vacated by my Master, he told us a tale, as we helplessly poked and sniffed at his "treasures".

On the edge of the Sea of Galilee, according to Morbi, there exists a metropolis that was cursed more than a millennia ago for rejecting the works of

Our Lord. And he told us of an encounter there with a man, who some called demon, who came up from a southern continent, having been expelled for an excess of wizardry and dark magic.

Now to the south there are civilisations, but not like our own. They are godless, and they do not write, but they have advanced mathematics which they express in calendars and tally-sticks and geometric figures of the kind Morbi showed us. And they do not have natural philosophies as we do, but they have herbs — drugs, powerful drugs, that can alter the mind, so that one sees the world in new ways.

"And," Morbi said dramatically, "liberated, the mind can *control* the world. Reshape it to its will. Explore it, but not as Europeans explore, footstep by footstep, on plodding horseback, in stinking, scurvy-ridden hulks of ships. The minds of those southern sages can fly over the oceans, at will. And *one can fly in the winds of time, back and forth, as one desires . . .*"

I, bewildered by the geometry on the scrap of skin, could barely take this in. My Master, though, has a finer mind than mine, and asked patient, plodding questions, to pin down this flight of the fantastic.

As to how this fellow came to the notice of Morbi?

That southern land was ruled by a recent and bloodthirsty empire. There, they water the stones of their temples with the blood of innocents, of human sacrifices, a sin the Carthaginians are alleged to have committed. The demon wizard was expelled from that place by the remote emperor's representative, the local Pontius Pilate, because of an excess of zeal — in a bloodstained land he killed *too many* wretches, and too gleefully. With a packet of enigmatic treasures and a memory full of dark miracles, this sanguineous priest wandered north, and came to a sea-coast, and at last he saw mighty ships with sails bearing the cross of Jesus . . .

My Master stood stock still, listening to all this. "You said, Morbi, *one can fly in the winds of time, back and forth, as one desires* . . . Are you serious?"

"So this monster promised the Crusaders who caught him. So he kept proclaiming as they transported him to that accursed city and, like so many others there, put him to the question for his evident devilry. So he promised even as they plucked out his eyes and burned him for the good of his immortal soul — if those strange folk of the southern continents have souls at all, and as I understand it that is an open question in the Pope's circle. The Crusaders could not make it work. Do you see? But they saw the plausibility of it. Oh, those new continents are full of herbs to addle the mind, Leonardo! Such concoctions suffuse their religions and their societies — that is what the Spaniards *and* the Portuguese say. Why, the common labourer will chew a leaf that deadens him even to the pain of a whipping by an overseer in some gold mine — that is what they say . . ."

"The alchemy of it is real enough, then," Leonardo said. "And if a man can be made oblivious to pain, can he be made oblivious to time as well? That's the question."

"Indeed it is. Think what one could do with such a thing, Leonardo!"

My Master frowned. "What would *you* wish to do with it, Morbi?"

"You could see your own birth — and death. You could see how you are to be remembered! You could see the outcome of the battle and advise the generals accordingly — imagine how the Borgias would prize *that* advice. Why, you could take a sitting of the Christ Himself, who you paint so obsessively, as man and boy, as an infant in the arms of the Madonna and a pasty-faced little wench *she* was, I can tell you . . . You could gamble with the centurions as to how long He would last on the Cross, and win!"

"You won't deflect *me* with your blasphemies,
Morbi," my Master said calmly. "I repeat my
question. Tell me why *you* want this."

Morbi spread his hands. "You know me —
well, actually you do not, you only *glimpse*
me, even you, Leonardo. The truth is I do
not *know* why I will need it. But my life
will always be complicated; it will be a
more than useful weapon to hold in reserve,
so to speak . . . To what purpose will a
newborn child be put?"

"Or a newly cast cannon," my Master said
darkly.

"Remember, the demon from the jungle
swore its account was true, even when put
to the question. But the Crusaders could
not make it work," Morbi repeated. "Which
is why this treasure fell into my hands,
Leonardo. But you, man — if there is
something there to be assembled . . ."

He was wily enough to say no more.
Evidently he knew my Master well enough to
know when he had been caught by a question,
as an angler hooks a fish. It was the same
in Milan, I was told by Salai, when Sforza
once challenged my Master — this was before
I was born — to build that lord an
equestrian statue to rival Bucephalus. My
Master did not rest until it was done.

Now it was the same. From the moment
Morbi left the studio my Master did not eat

or sleep, for all the entreaties of his
companions and servants, for all the
impatient snapping of his other clients.
Did not eat or sleep, and I too did
precious of either for he used me as his
principal assistant — until he called Morbi
back after a full three weeks, when the
Chronos Macchina was complete.

Once again Morbi irrupted into our studio.
This time, at my Master's advice, he wore
more substantial apparel: riding boots, a
heavy cloak, a wide-brimmed hat. We
intended to travel, after all. It was early
morning.
   Morbi walked around the *Chronos Macchina*
where we had set it up, in a cleared space
at the floor of the studio. "I cannot say
it looks like much," he growled. "Damned
unimpressive. I see a slab of stone, a
pillar. Scarcely taller than I am — it
would not suit a Pharaoh!"
   My Master patiently ordered me to show
Morbi its features.
   "Here," I said, "on each of the stone's
faces, is inscribed the geometric figure,
the distorted cubes, as shown on the scrap
of . . . leather you provided. The
traveller fixes his attention on the
diagram, and allows his awareness to flip,
to twist in a higher—" I had not the

vocabulary to complete the sentence. "But first one takes a pinch, as of snuff, of the herbs stored in these chambers cut into the stone face." I pointed these out; they had fine china lids. "This is the dried residue of the herbs you brought us, sir. Incidentally we took care to remove the seeds first; we have a new crop growing in an experimental garden attached to this villa as a reserve. We will show you this later—"

"Damned unimpressive," Morbi repeated, prowling around the column. "I expected more — what? — *flair* from you, Leonardo. The brightest mind in the brightest age, when thanks to savagery being inflicted at either end of the world — the Spaniards scything their way through the Indians of the New World, and the Turks in Constantinople driving the last Roman scholars westward into Christendom — there has never been such an injection of knowledge, not since Archimedes was a boy. Here we are in this new Athens — a place where they chuck their filth into the street, and yet genius and insight burns in a precious few heads. And in this ferment, you yourself, Leonardo, have sketched machines that fly and crawl and swim, and even, I am told, a machine that can add up numbers, a machine that thinks! Even if you do spend rather a lot of your brief life messing around with the properties of water, and suchlike. In such an age, why *not* a machine that can fly in time as in space? And yet you, the author of 'The Last Supper', have no more style and wit than to come up with this slab of rock!"

"It is functional," said my Master coldly. "And it is not mere rock. It is sandstone. And, if you look closely, you will see layers in the stone where once a sea lay down the sediment, and embedded in those layers the shells of oysters and snails long since deceased."

"What of it? Death is death, whether it occurred a second ago or a thousand years."

"Morbi, this piece I was given by accident, when I requested materials to create the great horse in Milan. The curiosity of it is that this slab was acquired, not by a sea-shore or under the waves, but at the high tops of the mountains. Do you see, Morbi?

"The Earth itself has age. The Earth is not unlike a human body. The Earth has a spirit of growth, and that its flesh is the soil; its bones are the successive strata of the rocks which form the mountains; its cartilage is the tufa stone; its blood the veins of its waters. And the vital heat of the world is fire which is spread throughout the Earth. But the Earth is under continual assault from the waters, as its surface is eroded by rivers and rain, and its inner cavities hollowed out. These processes result in shifts in the Earth — sometimes dramatically, when the interior caverns collapse. This is why marine shells and oysters, which have formed beneath the waters, are now found at so great a height, together with the stratified rocks once formed of layers of mud carried by the rivers into the lakes, swamps, and seas."

Morbi nodded. "This pillar is proof to your eyes of deep time, then."

"Yes. Time enough for the sea to exchange places with the highest mountains."

"And we can travel into that deep time. You say the *Macchina* is functional."

"I do."

"How do you know? Have you tested it?"

I, Giovanni, knew the answer to that, for I had been there when he went, and when he returned, and he would speak nothing of it, even as I salved his wounds and wiped away his bitter tears. He would only say now, "It is functional."

"Then let us go." Morbi precipitately grabbed pinches of the herbs and rammed them into his delicate nostrils, and took hold of the handles in the stone.

The house seemed to shake. The earth is restless in any part of Italy, but we all knew this was no common tremor. And then the sun dimmed, too, though the sky beyond the windows was cloudless — as if that great light had receded from the world it circled.

"Quickly, boy," my Master murmured.

Such was Morbi's impatience to go that neither of us was properly dressed for a jaunt, but we had no choice but to follow. We both stepped up to the column, took the snuff — it was bitter and made my sinuses ache — and grasped the smooth handles cut into the stone.

A wind seemed to roar.

Morbi asked, "How does one make this stone fly?"

My Master shouted back, "Consider the geometrical figure, Morbi. That is all. Embrace its shifting perspective. As it becomes loosely defined in your consciousness, so do we become loosely defined in this world."

"And how does one direct its flight in time?"

Now it was my Master's turn to grin. "That feature," he said, "is under development."

And the world twisted and fell away.

Of course my Master has travelled *this* world extensively.

I myself, Giovanni, am a city boy, born in the back streets of Florence. I have never been more than a day's walk from the Duomo, and I have grown to love the crowding, the towers of the churches, the sprawl of the private palaces, the way the terracotta tiles of the houses shine in the sunlight of the afternoon — even the great open sewer of the Arno — I cannot imagine living, no, *being*, anywhere else.

Imagine my shock then when the *Chronos Macchina*, having picked me up and hurled me around like a leaf in a tempest, deposited me on a beach. This was not a soot-strewn bank of the Arno as I was used to, but the shore of a semi-infinite plain of water, a grey mass. My Master assured me, as I sat huddled on the sand trembling with fear and a deeper twisted nausea, that this was merely an ocean, as Colombo and the other navigators had so recently conquered. "And if a buffoon like Colombo can master an ocean physically, then you can master it intellectually, apprentice."

"Yes, Master." I struggled to my feet, and tried to make sense of the world.

Before me, that ocean. Behind me, a forest, dense and drab and green, that washed down almost to the sea itself, leaving only the strip of gritty sand on which we stood. Beyond the forest, further inland, I saw mountains, made misty by distance, and I thought I saw smoke curling, as if from a volcano, from Vulcanus or Mongibello perhaps. I had a sense of the raw, the primitive — of the life force rampant in this world, in the jungle, the ocean. Even the sun looked odd to me, somehow shrunken, and the sky was littered with high scalloped clouds of a kind I had never seen before. (It would have alarmed me even more if my Master had told me then, as he deduced for himself immediately, that the rising sun that hung over the workshop from which we had departed had been instantly replaced by a *setting* sun on this far beach . . .)

Somehow I knew that we were alone in this raw world, we three — alone of humanity.

All that was familiar to me in this panorama of sea and sky and land were my own body, and the bodies of my two companions, my Master and Tomas da Morbi, and the pillar of sandstone which my Master and I had engraved and shaped in the studio in Florence — and which now stood in the sand like the gnomon of a sundial, as if it belonged here, as if it had always been here.

As for Morbi, he seemed unperturbed by the adventure. Laughing, he walked down to

the sea and let it lap over his riding
boots. "Another success for the mage of
Florence, the great Leonardo!"

My Master grunted. "Even your compliments
are taunting, Morbi."

Yet I was puzzled. I dared to ask,
"Success, Master? It is evident we have
travelled. But — where?"

He looked at me rather sadly, as if the
question disappointed him. "Where? The
better question would be, *when?* Into the
deepest past, I should think — or possibly
the furthest future. As to where — why,
this is still Italy, boy. Still Florence.
One day the Duomo will stand over there,"
and he pointed, "and the Roman Gate over
there, where the sea laps now. But in this
remote age the sea and the mountains have
changed their places, you see — in *this* age
the tiny creatures whose shells are
embedded in our pillar are, perhaps, still
swimming out their brief sunlit lives in
this archaic sea."

"Is it just as you imagined, then,
Leonardo?" Morbi called.

"Not as I *imagined*. As I *deduced* it would
be from my experience, from the existence
of the corals and the shells on the
mountain-tops. Nature begins with the cause
and ends with the experience. We must
follow the opposite course, that is

beginning with the experience, and from this investigate the reason."

Morbi pointed to the sky, over the drab trees. "Then experience *that*, philosopher!"

My Master and I together turned to look. I saw a flock of birds, I thought at first, bony, ugly creatures, flying in a loose formation not unlike geese in the winter. But these "birds" continued to approach us, and grew in my sight, grew and grew until they loomed over us, their wings leathery canopies like the kites of Cathay which can carry a man, and I saw their long beaks sharp as the pikes of the Pope's Swiss Guard.

My Master mumbled, "What are they? Not birds, not bats . . . Reptiles, surely, flying reptiles, of a kind I never saw before, nor any man . . ."

"And nor are they mentioned in your Bible," Morbi said dryly. "Speaking of which, it is hard to believe that we have travelled back no more than the few thousand years since the Creation it describes . . ."

"Crayons, boy, and parchment!"

My Master expected my pockets to be stocked with such things, even on that beach at the other end of time. And of course they were. I handed over the materials, and forthwith he lay on his back

in the sand and held up the parchment and
sketched and sketched, the beaks, the bones
seen dimly through the great translucent
wings.

For a while, as he worked, Morbi left us.
He plunged into the thick of the forest, on
some errand of his own. Even in that dread
place, and even with my Master's attention
entirely occupied by his work, it was a
relief for me to be out of Morbi's
presence, if only briefly.

I stayed close to the *Macchina*, as if
afraid it might be stolen away, and awaited
on events.

At length Morbi emerged from the forest. He
was breathing hard, his womanly face coated
in sweat and dirt, but he had a look of
triumph. And he carried something, in a
sack he had improvised from his jacket. I
did not get a near look at this, but it
appeared that he was carrying *eggs*, huge,
heavy, dark grey eggs.

My Master ignored Morbi, and Morbi
ignored him.

Instead Morbi came to me. He sat heavily
on the sand, having carefully set down his
sack of eggs. He had a pocket flask of some
liquor, which he sipped and offered to me.
I declined, for I feared that the drink
might reduce the efficacy of the southern

herbs which had brought us here, and which I prayed would yet carry me safely home.

"So," he said, "your Master is happy enough. Scribble, scribble."

"And you?" I had the courage to ask. "Are you happy with this commission you have yet to pay for?"

He studied me, and laughed. "Is that a hint, you petty little clerk? Oh, I will leave a bag of florins in his studio when we are done. As to the *Macchina* — yes, I am content enough, for now. I must learn its capabilities, and explore its use — I will break it as one breaks a horse."

"And then what? You said you had no definite purpose for it in mind."

"I will store it somewhere safe." He grinned. "Somewhere it will ride out the centuries in security, for no less than centuries are fit for consideration when one possesses a *Chronos Macchina*."

"Where, though, is safe? War suffuses Europe. Why, the Master himself had to flee Milan when the French invaded—"

"Pah! Europe and your squabbling post-Roman princelings. What a disappointment this age would have been to the Caesars — at least the ones I knew. England — an island fortress — *that* is the place for security and stability, as much as anywhere else. London, perhaps. I will think of something."

"You wish to keep the *Macchina* a secret," I dared say to him. "And yet *I* know of it, for I worked on its construction. And my Master knows of it, for he designed it—"

"I have no concerns about that," Morbi said. "Your Master will do with this what he has always done with his inventions, scribble a diagram in one of those endless journals of his, and move on to some new obsession. As for you—"

He eyed me, and it was as if Death himself stood before me, sickle in hand. He leaned closer and whispered, "As for you, boy — if you ever betray my secret, I will hunt you down. How will I do that? This is a machine that travels in time, remember, to future and past. If you ever betray me, even as a ninety year old whispering secrets on your deathbed, I will know of it. And my future self will come back in time, and I will return to *this very moment*, this beach, here and now, and that future Morbi will open your skull and spoon out your living brain, while I, the present Morbi, look on." He raised his hand. "At *this* moment—"

He snapped his fingers. My heart stopped in my chest.

And he grinned at me. "You still live." He ruffled my hair, probing at my skull with an odd regret. "Therefore you will not betray me."

When he released me and walked away, I could barely keep from a swoon.

Of the rest, the telling will be brief.

That was the only journey my Master and I endured together using the *Chronos Macchina*. Within days of our return Morbi had arranged for it to be crated up and shipped away, together with his relics from the east, and indeed with the young plants we had endeavoured to grow from the seeds we extracted. Nothing was left: we could not recreate the *Macchina* if we wished to.

For myself, I have never forgotten the threat delivered to me by the monstrous Morbi on that beach out of time. I have never been pious, but perhaps the feeling I have endured in the decades since then has been like that of a devout novice believing he is continually under the inspection of a judgmental God. If a man may travel in time, surely no secret is closed to him. And I have always feared that even though I have lived on peacefully and untroubled, if Morbi, as punishment or on a mere whim, were to return to that beach and open my skull as he threatened, my decades of life since then — my career, my loves, my children, my very existence — would all be snuffed out like a candle in a gale or changed in ways that I would be incapable to understand.

Yet I have determined not to go to my grave without leaving some record of what the man has done. For such a monster, with such a machine, has surely a power to rival Lucifer Lightbringer himself. And so I have contrived this deceit, a record scribbled in the shadows and unseen by any man, the words erased as soon as they are written down, the inscribed sheets passed to my poor Master who, obsessed, is now using them to scribble images of the flying lizards we saw in that distant age. If you read this, forgive me my lack of courage!

And as for my Master, it is true that he has never properly recorded his work on the *Chronos Macchina*. Its secrets will be forgotten when he dies, as with so much of his learning.

What has lingered for him, though, is the sense of abuse he felt at the hands of Tomas da Morbi, this monster of his past who once seduced him into sodomy, then lured him with corpses, and ultimately committed a kind of violation of the intellect by so using my Master as a means to his own ends. He became obsessed with Morbi, it seems to me, and his image.

And in the years after our venture into time he worked out this obsession in a strange way — strange, at least, for any man but him! He was commissioned to paint a portrait of a prominent woman of the city, the wife of the Secretary of the Ten of War. This he laboured at to an exclusive and excessive degree, even by his own standards. He worked the thing over and over, and took to carrying it around with him, displaying it as his finest work.

And only I, who worked with him on the *Macchina* and travelled with him in time, know its multiple secrets.

Oh, there are those who guess at its mysteries. Why is the background landscape so primitive, so fecund? Is my Master expressing his adherence to some natural religion? Perhaps, but this is also an indirect representation of that raw archaic world to which we travelled, a world of strong, turbulent life, a world entirely without mind.

And the face of the subject, that face . . .

It does represent the subject herself, yes. And yet my Master has sought to blend in the androgynous features of *another*, a little too heavy for the feminine, with a beauty of an unconventional, even uncomfortable kind.

What does that complacent smile conceal, do you think, that enigmatic smile of secret knowledge and control? An affair with the artist, or with another of the great men of our time, with Raphael perhaps? No! It conceals a far darker secret than that.

And if you, my reader, in your future age, still know of this painting and cherish it, know that in his most prized work my Master has bequeathed you not the visage of Signora Lisa Giocondo — but the face of Tomas da Morbi himself!

DownCount

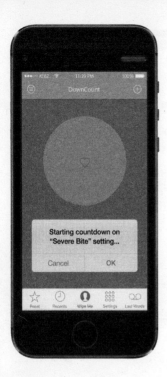

APP DESCRIPTION

Simple timer app, plus a few bells and whistles. Soon as you can after you get infected, press the big blue button. The bigger the bite, and the nearer your heart, the closer you should click to the centre. The app will then give you a countdown until you go Z.

It is *APPROXIMATE*, okay? I used to have the decay time linked to the official stats on turning rates, but the government server went down weeks ago so now it's just approximate.

I made the timings conservative, though, so it should be accurate enough to tell you how long you've got to say goodbye ...

... and to get the hell away from other humans, of course, and blow your own head off. Come on, people — let's be responsible here. You know you're going Z, do the right fucking thing. You don't got a gun, check out some of the suggestions under the "Wipe Me" tab. But get the job done.

(Sorry the app's kind of boring-looking but the dude who was doing my interface stuff got bitten when we were only half done. Though that at least made him a useful beta test, ha ha.

And, like, by the time you're pressing that big-ass button, who fucking cares how it looks, right?)

Peace out
Zeke @ ZApps

VERSION HISTORY

1.0 - First public release
1.1 - Added an option to reset the counter, case you find someone else's phone after they've gone Z.
1.2 - Added some more ways of smashing your own head open.

From: packrat <packrat@chatshack.com>
To: beherenow <beherenow@psychotrope.com>
Sent: TUE, Jun 11, 12:15 PM
Subject: Lehrer, von Braun and Moerbitz

Hey Bee

Check out this! I was trawling the NBC archives for cutting-room-floor shit
for my MeTube channel and a post on Friendface. Here's a demo of a song
by Tom Lehrer – yeah, the poisoning pigeons in the park guy. He wrote
satirical stuff every week for this old fossil of a show called That Was The
Week That Was. This was back in the 60s, needless to say, when you
could DO stuff like that and not get shipped to Gitmo by Homeland
Security, and whatnot. Well, Lehrer would demo the stuff on tape, and it
was sung by some woman on air, but TL recorded the songs himself later.

Anyhow this one week he lays into the space programme Nazis, you know,
Wernher von Braun and those guys. But here's the kicker. In the demo he
sings an EXTRA VERSE that was CUT from the broadcast version. I guess
somebody had better lawyers than SS General Herr von Braun!

Dig it, man.

Hope you're holding out here in Fortress Oxford. A "safe city", hah, yeah it
feels like it when you hear the screaming outside the barricades, and the
south London crater still glowing in the dark in the newsfeeds. But who
cares? In here for now it's nice and cosy and we got Friendface and search
engines, and we can still look up 60s protest songs like it's 2012 . . .

You still owe me that fifty quid BTW.
Laters P

. . . And let's not forget Wern's pal Tomas Moerbitz

Tom's up to his cuticles

In New World Pharmaceuticals.

"I've burned men. I've gassed men, blown babies to bits.

"Screams, schmeams. Buy my face creams!" says Tomas
  Moerbitz . . .

O
M
G

M
O   G

OG

Words are hard   They look funny
Meant things once   So many things
So many things   Gone now
  Most gone   Not all   Most gone
MG
  Oh
Dont remember it being so hard
Writing
  Dont remember so many things
Gone now
  Not the book   Not you
  Found you
  Mine   Not ours   Not theirs   Mine
  Mine mine mine mine mine mine
mine all mine not gone

  Names on paper   Names feel
scratchy under fingers   Maybe
fingers feel scratchy   Dont know now

Fingers feel like fingers
Feel
  Not used in so long Feel
Not feel Only hunger
   No think Only hunt
No live Only survive

  Changed
Changing Changing now Still
changing
Growing up

Maddy Wood have said growing up
Maddy Would Maddy Wood
Me
   Was me
Maddy was me Before

Names on paper Gone now Forgot
Mum Dad Uncle Jack Family
Charlotte Emma Mandy
Friends? Barbies Friends Alex
Sigh
George Friend too More than
friend BEST friend More than
friend?
George

Names on paper Words My words
Marks on paper pressed hard
Pressed almost through the page So
long since I wrote So long Dont
remember the words remember them
now words on paper No voice just
words

I DONT THINK WILL WRITE
ANYMORE
IM HUNGRY

I remember

EVERYONES DOWN THERE NOT
SO DIFFERENT FROM BEFORE
THEYRE WAITING FOR ME THAT
MAKES ME FEEL SOMETHING
GOOD NOT LONELY I WANT TO
GO OUTSIDE

They were out there I was in here
In this place Alone with everyone
else hiding from Them From US
In there out here Them Us
Hiding as the city burned As the
world changed As I changed We
changed Thinking silence would save
them Silence and darkness

I like the night We like the night
We own the night We own the
darkness We own the light We own
the city as it burns We are the city
We are the night We are we are we
are

It was so lonely up here I
remember Such a small space and
the only friend was you Diary
Mine George gave you to me George
was my friend
  More than my friend Made me
  Scratched me
  Infected me
  Didnt mean to Didnt know he had
But I couldnt let him go Couldnt
He told me he loved me I told YOU
and you told it back to me I
remember I remember all of it now
Not just the scraps Not just the
pieces Bite size
  I couldnt let him go and I wouldnt
let him go and he was infected and
I didnt know I didnt know and
couldnt know and I couldnt let him
go I didnt feel a thing Only my
heart breaking

They locked me away THEM Tried
to decide what to do with me like
they owned me Like I was theirs
Whisper whisper whisper in the dark
Quiet Secret Secrets secrets secrets
But we have secrets of our own dont
we? We did and we do and we will
Youre my secret Never found you
did they
   Scratch scratch scratch
   So I waited until it was night I
like the night
   By the clock tower my friends were
waiting Together A crowd A team
A pack
   A pack for hunting
   A pack for hurting
   Out there in here I needed to be
out there
   I waited
   They waited
   THEY slept and I let myself out of
the hatch that had kept us THEM
All hidden all secret all safe Or not
I let myself out and I climbed down
and I went to where the others were
waiting for me waiting waiting
waiting and it was like before

Before the city burned Before the
sickness came Before the school and
the army and the death and the
death and the death and the hunger
and the hunger and the hunger
  So hungry

  Dont go digging dont go digging
never know what you might find
  They dig and they dig and we pay
for their mistakes

  Alex Sigh Sound like Alex
Coming Alex coming

  They were waiting My friends My
George My George because he said he
loved me Mine Like you Mine
George gave you to me Mine Didnt
see couldnt see Didnt know couldnt
know couldnt feel Just heart
breaking
  They were waiting just like before
Barbies sitting on the steps below
the tower Alex standing Like he
was the leader like he was waiting
Waiting for me Alex Sigh Alex
And George

Nothing said Nothing needed
George held my hand Scratched my
hand Took my hand Held my
hand His
    Alex led the way The Barbies
followed staying close Sniffing at
him sniff sniff sniff Nothing
changes even when it does Even
when we do
    I see the flat windows before we go
All blind all dark And then the
tiniest crack of light A flicker No
more MR DRAKE Not so sleepy
Why didnt he stop me He could
have should have stopped me Too
scared Of me Good riddance bad
rubbish
    Hungry

The streets were empty Quiet No
gun battles No one running No
screaming no crying No one
Nothing Piles of rubble Piles of
chairs and tables and wardrobes
Litter blowing Holes in the road
Heads in the road Smells like
sweat and spoiled meat Smell
made me hungry Barbies stopped

together and picked something up
from the ground Dirty Burned
Smelled like barbecue
  Finger
  Finger food
  Funny
  Emma took it Emma ate it
Charlotte snarled and tried to snatch
it Emma bit her too Mandy made
a noise like a baby crying and Alex
stopped and Alex turned and Alex
just LOOKED
  Alex not Alex anymore Alex
something else All of us something
else Dont feel like me Dont feel
like anything Only hungry
  I didnt know the street Not any
more Everything was different
everything changed Like Id dreamed
it all before Like Maddy me school
Mum Dad all a dream from the
fever Fever dream Good dream
Bad dream
  Shop windows were all smashed
Glass on the ground Shiny brass
tubes by the handful Bullets Black
twisted things lying by the roadside
and Alex led the way Climbing over

heaps of broken things Broken
bodies He didnt stop to look at
them None of them did Just
climbed straight over
   No flies Where were the flies Are
all the flies dead too
   Flies were alive Had good life
strong life
   Am I dead I dont know
   Cant be 13 if Im dead
   Dont feel 13 Dont feel anything
Only heart breaking

   Used to be a supermarket where
Alex takes us Follow me follow me
follow the leader follow me follow
me down Strip lights hanging from
the ceiling all smashed Empty
fridges all full of black fussy mould
thick enough to stroke Like a dog
Good dog The floor covered with
something crunching under my feet
Snap crackle pop snap crackle crackle
pop
   Pop pop like gunshots
   Cereals All the boxes torn and
emptied on the floor
   It smells of dust and empty

Can you SMELL empty?

The Barbies go one way Alex
another George still holding my
hand Wouldnt know couldnt know
No warmth But George Mine Still
holding my hand Pulls on my hand
gently Wants me to follow I
follow Stairs all dark but I can see
How can I see No light but I can
see I like the night
A door Big Steel Broken
Swinging open and closed open and
closed open open closed closed A
flat roof Outside night The city
Stars Stars falling Fires still
burning Smoke on a hot wind
Silence Silence Silence George
still holding my hand looking
Waiting
Watching
Hunting
Everything quiet until its not

Whispers Whispers whispers down
below in the street Quietly moving
quietly creeping Footsteps Not ours
Theirs Not up here Down there

Them not us
 Hungry So hungry

 George moves first Faster than
before Fastfastfast and he pulls me
with him My face is numb and my
hands are numb and I cant feel
cant feel cant feel but hungry A
metal ladder on the wall Lets my
hand go starts to climb down Hand
over hand faster and faster My
hands and feet are numb Wont
move like his Wont follow Dead
meat moving Down and down and
then Im down in the little alley
beside the shop and waiting
Watching Listening
 So hungry
 I can hear George Running Hear a
scream Hear a bang like a gunshot
Hear falling Hear bodies smashing
together Flesh on flesh Teeth on
flesh One more scream Then
nothing

 Except

 Breathing

Breathing breathing very near   Very
near and very near and hidden
secret safe
Scared
Im not scared
Im hungry

Cardboard boxes plastic crates
Wrong wrong wrong   All piled up and
left behind   Left behind for who
Who wants them now
Cardboard box moves   Cardboard
boxes dont move   Not unless
I feel my hands   I feel my arms
I feel them now   Tearing ripping
pulling   Dig dig digging
They dig and they dig and we pay
for their mistakes
Hair   Golden hair   Rapunzel
Rapunzel let down your hair
Digging digging digging
Screaming   Not mine   Not me
Hands over the hair   Trying to hide
it   Hiding digging deeper   Screaming
screaming oh so hungry so hungry so
hungry
Face so small   So dirty   So
scared

Im not scared   Only hungry
Face so small   Hands so small
So small so small
Child
So hungry

Doesnt taste like chicken   Tastes
like tears

Tears tears my tears mine   Crying
Crying now   Crying over you   Over
me   Over this   Cried then over me
Over her   Little girl   Little girl gone
Little girl and little girl and gone
forever   Gone forever   Gone gone
gone

George in the street   Hear him
moving   Nothing else moves   Not
even the rats   Where are the rats
where are the flies where are the
people   Scared or dead or both
Not scared
Think Im dead
Still not scared

It was someone else   Someone not
Maddy   Someone else did it

Someone else ate Fed Fed like an animal Not like a person Not like me Because I am Maddy Am I Am I Maddy Am I am I am I
Am I mad
Am I dead
Hush hush voices voices
People in my head
Our head our head our head Maddys dead

Tired Was so tired Not hungry either First time in always No sign of the Barbies Alex sigh sitting on broken checkout Chewing Watching
So tired Just needed to rest An empty freezer Climbed in Head down Darkness Shivering cold but didnt feel cold Tastes like tears Tastes like tears Tastes like tears Im not scared

Days and nights and days and nights and eating hunting hunger hunger hunger hunt Barbies coming and going Alex watching George mine mine all mine

And then
A voice in my head   Not mine not mine no
Little girl   Golden girl   Rapunzel Rapunzel let down your hair
Rapunzel on a swing   Rapunzel in a playground   Rapunzel hair in bunches in a red and white checked dress   Shiny shiny black shoes   Sitting at a table eating not eaten   Eating dinnerfood not humanfood   Kitchen House   Garden
Not my house
Not my memory
Not my mind
Cassie   Cassie Cassie   Not my name
Not my memory
Rapunzel Rapunzel let down your golden hair

Hunger always hunger always hunt So few of them   Hiding   They run when we come   Run and scream and cry for help   Who is there to help Who is left   Only us   None of them All out there somewhere   But were in here   In HERE   In my head and

Im in you and you are all of us
together Are you hungry Im so
hungry
  It was Sylvie Sylvie Sylvie Hid
in the eaves Left by her sons
Sons Sons Shining a light Light
through the window when I left the
flat Sylvie Sylvie Georges mum
  Mum mum mums the word Dont
be glum Here comes the sun Here
comes the son
  It was Alex who found her out in
the street
  Theres no food You never came
back We were so hungry so hungry
she said We were so hungry and we
and we
  And she stopped
  HUNGRY We know hungry in here

  Alex who found her and Alex who
left her and she ran after him in
the street Calling his name and he
walked away And he DID walk
away I wouldnt have Couldnt have
  Couldnt
  Didnt And now my hands are red
red wine red blood red blood red

and she tasted of tears and fears
and sorry

Sorry

Sorry why Because shes dead or
because I was hungry or because I
knew her before when I was
Maddyme not madme Sorry
because shes dead or sorry because
Im dead

Sylvies in here Not out there now
Inside outside I can hear her in my
head

Can you hear her

I remember I remember I
remember I remember George My
George Her George Her son her sun
her son Smiling in a pushchair long
before I knew him Crawling on a
rug Chocolate biscuits held in
clammy hands Melting

Melting Im melting Im hot and
cold and everything hurts and
nothing hurts and everythings so
fuzzy

Scared Im not scared Im not
scared Im not Im not I am

Alex is different Alex sigh is
changing Not like we changed before
Not like that More and more
Smarter Sharper Harder He
watches us watches the darkness
Walks the streets Not hunting
Hurting Watching Thinking He
talks in his sleep He sleeps like we
used to I dont sleep dont dream I
just stop for a while He dreams I
dont dream I remember dreams I
remember waking up Bad dreams
I dont dream now I want to wake
up I want to wake up and
everything so fuzzy I want to wake
up and everything tastes of tears
I want to wake up
Im not scared
I want to wake up

Alex is different He sits and he
stares and looks like hes listening to
other people Other voices Maybe he
is Maybe he has voices in his head
Maybe he has room for them I
dont I dont have room Too much
Too many

Rapunzel Rapunzel staring at the sky
Georgie Porgie pudding and pie
Kissed a girl and made her die
No Not George Mine mine mine
all mine Safe in here in you Not
out there

Everything outside is grey and red
and somehow the fires are still
burning I dont know who starts
them They burn and theyre red red
blood red fire red burning red We
went to the fences in the winter I
know it was winter because the snow
was falling Snow like there used to
be Snow like Sylvies memories
Snow falling like white ash White
ash from the fires Winter should be
cold but I couldnt feel the cold only
numb and fuzzy on the outside
Inside Im hot and cold and
everything and nothing but outside
there was only the ash It stuck to
the chain link fences Alex pressed
his fingers through the gaps and
curled them round the wire There
were flakes on my eyelashes In my
mouth They tasted like warm

In my head George building a
snowman in the street Small George
Not my George Sylvies George Red
snowboots and blue gloves and a hat
that falls over his eyes Sylvies Alex
taller thinner smaller than I knew
eating fistfuls of snow scraped from
cars
No cars now No snow Where did
they all go
We stood by the fences and looked
at the falling ash All of us Some
of us Alex and George and the
Barbies and me and others Others
like us Like us but not us We keep
away They keep away One of them
looked at Alex Looked at him like
he was different Watched Alex
watching the snow
Alex IS different
Alex is changing
Alex is growing away
Alex is growing up faster and
further than me Faster away and
further away and Ill never catch him
now
I want to grow up
Can I grow up

Can I

I found a dress in a shop
Windows all broken Thought I heard
a sound I was hungry so hungry
Others had been there before Dirty
footprints all over the floor Broken
glass Broken lights Broken broken
all broken But in the corner a
plastic bag Forgotten or left behind
or
There was blood on the bag old
blood bad blood Inside a dress
made of flowers
Roses Sylvie likes roses George
likes Sylvie George likes roses
My head hurts
Everything hurts and nothing hurts
and George my George my heart is
breaking
I shook it out and pulled it on
Sylvie likes roses George likes
Sylvie George likes roses Does Alex
like roses
Something shiny on the wall
Behind overturned racks Beyond
rotting clothes Still shiny A piece
of mirror still in its frame In the

dark I could see and I looked and I
saw
 Saw roses
 Saw blood Saw hair longer than
ever Greasy Tangled Saw dirt
and grime and torn jeans under a
too big dress Saw broken
fingernails Saw shoes with holes in
and a lace missing Saw hands too
big for arms Saw broken teeth
Sharp teeth Broken teeth
Broken
 Saw Maddy saw me saw broken
broken Maddyme
 I raised my hand to push the hair
out of my face
 Almost me Almost
 The dress too big even over my
clothes
 Ill never grow up
 I want to grow up throw up Want
to grow up
 Does Alex like roses

 So hungry

 I wore the new dress Alex was
there sitting watching waiting He

had something in his hands Emmas
shoe turning it turning it round and
round

Sylvie in my head buying Alex his
first school shoes George learning to
walk Cassie Cassie Rapunzel Cassie
walking in her mothers heels

EMMAS SHOE

Alex Alex wheres Emma I wanted
to ask but no words came Only
sound Not words I lost my words
out there but in here I have found
them and I talk to you It feels
good to be talking to you again
Feels It feels good to feel But not
to feel

I dont want to feel

Im not scared Im not scared

I dont want to feel

Gone said Alex and he had the
words Where did he find them
Where did he keep them Gone he
said and he held up the shoe and he
smiled and I knew No no I know
now In my dress with the roses I
know and where is George my George
all mine all mine

Alex dropped the shoe and he
smiled and he looked at me and he
looked at my dress   Noticed my
dress   Noticed me noticed me
  But his smile kept going kept
growing and growing and he stood up
and behind him all that was left of
Emmas dress and all that was left
of Emma
  Alex is hungry

I dont want him to notice me

Alex is changing   Changing again

  I ran with the voices all of them
all of them   Cassie and Sylvie and
all of the voices   So many too
many and they tasted like tears
House still there   I came to the hatch
and the doorway was open   Ladder
hanging down   How long has it been
Time time ticking ticking ticking   No
clocks   No time   Only hunger   Day
and night hunger and hunger and
hunger is the time   Time to eat time
to eat time time tastes like tears
Ladder hanging down smells like

empty Smells like old red old red
dead

I remember climbing down quiet
and secret and safe To George to
Alex sigh Funny how now Ive come
back Alex is changing again again
Not funny Not laughing really I
can hear Sylvie crying in my head
Or maybe Im just remembering
Dont know The floorboards are
creaky under my feet Something
sticky on the floor Old blood dead
blood smells like red

Dust Everywhere dust and ash and
dirt What would Mr Drake say Mr
Drake and his rules Clean this clean
that do this do that dont look out of
the windows dont make a sound
breathe quieter breathe quieter breathe
dont breathe

Footprints in the dust Some old
scuffed Some new New Someone
here I can smell them smell the
meat smell the blood smell them
smell them so hungry

The kitchen reeks of dead Old
blood new blood smells like smells
like

Pieces of people Pieces everywhere
Arms legs bodies bodies Bones piled
in corners Leg bone connected to the
hip bone connected to the
   Ribs ribs spare ribs Bundles of
ribs tied with string Five ribs ten
ribs stacked along the eaves Bundles
of ribs Piles of small bones fingers
and toes What happened here
   A closed door Bathroom I
remember Sticky sticky on the floor
Sticky sticky all across the door
Open the door push it open the smell
the smell the hunger the smell
   Strips of meat hanging from the
ceiling from the shower from
everywhere Strips of fleshmeat thin
and swinging Fleshmeat freshmeat
six degrees of human bacon hanging
from the ceiling Cut and cut and
tied with string
   What happened here
   Knives piled in the bath Red
knives blood knives stained like rust

THERES NO FOOD YOU NEVER
CAME BACK WE WERE SO
HUNGRY SO HUNGRY SHE SAID
WE WERE SO HUNGRY AND WE
AND WE
AND SHE STOPPED

Sylvie Sylvie what did you do

Scrap of fabric in the bath stuck
to the biggest biggest knife Blue
and orange Know it anywhere Hate
it hate it Mrs Drake Mrs Drake
snoring in the bed all of us hidden
hidden secret not so safe Mrs
Drake dead Mrs Drake EATEN
Eaten eaten not by us
Oh Mr Drake Mr Drake what did
you do

So hungry so hungry
We were so hungry she said

Sylvie crying in my head

Noise below me Steps on the
ladder Someone coming Mr Drake

Mr Drake no more Mr Drake
Came up the ladder   Saw him see
me   Me mad Maddyme standing
with a book   His face all cut up
twisted nasty   Burns and blisters
One of them not one of us   Not like
us but just like us   Cutting eating
killed his wife   Not sick not dead
just mad   Mrs Drake in her blue
and orange dress   Mrs Drake snoring
in the bed and Mr Drake with his
knife
  Hungry hungry always hungry hiding
in your little flat   Stayed secret and
hidden and safe and forgotten
  Was the knife sharp   It didnt look
sharp   Looked like it hurt
Everything hurts nothing hurts I want
to wake up
  Mrs Drake Mrs Drake what did he
do

  Mr Drake standing in the door   Mr
Drake with a bundle in his arms   A
bundle of rags a bundle of rage and
looks at me with hate hate hate
Smell it on him see it on him   Hot
hate cold hate and what good does

hiding do Secret and safe and
forgotten and hungry and where is
your wife Mr Drake Hanging in
strips in the bathroom
  Mr Drake drops what hes holding
A hand falls out Small Small
Bitten down nails Rapunzel Rapunzel
let down your hair
  Not a bundle of rags and Im
hungry
  But Mr Drake has an axe in his
hand and hate in his eyes and he
sees me he knows me and YOU he
says and theres sounds in my mouth
but no words and Im smiling
  Me Mr Drake ME
  He rushes me at me and swinging
the axe and faster than ever I move
Out of the bathroom and into the
sitting room and staying ahead of
his axe He swings and the axe head
smashes a chair Smashes the table
Splinters splinters in the air He
roars and he howls and Mr Drake
you need to be quiet Mr Drake
theyll hear you
  Mr Drake theyre coming Theyre
coming Mr Drake Mr Drake Alex is
coming

Mr Drake Mr Drake what have you
done

Didnt see the trap on the floor
Didnt Steel jaws bear jaws bear
claws slam shut Didnt feel it
couldnt feel it couldnt move and he
has an axe Swinging swinging
laughing swinging and who is laughing
Mr Drake Not me not you not you
who
George George my George all mine
Climbed the ladder and has the axe
One hand on the axe one hand on
his shoulder and where can you run
to Mr Drake Laughing laughing my
George my George And where did
the gun come from Mr Drake
Mr Drake falling and Mr Drake
bleeding and a bang and a bang
and silence
Oh George oh George my George my
George and Sylvie screaming inside
my head Wheres your face George
wheres your face One shot two shot
both point blank and George is gone
and Mr Drake laughing and the trap
is heavy but Im strong enough He

cant run and lll drag it and drag it
and l cant feel it cant feel it only
my heart breaking

Funny how we end up here
Funny not funny and not laughing
really but should be because this is
where we started My George mine
and my heart is breaking and Mr
Drake now in a pool of blood
Hungry not hungry l dont know any
more because Alex is coming and
George is dead Shut up Sylvie shut
up shut up no room for us all no
room no room
Cant feel can't feel only heart
breaking
Heart breaking heart breaking l
want to wake up
Cant wake up cant wake up cant
grow up cant throw up and everything
everything grey and red.
Wine red blood red red red red
Mr Drake has a lighter in his pocket
metal shines like a star in the night
Follow the star follow the light
Second star to the right and straight
on till morning

Feel older Feel empty. Where did Maddy go Is Maddy me? OMG OMG Looks like my writing but not

I missed you I'll miss you

I miss Mum I miss Dad I miss George. I'm so lonely

So lonely again. The flat smells of lonely of empty of hungry of dead Mrs Drake

I remember I remember I remember.

Tastes like tears my tears mine every time

I remember.

Not living surviving Not living Not dying. I want to grow up I want to wake up

I want

His lighter feels cold feels heavy Old metal Not his Stolen I think Bad Mr Drake All your rules did they save you?

Thumbs feel too thick. Won't bend like they should Like gloves made of dead man's hands

Goodbye Mr Drake and good riddance

Goodbye George my George mine all
mine
  Goodbye diary Present from
George. What else did he give me
life not life

So much left but I don't think I'll
write anymore
  I'm hungry not hungry and my
heart is breaking

Goodbye Maddy Wood.
  Find a candle, light it up, and all
day long you'll have good

From: beherenow <beherenow@psychotrope.com>
To: packrat <packrat@chatshack.com>
Sent: THU, Jun 13, 19:25 PM
Subject: Sympathy for the Deathless

Hey Pack Man

Check out <u>this</u> on Friendface! It's a kind of mash-up based on the verses of that dusty old <u>Stones track</u>. It's kind of a scratchy video, the lighting's dark as a corpse's butthole, and the one-eyed dude singing it (if you can *call* it singing) has got the worst home-movie slasher makeup job you'll ever see, like a Zombie Klingon. AND it's verses only, the notion of a CHORUS seems to have passed him by, lame-oh. Kind of goes on and on until your head melts. But check out the lyrics: heads up, pop-culture refs incoming! How many can *you* spot . . . ?

Makes you think. The same name popping up the whole time across these various franchises (kind of) is a cool idea (kind of). Like a race memory expressing itself, or a ghost that haunts us. Or an enemy hiding in plain sight, almost. (You ever read Poe?)

Kind of cool. Or not. It is interesting that this was released at the end of April, *just before*, you know, the shit started flying out of All Hallows. As if this guy knew what was coming. Interesting, or not.

And BTW I know I still owe you fifty notes but since when did interest payments apply to transactions between best bros, get a life man . . .

. . . I ask no leave to introduce myself
As your strutting minstrel screamed
You know me, I am in your head
My face, my name, are in your dreams

I was there when awareness dawned
And you slaughtered your cousins with clubs of stone
And I'll be there to see my own kind rise
To flense your bodies and to rule alone

I saw your end, and I flew back through years
To an age of steam and greed
I walk your world in shade and light
While my other, my former self, sleeps with the dead

I let you glimpse me, let you hear my name
And I felt your fear echo in me
You smelled my blood, and you gave my name
To the white beast that haunts your inner sea

You gave my name, under Altair's light
To the mind that tore your star children apart
In your dreams I drank the blood of the Spider Boy
And I fought the Lords of Time on the wastes of Karn

You gave my name to the god of beasts
With his scalpels and his science and his House of Pain
I watched his heirs raise the swastika
And spill human lives like a fall of rain

I ask no leave to introduce myself
You know me all too well
But call my name when All Hallows falls
And you open the doors of your living hell . . .

EndNotes

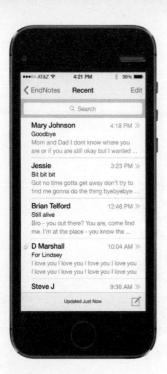

APP DESCRIPTION

You've been bit. Or you're just out there, lost and alone. You want to try to say goodbye, leave a message in case someone you care about is still around to hear it.

That's what EndNotes is for. Record your final thing, upload it. Hopefully your loved one/s will find it, and know you still cared.

Or just hear you say goodbye.

NOTE: Make sure you use your real name or whatever people are likely to search under. No point using a nick your mom don't know, if she's who you're hoping is going to find you.
NOTE 2: And be considerate, FFS. I'm going to try to keep this up and running as long as I can, but the rate servers are burning down, it's a losing battle keeping it up in the Cloud.

So I now got a 100 terabyte disk I'm storing it all on, and I plug it in the net wherever I can find a working uplink. This means:
— If you can't upload or search, try again later. I may be back online by then.
— Keep it short and sweet, friends. Storage space is running out *fast*. Pick your words carefully, and leave space for the next person. Don't make me start limiting messages to 140 characters or something. Like Twitter, right? Remember that? Ha. My first ever app was a Twitter app.

Seems like a *looong* fucking time ago now.

Stay sharp & stay human
Zeke @ ZApps

VERSION HISTORY

1.0 - First public release
1.1 - Removed the "Record Video" option — vids were using up too much space on my disk.
1.2 - Removed the "Record Audio" option. Ditto.
1.3 - Removed the "Final Photograph" option. You sensing a pattern here, people? Don't make me go to 1.4 ...

So this is the end . . .

June 2

Today is the first chance I've had to bring my journal
up to date since what happened. It's the first time
I've felt like talking . . . writing about what me and
my family went through. It's still all so . . .
  No, I can't. Not yet. I need another drink first. But
I will say this. It went down just like I kept saying it
would, more or less. They tried their best to cover
things up, but I know the truth. I'd predicted it, in
fact. I was always saying to Nat, one day they'll
really go and fuck things up and . . .
  Got to stop now, I can't get the image of little
Rosie's face out of my mind.

If you're reading this at some point down the line, if
there's anyone human still left to read it, that is,
chances are you probably know all about the last
several weeks. About the shit that went down with
that New Festival of Britain site in London, the cloud
of red insects we saw on the TV, heard about on the
radio - until everything got shut down and they
started to suppress what was really going on.

That the dead were coming back to life.

No, not life — not like Nat and my girl Rosie used to have. They were _so_ alive. On weekends when I got time off, or could rearrange my shifts — I was a workman for the council — we'd go to parks, go to the cinema, go out to eat. Rosie would order the most gigantic fudge sundaes you've ever seen in your life, then . . .

I need to stop thinking about all that. The life before. There's only this life now. I felt numb for such a long time afterwards, but now I'm just angry.

Now I just want revenge.

But I do need to get it all down, to explain our story and what happened to us. There needs to be some kind of record . . .

It was on one of those weekends when everything changed for us. We were at the local shopping precinct — yeah, I know, the irony wasn't lost on me either — when it all kicked off. We'd had a nice day out, even though I hate . . . hated being dragged round clothes' shops by Nat and Rosie. It was still a nice day out, and made a change from digging up roads for the local Council.

So we'd heard stuff was going on down south and, as I said, I'd been talking about something kicking off for years, though nobody really took me seriously: "Ssh, you're scaring Rosie," Nat used to say. That seems so ridiculous to me now. Scaring her? She should have been bloody scared - we all should have been. But I never thought it would hit us so quickly. I was worried, sure, and in retrospect I should have bundled my family up and made for the nearest harbour as quickly as possible, got off this island and gone . . .

Gone where? Is there any place that's safe anymore? It doesn't matter now anyway, as in the end I didn't do it. Maybe there was some part of me that couldn't believe the moment was actually here. That we'd gone and done it - caused the End of the World. They've been developing stuff like this for years, you know. Working on trying to reanimate dead tissue. But this time something went seriously wrong down south . . .

But that's all beside the point. There we were, sitting in the area where they sell food and drink. Looking back, perhaps I was trying to give them one final family day out, before the shit hit the fan. Because my radar was definitely up - something bad was coming our way.

I just didn't expect it to be a shopping mall full of fucking zombies.

Our first sense that something was wrong came when groups of people started running towards us. Nat put down her latte and looked over at me, frowning - that look she always got when she knew we were in trouble (usually financially, I have to say). Worried and confused and silently asking what we should do. That's the thing about having a ten-year-old around, you can't show your concern. You have to try and shield them, protect . . .

I got up, kicking back the chair I'd been sitting on. Trying to get a better look at exactly why those people were so panicked. Then I saw what was

chasing them and realised that we should be running too.

At first it didn't really register as anything other than more people, another group following them - attacking them to be precise. Dragging them down to the ground and, yes, I could see now they were biting into the ones they got hold of.

"Nat," I said, slowly, but seriously. "Grab Rosie. We need to get out of here. Right now!"

My wife, love her, did as I asked, and Rosie was frightened enough now to follow our lead. So we backed away, hoping to find some kind of emergency exit or something. Taking a look back over my shoulder, I saw more and more of the dead, all grey and shambling, mouths open wide and making those loud moaning sounds. Soon they were starting to outnumber the living.

The dead were spilling out of everywhere, filling the upper and lower levels.

And also ahead of us, surrounding us. They came upon us so quickly we never really stood much of a chance. I looked around for anything I could use as a weapon, snatching up a chair and slamming that into the nearest one as it came at me. It was only when I turned that I saw Nat and Rosie being dragged off, being pulled under the hordes.

I reached out, but was grabbed myself. They were strong those things, especially in large numbers. I managed to wrestle myself free, ducking out from under a pair of arms that were threatening to crush me. I dodged left, but another one had me by the arm. I punched backwards, not even looking, managing to escape and scan the food area for my wife and daughter. I couldn't see them - only a crowd of infected and . . .

So much blood.

Then suddenly there was pain - teeth biting down into my shoulder. My family had been torn apart and I didn't care anymore. Let them do their worst.

I really don't remember much more, because I blacked out. When I came to my senses again, I was lying in the car park. It was night and I was completely alone. All I can think of is that someone got me out of there, rescued me and pulled me free of the building, then had to leave me there for whatever reason. Rescued me, when I couldn't even do the same for my own wife and child.

Sometimes I wonder if I really did die that day, and if this is Hell.

I went back inside the shopping mall, of course, to see if I could find my family but, like outside, the building was now completely deserted. Red everywhere. No sign of Nat or Rosie. At least I was spared seeing what had been done to them. Though sometimes I think that makes it worse. You imagine even more appalling things, if that's possible.

I need to take a break now . . .

June 3

Okay, one drink turned into several. Yesterday turned into today. And I woke up realising that I hadn't finished my account properly. Hadn't told you about what happened next.

After the bite, which hurt like fuck by the way, I know what's supposed to happen - what I've actually seen happen after one of them gets you. Seen it up close and personal. It doesn't usually take long after that, either, before you turn.

Except I never did. Don't get me wrong, I was as sick as a dog - made my hangover this morning look like mild food poisoning. Luckily I had a place to hole up while I went through it.

I didn't tell you about my place, did I? My basement, or perhaps I should say "bunker" as that's what Nat always used to call it. The place where I'd organise my clippings about all the conspiracies. All the hidden agendas. It was a sort of hobby of mine, kept me off the streets.

It's what I did when I wasn't out on those streets labouring, but at least I knew them like the back of my hand. And now they're my hunting ground.

Night or day, makes no difference – it's not like I'm hunting vampires or anything.

The stuff I've compiled over the years is the reason why I always thought something like this – well, not exactly like this – was going to occur at some point. All those experiments scientists were doing, all those genetically engineered viruses injected into insects and animals. You think Bird Flu or AIDs or SARS came out of nowhere? That it was simply all down to Mother Nature? She had a massive helping hand, trust me.

They were playing with fire. Something was bound to go wrong at some point – it was only a matter of time. I think that there's a passage somewhere in the Bible about God destroying both man and beast from the face of the Earth. Maybe we just did it to ourselves first.

But I've gone off track again. Oh yes . . . the sickness. I locked myself away down here, knowing it was well-stocked – there's a concealed section with a refrigerator, tinned provisions, even some medicines (I'd treated the wound itself, but the virus was in me by then). There is also a chemical toilet and back-up generator.

Anyway, I was feverish one minute, freezing cold the next – then throwing up for England. It seemed to go on forever, but eventually I came out the other side. And, sitting there sipping from a bottle of water after my shakes had subsided, I realised that all this had been my body's way of fighting off the infection.

That I must be immune in some way.

Maybe that was why the dead had left me alone - because I didn't taste right. And that gives me an advantage.

Once I'd started eating again, got stronger, I went out armed with whatever I could find around my house - which I've since trashed, I should add: I've made it look deserted so as to hide in plain sight. I thought it would be hard, destroying all those memories, but in the end it was easy. I needed to wipe them out, become hardened.

I grabbed knives from the kitchen, tucked them into my belt, a hammer from the toolbox shoved into my pocket, plus a pretty lethal-looking handsaw and a short axe from my shed outside. Rough and ready, that's what I was. More than ready - and it wasn't as if there was now a shortage of them out there. I could take my pick.

And that's exactly what I did. I suppose I did go a bit Mad Max really . . . I went something at any rate. It wasn't the first time, and it sure as hell won't be the last. Especially now that I have better weapons – abandoned by some of those Army types in their bid to clean up the city, and failing miserably.

They're long gone, by the way, the authorities. They've given up on this place, just like they must have done with so many other cities across the country. Maybe they're concentrating on London still, who knows? Maybe everyone else has turned? I can't find out anything – I can't even get a signal on the radio up here.

All I know is – all I can rely on – is what I see out there. This city now belongs to them.

But I'm going to take it back.

June 15

Busy time again recently. I finally sat down and did some planning, and I came up with some better ways to tackle the infected. I mean, a stand-up fight is one thing, but it's still only me out there against all of them.

Fire's a pretty good deterrent, for a start. It's one of the reasons why I've rigged the street outside, and the house above - in case they ever find out where my base of operations is. Home-made explosives are not that difficult to make if you know what you're doing and have a grasp of basic chemistry. I might have messed about a lot in classes at school and wound up doing what I was doing before all this kicked off, but I've made up for it since. Plus I'm a fast learner.

I've also cooked-up some nasty batches of acid as well. That works a treat on the dead - and from a distance, if you spray it, it's like you're killing weeds in the garden. Which, y'know, isn't really all that far from the truth when you think about it.

Then there's the head thing. Everyone knows that you have to shoot or stab them in the brain to really kill them. But there are other ways as well. For example, you place a line of wire across a street - say between two lampposts - at a certain height. Then you show yourself, trying to attract their attention, which in all fairness isn't that difficult. After they start chasing you, you lead them into the street and then duck before they reach the wire. Hey presto, for them it's instant French Revolution, but without all that fuss with the guillotine. And thanks to their rotting flesh, you don't even need the axe to finish them off.

There are other methods I've used as well. For example, in my search of the city for anything I can use against them, I came across one of those industrial strimmers they use to clear overgrown wasteland with. A really tough model that makes those domestic garden ones look like a kid's toy. It makes a real mess of those things, and pretty quickly. Splatters them into tiny chunks of decaying meat.

Then there's simple brute force: if you ram them hard enough, and with a fast enough car (the thing about the End of the World is that there's no shortage of those - you can even drive them straight out of the showrooms now) then they tend not to get up again any time soon. Especially if you reverse a few times over their heads. I'd imagine I've become a bit of a local attraction doing that.

Whatever it takes. It all gets the job done.

Last night I took on a crowd of infected near what used to be old man Heston's place. I remember us being scared of him as kids, daring each other to run past his house in case he came out and tried to catch one of us. Looking back, he was just some confused old guy. I see that. And there are much, much worse things to be afraid of now.

But, just like I'm not afraid of old Heston anymore, so I'm not afraid of them anymore either. I'm still too upset to be scared.

Like when I waded into that group last night - there's nothing like getting back to that first hunt, that first fight. Getting down and dirty with them. Only now I jam pistols under chins, wedge serrated knives into skulls, hack off limbs with axes.

They try to bite me of course, try to infect me - not realising that they actually can't. Obviously, I wear padding - protective clothing scrounged from the local police station. I know I'm immune, but I'm not stupid - I don't actually want to get bitten again, because I can't risk being incapacitated, especially in the middle of a fight. I need to be able to get out of there before more of their kind arrive. Which they always do, as if they know when one of them is in trouble.

I like to make sure I'm long gone before then. I scope places out, so I know what my exit strategy is. I was caught on the hop once, and it cost me and my family dearly.

In my mind, I still see Nat and I growing old together, me worrying about Rosie when she heads off to university on her own. The amount of grey hair I'd get just from that! Nat telling me that kids have to find their own path, but me having trouble letting go. She was my little girl, you know? And I loved - <u>still</u> love her so, so much. I miss her.

I miss them both.

I need another drink now.

June 18

I think . . . I think that I might be going insane.

I've never had a hallucination before, unless you count that time when I was very little and I had a fever which made me see horses coming through the walls. But what I saw has got nothing to do with that.

Maybe it was lack of sleep then? Not surprisingly, my sleeping's not been great since the End of the World began. When I raided that chemist's for essential medical supplies, I came away with some sleeping pills that help. But I never really stay asleep for long. I fight it, you see. I've always been a fighter, just like my Old Man was . . . right up to the very end of his life. I wonder if he . . . ?

No, I can't think about that. Mum was cremated, so there's no chance of bumping into her out there. But Dad . . . ?

Off on another tangent, I know, but it does kind of relate to what I'm trying to say. Which is Rosie. I was out on the streets preparing for my next ambush and keeping out of the way of any infected, when I could have sworn I saw . . . it was a little girl, at any rate. Same kind of hair as my Rosie, dressed very similarly to how she'd been at the shopping mall.

Anyway, there she was ahead of me, turning a corner. I stopped, the breath catching in my throat. I could hardly swallow. Rosie. My Rosie. No, I shook my head. It couldn't be . . . and yet I found myself following, chasing after her. Or what I thought I'd seen anyway. Conscious now that I was out in the open.

Of course, there was nothing there when I got to the corner. No sign of any little girl. It wasn't inconceivable that someone like that might have survived the last couple of months or more, but at the same time . . .

She was so like my own little girl.

June 25

Last night I set another trap.
  Only this time it wasn't designed to bring down one of those dead things, but to capture it. I was thinking at first that I could study what I caught, figure out new ways to hurt or destroy them.
  The trap was a success, but when I'd got it back - "it" not "he" . . . I refuse to call it that yet - and secured it down in the basement, I got the sense that it was <u>watching</u> me, trying to work me out. It even opened and closed its mouth a couple of times like it was attempting to say something.
  It got me thinking. What if there is something left inside them - some semblance of humanity?
  However, I quickly dismissed such thoughts and set about what I was originally planning to do - study the monster. My enemy.
  I began by conducting some experiments of my own, testing the creature's limits of pain.
  I swear at one point I caught the thing looking at me with regret in its eyes.

June 30

I still can't shake the feeling that something might be living on inside them. That was one of the reasons why I stopped torturing that dead thing.

It probably wasn't even his fault he turned. He only looks young, although the rotting, peeling skin and greyish pallor will age any person. But it made me wonder about his previous life - like who he'd been, and what his ambitions were.

Maybe one day he planned on having a family of his own? Perhaps this dead guy would have felt the same way I do - would have done anything for his wife or child? Even given his life for them, if he could have.

The way he watches me, the way he looks so wretched even with those yellow eyes rolling back into their sockets the way they do. I've been thinking that perhaps I'm going about this all the wrong way.

What if he could be brought <u>back</u>?

What if I could restore his humanity, give him back his life? What if I could use my blood to do it?

I'm no scientist, but I know a little about what makes us tick. If you're immune, that means a cure can be developed from your tissue, your blood. And what I don't know I can find out from the library.

Now there's no Internet up here, we're back to the old ways.

Back to school. Doing things over, getting it right this time.

Putting all this whole damn mess right.

July 10

Well that didn't work.

I did what I said I was going to do - raided the City Library, an impressive building that looks like it belongs back in ancient Greece or something. But only after making sure there were no nasty surprises inside.

It was empty. So, after locating the science and medical stacks, I loaded anything that I thought might be useful into a backpack - not a hold-all, I needed to keep my hands free, just in case.

I made it back without incident, and began my studies. I pored over those books, taking in as much as I could. Learning how if someone has had a virus and appears to be immune, that they have developed antibodies and you can try and create your own cure from that. Like I said, I'm a fast learner.

It would mean another run for equipment, probably to the Hallamshire or Northern General Hospitals - maybe even both - but I sorted that out. I took a van this time and filled it up.

By the time I got everything back here and had set it up, my basement looked like a mad scientist's laboratory. Then came the hard part - drawing my own blood. You'd have thought I would have been the last person to be squeamish, especially after what I've had to do out there . . .

But eventually I got my samples, then I started work.

Once you know what you're doing, it's actually pretty easy. Or at least I thought so. The only problem is the quantities you're dealing with, because you never know whether it's going to be too much or too little.

Trial and error.

When I approached the boy I was trying to cure, I thought I detected fear or panic in his filmy eyes. He was chained to the wall. "I'm not going to hurt you," I promised, remembering my previous actions in that department. "I'm trying to help you. Don't you understand?"

There was perhaps some level of recognition there, but nothing you could call human.

Not yet.

I pulled out a hypodermic and pumped him full of my cobbled-together antidote. He immediately roared, straining against the steel shackles holding him upright. His milky eyes went wider than I'd ever seen them, and he snarled and shook and brought up a kind of black, tar-like bile. He was going through a similar reaction to me when I was first bitten, I noted.

Then something amazing started to happen. His grey skin began to gradually take on more colour. I'm not saying he looked cured, but any physical change was a good one so far as I was concerned.

"Come on, come on," I encouraged. All I could think about was giving him back a future that I'd been denied; the one he might still yet have. The one I might be able to give to all of the victims of this disease. And they were victims - I could see that now.

The boy was shaking so much I was worried that he might pull the chains out of the wall. But he wasn't trying to escape - his body was attempting to reject the antiserum that I had put into it. Then, as I looked on, he suddenly stopped shaking and his entire body slumped, only the shackles still holding him up. Black blood was running from his fixed, staring eyes.

He was dead. Truly dead this time.

There had been a time when I would have congratulated myself on creating such a weapon that could destroy those things, but now all I could see was failure.

And the fear and terror in that boy's eyes.

July 25

Test subject #10 has shown the greatest improvement yet.

Subjects #2 through #9 all displayed different - but always ultimately fatal - reactions to the serum, which I've varied with each subsequent injection. More failures, but I'm not thinking about it anymore. I need these subjects, need to carry out these tests so that I can get it right. Sometimes the end really does justify the means.

As in the case of #10, a woman who had been in her late forties by the looks of things, before she turned. I almost - almost - brought her back all the way.

I believe she even spoke a little, mouthing words I couldn't quite catch. They sounded like, "Help me . . ."

"Yes, that's what I'm doing," I told her, nodding.

That same fear was in her eyes as the colour returned to her pupils, the same as it did to her arms, face and body. There was the shaking, of course, but that was only to be expected.

"Please . . ." she begged, clenching and unclenching one of her hands. I stepped over and grabbed it, holding it as if that might actually help with the restorative process. But I'd done everything I could, and what was happening inside was up to her now. Her own private battle.

It was one that she ultimately lost.

Just when I thought the tide was turning, she suddenly let out a scream and slumped forward, hanging there on the wall. She was dead, just like the rest of my test subjects. But this time she didn't revert back to her grey, rotting form. She just looked peaceful.

Unlike the rest of them, I felt compelled to bury this one rather than take her to the incinerator. I even mumbled something resembling a prayer over the grave, though I'm not sure why. I was never much of a Church-going person before all this happened, and nothing that I've seen since has made me want to embrace any religion.

It just made me more determined to bring them all back.

August 1

I was doing my usual patrol of the city and I spotted something odd today.

Groupings of them, all heading in the same direction, joining up. I watched them through my binoculars from the top of one of the deserted buildings.

They were all heading towards the Town Hall. Congregating, as if following some silent summons - silent to human ears anyway. Like they had their own religion or something.

Although it was risky, I decided that I would try to get closer.

By the time I got to the ground floor, the crowd had thinned out somewhat - which at least allowed me to move a little more freely and catch up with them.

I peered around the corner of a building and saw a figure standing on a makeshift platform thrown together from debris and discarded trash. The zombies had gathered around and they seemed to be listening to him.

I wasn't close enough to hear what he was saying, but through the binoculars I got a good look at the zombie who appeared to be giving his very own Sermon on the Mount.

It was the Mayor, or at least the man who was standing again for that position at the time the End of the World began. My old fucking boss! Was he . . . were all of them just recreating some base memory from before the outbreak? Were they only going through the motions, doing something they could simply half-remember from their past lives?

That made me all the more determined to bring them back again.

I just need to find the right formula.

August 15

Subjects #20 through #25 were total failures.

Need to rest, need to get some sleep before I carry on with this.

August 20

Something's changed out there in the city.

I can't put my finger on it, but it's definitely something. Ever since I witnessed that gathering, since they listened to that speech.

It's been harder and harder to find test subjects, like they've spread the word or something. Like they know that I'm out there, setting traps.

I'm just going to have to think outside of the box a bit more . . .

August 27

Stupid, stupid, stupid.

I can't believe what an idiot I was today. I was out there trying to catch more test subjects - I'm running low now - and I saw her. Thought I saw her.

My wife. Nat.

As was the case when I thought I saw Rosie, I let my guard down. I followed her in a kind of daze, half-wanting, needing it to be her - even a zombie version of her. Something I could fix.

I think she was real.

Shit. My side hurts so much, and as for my ankle . . .

I'll write more later. I can feel the painkillers kicking in now.

I can hardly keep my eyes

August 29

Still not in great shape, but I'm slowly recovering.

Just read back what I wrote before. I nearly started again, but it's all part of the journal, the record of what I've gone through here.

My wife. Nat.

I followed her inside a building. It was a ruin. So much so that I didn't see any of it coming. I wasn't expecting it. I mean - I'm the thinking one, right?

It just didn't occur to me they'd be capable of . . . Maybe they were just going through the motions again, but it would still require . . .

I stumbled across the tripwire before I even realised that it was there. A lower-down version of the ones I used to leave for beheading them, only they didn't want me dead. Not if the spring-loaded piece of wood that hit me in the ribs was anything to go by.

It knocked all the air out of my body, sending me sprawling into a pile of rotting boxes. My knife went flying into a shadowy corner, out of reach.

Shaking my head to clear it, I started to clamber to my feet, then winced at the pain in my side. As if that wasn't enough, I'd barely taken a step or two when I trod on the mantrap, covered over with discarded rubbish.

I wear combat boots, which are quite tough, but they did nothing to protect me from those metal jaws as they snapped shut on my ankle. I yelled out in pain.

Already I could see shapes, shuffling movement all around me. I had to get out of there, and quickly. I shouldn't even have followed her inside without some kind of an exit strategy.

It took two or three attempts, but I eventually managed to prise open the clamp and get my foot out. Using some broken shelving to drag myself up, I scanned the room, trying to make out which direction might be the safest. One that wouldn't have any more nasty surprises in store.

In the end, I just thought <u>fuck it</u>, and launched myself sideways at the glass window not far away. I crashed through it and fell, tumbling over and over on the concrete pavement - which actually put some distance between me and my pursuers. Maybe even saved my life.

Not that it felt like it at the time, as I limped away down the street, looking back over my shoulder to check if I was being pursued. As I rounded a corner, I risked a final glance back, only to see a group of them outside the building. Was it only my imagination, or did one of them point and grunt some kind of instruction, like an officer giving orders to his troops?

There was no time to think about that then - I just had to get away. So, limping through the streets, I hobbled onwards - pausing only once to rip some material from my sleeve and tie it around the wound on my ankle. I needed to stem the blood-flow, not only for my own sake, but also so that they wouldn't have a scent to track. I've seen what their heightened senses can do . . .

I was conscious of the fact I was out in the open, and that I needed to get inside somewhere quickly. I chose a shop that looked deserted, gaining access through the smashed window at the front, most of the display having been looted a long time ago.

Once I made it to the back room I collapsed, deciding to wait until it was safe enough to be on the move again.

Under the cover of darkness (yeah, I know all about their heightened senses, but it at least made me feel better) I eventually made it home. Or what had become of it - I'd stopped thinking of it like that once my family had been snatched from me. After I'd trashed it.

Before the pills and whisky put me under, I began to consider what had happened. First Rosie, and then Nat. I'd seen both of them . . . or something that had looked like them, hadn't I?

Something that had led me straight into a trap, just like the ones I had been setting for my test subjects.

Using bait.

September 8

Healing . . . slowly. The pills and alcohol are helping.

Not able to get out, not able to find test subjects. Not able to do anything.

Useless, absolutely . . . useless.

September 11

I ventured out too soon, and they spotted me. Not surprising really. My injuries have slowed me down - I've lost my edge.

Not only did they see me, they <u>followed</u> me back here! They're organised now, much more than I had ever realised.

They began to gather outside the house. Not making a move while I watched through one of the upstairs windows I'd broken to make this place look like every other building hereabouts - decayed . . . just like them. I've come to think of this city like that. I once said that it belonged to them. Now it has also come to resemble them as well.

Within an hour there were probably hundreds of them shuffling around outside.

And the Mayor wanted to talk to me personally.

Yes, they can <u>talk</u> now - and not just to each other. I discovered that when he began calling to me from the street.

"You cannot possibly win Mr Nevill," he said.

It was a pretty good opening, and a realisation that I was reluctantly starting to come to myself.

"Yes, we know who you are. Are you surprised? We have known for some time. Only we did not know where to find you . . . until now. You have inflicted untold horrors on our people . . . " he went on.

Untold horrors, on them? What was he talking about?

"We found the results of your 'experiments'. What you've been doing to our . . . kin. Trying to go against the natural order of things."

Natural order? There was nothing natural about them. The world needed to be put right again - put back to how things were before . . .

My family . . .

And it was then that I saw them. They were standing close by him, like he was using them to somehow persuade me. Not Nat and Rosie, no, but they looked so much like them. Those dead people they had twice used to lure me into a trap . . .

"It is our time now," the Mayor continued. "We are the superior race, and we are cleansing the world of your kind. It is a New Era, and we are its Family."

New Era?

"The Family is one. Outside of the Family, there is nothing at all!" they all started to chant in unison.

That's when I remotely set off the explosive devices I had concealed around the perimeter of the house and outside in the street. Probably because of the nails and fragments of twisted metal that I had packed into each one, they shredded zombie flesh as easily as they would have done any human's.

And their screams of pain and outrage were as loud as any made by man.

I quickly retreated to the basement and locked the heavy wooden door from the inside. That is where I am now, writing this final account.

I can hear them outside.

Later

So this is the end.

It won't be long now before they break in here . . . I can hear them out there pounding on the basement door. There are too many of them for it to hold much longer.

I wanted to just finish this journal, get the job done. To leave something of myself behind.

God only knows what they have planned for me, after everything I've done to them. After all those experiments I conducted, trying to bring them _back_.

What have I become to them? A murderer? A thing of nightmares? A boogeyman that these things . . . these "intelligent zombies" . . . will continue to fear when I am gone. A legend that they will whisper to each other in the dark and use to frighten their dead children with . . . ?

I have lost. Lost everything. My family . . . myself. I am lost. I was crazy to think I could ever take this city back from them. It belongs in them now, as does this new world.

The door is beginning to give. There are only a few moments left before they'll be through it, but I still have my knife with me. Legends are written by the victors . . . and at least I'll not give them the satisfaction of that.

Welcome to The Shat Room!
(It's Chat, Jim, but Not As We Know It!)

02:16:12 14 June 2013

Online: \<beherenow@psychotrope.com>
\<packrat@chatshack.com>
Subject: Cool stuff from All Hallows

BEHERENOW: Hey Pack Man, check out this! I was snooping through the feeds that came out of this shit at All Hallows, back in like April or May, when they opened up that crypt? And the fleas came swarming out? And the next thing you know it's a plague of zomboids? I went back to it, wanted to get into the fuzz flicks — you know. Get the *real* gore. And I found that somebody hacked into this — crap knows how — and posted it up on the Anarchy TV site — just watch it, man, just watch.

> *Video feed: Early morning. A shaky handheld image of the church, groups of workmen in yellow hardhats, a police cordon, armed soldiers, TV news crews, protestors with banners and placards.*
>
> *Fleas erupt in a grainy tempest from out of the open church door and the excavated graves. We hear a low chuckle, off camera.*
>
> *And, dimly seen in the cloud of fleas — a quick zoom — a figure comes staggering out of the church door, spindly, dressed in grey rags, all but concealed by the swarm. As the throng of onlookers tries to move away, it appears that some people are starting to indiscriminately attack others in the crowd.*
>
> *A quick pan to reveal a stern male face, looking down into the camera from above, a patch over one eye, a cold grin. The cameraman says, "There he is. Right on time, after more than two centuries in the dark . . ."*

PACKRAT: Whoa, hello Jack Sparrow fright night!

BEHERENOW: Just keep watching, dork. Wait until you *see* . . .

> *Video feed: The viewpoint swings again. We are running, the image blurring, shaking.*
> *We move away from the church, the panicking crowds, to the left, then we sprint in the shadows back around the side of the*

church. And we see a figure panting, hiding in the cover of a graveyard wall. Fleas whining everywhere. Then a hand reaches from behind the camera, grabs a handful of grey shirt — it rips, crumbles to threads — drags the figure into a scrap of light. The figure stares into the camera, scared, bewildered. Freeze-frame.

PACKRAT: Urgh. So this guy was in the church? In with all those fleas? Fly, my pretty!

BEHERENOW: Yeah, he was in the church. Busting out of some sealed mausoleum they didn't open for, like, centuries. I mean is it possible?

PACKRAT: He doesn't look so bad, considering.

BEHERENOW: Right. Better than you, doofus. But look again. Doesn't he remind you of somebody?

Video feed: screengrab of "Captain Sparrow", the camera operator from earlier, brought up alongside image of fugitive from church.

PACKRAT: Holy shit. That's the same guy!

BEHERENOW: Got it in one. Give or take that missing eye, I mean. Listen what comes next.

Video feed: Voice off-camera: "You are Moreby."

Fugitive: "I . . . am Moreby." The voice is like old dust. "And you, sir?"

"I am Moreby . . ." from off-camera. "I have used a device that multiplies entities—"

Fugitive smiles. "Then you have used da Vinci's Chronos Macchina. You never were a fool."

"Coming from you, sir, that is hardly a compliment," says the unseen voice.

Image blurs as camera is manhandled; stabilises so we are looking back at "Captain Sparrow".

Sparrow: "Wear this device on your clothing. It will allow me to follow your progress. Do not ask how it works."

Fugitive's voice, now off-camera (we are seeing his viewpoint): "I do not care how. What must I do?"

"You are at All Hallows, Blackheath, wherein you were long incarcerated. You must make your way to Billingswell, in the village of Kensington, and to that land that lies between Brompton Lane and Honey Lane. There a great necropolis now stands."

A pause.

Fugitive: "I am far from my time. I can tell from the street lights, the carriages, that since I was last aware, in the year eighteen hundred and—"

Sparrow: "Fool. You have slept centuries, but London has not moved. Go find the Cemetery. Look for the sign of Anubis and it will point your way."

Fugitive: "Where?"

Sparrow: "Was I ever so slow-witted? There is an escape route for you, but it has been secured — you must unlock it. You will figure out the code. Go. The police, the scientists — the natural philosophers of this age — suspect there is danger here, at All Hallows. But they must not find you. Go now, while chaos and confusion reigns, and flee to a better time."

Fugitive: "But—"

Sparrow: "As for me, I have a war to win here."

Fugitive: "A war? Against whom?"

Sparrow: "Mankind. And also, in fact principally, against myself. You will see when it is your turn."

Fugitive: "But what will you do now?"

Sparrow: "Me? Why, I intend to give myself up. After a little pantomime resistance, perhaps."

Fugitive: "You would surrender to these peasants?"

Sparrow: "Don't be a fool. I said 'give myself up', not surrender. When I do so they will obligingly transport me into the heart of their strongest citadels — I believe the word is, 'rendition'. And when they do so, I will eat my way out of that heart. And the world will be mine — or ours. You will work it out yourself, when your time comes. Now you must go — it would ruin everything if you were to be caught."

Fugitive: "Then goodbye, Moreby."

Sparrow: "Goodbye, Moreby, until we meet again. Go, then, to Brompton — run, you clever boy . . .!"

Image blurs again, then resolves to a shaky image, a confusion of streets, houses and terrified faces . . .

PACKRAT: Did he say *Chronos Macchina*? That sounds like it means

BEHERENOW: Yeah, I grokked that too. Just when you thought the day couldn't get any weirder, huh? OK, so we do a lot of running and dodging and hiding . . .

Video feed: Fast-forward of a run through South London streets, traffic, fleeing figures. Stuttering pauses at distracting spectacles like TV stores, a brightly-lit fast food restaurant, a group of teenagers talking on their smart phones. People glimpse the camera wearer, recoil, scream. And he runs on.

PACKRAT: Gee. Kind of nostalgic, seeing London again.

BEHERENOW: You should worry. I've still got credit on my Oyster card.

Video feed: Slow to normal pace as a bridge is crossed. Curious stares from the rush-hour crowds on the walkways, people pulling away in disgust.

PACKRAT: That's Putney Bridge, right?

BEHERENOW: Well, it was. Yeah. He's on the right track.

Video feed: Fast-forward through more streets. Slow to normal at a great arch and the open gates to a cemetery, looking tranquil in the bright morning sunshine. Quick swings of the viewpoint, a feverish search along straight paths and through the long grass.

Then finally . . . a tombstone, an upright slab of weathered grey stone, inscribed with the legend JOSEPH BONOMI, SCULPTOR, TRAVELLER AND ARCHEOLOGIST. And below the dates, a carved symbol of Anubis, the Egyptian god of the dead, gazes off to the right. The viewpoint swings in that direction, and

some sixty feet away stands a tall, stone mausoleum with a huge copper door now stained a verdigris green. The camera rushes towards the door, but abruptly stops as it becomes apparent that no key sits within the lock.

Off-camera a rasping voice whispers, "A code, a code . . ."

Then the viewpoint swiftly moves again, hurrying back towards the nearby gravestone. The image stabilises for a moment on the figure of Anubis; the sound of ragged panting. Then another rapid search. Two hands reach out to lift a broken headstone, perhaps already vandalised; it is swung at the jackal-headed carving.

PACKRAT: Ouch!

BEHERENOW: I know. We're breaking some kind of deep taboo here. Keep watching . . .

Video feed: The rectangular carving shatters, the stone wielded with bloodied, dusty hands. Set behind it into the face of the tombstone is a glowing number display: six red zeros. Below is a keypad. The function is obvious, even to this refugee from another time. Bloody fingers desperately press at the pad, filling up the display with a random string of digits: a bleeping refusal. A muttered voice: "The code. Bonomi. Bonomi . . ." Again the camera swings, another frantic search. And a siren wails in the distance.

PACKRAT: Are the authorities on to him?

BEHERENOW: Onto what? He wasn't seen at All Hallows, nobody seemed to follow him here . . . Maybe somebody phoned in the vandalism at the graveyard, or more likely London is just coming apart.

PACKRAT: How ironic, Doctor Tombstone. Your elaborate plans for world domination foiled by a failure to consider a single simple detail, and even now PC Dixon of Dock Green closes in

BEHERENOW: Hush. Look. He gets to find it . . .

Video feed: Tattered fingers run down the face. And the fingers hover over a line: DIED 3RD MARCH 1878.

BEHERENOW: That's it, you clever boy.

PACKRAT: You know the ending. You're spoiling it.

BEHERENOW: Sorry. But keep watching.

Video feed: Fingers, trembling, slam in the code: 3-3-1-8-7-8. Then a frantic dash back to the imposing mausoleum. The fugitive stands back. With a hiss the copper door opens to reveal a shadowy interior, the walls completely covered in elaborate cabalistic designs. In the exact centre of the room stands a stone pillar, a monolith with handles to grip, an incision on the face of a geometric diagram, and chiselled sockets covered by flaps of china.

PACKRAT: Whoa! Now we're getting somewhere.

BEHERENOW: You ain't seen nothing yet.

Video feed: A shout of triumph; evidently the fugitive recognises this thing. A hand reaches out, smashes open an incised pot, and extracts a pinch of some dried herbal substance, brings it up to the face.

PACKRAT: Hardly the time for a pinch of snuff, my man.

BEHERENOW: For this next bit, please keep your hands inside the car.

Video feed: Two bloodied fists grasp the handles. Immediately, an explosion of light overwhelms the camera's capacity.

PACKRAT: Yow! Through the Star Gate, Hal.

BEHERENOW: You're not far wrong.

Video feed: Inside the corridor of light images appear for a split second before quickly being replaced by another, and then another . . . great cities burning, skies turned ashen with billowing smoke from a thousand fires . . . armies of corpses dressed in grey uniforms and distinctive steel helmets moving over the land in formation . . . a fleet of majestic airships making their way across the skies with the ZZ insignia starkly emblazoned upon their sides . . . giant flying reptiles swooping down upon fleeing figures and tearing them apart with their scissored beaks . . . and over every one of these visions the same superimposed face, yet each time subtly different, not quite identical . . .

The image stabilises again, though the colours are washed out; perhaps the camera has been damaged by the flash. A hasty pan around.

Now we're in artificial light, surrounded by fine furnishings — antique paintings hang on striped walls, a pair of plush couches facing each other with a square coffee table between them, an old grandfather clock standing to one side. No sign of people; this is a big spacious room with curved walls. The stone pillar is an odd intrusion in this clean, ornate space. The fugitive's breathing is loud.

The image flickers, breaks up for a moment.

Now the view swivels towards the other side of the room. Three tall windows frame an impressive antique desk. The image freezes on some kind of wall display, blurred by the pan.

BEHERENOW: So what do you think?

PACKRAT: I guess we escaped from the London cops.

BEHERENOW: Oh, we did a little more than that. The *Chronos Macchina*, remember?

PACKRAT: Did we move in time? If so, in space as well. Huh, so what, the TARDIS can do that, and it's not even *real*.

BEHERENOW: Yeah, but moved where? And when? I cleaned up the image a little . . .

Video feed: The wall display gets sharper, pixel by pixel. It has a time and date stamp, and various textual displays, including a DefCon level signifier. And three big mechanical clocks show the time in three cities.

BEHERENOW: Can you read that? The tabs under the clocks.

PACKRAT: Washington, London, Moscow. Holy mackerel. With Washington first.

BEHERENOW: You see what we got here, man. You see what we got. We're only in the Oval Office, in Washington. *In the White House.*

PACKRAT: How the hell do you know we're in the WH?

BEHERENOW: Well, where else in America would you find a circular room with a display like that?

PACKRAT: NASA.

BEHERENOW: Well

PACKRAT: F.B.I. C.I.A.

BEHERENOW: OK

PACKRAT: Wall Street.

BEHERENOW: OK OK. Come on, man, indulge me. And, plus — look at the date on the display.

PACKRAT: Day, month, year. Oh shit. 03:07:13. July frigging third.

BEHERENOW: That fugitive just jumped from London to Washington, and from May 1st to two months into the future, man.

PACKRAT: Technical point, bro. So how come the feed from the camera kept working?

BEHERENOW: I dunno. I guess it's feeding back through the time machine somehow. Look, it breaks down soon. Just watch what happens now. Hey, clever boy. He's behind you . . .

Video feed: Again the image flickers as it pans quickly, and settles on a figure, standing directly behind the fugitive.

PACKRAT: You figure this *is* the White House? That guy's wearing a suit like the President. He's even got one of those Stars-and-Stripes lapel pins like the President. But . . .

BEHERENOW: But that isn't the President. Not ours, anyhow. And . . .

PACKRAT: And he's wearing an eye patch. He's the guy from All Hallows. President Jack Sparrow! But . . .

BEHERENOW: But we figured that Sparrow and the running guy from the crypt are *the same guy.*

PACKRAT: Well, they would be. That's time travel for you. For God's sake, Moffat!

BEHERENOW: And notice the *other* guy lying on the ground behind the Prez. Kind of in the nip.

PACKRAT: Nice buns. You think he works out? Although it looks like somebody worked a pickaxe *into* his head, ha ha.

BEHERENOW: Close but no cigar. It probably wasn't a pickaxe. Did the job, though.

Video feed: The "President" lays his hand on the fugitive's shoulder. Then he plucks the camera off the fugitive's chest, more blurry movement, until the image settles so we see what the "President" sees — the dusty, bloody, grimy fugitive, standing in the subdued light.

PACKRAT: Shit! He looks bad in that light.

BEHERENOW: So would you, buddy.

Video feed: President: "So you made it. I'll check out the record on the camera. I imagine you think you're safe now?"

The image flickers, goes black for a moment.

Fugitive: "Well — since you are evidently myself, and you are apparently in command in this . . . this fortress of the future—"

Image cuts out for longer before coming back.

President: "Indeed, but it took much planning to get this far. And it finished with this . . ." He turns, and we're looking at the corpse on the ground. The President shoves it over with his foot, and the head lolls back, and the face is revealed.

The same face.

PACKRAT: Wow! Another one!

BEHERENOW: It's like what would have happened if the Nolan Sisters had ever really, really fallen out.

The video feed suddenly cuts out altogether. This time the screen remains blank.

PACKRAT: *No shit*! That's it? There's no more?

BEHERENOW: Sorry, good buddy, that's all she wrote. On the face of it, a time-travelling zombie conspiracy to take over the world.

PACKRAT: Or a hoax.

BEHERENOW: Quite. What do you think we should do with it? It's why I showed you, man, that's the key question.

PACKRAT: Well, there's two possibilities. We go public with this. The Americans, the U.N., whatever, are ready when these living-dead assholes try to take the White House. We save the world.

BEHERENOW: That's one. And two?

PACKRAT: We show ourselves to be the world's all-time number-one patsies when Dean at Anarchy TV crawls out and says he set it all up. Probably with outtakes from *Shaun of the Dead*.

BEHERENOW: I agree. That's truly an existential risk, man. Also, who's to tell? The N.S.A. probably saw it all already. They probably saw *us* seeing it already.

PACKRAT: God bless America!

BEHERENOW: Roger that. Hey, now check *this* out, somebody set the original *King Kong* to the soundtrack of *The Little Mermaid* . . .

"Both jaws, like enormous shears, bit the craft completely i atn."

. . . Of course the origin of the name of Herman Melville's most famous creation has always remained obscure.

The most plausible root would appear to be an infamous white sperm whale that became known as "Mocha Dick" to the whaling crews it encountered: "Mocha" for the proximity to that island, and "Dick" simply as a familiar name. Many such whales became notorious enough to earn names of this kind, "Dick" or "Jack" or "Tom", with a label for geographic location.

But how did "Mocha" transmute to its final form, as in Melville's book?

A clue may recently have emerged in a newly found archive of correspondence relating to American author Nathaniel Hawthorne. It is well known that Melville idolised Hawthorne, but the two men did not meet until 1850, a meeting which appears to have provided the final inspiration for Melville to tackle his masterpiece. However it now appears that Melville may have written to Hawthorne over a number of years preceding that first meeting, enclosing copies of his earlier books, manuscript fragments, even journal entries.

It is not clear if Hawthorne ever responded to these earnest communications, but the Hawthorne archive has fortuitously preserved elements of Melville's writings otherwise lost.

Of particular interest is a transcription of a journal entry made by Melville as a much younger man – perhaps sent to Hawthorne in the hope of electing praise for his precocity. In 1839 Melville, then twenty years old, had sailed from New York to Liverpool on the trading ship *St. Lawrence*. His experiences in the latter city would later inform his novel *Redburn*, published in 1849. The journal scrap contains writing that would later be reflected in the novel text, but describes an incident that was not later fictionalised:

. . . Previous to this, having only seen the miserable wooden wharves and shambling piers of New York. In Liverpool I beheld long China walls of masonry; vast piers of stone; and a succession of granite-rimmed docks, completely enclosed. In magnitude, cost and durability the docks of Liverpool surpass all others in the world. For miles you may walk along that riverside, passing dock after dock, like a chain of immense fortresses.

I turned into a street called Launcellot's Hey, for I heard the bawdy chatter of a tavern, quite clear, and desired to quench my thirst. But here I found a commotion. Next to the tavern was an old warehouse, with a cellar opening in the street; but that opening was barred by a heavy iron grid. The grid had been laid on the ground by a gang of rough fellows, seamen all by the look of them, who gathered around and stood over it, pots of porter and rum in hand, all the while goading whatever creature they had got penned up in the ground beneath them, under the bars. It was like a gang at a bear pit. "Back, Bear!" they cried. "Back in your hole!"

Curious, I ventured closer to see what the pit contained.

It was no bear, no animal. It was a man, bulky, blotchy, in stained shirt and pants, and with one eye cut out of a battered face. That was no unusual sight to me; at sea one becomes used to seeing such mutilations. But the man's cheerful rage was out of the ordinary, as he mixed fury at his captors' antics with a kind of savage humour.

For a time I observed their goadings, with a mixture of disgust and shame.

When he saw me the prisoner called out, "You, boy! From a whaler, are ye?"

I tried to stammer an answer.

To my alarm the fellow fair leapt into the air and hurled himself against his cage bars, as if to consume me, and the sailors raised a great cry, but the bars held.

"It's the whalers for me, lad!" said the man in the pit. "To see a man's limbs plucked off in the mouth of the god of fishes . . . To see in turn men scrambling over the captured carcass of the beast, like rats on a day-old corpse, slicing and cutting and amputating . . . Blood and knives, boys! And the sculpting of the flesh . . . That's the life for me!"

I was already enough of a writer to scramble for charcoal and paper from my pockets to make a note of this peculiar experience, and the man's memorable words.

When he saw my charcoal scratching, he grinned. "Yes, boy, write it down. Write the saga of a whale such as will whiten the livers of your landlubber readers with fear. And when ye do, give the man who hunts him down my name!"

The rude fellows laughed at that. "Ye're no captain, Moe!" "Look at your belly. He's more likely to name the whale for ye, Moe Beer!"

And then with a roar the fellow leapt at the grid again, and to my astonishment shifted it across the cobbles with a harsh scraping. Next thing I knew he was swarming out of the pit, like a demon released from Hades, like a white whale rising from the deep, and I and the rest of the fellows scattered and ran, each of us praying it would not be him he came after . . .

Monday, June 17

Bad enough on land, fog is, but I believe it must be worse at sea. It's not that I worry about us running into anything. More that it gives the illusion that we're hardly moving at all. There's no horizon. There's no sun. There's barely even a waterline down below. We're trapped in limbo, the world gone to a grey mist that even seems to suck the sound from the air.

Two weeks, give or take, this crossing is supposed to last. Two weeks aboard this ship of the dead. I've at least been able to resume my morning walks, ten circuits around the perimeter of the deck. It's good to have a routine again.

I have the run of the ship, as long as I don't go below, but I don't think I'd want to anyway, because when things are quiet and just right, sounds carry up through the ducts . . . weeping and sobbing and occasionally screaming that sounds very much like the living. It's only the screaming that doesn't last long. There's only one reason I can think of for the living to be down below. They are rations.

I've overheard remarks that seem to indicate that the ship's captain is still alive, too, but I've not seen him, as I'm not allowed up near the bridge, either.

I'm certain I remain alive only by Lady Cecilia's good graces, but by now I wish she'd just get it over with, either kill me or turn me, but don't leave me like this. Of the other vehicles' drivers, it appears that two were dispensed with before Cecilia and I even got here. Or maybe they're down below. There's only one left, a young woman named Bridget who serves one of the Seven that the others address as Charles, sometimes Lord Charles. He has a patrician look about him, as if he were born to order people around. Bridget keeps her hair skinned back and bound beneath a scarf, so you can really see her face, and so the resemblance between her and Charles is all the easier to notice. They have the same nose, the same high cheekbones.

Later she told me this: "He's still so much like my father sometimes. The rest of the time . . . I don't know what he is."

I understand this.

Otherwise, she's not had much to say to me, and keeps off by herself. I don't think she trusts me.

There are times I feel like such a traitor to my species.

Thursday, June 20

The other trucks and vans carry a similar cargo to our own, but the containers are a more eclectic mix. It's a collection of travel trunks and plastic drums and footlockers and crates and, yes, even the occasional coffin, too.

There's the eight we brought. Another nine in one of the other vehicles. Six in each of the other two. That's twenty-nine. Not much of an army, not even if all you're planning on taking back is a village, much less an entire country, or whatever outmoded impression they have of America, to still call it the Colonies.

I just don't understand this. And why bother rounding up the dead for transport at all, when they're going to be anywhere, everywhere?

Asking Cecilia does no good. Her answer: "Because our Thomas wants them."

Yes, but why? *Why*? I'm reduced to a child playing five degrees of why.

Cecilia: "Isn't it enough to know that Thomas wants them? For me, it is."

I could've asked how she and the rest of the Seven could be so sure, another pointless query, but I think I know already. It's something to do with the fleas, directly or indirectly. It's as if there's a hive mind at work. Of a fashion, it reminds me of quantum entanglement, when subatomic particles remain so inextricably linked that an action on one simultaneously affects the other, no matter how far apart they've become.

If the fleas all originated at a single point, perhaps they and all their descendants remain linked, and enable communication the same way. Just a thought.

Spooky action at a distance, Einstein called it. He certainly nailed that one.

Friday, June 21

So far, I've preferred to sleep here in the truck's cab, because I can lock it, and it feels safer that way. But sometimes I can hear them thumping around back there, inside their coffins, as if they're growing restless. Every now and again there's a muffled cry that, if I didn't know better, I would attribute to confusion.

Maybe I don't know better. Maybe they really are waking up to something more than pure instinct and hunger.

It's the same in the other vehicles. They grunt to each other through the walls of their prisons . . . I guess, to know they're not alone.

Fuck this. I'm going to have to find some other place to sleep.

Sunday, June 23

Still thinking about Einstein. I wonder what he would've made of all this.

I remember this from school, an age away: that he began to conceive of the theory of relativity one day when he was bored and daydreaming about riding on the front of a beam of light. It feels a little like that here on the ship, that I'm on some inexorable thing that I can't get off of, and that if I were to try, I'll just spin off into the void, faceless, placeless, trapped between two kinds of existence but belonging in neither.

I'm not dead, but I don't feel alive, either.

And so I continue west towards the New World, gliding over strangely calm seas, alternating between suffocating fog and the pitiless glare of the sun. At all hours of the day and night, our cargo moans and kicks and rattles at the lids of their containers. I'm tempted to let one of them out. Even if none of the Seven will do for me, maybe one of them would, if I ask nicely.

Cecilia sought me out a bit earlier. I wish I were seeing more of her on board, but I guess she keeps busy renewing acquaintances with her people. You'd think there might be lots to catch up on when you've not seen each other for 200 years, but then again, maybe not, not when you've been dead and buried the whole time.

I have no idea.

We stood by the railing near the back of the ship, where I've made myself a hidey-hole amidst some old crates, with a tarp overhead and a couple blankets. It's better than a cabin. I'm not trapped here. There's a lot less between me and going over the side, in case that starts seeming like a brilliant idea.

I asked Cecilia why I was still alive. It can't only be because I'm useful. I can't shake the feeling that my greatest use is that I'm nutritious.

Cecilia: "It has been a long time since I've had a pet."

Serious, or joking? I couldn't tell. Gerri was always easy to read, even for me. But not with Cecilia inside her.

Cecilia: "I have grown very fond of you. I really have. I was not expecting that, but here it is, so why fight it. Charles understands, at least. He seems protective of Bridget, and the Charles I knew, the only thing he was ever protective of was his status and his power."

I didn't mind when she touched my face. With Gerri's hand, cool as it was now.

Cecilia: "She must have loved you very much."

Is it possible for a person to feel any more used? I'll bet it was the same for Bridget. She would have done anything for Charles, so long as he looked like her father. The worst part is, I can't even say I've resented it all that much.

Cecilia: "What do you think of Bridget?"

Me: "I don't even know her. I've hardly even met her."

Cecilia: "I would have thought the two of you might have become inseparable on this voyage. You both have so much in common now."

Me: "Well . . . we haven't. I don't think she likes me."

Cecilia: "So you're mine, then. Well and truly mine."

I still didn't mind her touching my face. Just as she didn't mind when I touched hers. Our bodies had scarcely touched one another's since Cecilia had taken over. I think maybe we both missed it.

And that's about as far as I'm going to get into that. Other than to say that she knew how to do things Gerri had never known.

Wednesday, June 26

Land again. Thank God. Who's otherwise forsaken us.

It's a war we've landed in the middle of here in the States. The Capitol itself is under siege. The word amongst our party is that what remains of the military in the region has retreated to Washington to defend the politicians and their families and friends and whoever else has been deemed worth saving because they used to matter. We can hear the distant sounds of gunfire and explosions, and see plumes of smoke spreading out against the sky. I've seen all this before, in London, and look how that turned out, although here the stalemate has been going on for weeks.

Part of me was expecting to arrive and find that the Americans had held out. That Cecilia and the rest were travelling straight into their own extinction. I may have even been secretly hoping for it. If anyone was going to hold out, it was going to be the last great superpower, right?

But then, for the living, it's a war like no other, because every casualty can turn into a reborn enemy. Every loss is the dead's gain, a net shift of two.

Our freighter came in off the Atlantic and docked at the Port of Virginia, and although it wasn't as desolate as Liverpool, it was still lightly crewed by dead men who worked like slaves – the work of Thomas Moreby, I surmise. We got the vehicles off and consolidated the loads into the biggest two, me driving one and Bridget the other, and now here we are camped across the Potomac River from Washington, in a park at a place called Arlington.

I'm just catching a moment now in the downtime after being told to be ready to drive again. We're waiting for a pair of scouts to come back and tell us whether or not it's all clear.

Where? I have no idea, and still can't see what difference 29 more dead can make. The place is rotten with them.

Thursday, June 27

Dear God, it's all starting to make sense now. They may actually win this.

The scouting report came back all clear, because with the way things are, who can spare the manpower to guard cemeteries? Who would even think to?

Just before dawn, we drove the 29 anointed dead the last leg of their journey: to Arlington National Cemetery. The place where the Yanks have been burying their honoured dead for war after war after war.

Cecilia and the rest followed, moving camp. I've never been here and I'm all turned around. The streets are a mess, the way they get anywhere there's a river to work around. But I know we went in from the west side because we were heading into the sunrise.

It's their new base of operations, this giant cemetery. I've seen photos of the place, but nothing prepared me for the solemn reality of it. It's heartbreaking, really. Hundreds of acres of green lawn and trees, and countless rows of white headstones, each one of them somebody's tragedy.

I've always had a hard time pinning down what it is I believe, or if I believe in anything at all, but even I can tell this is holy ground.

When we got the trucks pulled in, more dead were waiting, two dozen of them in various stages of injury and decay. To an even greater degree than on the docks where we unloaded, these weren't the same mindless dead we left behind in England. They seem to be getting more intelligent by the day. They listen and follow commands and appear to be reasoning things through . . . slowly, perhaps, as though they're still groggy from an uncommonly deep sleep, but it's happening.

They're catching up to Cecilia and the rest.

I drove along one of the older stretches of the cemetery, judging by the dates on the stones, and Bridget down another. Every so often we'd stop and, under the direction of one of Cecilia's partners in life and death, the slaves – I don't know what else to call them – would unload another coffin or trunk or crate or barrel. Lord Charles went with Bridget, of course. Me, I had one they called Sir William, a man whose ashen face wore the most contemptuous scowl I've ever seen, as if there was nothing in the world of the living he didn't despise.

The slaves opened each container – some had latches, others needed crowbars – to free its prisoner. The stench, god, the stench of it . . . but that wasn't the worst. I'd forgotten the fleas that Cecilia had shaken into each of the coffins I'd sealed for her – like seeds, I thought at the time – and obviously the others had done the same in theirs.

During their weeks of being sealed up, the fleas have multiplied into multitudes. Each body came out engorged with them, a mass writhing with a living carpet the colour of rust. They seethed with them, wore them like a cloud. Sir William whispered a few words to each newly freed dead man and, with great violence in his movement, made a sign in the air before them, then we moved along.

Even that wasn't the worst. It wasn't until the third or fourth they let out that the dawn was bright enough to allow me to see what was going on behind us.

In the past few hours, the slaves must have been at work breaking through the turf into the topsoil. It gave their comrades a target, a place to start.

It no longer seems a coincidence that each and every one of them has a frame that's tall and lanky, long and lean. This is an asset. This was by design, all the better for them to burrow into the earth like worms. Like grave worms.

I would never have guessed they could even do something like this, let alone do it in such frenzy. But they don't know pain. Don't need to breathe. They don't get tired. Don't get distracted or discouraged. They're only eager to finish the mission of the plague ship that carried them here.

As we progressed, unleashing corpse after corpse, Sir William grew louder, until his voice equalled the force of his movements, and I could hear the incantation that he sent each of them off with:

"Dust thou were, and dust thou art. Now dig, as though Lazarus returned to the tomb."

I'm remembering that encyclopedia entry about Cecilia that quoted Boswell on the area around All Hallows, about reports of the dead gnawing each other's bones under the ground. It doesn't seem nearly as far-fetched this afternoon as it did then.

Monday, July 1

The first of them started breaking free of the earth on Friday morning. A few here and there to begin with, then more throughout the day, and even more Saturday, and exponentially more yesterday, a chain reaction like nuclear fission, until the process hit critical mass and the earth churned with constant eruptions. But rather than head off one by one as they rose, they simply waited. They waited with the discipline of soldiers.

There must be thousands of them by now. Tens of thousands. They're all of one mind, a true army of the dead.

I've never seen anything so wrong in my life. Who's more deserving of eternal rest than the people buried here? I can't help but think they'd all have opted for cremation if they'd known that one day they would rise to take up arms against the country they'd died fighting for.

But the old allegiances are gone, and there is no sovereign more universal than Death. No brotherhood more bonding than that of the emptied grave.

I've seen Death's master now. Moreby. I've seen him. No one had to tell me who he was. I knew at once who it had to be, that figure that appeared at the top of a marble tomb in the distance. The dead knew before I did. There was a great rippling in the ocean of corpses standing at attention throughout the cemetery, and eddies of red as the fleas churned with . . . what, excitement? . . . as they all turned to face him.

Their commander-in-chief, I believe would be the proper term.

I don't think he spoke. Not aloud. How could anyone's voice have carried over such a distance? But I don't believe he had to. He spoke on a level that's still denied me. They simply knew that it was time, and began their march to the east.

I followed for a while, like a camp follower bringing up the rear.

They poured along paths and drives, surged over hills, sluiced around headstones like they were rocks in a stream. Fences and gates fell before them. Their numbers swelled as others freed themselves from their graves at the last minute, and joined the procession.

Weapons stations had been set up on the cemetery's east side. I hadn't known. They paused just long enough to arm themselves, then moved along, streaming out of the cemetery with their sights set on Washington D.C., on the other side of the Potomac. Some broke north and others south, but the bulk of them continued east. Some went for bridges, whilst others plunged straight ahead into the river.

I watched until the first of them began to reach the other side.

Then I came back here to my tent to wait for the inevitable, even if I don't know what it is, now that my purpose has been served.

Found a flea on the back of my hand a while ago. Even it doesn't seem to know what to do with me.

Wednesday, July 3

And that's that. Word came back not long ago, and it's safe to say there's no such thing as America anymore. What's a country but an idea that everybody agrees on? What's left when the idea has been replaced by something else?

Whatever their nation is now, Moreby is planning on addressing it tomorrow. Fourth of July, the Independence Day they always celebrated here, launching fireworks over the fact that they broke away from us. Funny how things work out.

At the moment, Cecilia and the rest of the Seven are doing some celebrating of their own. Feasting on the spoils of victory. Chanting their incantations. Not a thing I really want any part of.

I'm still trying to sort out how I could've thought I ever did.

Thursday, July 4

My dear Gerri,

Losing you a little at a time . . . at first I thought it would be easier that way. Like anything I might've loved, or been addicted to, but had to give up, and wean myself off it gradually. Now I wish I'd got it over with all at once.

You're gone now. Truly gone.

I found what was left of you laid outside my tent this morning, cold and wet with dew and emptied, finally, of every last semblance of life. I've seen parts of you now that I hoped I never would. Cecilia's way of letting me know that this journey, this mission, has reached its end.

You know, I'd always hoped Cecilia would come to accept the body she took from you, maybe even come to like it. I always did, because it was yours. I never could understand her contempt for it.

Instead, she bided her time until she could trade you in the same way she traded in that ruined old carcass that first beckoned to me and asked for help.

Cecilia joined the feast last night, all right, same as the rest. I was just too blind to expect that she might've spent the time serving instead of eating, feeding you bit by bit to Bridget, until she could make the crossing once again.

Bridget's scarf is gone now. Magnificent red hair. I didn't know, and can't help but think this was what cinched it for Cecilia. When she heard me weeping over you outside the tent earlier, and first showed herself to me, I didn't even recognize her at first. Oh, I recognized her as Cecilia. It just took me a moment to recognize the body she's wearing for now. I wonder if Bridget tried to look as plain as she could during her travels, thinking it might be safer that way. It's a body that suits Cecilia, her vanity. I admit, she really is quite striking now. She's done so much with it already.

But it isn't yours. And the things about her that reminded me of you . . . they're fading already. Along with whatever fondness she may have felt for me.

She's been true to her word, though. She put the bite on me hours ago. Using Bridget's teeth, she broke through the skin of my shoulder like it was the peel of an apple. My overdue reward for helping topple a nation? A shoulder wound, this red badge of apathy.

Shouldn't it be taking hold by now? So far, the worst I've done is bleed.

It's got me wondering: remember, when we were still at home, how I always said the dead didn't want me? Suppose it's really true. Suppose the more mindless, animalistic ones sensed something or smelt something about me that the ones like Cecilia, with their higher faculties intact, overlooked.

Suppose I'm immune. In which case, maybe there are others.

I've read that no virus, no disease, however virulent, is 100 per cent contagious. And the best chance for saving everyone else is to study the ones who don't contract it.

I could've saved the world, if only I'd known, and got to a research facility in time. I could've saved the world. I could've made you proud.

But I don't care about that now.

Because all I want is the only thing remaining to me. Cecilia left me you. What remains of you. Maybe she's not entirely cruel. So I brought you into the tent and shooed the flies from your face. My wish is to turn, to make that final crossing to death and back again, and take the rest of you into me the only way I'll know how, in hopes there's still some spark of you left to hold close. So we can stay together, the way you wanted, the only way they've left to us.

I'd know you anywhere, even on the inside. I have to believe that.

Had to, anyway. I've clung to it as long as I can, but I don't think it's meant to be.

Could any joke be greater than the one that's been played on us . . .?

Dead to the old world, and dead to the next.

Eternally yours,

Malcolm

From: Josh <josh73805@postapok.com>
To: GeeEyedJane <GeeEyedJane@safety.net>
Sent: SUN, June 2, 10:42 AM
Subject: World of Ice!

Hey Janie! How you doing? Good, I hope. Just wanted to check you're okay.

Well, here's the promised report:

Made it to Nunavik, more than 440,000 kilometres in Canada's north, with only 12,000 inhabitants in this frozen tundra. I remembered you like translations and I found out that Nunavik means "vast land". They got that right!

Flew into Kuujjuaq, on the southern shore of Ungava Bay—that's where the administrative centre is situated, in the "big" village—under 3,000. I needed to meet with the Inuit elders so they could assess whether or not I'm a nutcase—that's just the way they roll—gotta respect that personal touch. Really nice, family-oriented people. Open, genuine, happy, even in a world gone to hell.

Remember that time we did the shoot in Palmerston—9 days in a boat from Rarotonga to get to that tiny South Seas coral atoll of 62 happy and peaceful people? Well, this is even further from civilization, though I got here faster, mostly by small plane, dog sled at the end. Palmerston, as I'm sure you remember, was a paradise, every day 27C, although I recall you suffered morning sickness off and on. Where I am now is north of the 55th parallel and beyond freezing—it's -37C at the moment—and except for a couple of stills shot from the plane with the Nikon (attached), there's not much alive here that I can see. I still find the Canon better for video—yeah, I know you disagree. LOL! Well, I didn't come for wildlife or indigenous peoples, per se. I came for the indigenous zombies.

My final destination—arrived yesterday—changed at the last minute, based on the most recent sighting, well, not exactly sighting but more the expected arrival point of the living dead. When the Inuit get infected, they're strapped to their dogsleds and sent off on their own or with their infected loved ones until they die then change and by then they're far from living people. The elders say they estimate how long the dogs can run without rest, since the infected aren't likely to be living for long and the dogs won't rest until the lead dog gets exhausted. Besides, they attach a beeper to the lead Husky, so they pretty much know where the team stops. And unless the dogs escape, the Zs have at least one fleshy meal, then, nothing. So far, no Zs have returned to any of the villages, so I suppose with all this land, it's a reasonable way to get rid of them.

I'm about eight hours by sled from Kuujjuaq, on Baffin Island. This safe house seems pretty secure. Hard to believe, but they're right, it's a dry cold, not so bad, I guess, though I was pretty glad to get indoors. The one room house runs on solar power, which makes sense, since it's 20&½/7 daylight up here right now. I can charge the cameras and the portable drives, and the cellphone—which doesn't work here, of course. There's a CB and also a crank-up radio. Three-quarters of the building is underground for insulation. A toilet, sink, shower, all of it hand-pumped. Bit like a hunting lodge. The six windows are these weird rectangles that remind me of that castle we shot in Wales, just slits in the stone, in this case in the wood. With a sweater, it's warm enough inside. There's canned and dried food, 18 litre bottles of water, a few rifles and some ammo. Everything a man could want. Ha!

I've got my iPad, and there's a computer here, an ancient Mac I could sell on eBay—if it still existed!—for a pretty penny. Internet is erratic and flips off unexpectedly—it was quite stormy en route and likely that affects satellite service. Like I said, there's also an old crank radio like my dad used to own. You'd laugh, Janie! Gotta turn the damned crank sixty times to get 15 minutes. So far I've only found one live station and it's in Inuit. They play a bit of music, everything from Celine Dion to local garage bands that do all kinds of blends of rap and native sounds. There's a lot of radio-host talk but I don't know what about, and they conduct ceremonies every few hours, with drums and chants and it sounds religious or mystical or something. You, more than anybody, know I've never been a mystical kind of guy; you're the person who knows me best. Well, I guess that's what married couples are like. I mean, when we were married. I know, I know. I'm not "starting". Just saying. We've both moved on. Only chatting the time away 'till something comes into the range of my viewfinders. So, Janie, send me some news, let me know you're well.

XX

Josh (the Other Ex) :-)

From: Josh Magnusson <JoshMagnusson@proshot.com>
To: Christie Sinclair
            <CSinclair.editor@internationalgeographic.com>
cc: Art Levinson
            <ALevinson.assteditor@internationalgeographic.com>
Sent: FRI, June 7, 2:32 PM
Re: Touching base

Hi Christie and Art,

Did my email on arrival get through? I didn't receive a reply, but Internet is wonky here.

I'm all set up but for the live feed camera, which I'm working on—having problems with the sound. Three walls here are completely underground, the fourth is about half-underground and the four windows like gunwales near the ceiling. I've got a camera set up at each, two video (one a wide angle), two still, recording or ready to shoot whatever comes into view. So far nothing but ice and snow, mostly blowing.

I did get some great landscape shots as we flew into Kuujjuaq, which I've tagged and attached. I know you're not big on landscapes but just in case you want to use one for an overview lead-in of this whited-out land. Ice. Snow. Mountains. Beautiful rivers of green glacier water. When it's not storming, the sky sometimes reflects the snow, what they call "snow-blink", and I have a couple of shots of that. It's pretty, though, all this non-colour, glistening under the sun, as if the snow and ice are sprinkled with jewels. Well, I'm waxing poetic here! :-) Anyway, I've got one close-up of two adult polar bears with a cub on a berg as I flew overhead, an asteroid crater, and a few locals from the village. Sorry, no zombies. Didn't see any from the air, or the ground as we sledded here. I'm sure they're around, like everywhere else, and the minute I see any I'm ready to record them. The audio on the live-feed isn't working and I'm trying to figure out why and get that happening. The minute it's up, I'll stream a test to you. Oh, and I also hauled up the Hasselblad so I can get some top-of-the-line close-ups. And no, don't worry, I'll follow protocol—won't make my presence known and won't venture out of this hut until the sledders return for me in, what, another three weeks or so.

Christie, Art, let me hear back from you guys that you received this email and the attached photos. Hope you and your team are doing well.

Josh

From: Josh <josh73805@postapok.com>
To: GeeEyedJane <GeeEyedJane@safety.net>
Sent: FRI, June 14, 7:12 AM
Subject: Repetition Makes the Heart Grow Fonder!

Hi Janie!

Haven't heard from you and it's been two weeks since my first email and this is my tenth. Hope I'm reaching you. Net is unpredictable. Let me know how you're doing. Yeah, I worry—you're still my best friend, even if you are The Ex! :-)

Been here fourteen days with no Zs in slight. Haven't been out of The Lodge—Christie and Art would skin me alive if I went out—you must remember how they are. Going stir crazy. All I'm getting is snow and more snow on the videos. Not even an animal passing by. I feel as if I need to go out there and find the shots instead of waiting for them to come to me, but of course this is literally the middle of nowhere and I wouldn't know which direction to head in and I likely couldn't find my way back. I didn't even see this house when we rode in on the sleds, it blends so well with the landscape.

I'm only here another nineteen days—yeah, ticking them off on the calendar! Hell, if I go back with nothing, Christie and Art will have my hide for that too, since this is such an expensive project! Why they even approved it is beyond me. All zombies look alike, just different shreds of clothing and various stages of physical decay.

Don't want to keep writing into the void, so let me know these are reaching you. I can't get any news that I can understand, and I've tried the CB a few times and, nothing. My world has shrunk to this room. Isolation never bothered me before in the jungle, or the dessert, or on any of the islands, but boy, here? I don't know. It's like the Earth has frozen over and we've moved into a new Ice Age. One with zombies strolling around, just not up here. Not yet.

Write me, Janie. Please.

XX

Josh

PS: Was thinking about when we went to Siberia to shoot the Kazakhs. That was right after Jenny was born, and we took turns strapping our papoose to our bodies when we rode out with the eagle hunters! She never cried, remember? Not once. Even the most fierce-faced eagle perched on the arm of a hunter just made her smile! I was so proud when the translator said the senior hunter declared that Jenny had the gift to train eagles! Sorry Janie. Guess I'm going nostalgic again. Signing off for now.

From	Josh Magnusson <JoshMagnusson@proshot.com>
To:	Christie Sinclair
	<CSinclair.editor@internationalgeographic.com>
cc:	Art Levinson
	<ALevinson.assteditor@internationalgeographic.com>
Sent:	MON, June 17, 5:11 AM
Re:	Another update

Hi Christie and Art.

Haven't heard from either of you so I'm not sure any of my emails have gotten through. I've fixed the sound on the live feed and streamed a test. Now I'm streaming full time, or at least as much as the near constant storms allow. You should be getting something. I've alternated the stream between me indoors, and the blizzard outdoors.

I'm a bit past the two-week point and, sad to say, nary a Z in sight. Just snow. Every day. The sledders will be back for me on July 1st and I'm feeling I need to go out there now and survey the area. I know that's against protocol, yours, the blog's, hell, the procedures set in place by every government in the world—Don't Put Yourself or Anyone Else in Harm's Way! But at this rate I'll return with tons of tape and stills of the ongoing Arctic Circle storms, and you'll get a stream of those same, seemingly endless blizzards, and the bearded guy in a Hudson's Bay sweater hovering indoors rattling on about the snow, and the zombies he *isn't* seeing!

I'm thinking . . . hold on . . .!

Thought I heard something that is NOT the wind, but no, nothing. I poked my head out the door—guess as long as my foot doesn't touch the outside I'm still in compliance! Saw nothing in any direction.

Anyway, I need to hear from you guys. I don't have much time left so now's the moment. Give me the go-ahead. I'll assume the risks in going out. And let me know if the live feed is coming through! In fact, just let me hear from you.

Josh

From: Josh <josh73805@postapok.com>
To: GeeEyedJane <GeeEyedJane@safety.net>
Sent: SUN, June 23, 9:02 AM
Subject: 3 Down, 1 to Go!

Hi Janie,

Three weeks and counting. I swear, if I hear one more incomprehensible native ritual on the crank-up, I'll shoot myself. In fact, I have shot myself, with the little Lycra, photo attached. Yeah, I have a beard. Shaving got to be a chore three days after I arrived, even though it was entertainment for a while. Now, I just don't care. I'm bored out of my skull.

Never been on an assignment like this, Janie. When you and I worked together, we hit some crazy spots. I was just remembering the other day about us in Rwanda shooting the 20th anniversary of Fossey's murder and we had to hike two days to get to the mountain gorillas and how hot and bug-bitten we were—when we weren't drenched by the daily downpour. Some honeymoon, huh? LOL! That was hell—but for being with you, of course! At least there were things along the way to engage us, like the animals—especially the birds! And of course neither of us will ever forget that ogre-faced spider with the binocular eyes! Wow, talk about the living dead! We screamed at the same moment, me louder! LOL But sometimes the most horrifying creatures are the least dangerous, and that one was, thank god, because I was so close it almost bit me and you probably remember we were at least a day's walk from camp.

We had some adventures, Janie, we really did. I miss that. I loved going on shoots with you. We had such a good time, even when we had bad times. Well, I had fun, anyway, but I think you did too.

Life sure can take some terrible turns. I know you don't want me to bring it up, and I'm really sorry, Janie, but I guess the isolation is getting to me. I think about Jenny all the time. Funny how all our names start with the same first letter—people always used to comment on that. Remember how my mom said we were three parts of the same person? I remember how we talked about it, when we named her, whether it was a good idea or not, then decided it didn't matter, *we* liked the name Jennifer. She would have been eight years old this month. I miss her so much. I miss you.

I'm sorry, Janie. I know how it is, what we went through. It's hard to come back from a devastating loss—everybody says so. I wish we could have. I wish we were together. You know I'll always love you, but I understand.

I'm sorry. I shouldn't go on like this. I know I promised we wouldn't cover this ground again. Just let me hear from you, Janie. Please. I haven't gotten an email from anyone. Nobody's on the CB, only the Inuit channel on the crank up. I'm not even sure my emails are getting through. I've written you just about every day, and, nothing. Maybe I'm the last man on Earth. Ha! Wouldn't that be something? Something horrible.

XX

Josh

PS: I'm ccing you the live feed, just in case you're interested. I think I'd tell Robert Frost that if the end of the world is a toss-up between fire and ice, I'd go with ice—it's a sure thing.

From:	Josh Magnusson <JoshMagnusson@proshot.com>
To:	Christie Sinclair <CSinclair.editor@internationalgeographic.com>
cc:	Art Levinson <ALevinson.assteditor@internationalgeographic.com>
Sent:	SUN, June 30, 6:09 AM
Re:	Final email

Hi Christie, Hi Art.

Haven't had a response from you yet. The live feed is on day and night and should be working from your end, when the storms calm and the Internet is behaving at my end.

Just to remind you, the sledders are scheduled to return tomorrow, so this will be my last email for a bit. I can't say I'll be sorry to leave here.

If there are any zombies out in this icy wasteland, I haven't seen them. I've stuck my head and even my foot out the door a few times but haven't ventured further. Frankly, the storms are so constant and so severe it's a near-perpetual whiteout and I can't see more than a couple of metres in front of me, so likely I wouldn't find my way back and I can't find a rope long enough to tether myself to the shelter that allows me to go more than six or seven metres.

Anyway, I'll call the minute I get within cellphone range, which I guess will be within the week. Sorry this has proven to be such a write-off. I'm hoping that when we get back to Kuujjuaq, if there's anyone infected and they're about to send them out onto the ice fields, I can at least get some stills and video and I'll stream that for the digital site. Better than nothing.

More when I have more. Meanwhile, here's a one minute video of the swirling storm (attached). If you're getting the live feed, you'll see it there too.

Josh

From: Josh <josh73805@postapok.com>
To: GeeEyedJane <GeeEyedJane@safety.net>
Sent: SUN, July 14, 4:01 AM
Subject: The Good, the Bad, the Abandoned!

Hi Janie!

First the bad news. It's been six weeks since I arrived and I've had no contact with anyone. I'm running low on food, but not so much water—can always melt snow! The sledders are two weeks late. I think the delay has to do with the most recent storm, a real doozy. I'm worried, but not too much; a lot of people know I'm here. If only I could make contact on the damn CB! Or even get an email response!

   The other day I was looking through some pix on the portable hard drive I brought along. You, me and Jenny, when we were in Papua New Guinea, shooting the Asaro Mud Men. Jenny wasn't frightened of the warriors' fearsome mud masks with the tusks. She was such a brave little six-year-old; took after her mother. :-) I remember that night we had a grass hut to ourselves, crashing on top of our sleeping bags, covered in stinky mosquito repellent. Her eyes were big and round in the moonlight that shone through the opening as you told her the story of the Mud Men running from their enemies at dusk, falling into a mud hole, emerging covered in mud, how the enemy thought they were evil spirits and ran away terrified. Remember what Jenny said? I do—I have it on tape. In that sweet little voice of hers she says, "Good! But they don't scare me!" "You mean the Mud Men?" I asked her. "Of course not, Daddy! The enemy!" God, I miss her. I miss you

I wish we could go back to the beginning, before all this, before Jenny got infected, before we split, before the fucking world fell and landed on its head. Janie, I'm so lonely . . .

Okay, I promised I wouldn't go on, but we also promised neither of us would ever hold back from the other. You and I have always believed in honesty, even when it's painful.

So, the good news: Unless it's a Fata Morgana—a shifting mirage—I saw zombies! They arrived last night. I was asleep and when I reviewed the overnight video I spotted them, a kind of family I guess, what must have been the father, the mother and a little kid, a girl, I think, but it's hard to tell because they appeared during the three dark hours. Even from this far away, I can see that the adults are pretty messed up. It's grainy, but should be on the live feed, which I hope you're seeing. I'm switching to that now, because there's something to record. I'm using the new Go Pro with the hard drive and wifi connection so I might just step out for a sec and see if I can film them without the glass between us. Don't worry, Janie. Long gone is that baby-faced guy you married, ready to plunge into the most dangerous situations at the drop of a hat. Jenny's death sobered me. Our divorce cured me. I'll be careful.

XX

Josh

PS: Let me hear from you!!! XX

This is Josh Magnusson, for *International Geographic*, reporting in from near the top of the world, half a day inland off the east coast of Baffin Island in the Arctic Circle. I've been here six weeks plus, and this is my second live report. I've come to photographically document the never-before-seen Inuit zombies.

A small group of zombies has appeared in this area. These formerly-living originated in a village of 3,000 called Kuujjuaq. Once infected, they were strapped to their dog sleds and sent into the frozen wilderness. As you can see, there is a large adult, a smaller adult, and a child roughly the size of an eight or nine year old, each wrapped in filthy, bloody furs. Like ghostly apparitions, they appear and disappear in the howling, swirling storm, which makes them nearly invisible—ice and snow are the norm here. Like most of the undead, they wander aimlessly, moving in circles, about fifty feet from the windows of my hidden base camp, which you saw in my previously streamed report.

This "family", despite what they must have suffered—the infection and the tragic end of life that led to their present state—they remain together, which speaks volumes about how closely knit the Inuit are in life. Of the three, only the child seems to have retained any traits of the living. You see her head sway from side to side, as if observing what's around her, from this distance making her appear alive.

Living or dead, the Inuit are used to this frigid Arctic cold. They often travel in small bands days from their village by dog sled to hunt, and spend weeks in -35C. They are incredibly adept at survival in this extreme, unforgiving climate and dieticians believe that the large consumption of fat in the form of blubber in their diet is responsible for the ability to tolerate temperatures that most of us could not withstand. These zombies have that in their history, their DNA, more so than most zombies, I'd imagine. It's a good bet that they, too, will survive, despite the cold and the lack of resources.

The trio hasn't come close enough for me to get a good look at their faces. And while I've zoomed in with high-powered lenses, they keep their heads down in the storm, likely behaviour by rote, carried over from life. Of the three, the little girl is the most curious, if I can use that word. Despite the thick fur hood of her colourful parka, I've been able to capture this partial facial shot from her left side. Isn't this astonishing? You can see for yourself—her cheek and jaw and the side of her nose— no decomposition! It makes me wonder if she even is a zombie. The parents have clearly turned. That's obvious in their lurching, and mindless actions. The smaller adult—the mother—is missing an arm. The larger has the most stains—likely blood—down the front of his parka and the fur surrounding the hood. But the little girl . . . I see nothing that convinces me she's turned, and, unlikely as this might sound, perhaps she hasn't! We've all seen the reports of zombies around the world with a rudimentary consciousness, as scientists have described it. Is it possible these parents are aware of their child and refuse on some level to attack her? Is that conceivable?

Josh Magnusson, for *International Geographic*, here on Baffin Island, recording live the Inuit zombies.

Sometime during the night the two adult zombies vanished, leaving no trace. Only the little girl remains. She wanders alone in a circle, or stands still, forlornly staring into the distance, her profile still not showing decomposition, and she has the posture of a child being brave in the face of abandonment.

She looks like any other eight year old, trying to make sense of what's happening to her, around her. As I zoom in, you can see her trembling. It begs the question: can the revived dead experience cold? And if they cannot, is this child really dead? She reminds me of my daughter, Jenny, about the same age, of similar size, and I know that many of the mannerisms I see are ones that Jenny used, that any child of this age would. It forces a conundrum . . .

I've named her Jenny. And I've come to believe she is not a zombie. I've never seen a zombie tremble with cold. This child must be starving. She's been alone for about thirty hours, no sign of her parents. I believe they've abandoned her to save her from themselves.

I feel torn about Jenny. My head tells me to obey the rules and not to go out there to see for myself if she has or hasn't turned. My heart sends another signal: if she's alive, she won't be for long without intervention. How can I leave a child alone in the cold, starving, dead or alive? She is, after all, an eight year old, and I'm an adult man; she can't really hurt me. It occurs to me that I can bring her inside, feed her, check her out and see what's what. Maybe I'm wrong. Maybe she's turned. On the other hand, what if Jenny is only a child, caught here, alone, unable to take care of herself?

Oh! You see that? Jenny's fallen, sitting in the snow as it blows around her. Her head's bent—maybe she's crying. She's still trembling. She's growing weak. I've got to save her!

I'm going to bring Jenny inside! I know this breaks every rule in the book, but if she isn't infected, or if, maybe, as some scientists have postulated, some are or could be immune to this disease, maybe she's one of those. And if she is infected, I can control Jenny, I know I can.

All right, I'm opening the door. I've got the GoPro camera strapped to my forehead so you're seeing exactly what I see, nothing in any direction but Jenny and the falling snow rapidly covering her little body. That sound you hear is my boots trudging through the crust towards her—she isn't even looking up!—and my hard breathing—you can see the condensation. Skin freezes in seconds and this cold is so biting that the exposed bits of my face are already numbing. I wish I knew how the Inuit hunters manage to survive without frostbite.

Jenny? Come on, honey, look at me. She's not looking up. I hope I'm not too late. There, she's lifting her little head but her eyes are closed as if she's sleeping—people sleep when they're freezing to death. She's not infected! I can see that clearly now. Her entire face is unscathed and while she's pale, it's not the blue-white of the dead. There's nothing there, no signs of the disease!

Come, sweetie, let's go inside. You can warm up and get some food. Take my hand. I'll help you stand and—

Wait! What's wrong with your eyes? My God, she's already turned! Jenny, what are you doing? No! Stop that. Don't bite! I'm here to help you. I'll just get behind you and—where did those two come from? I've got to get back to the house! Oof! Get up, get up! Get—No! No!! Jenny . . . !!!

From: Janie <StillABreather123499@hope.net>
To: Josh <josh73805@postapok.com>
Sent: FRI, August 9, 3:16 PM
Subject: You

Josh, I need you to contact me immediately. I've just seen the live feed and I don't know what to think. Please, Josh! Get in touch right away. Please. I'm so worried.

Love you,
Janie

Diary of Dr Clare Fremont – Day 6 New Era (NE)

Today I feel like giving up.

The results of my experiments are gone, and all my notes destroyed. That is why I'm having to start this log again from scratch. There is little point in my recounting what has happened in detail. My recent experiences have taught me that there is no place for independent will in my experimental subjects. The location of the will within the brain has been the subject of much philosophy and little science, despite at least one popular filmed entertainment of the old era using the concept for both shock and comedic effect.

There is nothing humorous about what I am doing here.

Right now there is little to show for my efforts, either. And so I must begin again, just as I must begin this log again, so here goes:

My name is Dr Clare Fremont, and I am nearly one week old.

This is by new era reckoning, of course. I had an old life, a human life, but I try not to think about it anymore. It isn't difficult. I was created by a surgeon called Graham Harman on a godforsaken windswept place called Ramsey Island. The experimental facility there had been put together in an apparent attempt to halt the zombie plague and find a cure.

What happened there was something else, entirely.

They're all gone now, my ex-colleagues. All dead, their notes and records destroyed. I should know. I was the only one who walked out of the wreckage of the place once I had set the charges.

As far as I can tell I cannot die.

I can rot, which is the major problem for myself and my kind, and what my current work is intended to address, but I cannot die. My experiments in this area are summarised in Table 1. As I have already explained, all notes previous to what I am writing now have been destroyed, and therefore the beginning of this document is from memory. But it is better than nothing.

Table 1: Attempted Methods of Self-Despatch & Their Outcome

Method	Materials	Outcome – Viable Tissue	Outcome – Necrotic Tissue
Puncturing of Major Blood Vessels	Scalpel	Viable tissue quickly forms clot and seals wound	Tissue does not bleed
Thermal Injury	Blowtorch	Burned tissue sloughs to reveal healthy viable tissue beneath	Tissue does not burn
	Ice	As above	As above
Chemical Injury	Concentrated Sulphuric Acid	Tissue dissolves on contact but regenerates within minutes–days depending on dose administered	Tissue dissolves and does not regenerate. Avoidance of toxic chemicals therefore imperative
Blunt Trauma	Vertical Descent From 100 Feet	Bones break and blood vessels burst but tissue heals within 24 hours, during which subject remains immobilised. Danger from immobilisation greater than from trauma	Tissue ruptures, is destroyed and does not regenerate: avoid blunt trauma for this reason
Poisoning	Warfarin	Profuse bleeding but bone marrow is able to keep up production of new cells. Unable to say for exactly how long but at least three days	No effect on dead tissue

Why death is impossible I have no idea. One of the training videos we were required to watch in my previous life suggested a reason that we all laughed at at the time. But perhaps there really is no more room in Hell.

My failed attempts at self-destruction, and my persistently decaying state have, however, provided me with a research project that, if it proves successful, should help me and others like me to live long and relatively healthy lives.

I use the word "life" quite specifically. There has been enough talk of death these past couple of months. It is time for that to change. It is time for us to embrace who and what we are. Being a living human being carried with it its risk of diseases and disorders. The same is true of our new selves. It is just the morbidities that have altered.

The most significant of these is corruption, and it is my belief that there is only one way to fight it. Before the Apocalypse, significant progress had been achieved in the field of cloning. While many of these techniques have been lost now, I intend to develop my research along the same principles, taking cells and developing them in a suitable nutrient environment such that they can grow into specimens that may then be harvested for replacement parts. Cloning of my own cell lines is probably too ambitious a project to begin with, however, and therefore I have settled on something no less important but hopefully more practical.

I intend to create life in this laboratory,

Diary of Dr Clare Fremont – Day 7 NE

I have read last night's notes and, while I have no wish to correct any of what I have written, I appreciate that they may come across as a little more hysterical than I intended. The creation of life is nothing new. Humans, and indeed all animals, have been achieving it for millions of years by the simple method of sexual reproduction. It is my intention to broadly employ the same process, but within an artificially created environment. To this end I have outlined the materials I shall need as follows:

Gametes

a) Ovum: it is my intention to harvest a number of oocytes from my own ovaries using standard endoscopic techniques.

b) Spermatozoa. There are a number of male subjects wandering the wastelands outside this facility and it is to be hoped that a suitable individual might be examined under anaesthesia and a testicular biopsy containing appropriate specimens obtained.

Fertilisation Medium

I am in the process of preparing an appropriate medium for both fertilisation and cultivation of the resultant zygote. Detailed notes to follow.

Uterine Tissue

Once the zygote has developed successfully into the morula and this in turn has become an implantation-competent blastocyst it will need receptive endometrium to be present during the so-called "implantation window". My intention to use my own uterine tissue has had to be abandoned after hysteroscopic examination has revealed the quality of the endometrium to be unsuitable. Quite why my own womb has become necrotic I cannot say. It is possible I have developed a thrombosis of the anterior division of one or possibly both of my internal iliac arteries. I should investigate the likelihood of this further but my current work is more pressing.

This need for uterine tissue has led to me acquiring a number of recently deceased female specimens that are at present being stored at a temperature of $-200°C$ on the sub-basement level. It is hoped that at least one of these should be able to yield a viable organ in which to implant the blastocyst obtained from the fertilisation stage above.

Gestation

Nine months is a long time to wait for potential failure, and so I intend to bombard the developing foetus with a combination of gonadotrophins, growth hormones and steroids to achieve significantly faster rate of development. If the resultant specimen is unsuitable as a result, then dosages and hormones will be adjusted accordingly in the second phase of the study.

Delivery

It is intended that once full term is reached, the foetus will be extracted via surgical incision of the uterine tissue. If the tissue seems viable for a further, future specimen, the wound will be closed and the tissue preserved until needed again.

nic
e,
poor
of

25

ke

ed and accurate record of my first
iable zombie foetus under laboratory

i Female Gametes for Fertilisation

ind well-recognised technique was employed.
t (myself) was given a self-administered trigger
of human chorionic gonadotrophin (hCG) and
ng hormone (LH) thirty-six hours prior to oocyte
al. The transvaginal route was deemed appropriate for
ss and a 16-gauge aspirating needle was passed under
asound guidance. Once ovarian access was achieved,
ggs were recovered by a foot-operated pump. The
procedure took slightly less than half an hour and there
appear to be no ill effects. After my personal experiences
listed in table one I would have been surprised if there were.

b) Male Gametes

The ideal choice of sperm donor would have been a healthy
adult human male. Unfortunately such specimens are rare
and therefore I had to make do with what I found during the
course of three expeditionary trips outside the facility. Male
individuals were immobilised (and in two cases, terminated)
via an abrupt blow to the head. Testicular tissue was then
obtained via several core needle biopsies taken via scrotal
puncture. Specimens were preserved in dilute Bouin's
solution for transport back to the research centre.

2. Fertilisation

The technique previously known as ICSI (intra cytoplasm
sperm injection) was decided upon as being most effecti
especially as even the best sperm to be recovered was o
quality and low motility. Oocytes were incubated in groups
five in a media of 150 microlitres of oil. Traditionally, 22500
sperm should have been added to each group. In this case
were added due to circumstances.

At twenty hours it was noted that five specimens showed
evidence of pronuclei. By day three, based on cleavage rate, si
and appearance of the blastomeres, and the presence or
absence of nucleus, three of these were deemed to be of Van
Royen grade 1 or 2 and thus of sufficient quality to proceed with.

Transcervical embryo placement was performed at day four
under ultrasound guidance, with the embryos being placed in
the mid-cavity of the uterus via a Wallace catheter as per
standard techniques. The details of the uterine tissue used are
outlined below.

3. Uterine Tissue

To minimise damage to the uterus when harvesting the organ
from its female subject a radical procedure was performed
through a midline abdominal incision. The round ligaments were
divided and the uterine arteries clamped and ligated, leaving
good lengths on the specimen for the attachment of artificial
nutrient fluid pipes. The rectovaginal and uterovesical spaces
were dissected out and, once the ureters and the vaginal cuff
had been divided the specimen was ready to be removed and
transferred to the laboratory. Modified cardiac bypass
equipment was attached to the uterine arteries and veins and
as soon as the equipment was activated the specimen quickly
achieved optimum temperature. It is my intention to perform

similar procedures on the four other specimens I currently have in cryopreservation but for this initial run it is proposed a single uterus be used.

4. Gestation

As noted above, it was hypothesised that the gestation period of the embryos be accelerated by the application of appropriate hormones. The most viable embryo was selected at one week and the others removed from their areas of implantation and frozen for possible future use. Then, increased quantities of gonadotrophin releasing hormone were introduced via the umbilical vein, maintaining the normal circadian fluctuation to avoid interference with normal processes. At forty-eight hourly intervals extra quantities of luteinising hormone were administered, along with a high dose of testosterone once the developing foetus could be identified as male. The initial accelerated growth pattern of Adam (as I have christened him) is illustrated in part in Table 2.

Table 2: Growth Rate of Adam Compared with Normal Human Foetus

Developmental Milestone	Normal Human Foetus Timeline	Timeline of Development of Adam
Brain & spinal cord develop	4 weeks	6 hours
Heart begins beating	5 weeks	8 hours
Face begins to form; Limb buds appear	6 weeks	10 hours
Internal organs start to function	10 weeks	11 hours

5. Delivery

Term was achieved in just over twenty-four hours – a remarkable achievement if I say so myself. To minimise damage to Adam he was extracted from his birth womb via a Pfannenstiel (ie Caesarian) incision through the uterine wall. Adam was successfully removed, although his thrashings during the procedure of clamping and cutting the umbilical cord means that this uterus has been rendered useless for further gestations.

6. Preliminary Examination

Adam appears to be a healthy full-term baby boy. The only anomalies are his nails, which are extremely sharp even by newborn standards, and his teeth, all of which are pointed. I am assuming this is to assist him with his essentially carnivorous diet. I realised having examined him that I had given little thought to his neonatal diet! There was little in the way of milk available and I despaired until my eyes alighted on the now-redundant and all-but-destroyed uterus from which I had extracted him. I morcellated a small quantity, reducing the tissue to an almost liquid consistency. The resultant pulp was fed to him via a pipette as I was unsure how he would react. He took to the food like . . . well, like a babe at its mother's breast, and he was so hungry for more that his tiny teeth bit through the so-called unbreakable plastic of the feeding tube! One more pipette full and he was satiated. He is now resting in the incubator I have prepared specially for him. The monitor leads register pulse, blood pressure and oxygen saturation as all satisfactory. The little fellow even tried to nip me as I attached them!

I must remember to keep my hands away from his mouth.

Diary of Dr Clare Fremont Day 35 NE

I still find it hard to believe how short a time it has been since my original outlining of this project and its success so far. Adam is putting on weight and has now hit the milestones one would expect of a six-month-old child. And yet it is only just over two weeks since his "delivery", and only just over three since the fertilised egg was implanted in the uterine tissue! He is already able to crawl, and it has become painfully obvious to me that his only interest is the pursuit of food. Despite my best efforts to keep him adequately fed, his appetite remains voracious. I suppose it is not surprising considering the rate of his development! I ceased the administration of extra stimulatory hormones at his birth, but considering his rapid growth rate, I very much suspect that his own hypothalamo-hypophyseal system has developed a high metabolic rate autonomously. Whether he will continue to develop at this speed only time will tell, and we will have to wait to see how this affects his ultimate life-span.

I must confess I find myself utterly fascinated by his progress. As a consequence I have delayed further attempts at fertilisation and implantation in order to study him more closely.

Diary of Dr Clare Fremont Day 37 NE

Adam is dead.

My obsession with following his progress has meant I have neglected this journal for the past forty-eight hours. There is no excuse for this. I have no one and nothing but myself to blame, and all I can do is promise myself within these pages that such sloppy record keeping must never happen again. If I had made more copious notes (or any notes at all – stupid woman!) I would at least now be able to go over them in detail, to try and discover at what point everything started to go wrong. I will perform a full post-mortem examination tomorrow when my nerves have settled, but right now all I can bring myself to do is take his body from where I found it near the exit door to this facility and keep it at a low temperature pending further examination.

I wish there was some alcohol here. But then again it is probably a good thing there is none.

Diary of Dr Clare Fremont Day 38 NE

Adam died of a huge myocardial infarction. Basically his heart died because it was growing too quickly, and his blood vessels were unable to keep up the same rate of development. His coronary arteries were too small to keep the cardiac tissue properly fed with oxygenated blood, and when he tried to over-exert himself everything just gave out.

His gastrointestinal tract also provided some findings of interest. Oesophagus and stomach were normal but both small and large intestine were much shorter than they should have been, presumably because Adam was designed to enjoy a protein-only diet, eliminating the need for much of the digestive process. His pancreas was small and ill-formed, suggesting his system had little use for insulin. At least my creation would never have become a diabetic! Dissection of the anterior part of the head and neck revealed atrophied salivary glands, again in keeping with an organism that only eats protein (cats, for example, produce very little saliva as there is no need for digestion of starch to begin in the mouth). Multiple sections taken through the brain tissue revealed a grossly hypertrophied hypothalamus and a significantly enlarged anterior pituitary gland. Both of these findings I would have predicted. What I did not predict was the hypertrophy of a part of Adam's brain the function of which has been long debated by anatomists. Instead of a tiny area of redundant tissue, this organ appeared to have a good blood supply and was actively secreting a hormone the function of which I am unsure of.

I wonder why Adam needed such a large pineal gland?

Experimental Log Book of Dr Clare Fremont – Entry Number Two

I have commenced stage two of my experiment. I am determined to minimise the errors I made with Adam, and so, instead of concentrating on a single specimen, I am currently gestating three separate foetuses in three separate uteri. How strange they look, side by side on my laboratory bench, standing vertically and pulsating rhythmically. I have connected one to the other by their own blood vessels. The arterial supply for specimen one comes from the heart bypass unit, passes through specimens two and three, and is then returned to the bypass unit for reoxygenation. The artificial blood is sufficiently rich in oxygen that even by the time it reaches specimen three there should be enough for its needs.

I have already identified the sex of my new children. This time there will be two boys and a girl, and I have named them in order of implantation. Specimen 1 will be Ben, specimen 2 will be Christine and specimen 3 will be David. Each is being fed a mixture of hormones to accelerate their growth rate, but at lower doses than were administered to Adam. Obviously greater doses of oestrogens and progesterone are being given to Christine compared to the other two.

Now all I have to do is wait.

Diary of Dr Clare Fremont Day 60 NE

My new babies are not quite yet at full term, but today something so interesting occurred that I feel duty bound to record it. Over the last few days there has been a significant increase in the number of walking dead outside this facility. At first I wondered if they were drawn to the smell of the remains of female corpses I have disposed of outside. Now I have their living uteri I have no further need of the rest of them and so, having denatured them to prevent their resurrection, I dragged their bodies a reasonable distance from the compound in the hope that any passing dead would act as nature's refuse collectors and consume their remains. Certainly some interest was displayed in the four bodies, and there is little of them left now. But instead of moving on, the dead have stayed close to the complex, and others are gathering as well. The last time I looked there must have been close to thirty of them. I am unsure as to what is attracting them. I am buried too deep within this complex for them to be able to detect either my presence or the noise of my machines.

My specimens are progressing nicely, although there does seem to be some problem with David's lower limb development. However, the rest of him appears to be quite healthy, with some significant over-development in his arms and upper body. Oxygen saturations and pulse rates are satisfactory for all three.

But now I come to the most fascinating of my observations to date. This compound that I have made my home for these last couple of months was obviously some kind of medical supply in the Old Era. This is how I have been able to create my own laboratory from what I have found in the various storage wings. During one of my most recent exploratory trips I found an EEG monitor, which means I am now able to monitor my specimens' brainwaves.

The results have proved even more interesting than I could have predicted. Each of my growing babies is demonstrating frequency oscillations far faster than one would expect for a neonate. Also there is a significant beta activity, suggesting that they are awake in there, and not just awake, but actively doing something.

I wonder if they are talking to each other?

Diary of Dr Clare Fremont Day 63 NE

Each uterus is now at a size that suggests my specimens are close to term. I have given detailed consideration as to how best to deliver them. Once these uteri are gone I shall have no more, and my experiments will be at an end. I have therefore elected to try and deliver my new children normally, via the cervix of each uterus and with the aid of a set of Kjelland forceps I have obtained from the stores. In delivering them by this method it is my hope that at least two uteri may be preserved for further experimentation, but I shall have to take great care. Oxytocin will of course be administered beforehand to encourage uterine contractions.

The number of dead at my door is now too great to count. One who is able to speak has clad himself in what resembles a priest's robe and seems to be trying to organise them. Through the intercom I can hear him rambling in his throaty voice about the "New Messiahs" and the "Coming of Our Saviours". I would prefer to think it coincidence that they have amassed here, but the ever-increasing EEG activity over the last few weeks has made me think otherwise.

Suppose my babies aren't just talking to each other?

Suppose their minds have become so powerful they can influence those gathered outside?

And, if this is the case, why have they not tried to influence me? Or have they?

Diary of Dr Clare Fremont Day 64 NE

A very restless night as I contemplated my observations from the last forty-eight hours. My mind is replete with theories and hypotheses, but at the same time I am beginning to wonder whether these thoughts are my own, or whether they are being manipulated by creatures yet to be born. I felt a twinge at the back of my mind when I first thought of the "c" word, suggesting that my new offspring are unhappy with being regarded as such. Let me think of them as creatures again.

That actually hurt.

So this brief experiment, conducted here in the darkness of my sleeping quarters, confirms that specimens B, C and D have access to my thoughts and may well be able to manipulate them. Which begs a new question.

Is it all of them? Two? Or just one? EEG activity is similar between all three but I find myself returning to the question of Adam's greatly enlarged pineal gland. All three specimens have been fed high dosages of hormones at different rates and therefore it is unlikely that all three will turn out the same. David's legs are shrivelled and useless. The others look anatomically correct on ultrasound scanning but how can I learn how their individual physiologies differ?

I know the answer to that, of course, and now, for the first time, I am beginning to fear the moment of delivery. I have staved it off for as long as possible, and I believe they are aware of that. There is a clawing inside my mind that was not there before. They are growing impatient to be free of their fleshy prisons.

Tomorrow will be the day.

Diary of Dr Clare Fremont Day 65 NE

How peaceful they look. Each uterus still gently pulsing away, each now holding a full-term foetus. Each harbouring something of which I am now equal parts fascinated and terrified.

It is time.

I shall resume this log when I am able.

Diary of Dr Clare Fremont Day 69 NE

Four days! Only four days! And yet it feels like a lifetime. I am writing this having locked myself in one of the sub-basement freezers. It seems to be the only place their thoughts cannot penetrate, and I must make this record now, before the reach of their minds extends even to this place.

The deliveries went as planned, but each uterus was destroyed in the process. I think now that was their doing, and that I was not to blame for the clumsy way in which I extracted each of my new children from the wombs which had nurtured them. I believe now that it was part of their plan that there be no chance they be replaced, that their positions be usurped.

Positions? Forgive me if this narrative seems incoherent but I have so little time to get everything down. Because of the state each womb was in, and remembering Adam, I fed each of the infants with the pulped remains of the organs I had drawn them from before subjecting each to a routine examination. Both Ben and Christine possess normal anatomy, apart from the pointed teeth that Adam exhibited.

David's lower limbs are nothing more than tiny, atrophied remnants, useless for locomotion and equipped with only the merest slivers of muscle tissue, meaning that apart from intermittent twitching there is little movement. They are, of course, made to look all the smaller because of the sheer size and muscle bulk of his torso and upper limbs. His head is also larger than it should be, but the thick musculature around his cervical spine seems to offer good support. As he lay there, watching me or rather, studying me, I got the distinct impression that he did not seem like a child at all. The others seemed intelligent, but David was something else again.

I had scarcely been able to feed and examine them before there was a noise from outside. Through the observation window I could see the massed crowd being directed by the preacher to break down the entry gate. It is made of reinforced steel and is still holding four days later, but there are more of them every day, and I am convinced now that their movements are influenced by the children in my care.

While I looked out, I could hear what the preacher was saying. Rambling nonsense about "Freeing the saviours" and "Let us behold our messiahs". Of course now, I have to wonder how much of what he was saying was of his own volition and how much was due to the creatures my experiments have produced.

There was a twinge then. I'm sure there was.

It would be foolish of me to think their reach would not get to me here eventually, but I had been hoping it would not be so soon. The three of them have been developing rapidly. Ben and Christine can already walk and, worse, can lift David and carry him on their shoulders, creating a hideous dwarven quadruped with telepathic powers that are as terrifying as they are powerful. They are gathering new followers every day, and their almost continual need for food has become difficult to satisfy.

In fact, there is very little left here that is edible.

Except me.

I'm sitting here, pressed up against the freezing cold steel wall of this storage unit. The door is firmly bolted but I know they are outside. Of course, David cannot reach the handle, even with the aid of the others, but maybe he won't need to, not if their mental reach can get past the steel and

I dropped my pen just then. It may simply be anxiety on my part, but somehow I don't think so. There are images now, at the very edges of my perception, creeping into my consciousness no matter how hard I try to keep them out. Images of the world outside, of those who have come in their hundreds, their thousands, driven by something they do not understand. An instinct, buried deep within their flesh, both dead and living, an instinct that has called them to this place, to these children, to this new way of life. The preacher has done little to calm them — indeed, I believe it is he who has organised their assault on the gates.

It would appear that I have inadvertently created a new religion for this New Era. But then, who knows how religions are truly created anyway? This way is as good as any.

The gates have given way now, and the dead are entering. They are led by the preacher. Up until this moment his face has been a blur but now, finally, my children are permitting me to see it.

No. No, I cannot believe it. I refuse to believe it. He died. He died in that disaster back on Ramsey Island. I should know because I killed him. I killed him after he created me.

From living surgeon to living dead religious leader in just a few short months. Oh Graham, was this what you hoped would happen when you began those terrible experiments all that time ago? Was your death and resurrection part of your plan? Just as I was? Just as the children are? Or are all these things the result of some Greater Power — perhaps the intelligence that created this New Era? Are you Frankenstein and John the Baptist rolled into one Graham? Am I your virgin Mary? Are these children — who even now are trying to get my fingers to release my grip on my pen and reach up to unlock the door and let them in — are they this world's Unholy Trinity?

I may never know. The urge to drop the pen is becoming too great. The New Messiahs will eat of my flesh and drink of my blood in the First Communion of the New Era.

If death is not the end, what will become of me then . . .?

"Thus is was that the Holy Three, having partaken of the Holy Virgin Mother, were carried abroad by their disciples. And he who had led the disciples to the Most Holy Place of their birthing became the First Prophet of the Religion of the New Era. By using the voice of the prophet were They able to speak. And through the bodies and limbs of what was left of Their disciples were They able to act. Thus was the First Church of the Religion of the New Era built that others might come and worship at Their feet in Their Holy Name."

—Excerpt from *The Testament of The New Era*
Chapter 4, verses 5–9

File dated: June 27

ALL right, time to make some sort of plan. I suppose, first, I should jot down where I'm at.

I'm an ex-reporter, ex-husband, ex-father (I presume, anyway). I wasn't particularly good at any one of them. But there: the darkest days are behind me, aren't they? I promised myself a new start — that I'd achieve *something* before the end.

I left my family to die.

I promised myself I'd be honest, and there it is, fact one. I was fascinated with Haitian *zombis*: fact two. This was before the zombie uprising, when it was only of interest to the types who browse the "Paranormal" section of bookshops. But there was that case of Variola Savain, the Haitian girl found working as a house-slave in London, where the "owners" claimed she didn't need human rights because she wasn't human. She'd been made *zombi*, they said, and they'd bought her fair and square.

So I came to Haiti, to find out if *zombis* really did exist — human interest at its finest — just as, at home, the new zombies rose from their graves and the world went mad. I always did follow the wrong fucking lead. Feel free to laugh: I did.

Course, I was mostly drunk, especially after the planes were grounded and I couldn't raise Angie and little Debs any longer. I know I couldn't have done much if I was there, but – I could have done *something.* Anyway, after the phones died, trust me – I laughed a whole lot.

So that's me, all-round failure as a human being. If you're reading this, you'd probably hoped for someone better, but tough shit: you get what you get. And all I've got is this, so we're pretty much all losers together. Ha ha.

RECIPE FOR *ZOMBI* POWDER (as far as I can ascertain)

- Tetradotoxin (from puffer fish) -- causes state of catalepsy – victim mistaken for dead.
- Datura (also known as moonflowers or angel's trumpets) – cause of dissociative state after 'revival'?
- Ground glass or other skin irritant. (Breaks skin, allows powder to enter bloodstream.)
- OTHER STUFF. Dried lizards, toads, snakes, spiders' legs, other nasties for effect: slugs and snails and puppy dogs' tails.
- Dried herbs/plants – particular mix unique to the Vodou *bokor*, or sorcerer. (Purpose? Who the hell knows.)
- Human remains.

Conversation with a *Bokor*
by Archie Reynolds

The *bokor* lived outside a small village in the Nord-Ouest *département*, somewhere to the south of the legendary island of Tortuga, famed for its connection with the pirates of old. The *bokor* is the sorcerer of the Vodou religion, said to "serve the *Loa* with both hands", meaning they practise both light and dark magic. Chief of the black magic arts is the creation of *zombis* or living dead . . .

(God, I'm writing this as if it's going to be in *National Geographic*, one of those artsy atmospheric pieces: who am I trying to kid?!)

When I locate the shack the *bokor* is outside, staring down the dusty path that winds between scant sea grape trees, unblinking and expressionless. It's as if she is waiting for me – for it is a she, a Vodou *mambo* (priestess) rather than a *houngan* (priest). When I draw near she passes inside, ducking under the door, but her look tells me to follow. It's all very much like a movie, save for the gaudy skirt and frayed yellow T-shirt she wears.

Inside, she is surrounded by strange objects: Vodou dolls designed to house spirits or *Loas*, stones, candles, herbs, fetishes, the dried skin of a snake, and offerings – fruit, corn, bottles of what looks like alcohol. There is row upon row of dirty, empty-looking jars and a skull, which

Looks frightening until I see that it's made of plastic; it's also wearing, at a jaunty angle, a sequined top hat.

I start to introduce myself and she waves away my words with an "I already know" gesture. She starts to explain, touching objects as she speaks in a mixture of French and English: about how she claims her victims with *zombi* powder, later raising their dead body from the grave and capturing their *ti bon ange* or "little good angel", the part of their soul connected with the individual, making them her slave, setting them to work in the fields or selling their services.

Of course, theory has it that this powder merely puts the victim into a deep coma, so that they are buried alive. When exhumed, believing themselves to be dead and in another's power, they suspend their own conscious will, choosing to behave as they think a *zombi* should. It's an explanation, but it's difficult, on these shores, not to believe there might be more to it. After all, once "the pearl of the islands", Haiti *is* a kind of *zombi*. The victim of deforestation and desertification, ravaged by earthquake and corruption, stripped of its spirit – who knows if this blighted place can rise again? And the fear of being trapped in eternal slavery remains prevalent among its population, perhaps a remnant of the dark days of human traffic . . .

~~Notes for news item: The Rise of Baron Samedi~~

~~There was panic on the beaches of Haiti as many mistook the arrival of the new zombie threat for the advent of Baron Samedi's rule on Earth. Wearing a top hat and a long black coat, it seems he was bitten on the way to a fancy dress party, or dressed to entertain the in/out cruise ship tourists: the glare of exposed cheekbones beneath his skin was no doubt incidental. It certainly gave the impression of myth brought to life as he came across the water . . . .~~

Jesus. I promised myself I'd tell the truth, to do something real, not just churn out whatever I think is acceptable copy these days. Failed again, even now. All right (deep breath). What I really saw:

They came at sunset, when everything was dying, even the sun abandoning the world. At first there was nothing but an indistinct shape, as if a new island had formed on the horizon. Then it grew darker, and closer, and clearer.

They had built rafts of the dead. The sight kept people on the beach, fascinated, mesmerized long past the time when they should have run. The sound of them drifted across the hiss of the waves — wailing and keening, a hungry sound, and beneath that, the gurgle of seawater in windpipes and body cavities and wounds and empty gullets.

There were hundreds of them, lashed together so that the rafts didn't disintegrate when their limbs failed. They writhed, a constantly moving mass, their cold, swollen bodies half-immersed in a sea that was warm as blood.

Baron Samedi was at their head. He stood on the backs of his army, and others stood with him; they rowed, while he stared at the shores of Haiti as if it were his Promised Land. He was much taller than anyone else. He bore a black cane and it became clear, as he drew closer, that it was topped by a human skull, shreds of flesh still attached to the bone. His dark skin was greyed with the pallor of death and his cheekbones shone through the decaying matter. His eyes, though, were bright: bright and yellow.

Brighter still were the chevrons marking the sleeve of his coat. There were seven, some military insignia that made me think of the Well of Seven, Moreby's cursed generals, the subject of some of the wilder reports coming out of England before everything went dark.

But what I saw was more than that, because if I'm really going to be honest, what was foremost in my thoughts – what I couldn't keep out – was the origin of the Haitian word *zombi*. I already knew that it came from Africa with the slave trade, its roots evidenced by the similarity to the Kikongo word *nzambi*, and it doesn't mean *undead* at all. Seeing Baron Samedi – if it was indeed he, though a part of me could not doubt it – I understood why its true meaning is *god*.

There was a man who swept the floor at the coffee stand at the back of the beach. He had a blank look, and I'd always taken him for someone with learning difficulties. When Samedi landed, I saw him again. He was the only motionless thing in a world where everyone was running, screaming. A zombie – one of the quicker ones, the more *sentient* ones I think – ran after a young woman and sank its teeth into her shoulder, her blood spurting into the ruin of his face, and the man just stood there, his expression as blank as always, and he did not move.

I saw what happened when the zombies reached him.

Nothing. Nothing, that's what happened. They looked at him and disregarded him, as if he were *less* than nothing – as if he was of no interest to them at all.

I knew, suddenly, what the man was: a *zombi*. And the new zombies had no interest in him.

I couldn't think about it any more, not then. I had to get away.

The *ti bon ange*. Is that why they didn't recognize the *zombi* as prey — because a part of its spirit had been removed? Is that what zombies must consume, along with living flesh — must they also feed on our souls?

NOTE: something else from the news reports, before they stopped. Moreby's idea of preserving "essential salts". Do essential salts = *zombi* powder? Who knows?

No time for more over the last day or so. Had to put distance between myself and the zombies. Odd to see them at last - not like the news footage or movies or anything I can think of. And they feed. They *feed*.

Jesus, the blood. Not prepared for that. Should have been, perhaps.

The *bokor* was at home when I reached her shack, but I couldn't get close. It wasn't surrounded by the dead, but by the living. I wasn't the only one who'd noticed that *zombis* appeared to be safe.

There were people clutching purses, silver necklaces, candlesticks. The form of payment might have been different but the looks on their faces were all the same. It wasn't just fear; it was the look of people who still had a hope of salvation left.

I caught glimpses through the window. The *bokor*, weighing a pouch in her hand. *Zombi* powder? She didn't appear to have very much left, but then, I didn't know how much she needed - how many she could save, or how she would choose among them. Then I heard her voice out front, something sharp and loud that sounded like a question.

The horde outside started to bay. There's no other word for it - they *bayed*, shouting pledges, promises, numbers. They waved jewellery in her face, pulled rings from their fingers. One had what appeared to be a fistful of gems and she bent over them before beckoning him inside.

A sigh ran through the gathered host. They did not disperse but settled down to wait. One took a knife from his pocket and stared at it, as if it might hold the answer.

Inside, through the window, I saw a flash of light. The powder strike, perhaps.

I found an abandoned farmer's shack on the slopes beyond
the *bokor*'s house – overgrown and cracked apart by roots,
but there are a couple of sacks of rice not yet too mouldy.
I don't know what happened to the owners – I keep telling
myself they were probably forced off the land when cheap
rice imports turned farmers into sweatshop workers.

There's no power. I hope my laptop battery will last.

I heard a car today. I crept down in time to see bulky
types in dark glasses and ear-pieces demanding the *bokor*
come out of her shack. In the end they went in, though
they didn't look happy. One had a machine gun. I heard the
bokor demanding ingredients for her work and they left.
Someone was waiting in the car – I saw a hand, laden with
gold rings, resting on the open window. An official from
Port-de-Paix maybe, though I never saw his face.

Later, I heard screams coming from the other side of the
hill. I knew I should investigate, but I couldn't move.
Literally couldn't. I crouched against the wall and shook,
until it stopped. Later I realized this took less than an
hour, though it seemed longer.

They're getting closer, I think.

The officials came back. They handed stuff over to the *bokor*; one of them bowed. So much for their guns. This time Mr Bigwig went in with them. Fat, sunglasses, actually wearing a white suit. Smug-looking, had "official" written all over him. Probably a sweatshop boss too.

It occurs to me now that I could ask for her help myself. I can still hear the screams of those who were eaten. I can't imagine teeth taking pieces of my flesh, reducing me to nothing — nothing but pain, anyway, and after that, who knows?

Belief has it that after death, Baron Samedi gathers men from their graves and brings them to Heaven — unless they have offended him, in which case he makes them a *zombi* slave for evermore. I can guess which option he'd offer me.

Jesus. I saw a sight today. Early on, I heard a helicopter beating the air, so loud I wanted to burrow into the ground. Scared: I thought the noise would bring zombies fast. I didn't see any, though.

The helicopter was outside the *bokor*'s place, bright and shiny against the dry earth. Men with guns kept the locals back — there were fewer of them now, and many of them in a bad way. Then someone stepped out. I recognized him. Dark glasses and a hoodie, but he was unmistakable; the shreds of Hollywood glamour still clung to his skin. He went inside. This time, I waited. It was hours before he came out again, and when he did, he looked different.

It seems someone is getting word out. Haiti is no longer an abandoned pit with pretty beaches — it's the salvation of humankind, if they have money enough. Money enough to make the *bokor* work her *zombi* magic.

The President was here. And that was only the start. They stay a while and then, when they leave, led by their bodyguards, they stumble. Their heads loll on their shoulders. I've seen a rapper from Miami, the actress from some sitcom — I'm cursing myself for leaving my camera. Not that I ever wanted to be a pap, but I'm shit at names. I knew plenty of the faces, though.

They must hope there will be an *after* — some kind of world where the zombies are dead, or *re*-dead, and long live the *zombis*. Maybe they think they'll get their spirits back again. She keeps them in jars, doesn't she? The row upon row of jars. The *ti bon ange*. She must have a way to put it back.

NOTES FOR NEWS ITEM

Blair	Shatner
Khan	Jackson
Cameron	Zidane
Cohen	Mendes
Iglesias	Ford
Bush	Cruise

Shit, what's the point? No one will believe this.

<u>She keeps them in jars</u>.

Conversation with a *Bokor* (2)
by Archie Reynolds

There were still a few poor souls sitting outside the shack. They hardly troubled to lift their heads at my approach. Someone was sweeping the yard, a nicety that verged on the ludicrous.

When I reached the doorway, I saw that the *bokor* had gained some servants. A huge man stood there, and he blocked my way, though his eyes remained blank. The *bokor* ordered him aside.

Inside, at first, all I could see was silver and gold. Instead of corn and fruit there were candlesticks and jewels, rings and watches heaped on the altar among the rest. I blinked. *Offerings*. I had imagined her selling the stuff, going away somewhere, a nice new home; not this.

She saw me looking and nodded. "The *Loa* are angry," she said. "This thing – this curse – it is because we are not in harmony. All men should be in harmony, with the world, the land, the spirits, everything. This – *being ill-with* – it is the spirits. They take revenge." She jabbed a finger towards the offerings, as if they would fix everything.

A movement caught my eye and I turned to see a man on his knees, cleaning her floor. He must have been there all along; with a start, I recognized his shabby white suit.

"They came back," she said, "to take me away. To make me their slave, to do what they want. I powder-struck them; the guards too. They didn't fight. I think they wanted it, no?" She laughed, revealing slabs of yellowed teeth.

I could only stare. I knew, suddenly, that it would be the same for them all. It didn't matter if there was an *after*: no one was getting their spirit restored. They were her puppets now. *Zombis* forever. If their bodyguards objected, she could buy them; she held the ultimate temptation in her hands.

I looked at the jars. They glinted softly, some shining back soft colours; it almost looked as if there was something inside. When I turned to the *bokor*, she looked amused.

"But if they need the *ti bon ange* to feed," I said, "and the *ti bon ange* is here – what then?"

Her smile broadened. "The *Loa* are angry," she said. "We offer what we must."

They came later that day, as the sun spread itself against the horizon. I heard them first, an unearthly wailing that reminded me of seeing Baron Samedi outlined against the sea, that first time. I remember thinking: *nzambi. God.*

Now the Baron led them again. He stood by the shack while his minions gathered, circling it so that I was afraid they'd discover my hiding place in the bushes. The other people had run away. I could still hear them crashing through the undergrowth, but the zombies didn't follow. They had other business, were after easier meat.

The *zombi* guards were dragged outside. Samedi had to duck to get into the shack: somehow, it didn't look undignified. A short time later I heard glass shatter. I couldn't see, but I heard the jars smashing one after the next and suddenly the *zombi* outside, the one that had been guarding the door, dropped to the ground.

He appeared to be insensible, or dead — blessedly dead, perhaps. I found myself wondering if the zombies envied him that, and then they were upon him. They blocked my view but the sound was terrible. The tearing. The moaning.

Then I heard a scream, and I remembered the *bokor* was still inside.

Samedi had come for her himself, at least. It seemed right somehow, that he should receive her offering in person.

And then I thought of the *zombi* powder. I never had got the actual recipe, only hearsay and guesswork, and now — oh, those sounds — it would die with her, God help us all.

I wondered what was happening to the others, the *zombis* she had created. Whether they were now prey. Whether they were already dead.

I'm typing this in the shade of the trees upslope from the *bokor*'s shack. I'd go closer, but I can't see my screen in the sun — it's still shining down, like the punchline on some cataclysmic joke. Ha ha, God.

Actually, I don't think I believed in God until all this happened. But there has to be someone to blame, doesn't there? For everything being this royally fucked up.

OK, I admit: I never did do the right thing, not by my family, my job, anybody. But it struck me that I have one chance left. To investigate. To find out. After all, I promised myself I'd achieve something before the end.

Course, it's too late (ha ha again), since I'm stuck here with no phone and not even a dial-up. All I have is this laptop — old faithful — and when I'm done I'm leaving it here under the trees. It can take its chances.

The way I see it, there's only one thing left to discover. That big bastard — is that really Baron Samedi? Is he a *Loa* — a spirit — or something else, just a dead thing walking? I need to know if the *bokor* was right. Maybe the key to understanding all this was in Haiti all along. Maybe I wasn't really that wide of the mark.

Only one way to find out.

Still, my grand hurrah as a journo will take place when there's no one left to read it. No one left to write it, probably. Shit. My fingers are shaking. I'm fucking terrified, if I'm honest. Writing this is probably just the delaying tactic of the shit scared, and amen to that.

Or am I just giving up — being a coward? Is it just that there's no rice left and nothing to eat in Haiti but fish and people, and let's face it, the people are easier to catch?

But I need to *know*. Baron Samedi is supposed to gather in the souls, right? Heaven or *zombi*, that's the choice. And I thought the Heaven part was bullshit, but then I thought — is it? What if it isn't an either/or deal at all — what if it's the *same* thing? Because those things down there, they may not be happy, but they sure as hell don't look sad. Some of them probably never had a full belly in their lives until they got turned. To steal the words of some old hymn: They do not want. They do not sorrow. They do not have to miss the people they loved, because they do not love. Those things down there, Samedi's slaves — they don't even have to think. They're *free*.

So I'm going down there as soon as I'm done writing this. I'm going to meet the Baron. I don't suppose that meeting will be painless, but I can hope it will be quick. And then I'll know. Course, there won't be anything left of me to tell the tale, but — *I'll* know, won't I? I'll know the truth.

Isn't that all any of us needs?

Angie and Deb — maybe I'll see you again some day. I hope I'll recognize you if I do.

[End of file record]

River Bottom Blues
(or What to Do When We Get There)
by Will Halloway

I have love in me the likes of which you can scarcely imagine and rage the likes of which you would not believe. If I cannot satisfy the one, I will indulge the other.

— Mary Wollstonecraft Shelley
from *Frankenstein; or, the Modern Prometheus*

In those days, those long-ago far-off days when everything was possible—and I mean *truly* possible—and God smiled down on the traveler, salesman and Okie alike, the dust of the cities blew off along the Main Streets and out onto the Interstates and the Highways, pretending like it had someplace to go. But it didn't. It just had someplace to be away from, someplace behind and already gathering distance, its voice growing mercifully softer and merging with the wind and the throaty song of the cicadas as evening gave up the fight and accepted nighttime . . . as one day we all must do.

<ring ring . . . ring ring . . . ring ring . . . ring rin—>
Hi there, you've reached the home of Dylan, Sofia and Alexandra Spaulding. We can't get to the phone right now but leave us a message—and maybe a return number—and we'll get right back to you. Here comes the beep: <beeeeeep>
<click>

J.W. Fletcher: "You see the thing in the *Post*?"

W. Leonard Paryder: "You got a newspaper?"

JWF: "It's weeks old. It's . . . it's February. 17 February."

WLP: "And you're asking me if I saw it? How the hell could I remember reading a six-month-old—"

JWF: "You'd remember this. Charlie Chicken?"

WLP: "Charlie Chicken? You're worrying me now."

JWF: "I'm not calling you Charlie Chicken. That was the name in the newspaper. The headless chicken."

WLP: "As in 'running around like a headless chicken'?"

JWF: "The very same."

WLP: "Okay, I'll bite. Is there a punch-line to this?"

JWF: "Pacific Northwest Research lab. They managed to keep a headless chicken—"

WLP: "This is Charlie, I'm guessing, right?"

JWF: "Right. Charlie. But actually it's Mike who was headless."

WLP: "Mike. Not Charlie. I thought it was Charlie, this chicken."

JWF: "Yeah. There are two. Mike Chicken and Charlie Chicken."

WLP: "And Charlie was . . .?"

JWF: "Charlie was bodyless. They got the idea to do this—"

WLP: "They?"

JWF: "The folks over at Pacific Northwest. They got the idea of severing Charlie's head from what happened to Mike."

WLP: "Tell me about Mike."

JWF: "Okay. This is from Wikipedia. You can look it up."

WLP: "I trust you. Go ahead and read it to me."

JWF: "You got time?"

WLP: "What else am I going to do? Read it to me."

JWF: "Okay. 'On September 10, 1945, farmer Lloyd Olsen of Fruita, Colorado, was eating supper with his mother-in-law and was sent out to the yard by his wife to bring back a chicken. Olsen chose a five-and-a-half-month-old cockerel named Mike. The axe missed Mike's jugular vein, leaving one ear and most of the brain-stem intact. Despite Olsen's failed attempt to behead

Mike, Mike was still able to balance on a perch and walk clumsily; he even attempted to preen and crow, although he could do neither.'"

WLP: "Ain't life a bitch."

JWF: "There's more. 'When the bird did not die, Mr. Olsen, who was surprised—'"

WLP: "Now there's an understatement if ever there was one."

JWF: "'—Mr. Olsen decided to continue to care permanently for Mike, feeding him a mixture of milk and water via an eyedropper; he was also fed small grains of corn. When used to his new and unusual center of mass, Mike could easily get himself to the highest perches without falling. His crowing, though, consisted of a gurgling sound made in his throat. Mike also spent his time attempting to preen and peck for food with his neck. Once his fame had been established, Mike began a career of touring sideshows in the company of such other creatures as a two-headed calf. He was also photographed for dozens of magazines and papers, featuring in *Time* and *Life* magazines.'"
[PAUSE]

WLP: "Is that it?"

JWF: "Almost. All of which brings us to Charlie, the latest in a long line of chicken experiments . . . and this one is more successful. With Charlie, they tried it the other way around. They kept the body, same as before—"

WLP: "Same as Mike?"

JWF: "Same as Mike. But this time, they concentrated on a bodyless head."

WLP: "Which is . . . which is a *good* thing?"

JWF: "Depends on which way you look at it."
[PAUSE]

WLP: "Give me the opposing ways."

JWF: "Well, there's really just the one. Normally, you separate the head from the body, both die, right?"

WLP: "That's the way I've always figured it would be."

JWF: "And then we got Mike, a body kept alive after the head had been removed for, for what? Couple years?"

WLP: "Couple years. I feel like I'm in a dream here."

JWF: "And then you get the article in the *Post*."
[PAUSE]

WLP: "Which says?"

JWF: "Which says they've got a bodyless chicken—"

WLP: "Charlie."

JWF: "Charlie, yes, that has managed to stay alive without any in-built oxygenization—"

WLP: "Is that even a word?"

JWF: "Who the fuck cares."

WLP: "My very sentiments exactly."

JWF: "—or any mechanism for pumping blood or . . . or anything at all. But it still ingests food."

WLP: "And that's it?"

JWF: "Yeah. Sound familiar?"

WLP: "Familiar how?"

[PAUSE]

JWF: "Think of the zombies."

WLP: "Think of— [PAUSE] Fuck! We did it again: first AIDS and now this."

JWF: "Yeah. Looks like nobody's got clean hands on this one."

WLP: "Fuck!"

JWF: "Yeah."

WLP: "We need to stay shtum on this."

JWF: "Stay shtum?"

WLP: "Not let it get out.

JWF: [LAUGHTER]

WLP: "What's funny?"

JWF: "Hell, way things are going, there's gonna be no fucker left for it to get out to."

WLP: "Fuck!"

[PAUSE]

JWF: "Yeah. But you know what else?"

WLP: "Surprise me."

JWF: "I heard from Jake Carter—you know Jake? Down in Atlanta at the Academy for Medical Research?"

WLP: "I know Jake: pimples, overbite . . ."

JWF: "That's the fella."

WLP: "What about him?"

JWF: "I hear they've found the Fountain of Youth. Or should I say they found someone who found it. They've had him there for years. Well . . . strike that. They've apparently had him there or in other secure facilities for more than two centuries."

WLP: "John, are you smoking something that—"

JWF: "No one knows his name, but he claims he's three hundred and seventy-nine years old."

WLP: "And? Tell me why I should give a rat's ass about this fella."

JWF: "Carter and his cronies are working on using his cells—"
WLP: "His three hundred and seventy-nine-year-old cells?"
JWF: "—using his cells to counteract the zombie virus."
[PAUSE]
WLP: "And how hopeful is he?"
JWF: "I guess he figures it's worth a shot."
WLP: "Anything's worth a shot."

<ring ring . . . ring ring . . . ring ring . . . ring rin—>
Hi there, you've reached the home of Dylan, Sofia and Alexandra Spaulding. We can't get to the phone right now but leave us a message—and maybe a return number—and we'll get right back to you. Here comes the beep: <beeeeeep>
<click>

▼ [Extract from *The Island of Eternal Life* by H. Abraham Greenberg (John Hopkins University Press, 1887)]

The so-called Fountain of Youth is believed by the *Arawaks* in *Hispaniola*, *Cuba* and *Puerto Rico* to lie on the island of Bimini (or Beimini or Beniny). This fictional island (for no proof of its existence has been put forward) was considered a place of great health and prosperity, the wealth—it is alleged—originating from the New World over the early part of the 16th Century and believed to having been made to preserve the miraculous waters of the Fountain. In 1711, however, any reference to either the Fountain or the Island of Bimini being expunged. The last recorded reference was in respect of Sequene, an Arawak chief from Cuba, who is believed to have succumbed to the lure of Bimini and its restorative Fountain. He gathered a troupe of adventurers and sailed north, never to return. However, a man called Lungderry was discovered in Livonia professing to be more than 200 years old.

<ring ring . . . ring ring . . . ring ring . . . ring rin—>

Hi there, you've reached the home of Dylan, Sofia and Alexandra Spaulding. We can't get to the phone right now but leave us a message—and maybe a return number—and we'll get right back to you. Here comes the beep: <beeeeeep>

<click>

Saturday, 8:20 am

I don't know any more. Don't know anything any more. No messages from dad. No message from Leaf. I check the window all the time but her house is still. House is still? What the hell else would a house be? It wasn't this morning though, around six o'clock. That's two hours ago. It's 8:20 now. Nothing on the radio. In fact, electricity in general is hit and miss. This morning there was someone over in Leaf's house. I saw movement. Don't know who it was but

<ring ring . . . ring ring . . . ring ring . . . ring rin—>

Hi there, you've reached the home of Dylan, Sofia and Alexandra Spaulding. We can't get to the phone right now but leave us a message—and maybe a return number—and we'll get right back to you. Here comes the beep: <beeeeeep>

"Oh, come on. Answer the fucking phone . . . Leaf, it's Jeffrey. Pick up. Come on, Leaf, pick up the damn phone will you! I just saw you—just saw somebody anyways . . . Look, I know it's you. It's not your father because . . . well, we know why it's not your father. I just want to know how you are. *Please!* I'm . . . I'm not doing so good—first mom and then dad. Talk to me, *please*. Before I do something stupid."

[A bank of TV monitors on a wall above a desktop counter. On the desktop are telephones—all of them off their cradles—and a keyboard and computer screen. The monitors are showing different areas. On each of the numbered monitors is a legend that states ACADEMY FOR MEDICAL RESEARCH. Some of the monitors show empty rooms, others show people working and one shows a man sitting reading a newspaper. On this screen is the additional information JOHN DOE. On the right-hand side of the bank zombies are approaching the building. The security guards are firing into them but there are too many zombies and, one by one, the guards go down. The zombies then spill into the rooms and corridors beyond the reception area—they appear on other screens until, at last, the man reading the newspaper looks across at his door startled. Within a matter of seconds, the door buckles inwards and a crowd of zombies enters the room. The man drops his newspaper on the floor and backs away. A man's head is slumped on one of the keyboards in front of the bank of screens. There is blood everywhere and the man is missing the right side of his head and his right forearm. On the screen, more zombies enter the room and swarm onto the hapless man. One of them looks around the room until she stares straight at the monitor's camera. She advances dragging a chair. She stands on the chair and reaches up . . . and the screen goes blank, with the hiss of static.]

▼ [Extract from *The History of Patchwork Quilting* by Lucinda Cantor-Napier (Alfred A. Knopf, 1954)]

Patchwork quilt-making came about as a result of two things that were, in essence, just one: the Depression of the 1920s and 1930s.

The first element was the need for covering and warmth, with the lack of materials in any large amounts resulting in what was available being cut down into manageable squares and then stitched together. Into each of these squares a small amount of filling was inserted, with the square then being stitched.

The second involved the mobility of the American people.

"Work was in short supply and, inevitably, so was food and drink. So families were forced to move in the hope that something would present itself around the next bend in the road. Briony Napier, aged eighty-six, recalls:

"'Ma and Pa sat up front in our old truck, a course, while the twins, plus Josh and me, well, we spent whole days sittin' on the flatbed while our pa moved up and across and back and around, lookin' for some work. We found it ever once in a while but it was a hard slog. When I look at the old maps my husband George hid away from me—God rest his soul, passed away some twenny years ago now—it's hard to figure out any sense in our route. Didn't seem to be any real order or plan to it. And still I marvel at the huge columns of dust and grime the good Lord tossed up at us, day in and day out. Yes sir, they was mighty tough days.'

"Although Nebraska was not the center of the Dust bowl area—southwest Kansas and Panhandle Oklahoma were far more drastically affected—and Adams County was not hit so drastically as counties farther southwest in Nebraska, still those years created psychological scars that exist in Adams County people even now, all these years later. Drought and heat and crop failure the people had known before, but never before had the land itself been imperiled, the topsoil just up and blowing away. Land had always been the one stable element in an environment where everything else was a gamble.

"Briony again: 'Only thing kept us sane—partickerly after Josh passed on (which near on killed my ma)—was the quilts my ma done made for us, one each for me and the twins and one for Josh. Pa buried him in that. A sad day. But ma, she sewed little pickshers on the squares—one I remember was a apple tree with apples layin' on the ground—and me and the twins would make up stories taking the squares in a different order every day. Stories. Stories we made up. And although we was poor—and by golly we was poor—we did a lotta laughin'. So happy days, in spite of stuff.'"

Mr. Paryder,

Doctor Gilray has asked me to tell you that we have made contact with our patient. He thought you would like to know.

And John Doe has been terminated.

Lois Chapelle
Assistant to Dr. Brewster Gilray
NWP

<ring ring . . . ring ring . . . ring ring . . . ring rin—>
Hi there, this is the Willson residence. We're either out or fielding calls so speak and maybe leave us a message. If we don't pick up, we'll call you later. Maybe. You know what to do:<beeeeeep>

"Jeffrey, I don't know if you can hear me. It's dad. Fact is, I don't even know if you're alive. (Christ, I say that so casually: 'Don't even know if you're alive!' Hey ho! Ridiculous.)

"It's amazing how hard we've all become in such a short time. How accepting we are of what we've always considered cheesy drive-in horror fare. I mean . . . *zombies* . . . !

"I've called a couple times and then, when it started to go to the answer message, I killed the connection. I couldn't bear it . . . hearing mum's voice again. I don't know if you <bump!>—whoah! Fuck! Get the fuck off of—<screeching noise>

<bump>
<bump>
<bump>

"Shit. She's gone. Don't know if you heard that but I just ran one of them over. Old woman . . . well, late fifties I'd guess. She bent forward over the hood and—fuck me, for Christ's sake . . . she's still there, crawling up from the grill.

<screech>

<screech>

<crunch>

"Hold the line. Where's my shovel? It's in here some— Ah! Here it is.

<bing . . . bing . . . bing . . .bing . . . bing>

<slam>

"Okay sweetlips, you ask—

<guttural growl and a high-pitched whine>

"I said, you asked—

<thunk>

<thunk>

<thunk>

"—you fucking asked for it, lady.

<thunk>

<thunk>

<bing . . . bing . . . bing . . .bing . . . bing>

<slam>

"Okay, let's—no, lock the doors first . . .

<clikcclickclick>

"Okay, we're getting out of here right now . . .

<bump>

<bump>

<bump>

"There. We drove over her. I just—anybody there yet . . . ?

"No, okay. Nobody there.

"I just checked in the mirror and she's still there, there in the road. And, incredibly—<laughter>—hey, I'm laughing and there's not really anything to laugh at but it's funny. Like that Maughmstein guy: you know? The stand-up? Anyway, I'm looking in the mirror—we're out of sight of her now but, you know . . . she was there—and the old woman was still waving a hand. Was she mad at me? Who the hell knows? Was she waving me goodbye ('You take care now, young man.') . . . ?

"That's what my mom used to say to me: 'You take care now.' I am so glad she didn't live to see this. So glad."

Trooper Clifford Olengo: "Hazey?"
Hazel Pennyman: "Cliff? That you?"
CO: "Yeah, it's me. I'm getting too old for this shit, Hazey."
HP: "Why you whispering, Cliff?"
CO: "Well, you know . . . I have no idea. [PAUSE AND THEN HE SHOUTS]Hey! *Hey!* I'm *talkin'* to ya."
HP: "You talking to me, Cliff?"
CO: "Nope. You wouldn't believe who I'm talkin' to and what I'm seein'here."
HP: "These are strange days, Cliff. Try me."
CO: "Okay. I'm parked up on the beltway. Doin' nuttin'. I tell ya . . . it's like a morgue out here."
HP: "Like a morgue everyplace, Cliff."
CO: "Well, yeah . . . but this is different. It's like that old crappy horror movie about a Plan from Outer Space?"
HP: "'Fore my time."
    [PAUSE]
CO: "Some alien race activates dead folks to turn on us?"
HP: "Cliff, I gotta go do—"
CO: "There's a bunch of folks walking down the road and they don't have heads."
    [PAUSE]
HP: "Cliff, you been in the evidence cupboard?"
CO: "I wish."

Saturday . . . I think.

I have absolutely no idea of the date – oh, wait, I can work it out: if it really is Monday, then it's the 13th. But really, who gives a shit. Not me any more. Really. I just do not know why I'm writing this stuff any more. Anyway, I went down the street to Courtney's Provisions store today. I moved real slow, waiting at each stop to make sure nobody saw me. It was late afternoon, early evening, with the twilight only just coming on. The only real problem was in the store because the electric is off. I picked up some cheese crackers, peanut butter, sodas and a few comic books from Old Man Courtney's spinning rack. I haven't seen anyone outside for almost two days now. Day before yesterday there was a guy wearing a motorcycle helmet came walking along past the filling station just across the street. He was long gone, I think, staggering and dragging his leg a little, arms outstretched like he was going to fall over. He stopped by the fire hydrant and seemed to look around, head thrown back like he was sniffing. I had the living room window partly open and I wondered if maybe he could smell me. So I closed the window real slow, but even then it squeaked but so low you could hardly hear it. But he heard it, I'm sure he did and for a minute or two I thought he was going to come across to my side of the street. But a noise from somewhere up ahead – like something falling onto metal – made him turn around. And he threw back his head again, dislodging the helmet and sending it to the ground as he let out a hoarse roar. They do that. Dad told me it's marking territory for them. It's almost a week since I got the call from dad. I watch out for them. Dad told me I had to do that. And that I hadn't got to be frightened. I should just do what I had to do, he told me. I miss him. I miss Leaf.

▼ [Telephone conversation between Edward Zilasker Jr. and Abraham Capel, Cedar Rapids, Iowa]

```
Edward Zilasker Jr.: "Abe? It's Ed."
Abraham Capel: "I know who it is."
EZ: "Well, I thought-"
AC: "I mean, who else is it going to be?"
EZ: "Abe, look outside."
AC: "I'm looking."
EZ: "Can you see her?"
```

AC: "I can't see anybody. It's dark."

EZ: "Go to your front window—the one in your dad's study—and take a look up the road, around the old furniture store. See her?"

AC: "I'm looking . . . leaning against the glass—"

EZ: "I can just make you out now. Stay a little to one side. You don't want her to see you."

AC: "I still can't see any—Oh, I see her."

EZ: "Yeah, you see her?"

AC: "Jeez, I *see* her."

EZ: "Keep back, Abe."

AC: "I *see* her."

EZ: "Abe, isn't that your mom's dress?"

AC: "Oh, God, Ed. *Oof . . . Shit!*"

EZ: "What happened?"

AC: "I walked into the hall table. That's the problem with keeping the fucking lights off."

EZ: "Well, you know they told us at school why we have to do that, right? We have—Wait a minute. The *hall* table?"

AC: "Yeah, damn thing near on broke my leg."

EZ: "I can't see you anymore. At the window, I mean."

AC: "I know. I'm in the hall."

EZ: "Abe, don't open the door. Do not open—"

AC: "What?"

EZ: "I know what you're doing. You walked into the hall table because you're going outside to see your mom."

AC: "I'm not—Shit! The sensor light!"

EZ: "Abe!"

AC: "I know, I know. It'll go out again."

EZ: "Too late, Kimosabee. She's seen it."

AC: "There: it's out."

EZ: "Too late. Get back in the house! She's heading your way."

▼ [From *The Dawning of the Long Dark Night* by Timothy Gregory MD and Professor James Lang (The American Psychiatric Association, November 1973)]

Numerous conversations with terminally ill patients have unearthed a common concern. Namely, do long-time familiar things assume a new status or image when the patient finally comes to terms with the fact that he is going to leave it behind.

Patient: G.A. Moody

Diagnosis: pancreatic cancer

Prognosis: estimate given of four to six months.

"I couldn't stand to look at my Levis Timberline (or Timberland: I can never remember) coat when the Doc over at Fairfield gave me around six months to go. It was the idea that the coat and I had been, like, inseparable—you, I mean . . . I'm just thirty-three right now so it's a bit of a bum deal—I kind of felt it was gloating. Does that make any sense?

"Now, with just a little over four weeks to go—though I have to tell you I'm doing okay (the morphine helps)—I sleep downstairs leaving Cindy to our big double bed. I watch a lot of TV, mostly sitcom re-runs, and I keep the volume as high as I can without disturbing Cindy. But I can still hear them . . . my racks of vinyl albums (mostly progressive rock). And they're all going to still be here when I'm gone."

▼ [Transcript of cell phone conversation between Precinct 14 Dispatch Manager Benjamin Wos and Officer Jerzy Glunreedie, Monday, July 15, 11:33 am]

```
Benjamin Wos: "Jerzy, just—"
Jerzy Glunreedie: "I mean, Jesus fucking H. Christ, Benjy,
    Jesus fuck—"
BW: "Take a breath, will yo—"
JG: "He's hanging there like a side of beef, Benjy.
    <sobbing> I need to cut him dow—"
BW: "Jerzy! You cannot cut him down."
JG: "Can't cut him?"
BW: "Jerzy, it's a crime scene. You cannot disturb—"
JG: <laughter> "Are you kidding me here, Benji? I mean,
    really? The whole fucking planet is a crime scene and
    there's getting pretty damn few people to disturb it. A
    crime scene!" <more laughter>
BW: "Jerzy, tell—"
JG: <sobbing> "I cannot believe this. I really—"
BW: "Jerzy, easy. Go easy, girl."
JG: "I think it's that Willson kid. The one who's father went
    missing. They strung him up and then . . . and then—"
```

BW: "They wouldn't string him up, Jerzy."

JG: "Hey, I'm looking at him. He's just a kid. There's a rope fastened onto the fan—one of those big circular fans, you know?"

BW: "I know the ones."

JG: "Fan's not on."

BW: "Right. Okay. The fan is not on. So where is he? Where is he?"

JG: "He's hanging over the balcony of the upstairs floor so the rope comes down from the fan on the upstairs ceiling—Jesus, the smell!"

BW: "Jerzy, stay focussed."

JG: "I'm focussed. I'm fucking focus—"

BW: "Yeah, well just stay focussed."

JG: "And . . . and . . . hey."

BW: "What is it?"

JG: "They didn't put him up here. I can see that now."

BW: "You said . . . you said they'd hung him like a side of beef?"

JG: "I was wrong, Benjy. *He* did it. *The kid.* He hung *himself.*"

BW: "And then . . ."

JG: "And then somebody's eaten parts of him. The throw rug in the hallway, man, it's clotted and thick with blood. Parts of his—oh shit, oh my good lord—they ate his pecker, Benjy; ate his balls, scrotum sack, parts of his lower stomach and his belly, his ass . . . and I'm standing right in the middle. [PAUSE] Hey, Benjy?"

BW: "You're whispering. Why you whispering?"

JG: "There are footsteps."

BW: "Footsteps?"

JG: "Yeah, going through the blood and guts on the carpet and carrying on across the floor."

BW: "You mean foot*prints.*"

JG: "Yeah. Footprints—first it just looks like splashes, and that's why I didn't notice them. But it's footst—prints, foot*prints.* And they go—"

BW: "Jerzy . . ."

JG: "And they go over to a door."

BW: "Jerzy, stay away from the door, girl."

JG: "It's like a cupboard door, you know?"

BW: "Is there glass? Is there any glass in the door?"

JG: "Uh uh. It's just wood."

BW: "Is the door open?"
    [PAUSE]
JG: "It's slightly open. Not snecked, you know? But it's
    pulled—"
BW: "Jerzy, get out. You listening to me here. Get out
    now!"
JG: "I got my gun out. It's cool, Benjy. It's coo— [PAUSE]
    Wait a minute. The door is pushing open."
BW: "Jerzy, get out of the house. Get out of the fucking
    house, girl."
JG: "Hey, *shh*, will ya. My heart's beating like a trip-ham—
    Oh . . . [PAUSE] It's a girl, it's a young girl. Can't
    be more than seventeen . . . maybe not even that."
BW: "What's she doing?"
JG: "She's just standing there. Oh, she's crying . . ."
BW: "Is she . . . is she—?"
JG: "She's got her arms up over her face and she's watching
    me. Hey, sweetie, how you doin'? You okay? Are you?
    She's frightened, Benjy. [PAUSE] Look, you worried
    about the gun? Well, look right here now . . ."
BW: "Jerzy, what are you—?"
JG: "Oh, hey . . . she's lowering her arms now—I think
    she's okay, hey . . . that's a beautiful T-shirt . . .
    it's a single leaf, a really big one, just lying on the
    ground . . . and above it, it says, *I've fallen for
    you*! [PAUSE] She's still crying but she's calming now.
    There's a bloody sweater on the floor next to her. And,
    hey . . . wait a minute—"
BW: "What is it?
JG: "She's got something in her— *Fuck*!"
BW: "Jerzy?"
JG: "In her mouth! She's spit it out—oh, for the love of
    God"
BW: "Your gun. Use your gun, Jerzy!"
JG: "It's a fucking . . . oh, Christ . . . it's the kid's
    fucking—"
<roaring sound and lots of clattering, then a scream, and
a gunshot. It's clear that the cell phone has been dropped
. . . then the policewoman's high-pitched scream . . . and
then a crunching sound. And then silence>

W. Leonard Paryder: "Lois?"

Lois Chapelle: "This is Miss Chapelle. How may I help you?"

WLP: "Lois, you know who this is, so take your thumb out of your ass and tell me what Brew means about making contact with Dr. Willson."

<silence>

WLP: "Lois? You hear what I asked you?"

LC: "I heard."

WLP: "And?"

LC: "Does it matter?"

WLP: "Does it matter? Are you kidding me here?"

Brewster Gilray: "Leonard, this is Gilray. What's your problem?"

<the line clicks as Lois Chapelle signs out>

WLP: "My problem is—"

BG: "We helped him leave."

WLP: "You *what*?"

BG: "We helped him leave. He is in good shape now with all the patchwork regenerative work we did. And he can help us."

WLP: "Help us how?"

BG: "He's gone after Moreby."

WLP: "Is Moreby still with—?"

BG: "Willson's wife? Yes."

<a muffled moaning sound>

Marianne Willson: "Are you going to leave him in there the whole trip?"

<silence>

MW: "He's getting on my nerves."

Thomas Moreby: "*Estoy con miedo lo que no es posible, mi querido.*"

MW: "I cannot believe that I'm saying this to you because I know damn well you know this already. But I'll say it anyway: I don't understand what you just said."

TM: <laughter> "You did not understand me? <more laughter> I said it is not possible. *Non possibile, mia cara. Nicht möglich, meine Liebe.*"

<muffled sound is now interspersed with banging noises>

MW: "You are just showing off."

<silence . . . then someone starts whistling>

MW: "Please do not do that. Can't I just have some silence
while I drive?"

<banging noise starts up again>

TM: "Stop the vehicle."

MW: "Why? We're still miles from Washington. Why stop
here?"

TM: "Stop the vehicle. *Now*."

<sound of screeching tires. Engine stops and the banging
also stops. A door opens and the security beep sounds
repeatedly to indicate that whoever has opened the door
has left it open>

MW: "What are you going to—?"

<sound of a trunk door being opened>

TM: "—am not a patient man, Mister Carrier. Oh, yes, I
remember now—it is Carpenter, is it not? Is that not
correct? Mister Carpenter?"

<muffled response>

TM: "Oh, my . . . you were making so much noise just a few
minutes ago and now, well . . . the cat has got your
tongue, has it not? And still you remain silent. As,
indeed, I had asked you to. And yet a moment ago you
persisted in making—"

<sound of something wet being torn out and swallowed. A
muffled scream, followed by a steady whimpering>

MW: "His eye, Thomas."

TM: "What about it?"

MW: "It . . . it's gone. It's not there anymore."

TM: "My, you are certainly observant my dearest Marianne."

<whimpering continues>

MW: "Where is it?"

TM: "'And if thy eye offend thee, pluck it out, and cast
it from thee: for it is profitable for thee that one
of thy members should perish, and not that thy whole
body should be cast into Hell.'"

Special Agent Philip "Flip" Carpenter: ". . . It . . .
hurts."

TM: "Oh, I am very aware of how much it hurts to lose an
eye, Mister Carpenter. As you can seen from this
tattered patch that covers my own gaping socket."

MW: "But why—?"

TM: "He irked me."

FC: "Help me . . . you can help me . . . *please*?"
TM: "Nobody is going to help you Mister Carpenter. Not on
     a road at night, where two people are standing with
     their vehicle's doors open, looking down at a trussed-
     up naked man with an eye missing and a face smeared
     with blood. It is a whole new world out there now."
MW: "That's it? He pissed you off so you stripped and
     bound him, put him in the trunk, and now you've eaten
     his eye?"
TM: "He had the upper hand—or thought he did—but now he no
     longer does.[PAUSE] Are you hungry my dear?"
MW: "Are you sayin—?"
TM: "Think of him as a picnic lunch . . .
<noise of a truck going by>
TM: ". . . and anyway, even us dead folks have to eat
     sometimes, right?"
<sound of air-brakes squealing noisily>
TM: "I was apparently mistaken. I do believe that this one
     is stopping. It is our lucky day."
MW: "He can't have seen—"
Truck driver: "You need any help?"
TM: *[soto voce]* "Heh, we have got ourselves a live one
     here. And those are the juiciest.
<sound of a cab door opening and feet dropping down onto
gravel>
TM: *[normal voice]* "Certainly, please come on over here."

            <ring ring . . . ring ring . . . ring ring . . . ring rin—>
*Hi there, this is the Willson residence. We're either out or fielding calls
so speak and maybe leave us a message. If we don't pick up, we'll
call you later. Maybe. You know what to do:* <beeeeeep>
    "Jeffrey, I can't talk for long. So listen to me. If you get this. Hell,
maybe you've left. Taken off for the border . . . I just don't know. Don't
know anything any more. But I just wanted to call you one last . . .
    "I may not see you again, son, so I just wanted to say—shoot, what
did I want to say? I don't know now. You know? Everything was so
clear a few minutes ago, just before I made the call, but now . . . hell.
I love you boy. I hope you can survive all of this . . . go with Leaf, get
out, try to hole up until— Hah! I was going to say 'until all of this blows

over' and, of course, it's not going to blow over. Not ever. The world is finished. It is the breakdown of everything . . . false hopes, crazy notions, bizarre concepts and the destruction of humanity in all of its myriad guises . . .

"I've seen some things, Jeff . . . stuff you wouldn't believe.

"I've seen a burning woman with her child, both of them burning, waiting at the side of the road. No idea how it happened. I thought she was going to walk out right in front of me but she just stood there, watching—at least I think she was watching.

"And I've seen headless people, some of them at the side of the road, too . . . and others walking along the street. How do they see? How do they breathe—no, scratch that: they don't breathe.

"And when I pulled up to take a pee, keeping an eye on a collection of corpses, I saw a head watching me, its eyes blinking and the mouth moving, like it was trying to speak to me . . . mouth moving like a fish. I don't know where its body was.

"Anyway, I'm going after . . . I'd sooner you heard it from me than from someone else. There's this man you see, if you can even call him that, and he's got your—"

<click>

> ▼ [Recording of a conversation between repair truck DC7 and the out-of-hours office on Western Avenue, three blocks from the Capital Beltway leading into downtown Washington D.C., Saturday, 29 June, 2013]

```
Office: "Hello?"
Truck:  "Hello."
Office: ". . . Who's that?"
Truck:  "Who would you like it to be?"
Office: "Where are you?"
Truck:  "Where am I?"
Office: "Downtown. Leastways, I thought you was downtown."
Truck:  "As a matter of fact, we are currently in your
        immediate vicinity.
Office: "I don't—"
Truck:  "Western Avenue, right? That was the address
        engraved upon the side of this vehicle."
Office: "Yeah, I can see you now out the window."
Second Office Voice: "Who is that? It don't sound like
        Hank."
```

<bing . . . bing . . . bing . . . *slam*>
Office: "Hey, sir? Don't do that."
Second Office Voice: "What's he doing?"
Office: "Whoever he is, he's getting out of the truck. Sir,
        please stay in— Sir,can I ask you to stay inside
        your vehicle? Please? Will you— He's out of the
        truck now. Out of it completely."
Second Office Voice: "Tell him to stay inside the
        vehicle."
Office: "I just said, he's out of the truck."
Second Office Voice: "Just tell him to stay where he is."
Office: "I told him, already. Didn't you fucking hear me
        tell him?"
Second Office Voice: "I heard—"
Office: "Sir? He's coming across . . ."
<bing . . . bing . . . bing . . . bing . . . *slam*>
Second Office Voice: "Now what?"
Office: "There's a woman with him. Maybe it's his wife . . .?"
Truck Voice: "My *wife*?"
Second Office Voice: "How . . . how did he do that? He's
        not in the truck so how did he come over the
        inter—"
Office: "They're both coming over here."
Second Office Voice: "Who the fuck are these people?"
Office: "We need to stop them."
Second Office Voice: "You want me to go out there? Scratch
        that. I ain't goin'out there, man. This is too
        fucking weird."
Office: "We need to— Wait a minute . . . where is she?"
Second Office Voice: "Who?"
Office: "The woman. I can't see her no more."
Second Office Voice: "Is she back in the vehicle?"
Office: "No, she is not back in the fucking vehicle. And
        will you fucking stop calling every fucking thing
        that comes in here a 'vehicle'?"
Second Office Voice: "Geno, she outside. She outside the
        door, man. I'm looking at her through the glass."
Office: "What's she doing?"
Second Office Voice: "Now the guy has disap—"
<grinding noise as the door is ripped from its hinges>
Woman's Voice <over the sound of the door being thrown
        across the forecourt>: "Hello, boys."
Truck Voice: "Okay, you gentlemen are not going to say it

so I will: 'Welcome to Washington, Mister Moreby.'
    Why, thank you kind sirs. By the way, do you know
    where we—"
Office: "Sir, you need to get out of this office right now.
    I don't know how you got in here but—"
Truck Voice: "—where we can get somebody to eat?"
Woman's Voice: "Turn off the recorder."
Second Office Voice: "Don't listen to her, Geno. Don't
    listen to—"
Truck Voice: *"Oh, me temo que el tiempo para no escuchar
    es cosa del pasado, caballeros. Atrás quedaron."*
Office: "Sir, I have to ask you one last time not to touch
    the interc—
Truck Voice: "Oh, I'm afraid the time to listen is not a
    thing of the past, gentlemen. Gone are—"
Office: *"Aaiiieeee!"*
Truck Voice: "My oh my, what a lot of goodies to choose
    fro—"
<click>

For you provided me Washington—and now these also.

—Walt Whitman,
from *Virginia, The West*

<ring ring . . . ring ring . . . ring ring . . . ring rin—>
*Hi there, this is the Willson residence. We're either out or fielding calls
so speak and maybe leave us a message. If we don't pick up, we'll
call you later. Maybe. You know what to do:* <beeeeeep>
"Oh, Jeffrey . . . <sob>"

<click>

"Time isn't linear. Every moment that's ever happened or that ever will
happen is happening right now. We just choose to live in this moment to
create some illusion of continuity. So, really, we have already died and we're
also not yet born."

—Jessa Johansson (Jemima Kirke),
from *Girls* (Season 3, Episode 4: "Dead Inside")

This didn't start with science or medicine.

It started with magic.

Sure, science can help us understand some of it. Yes, the HRV <u>does</u> activate a dormant gene in us all. Yes, we're working to switch it off again. Yes, the human body simply can't exist as it's meant to with the gene turned on. That's what makes the dead walk, what drives them to eat the living. (Q: are they trying to stop? Are they trying to take into themselves the trigger that will shut things down — by eating life? Consider further.) But science didn't start this.

The Death.

The Lazarus Virus.

The Dark Hope.

It started with magic.

It started with Moreby, architect, black magician, wife murderer, zombie master. Arsehole-in-Chief.

My reading and research have become, since the outbreak, somewhat stranger than before. More esoteric. Not the stuff you reference in conference papers, not unless you want to be laughed out of your profession and have "nutbag pariah" tattooed on your backside. Lucky for me there aren't any conferences to worry about anymore, no peer-reviewed journals, mainly because most of my peers have been eaten and/or turned. Not that I was fond of many of them, but even Professor Nielsen probably didn't deserve to have his brains used as tapenade.

And these notes won't be going anywhere near what remains of the official channels — this is my diary, one of the few private things I've got left after all this time. When the world's threatened, the private becomes so small, so unimportant; the whole of existence kind of overwhelms it. The public, the common good, becomes everything. This is secret, confidential, the place I can vent and rant and posit ridiculous theories.

And while I'm waxing philosophical, the past, which I've been thinking about a lot lately, becomes so very, very insignificant. That's what I'll say to my sister, when I see her . . . sister, half-sister, doesn't matter. Forget what's happened, I'll say, forget the spite, forget everything we said to each other, every carefully placed dart. It doesn't matter who slept with whose husband. I'm sorry for all the times I wasn't there for you, I'm sorry I didn't give you enough attention. Forget it, there's just us now. We're all we've got.

That's what I'll say when — if — we find her.

From: Lieutenant General Barry Cosgrove,
Task Force Lazarus Email Blast, Medical Research Division,
Australian Combined Forces, Fortress Brisbane,

Recent recon flights from Fortress Adelaide over the northern parts of the state show large tracts of land to be fairly clear of Lazarite activity, most particularly around Kati Thanda-Lake Eyre basin. Further flights from Fortress Brisbane over the Queensland sectors of the basin show similar results. It has also been noted that several remote communities appear intact despite having no walls or electrified fences. Until recently there was no reason to believe that this was anything more than a coincidence – the majority of the population has always lived at the edges of Australia, so prevailing thought was why would the zombies be any different? That's where the food is, after all. No effort has been made to investigate this.

The receipt of email contact from a Dr Susan Perry, a GP at the Sturt's Folly Medical Center located not far from the upper reaches of Kati Thanda-Lake Eyre has changed that. She reported that she had treated a woman, Lynda Russo, an RFDS pilot (and one of the first witnesses to the Lazarite landfall) believed lost in Gulargambone, NSW, at the outbreak of the epidemic. Dr Perry (Susan) reported the woman appeared healthy, if a little dehydrated, and somewhat delusional. Russo claimed she'd eaten the flesh of Lazarites with no ill effects, and that it was the key to keeping the creatures at bay. That digesting the undead renders a living person somehow "immune" – or at least unappetizing. The woman has since disappeared, but Dr Perry (Susan) was able to take samples of her blood, sputum and tissue.

Her lab is too limited to allow proper testing, and she does not have the means to get to Brisbane, so a small detachment is being sent to collect her. Dr Maisie Perry, who is currently heading up the researches in Fortress Brisbane, has been very insistent about being allowed to accompany the team and, when she wasn't shouting abuse at me, was able to present a cogent and convincing argument, not based solely on her desire to help her sister. Dr Perry (Maisie) has made some headway with temporarily reversing the effects of HRV and, in the interests of preserving the data via redundancy, copies of her results and current work have been sent to Task Force Lazarus Med Centers in the remaining major city Fortresses of Adelaide, Melbourne and Perth. Researches will be continued while she is in the field.

Of particular interest has been her work with the flea specimens sent from Zombie Ground Zero, the crypt of All Hallows, before London went nuclear. Dr Perry managed to formulate a pesticide that kills the bugs – something that had yet to be achieved. Dr Perry was insistent that it was the place to start, that it wouldn't matter if we got rid of the Lazarites and HRV if the insects were still floating around, ready to resurface. She has refused to share the origin of her breakthrough, but reports that arrived before we lost international communications were that the oak-based solution was being used with great effect. Pity it was too late for London and much of Europe.

Despite unsubstantiated rumors of a resistance Government set up somewhere in Washington D.C., efforts to re-establish contact with the rest of the world have so far remained mostly unsuccessful. We are uncertain as to what kind of infrastructure, if any, has survived; if there are any other centers of civilization left or if everywhere else is simply a mix of a few outposts of humanity and large bands of wandering Lazarites looking for food.

The Australian Combined Forces are determined to continue these email blasts in an effort to render aid to anyone who might be able to utilize the results of our research efforts. We are able to access many overseas servers and the information contained therein, but we have yet to receive replies from any CDC or other government-affiliated organization.

Feels like we're travelling in a mortsafe, those things they used to cover graves with so resurrectionists couldn't dig up bodies and sell them to medical schools. Kind of appropriate. Yesterday afternoon, we landed at the military airfield at Port Augusta - the closest place we can safely set down and refuel. The ACF provided these specially adapted Humvees that they've tricked out with fine, tough mesh wiring to keep the walkers out; even - especially - the windows are covered. Very <u>Mad Max.</u>

It's a bloody long drive to Sturt's Folly and we pulled over late last night to get some z's, then woke a few hours later to find that's exactly what we'd got: a whole herd. They were moaning and rocking both Humvees, almost six tons of metal and glass, not to mention us. Luckily, there wasn't much intent in the action other than to try and get to us; if they'd managed to tip us we'd have been in trouble. We got out of there pretty quickly and decided no more naps; driving will be done in shifts. Tired soldiers are careless soldiers, and careless soldiers end up as walking dead soldiers. Our driver and his buddy are talking non-stop, trying to keep alert and lighten the atmosphere. The two grunts in the back with Atherton and I are sleeping upright while they can, and I imagine the team in the second vehicle are doing the same.

Don't know their names. I stopped learning names over a month ago – may as well give them all red shirts. I only remember Atherton's because he's been my bodyguard for longer than that. No one's ever lasted that long. Besides, he's good in bed and things go better there if you remember the right name.

Before the rude awakening I was dreaming. Biblical dreams if you must know, resurrection miracles. Jesus raised the dead then sent his disciples out to do the same, yet we find no records of those same dead going on to either live productive lives or heading out for an all-you-can-eat human buffet. Understandable, I suppose, as that would definitely count as bad PR for the Church. But it makes me wonder what he did and if Thomas Moreby – a mage, you'll note – somehow discovered and duplicated it.

Then there are those bloody carriers, the fleas. They can live for a very long time. Somehow Moreby knew what they could do and planted them like depth charges or landmines. Somehow he created the best conditions for them to hibernate. Somehow, he left a spell that was set to release the fucking things when the All Hallows' pit was opened. Somehow. If I hadn't started looking for out-of-the-box ideas, if

I hadn't started looking at those conspiracy sites I'd have never found the leaked documents. I'd have never found the information Margaret Winn and Simon Wesley were able to get out – it's still there, all those pages of confidential stuff floating around on the web, even though Prof Winn and Dr Wesley are well and truly gone. Without the so-called nutters, I wouldn't have found those redacted bits of Boswell's *Life of Dr Johnson*. "Oak! Oak!" What a stupid spell; what an effective pesticide. At least that's one run on the board, but fuck knows we need a hell of a lot more. We need to stop HRV in its tracks.

Maybe I'm just getting desperate. Maybe I'm just getting demoralized. I thought we'd made a breakthrough, and honestly, for a few days we had. Captain Morvain responded to the retrovirus; for a good three days he was lucid, showing no signs of deterioration and, most importantly, wasn't in the least bit bitey. He was a good patient because he could respond verbally to my questions, he let me know when he felt different – half of effective medicine is getting patient input.

But on that fourth morning, he'd gone bad: fever, necrotized flesh around the original bite site and creeping up his arm, then delirium. He died around lunchtime, and started wiggling about five hours later, which was a long time given what we're used to seeing. Maybe it's a sign that the retrovirus was still having some effect, that, even though it had failed to beat the HRV, it was still trying to keep the victim dead. Morvain took about ten minutes to get free, but I'd had enough time to get the blood and tissue samples I needed. Sergeant Atherton shot the Captain when he broke the first restraint. Nice, clean headshot, minimal spatter (a lot fewer infections spread that way) and I could get some good slices of his brain.

I didn't get a chance to run the tests before I left - Bateson is doing that while I'm away. I hope he's careful. Honestly, I have doubts about his ability to use a toaster without inflicting self-injury, so I hope I don't end up flying back to Fortress Brisbane and find it filled with Lazarites all because Bateson forgot to wash his hands. Maybe that's unfair; he's not that bad, but he was an academic before he came to us, good on theory, not so much on the research side. He thinks in straight lines, always wants to test and prove his hypotheses before he blurts them out.

I'm wondering what we'll find when we get to Sturt's Folly. In the three days it took to get this expedition together (mind you, that was two days of me arguing, one of actually assembling men, machines and making a plan), we lost contact with Susan. The emails still seem to be going through, but there's been no answer. When dawn broke this morning, we could see a few shamblers through the trees, but there didn't seem to be too many of them, and they didn't take too much notice of us despite the noise of the engines. Then our driver raised his voice, said we were ten minutes out of Sturt's Folly and we should get our shit together.

▼ [Loose folio, Note from Dr Susan Perry, inserted in private diary of Dr Maisie Perry, date unknown]

Maisie,

I don't know if you'll get this, but I hope you do. The town's been overrun — which, I guess if you're reading this, you may have already noticed.

We were clean and clear, right up until that Russo woman came. Word got around, all the things she'd said about the effect of eating zombie flesh and some of the half-wits around here (men in their twenties are a blight on the earth), thought it was a good idea to go and find a couple of those things, bring them home for a town BBQ. Get everyone immune.

You can imagine how well that went. Five of them headed off, don't know how far they got, but apparently they managed to find what they were looking for. Three were, apparently, eaten; the other two came back, one bitten. I had him in the infirmary, handcuffed to the bed. When he resurrected he just took off his own thumbs, slipped the cuffs and then made a snack of his buddy. This all happened while I was at home having lunch. When I got back, they were gone, and a steady stream of folks were turning up here with bites and scratches.

I sent them all home with Panadol and orders to take a hot bath, told them you were coming with a fancy new cure. Told them not to worry because help was on the way in the form of my big sister. I told them I'd do home visits as soon as the cavalry arrived, but what I'm actually going to do is gather up the children who've come for their checkups, pile them into the car and get the hell out of here. I won't waste time looking around at everything I've built, or thinking about the things I'm leaving behind. I'm heading to the national park, there's a few travelers' huts out there, we'll see how long we can last. I've got all the samples with me from that Russo woman, just in case any of your military brethren think we're not worth rescuing. Call me suspicious, but just come and get me.

You'll remember the spot — it's where we scattered Dad's ashes, and where you and I had our last fight.

Sue

The kid is maybe eight, it's hard to tell coz she's very small, bones like a bird, big eyes, dark hair, brown skin, pretty; I keep thinking she looks like Sue when she was that age, but maybe I'm just getting nostalgic. She kept trying to climb into my lap but it made writing - hard enough with the bumping and bouncing of the vehicle - nearly impossible, so I finally convinced her to stay on the seat beside me. Now she's snuggled up under my left arm. There's plenty of room in the back since we left Sturt's Folly.

We hit the town in the early afternoon, and several Lazarites, too, by the time we pulled up outside the Medical Center. Atherton told me to stay in the Humvee while they cleared the clinic, and enforced his point by locking me in. Can't say it wasn't a relief to not have to go in then, but I didn't like being treated like a child. So I sat there and pouted, listening hard, trying to pick up the whisper and thud of crossbows, the peculiar sound of a silenced gun, and the occasional scream that I've come to associate with the living getting bitten. After a while Atherton, someone else's arterial spray across the left leg of his combats, let the daylight in and nodded, saying "Be quick about it."

"You've got red on you," I said as I climbed out, coz I couldn't resist it. I don't care what anyone thinks: civilization has gone to hell but that line is still funny.

The building was a long low rectangle, single story, separated into rooms by thin partitions. As I strode past a space filled with privacy screens and six beds, I noticed some had half-eaten bodies draped across them, others empty but spattered. I almost slipped over in a puddle of something a little red, a little grey, and Atherton caught me. In a small examination room I saw four sets of army boots, the white earth and tiny shards of gravel from outside caught in the grooves of the soles. They were all face down, well-trained, hadn't run, just knelt away from their commanding officer and let him shoot them in the back of the head with a silenced Glock. Safer for everyone. No one wanted to turn.

In the office, most of the equipment — medical, computer, assorted — had been smashed. Lazarites don't go in for mindless destruction unless they're trying to get through a door to a meal. I could see the shelves in the dispensary had been cleared out too, so Sue must have taken as much stuff with her as she could. In the middle of the whiteboard was a single piece of paper, held there with magnets, big red arrows pointing towards it so it couldn't be missed.

Didn't take long to read it and win the argument with Atherton that we had no choice but to go after Sue and the samples.

It occurred to me, as he and I stood there, that this was why we get infected so easily: we let our hearts rule our minds. We went back for family members when what we should have done was run as far and as fast as we could in the opposite direction. When what we should have done was put a bullet or a blade through Mum's or Dad's or Aunty Norma's brain the moment they started to look at us as if we were canapés. I wanted those samples, sure, but mostly I wanted to go after my sister. In spite of everything, I wanted to find Sue.

It was only when we were about to leave that I heard a sound from the only cupboard that wasn't hanging open.

"Thought you said it was clear," I hissed at Atherton and we took up position. Then I realized the sound was sobbing, not moaning, not shuffling, not the wet noise of tearing and chewing. On three, I pulled the door open.

The kid was hiding, fairly ineffectually under the bottom shelf. She had a battered old teddy with her and was hanging on to him for dear life - looked just like the one I had and passed on to Sue. But then, with love and years all teddies end up looking the same. Her name is Rosie and she kept repeating:

They left me behind, they forgot me, and I'm newly angry at my sister for being so careless. It's not like her, but if I've seen one thing over and over during this time it's that panic in the face of the unthinkable hits everyone no matter how smart or otherwise well-organized they are.

There was a shout from one of the remaining grunts that the Lazarite presence outside the med center was increasing and that we should, as he poetically put it, Get the fuck out of there.

We're on the road out to the national park, we've been seeing more and more Lazarites, but again, they're not taking much notice of us. It's weird. The driver started to slow and the movement of the Humvee felt different. I looked out through the windscreen and saw we were on the salt flats. The change in the weather patterns means that there's been very little rain out here. Don't know the last time Kati Thanda had water in it - once, the traveler's hut was on the edge of the lake, but now the shore has crept back almost a kilometer, leaving the shack marooned.

But that isn't the strangest thing. Around the lakeshore, as far as the eye can see, Lazarite corpses, some still twitching, most not moving though. All with at least one arm outstretched towards the shanty . . . no, not towards it . . . towards some spot on the horizon.

Around the hut itself there are no bodies, not for a good twenty meter radius, and that's a relief – just an older model silver 4WD, covered in dust. We're pulling up now. Rosie can wait here; we won't be long.

When I heard the vehicles I couldn't quite believe it. We'd been out there for three days, hiding in the darkness with the windows boarded up, and I was wondering how long the food was going to last, what we were going to do when the water was gone. Wondering if I dared make a run back to Sturt's Folly or try the deserted eco-resort in the national park. Wondering if I could force myself to go past those twitching dying Lazarites spread across the salt beds again. Wondering if I could leave the kids here and just make a run for it – but I rescued them as a salve to my conscience and I don't think I can be without them now. They're filling an absence, plugging a hole, keeping things in, and I don't know what will happen to me if they're gone.

When I heard the opening and closing of doors, the chatter of soldiers, the sound of weapons being readied, I was so happy. Irrational happiness, the sort you get when you think all your problems are over, when you think someone else is going to solve everything and you can relax. My sister was there and she'd fix everything.

Then I opened the door, Maisie wasn't there — or rather, she was but she wasn't where I expected her — needed her - to be: near me. There were big men in camouflage, armed with an assortment of crossbows and handguns with silencers, machetes strapped to their backs, fanning out and taking in the sights. I shoved the kids inside and took a few steps out and there she was, crouched next to the closest body, rubber-gloved hands creeping over the dead thing, examining it with that faraway focused look she used to get when we were kids and she found something more interesting than me. She had a kit on the ground beside her and was taking skin and blood, then I watched as she stood, kicked at the skull so it cracked open with the friable ease that seems to be a characteristic of the Lazarites, and took smears from there too.

I hadn't seen my sister, or spoken to her in almost ten years, and she was off playing in zombie brains. So, I got angry, I admit. I was thrown back to being a child and wanting her to pay attention to me and only me. Thrown back to all that disappointment, back into that bottomless pit where all the yearning and resentment and fear of not being good enough live, and I found something new: the certainty she hadn't come out here for me, that I was just incidental to looking over dead things. I didn't wait to hug her, to say it was good to see her, or thank her for coming. I just yelled at the kids to hurry up, grabbed the bio-med cooler box with Russo's samples in it and asked the nearest soldier which Humvee we were in.

By then Maisie had finished examining the body and was scooping up handfuls of salt from around her and putting it into a plastic envelope. When she finally sealed that shut she looked over at me and smiled. I turned away, followed the kids to the second vehicle and climbed in. I don't know how she looked. I've asked Atherton and he says he doesn't know, but I think he was lying.

I stared at all those bodies, in some places five or six high, forming a fairly imperfect wall. Obviously I stayed away from the ones that had tremors going through them, the ones that were still trying to dry-swim towards wherever they were driven to go. But those closest to the hut were decayed, yet not decayed in the usual manner of the Lazarites, who normally have the marks of their deaths written upon them – they get to a certain point and don't seem to get any worse. Those beyond the hut were much worse.

These ones displayed different levels of decomposition, some more revolting than others but all showing signs of continued putrefaction. The heads and shoulders of those furthest out on the salt flat were almost gone. They showed a gradation in mortification: from the waist down there was still intact flesh, but from the waist up, only skeletal remains. The closer to the skull, the more obvious was the deterioration, the bones were weaker, more brittle, severely pitted and eaten away until some had only piles of red dust where the tops of their heads had once been.

It looked almost as they'd gone partway through a doorway . . . or dematerialized badly. What if . . . what if something is drawing them to a gate, a crossing space? Because these Lazarites aren't trying to escape from it, they're moving towards it, whatever the it is, the liminal space . . . a threshold . . . somewhere between living and dying, really dying, not just ambling about with the sole purpose of eating others.

True death.

But they can't actually seem to get there . . . I mean they are dead, those furthest away from the shore, those closest in to where the salt is concentrated.

So I've been thinking about salt.

The salt is what's slowing them down even as they're trying to get towards whatever doorway there might be for them. The salt seems to be mummifying them.

Salt.

It's been used to preserve people and food. It's been used for healing and purification and protection. For magic. Old-time zombies, those before the Romero crop, were supposed to return to their graves if fed salt. In Ancient Egypt it would preserve the bodies of the truly dead - what might it do to the faux dead?

Obviously those that Russo saw coming ashore at landfall didn't succumb to the salt in the sea water, but maybe that was too diluted. Maybe it needs to be this salt right here, on Kati Thanda. What if we could have just been throwing table salt at these fuckers from the start? Are they like leeches, do you just sprinkle it on them? How much do you need to feed a Lazarite before this happens and how do you get them to ingest it? Or will it only work out here?

I still need to talk to Sue. I could see from her face that she had the shits, that I'd somehow failed her yet again. Didn't seem to matter that I was there, or what I'd risked to come for her . . . there it was, that look, then she just turned her back and headed to the second vehicle with those kids around her like imprinting ducklings. Before I could follow, Atherton hustled me into the lead Humvee, muttering about getting my big brain back to Brisbane. I'll talk to her on the next pee break. We've got a long trip, there will be time.

The kid is squirming a lot, she's bored I guess, playing with the rings on my left hand . . .

I take full responsibility for the omission. Our extraction from Sturt's Folly med center was precipitous and by the time we were out of danger, no one thought to examine the child.

We reached the national park and collected Dr Perry (Susan) and the four children she had with her. Dr Perry (Maisie) examined some of the Lazarite bodies and the salt flats, taking samples, but we didn't delay. Dr Perry (Susan) and the children were in the second vehicle, as a result they didn't see the child, Rosie.

About five minutes after we'd left the travelers' hut Dr Perry (Maisie) yelled. Her hand was bleeding profusely. The little girl's mouth was ringed with blood, but she seemed more afraid than aggressive, and was whimpering "I'm sorry, I'm sorry."

For some reason the effects of HRV had been slow to show themselves on the child. Dr Perry (Maisie) suggested it might have had something to do with the proximity of the salt flats. She examined the girl, observed that Rosie had developed a fever and was sweating profusely, then pulled up the girl's sleeves; the bite mark was obvious on the upper right forearm. Dr Perry (Maisie) called a halt and took blood samples and skin scrapings from herself and the child. She remained quite calm throughout.

We stopped and I had to argue with the soldiers in the back to let me out so I could see what was going on. Maisie was there and a small figure, that made my heart contract as if it was drying up as surely as all those Lazarites, hung onto her leg in terror. Sergeant Atherton was threatening to do what I hadn't, what I couldn't, his sidearm drawn and pointing at the child.

At Rosie.

"No," Maisie said and touched him on the arm. He was slow to lower his gun, but he did it.

"It's orders," he said lamely and she smiled at him like I've never seen her smile at anyone before, so tender and kind.

"You don't need to worry about that. I'll take care of us both."

"Come back, we can try for a cure."

She shook her head. "No cure yet, just a way to get rid of these fucking things. No way but death. It's too dangerous to take us back."

She knelt next to Rosie — the daughter I'd left behind because she'd been bitten and I lacked the courage to either stay with her or send her to oblivion - and smiled at her, too, a gentle resigned smile that set my teeth on edge. I heard her say as I came closer, "We're going for a walk."

And my daughter nodded, then noticed me . . . and stared through me as if she didn't know who I was. She just held onto my sister's hand and all I could think was that I didn't have to tell Maisie what I'd done. I didn't have to tell my sister that I'd never told her she had a niece, that her husband had stayed with me long enough to plant a child. Whether the virus had taken out Rosie's memories already, or she'd simply cast me aside as easily as I had her, I didn't know, didn't care. I was just grateful that my sister would never know what I'd done.

She saw me, then, and smiled again.

"I'm sorry, Sue," she said. "For everything."

And I didn't have words, not one. I should have said I'm sorry. I should have said It doesn't matter, it never did. I should have said Don't die. But I didn't manage anything, just swallowed and swallowed yet the big ball in my throat wouldn't go anywhere. She hugged me quickly, then handed me the diary. "Get this back. Let Bateson have a look and make copies."

Then she turned away, said to Atherton. "Get back on the road. Don't stop until Port Augusta."

"What about you? And her?" He pointed his Glock at Rosie, whose eyes had begun to glitter.

"Back that way," she said, pointing towards the salt flats, to where the dead and almost dead Lazarites had found a gateway, a true death. "I'm making my own choice, better that than you putting a bullet in my brain."

And that hurt him, I could tell, and I wondered if she was hurting him in the hope he wouldn't miss her as much; so when he thought of her, he'd think what a bitch she was in those last moments. Then, as if to soften the blow, she kissed his cheek, and spoke quietly enough to him that I couldn't hear what she said, but he closed his eyes for a moment.

Finally, she offered her hand to Rosie, and said sternly, "No biting."

We didn't hang around, but I looked out the back of the Humvee, watched them moving away, and grow smaller and smaller with every step as they headed towards an ending of some sort.

From: Lieutenant General Barry Cosgrove,
Task Force Lazarus Email Blast, Medical Research Division,
Australian Combined Forces, Fortress Brisbane

The loss of Dr Maisie Perry has been an enormous blow to our program, but her diary notes and the samples that have been brought back are being put to good use. In particular the Kati Thanda salt specimens are showing positive signs of being an effective agent against Lazarite lab subjects. Dr Bateson says he is hopeful. We all must be hopeful. The Russo samples are yielding some similarly interesting results, and, in hope, I append a file with our findings to date.

The dead were at the gates again today.

It was another unexpectedly lovely afternoon,
blue skies, warm sunshine, just enough of a breeze
to keep the midges away. The water in the loch
sparkling, heather purple on the brow of the hills
that rise on either side, above crowded ranks of
pine trees no one will cut down for at least a
generation, now.

The dead stay under the pines usually, catching
mice and rabbits and unwary birds. They eat
crickets and beetles and woodlice if there's
nothing else. I once saw one ransacking the litter
pile of a wood-ant nest for tasty grubs. But
sometimes two or three of them
will wander down to the shore of the loch and
mumble around the gate of our little research
station. We have names for the regulars.
Stinkfoot. David. The Nudist. Mr Bones. They're
mostly harmless. Skinny and ragged, in ragged
clothes. Sometimes we have to drive them off.
Usually they wander away on their own, when some
new impulse stirs in what passes for their minds.

It was different today. There was a crowd at the
gate, clinging to the fence. Sixteen, Chris Lovell
told me, when I wandered out of my lab to see what
was going on. And amongst them was one I
recognised. Not one of our regulars, but someone
from my past. From where all this started, for me.

HIM. C— W— The former King.

The last time I'd seen him he'd been dressed in
navy-blue pyjamas, his coat of arms on the breast
pocket. I'd been treating him for late stage HRV,
and when everything went to hell Ralph and I
turned him out into the wild. And here he was
again, dressed in a kilt and a ruffled white shirt
that flapped open over his ribs and the hollow of
his belly. He was very skinny but mostly intact,
although somewhere along the line he'd dislocated
his left arm: it hung from the hump of his

shoulder like a chicken wing. But he was in pretty good shape, considering.

Some zombies continue to grow hair. Some grow hair all over their bodies, or grow spines, or mats of razorish barbed stuff. Some don't. The King didn't. What had been left of his hair was entirely gone and his bald head shone white as bone. But the lugubrious face and that poached-egg gaze, those wingnut ears (even more prominent now), were unmistakable.

He stood at the back of the crowd around the gate. Watching quietly while the rest of the dead pawed at chain-link and slobbered and moaned. He stood straight-backed and seemed alert, his head smoothly turning back and forth. And then it stopped turning and he was staring straight at me.

It gave me goosebumps, there in the sunlight. Joe McIntyre, always alert for frights and upsets, asked if I was okay. I pointed to the King, asked Joe if he recognized him. It took Joe a moment. He said, "I thought he was dead. You know, really dead."

I said that he'd turned near the beginning, that he'd escaped . . . no point explaining my role in that. Mine and Ralph's. My very own spook. Who should have been there to see our visitor too.

Joe's three post docs craned to see their VIP visitor, made jokes about painting the toilet block, putting up a ribbon he could cut, a plaque he could unveil. Then one of the dead, David, threw a stone. Which is why we call him David. Sometimes he swallows the stones he picks up (his belly bulges like a miser's coin sack) and sometimes he throws them. This one rattled off the snarls of barbed wire above the gate, and several of the dead stirred and started to throw stuff too. Twigs, handfuls of dirt, more stones. Daisy Callaghan and Steve Finlay dragged out the fire hose and turned it on the dead, blasting some of them off their feet, drenching the rest. Slowly, sullenly, they retreated, plodding away up the road towards the shelter of the trees. The King last of all, pacing after the others with straight-backed dignity, like a shepherd driving his flock.

How did he find me? I can't believe it's a coincidence. Oh, perhaps he drifted north to Scotland, drawn by fading memories of his schooldays, or holidays in Balmoral. The dead often migrate to the places of their childhood, as if the oldest memories are the last to go. They cluster around schools, playgrounds and shopping centres in macabre reunions. But we're on the west coast and Balmoral is up in the Highlands. How did he make his way here? And who dressed him in that kilt and shirt? Socks too, and presumably shoes, although he'd lost those and the socks had worn from his feet, leaving only filthy ruffs of tartan around his ankles.

Perhaps some monarchist took him in, and he escaped and just chanced to wander in this direction. Stranger things have happened in these strange days. But I don't think it's any kind of coincidence. I want to talk it over with Ralph, but he isn't due to return for three days, and we still haven't fixed the radio problem.

Anyway, this is why I started this entry, the first in a while. The first since Ralph and I settled here. It's been a good, peaceful time. Hard work and hope. But I think that's about to change.

Dr Alison McReady's journal, 16/09:
He came again. The King. With twenty-eight
followers this time. All of our regulars, plus a
number of skeletal stragglers. One of the latter
was a little boy, very quick and agile. He tried
to climb the gate and Steve F had to use the shock
pole to drive him away. David and the other
regulars were hurling stones all the while; one
cut Steve, a scalp wound that looked worse than it
was. The scent of blood sent some of the
stragglers into a frenzy. It took a long time to
drive them off, and some are watching still, along
the tree-line. There was talk over supper of
sniping them, something we've been reluctant to
do. If we kill the regulars, unknown dead will
drift in to take their place, better the devil you
know etc etc. Still, we're all a bit rattled,
despite a pep talk from Joe. I backed him, saying
that this was just a temporary blip, a scattered
herd of dead passing through, things would soon
settle down again. But I wish Ralph was back right
now.

Dr Alison McReady's journal, 17/09:
Forty-two today. The King is standing at his usual
place, like a general behind his troops. The sense
of a commanding presence is uncanny.

The little boy got over the fence, and Steve F
shot him. I should be used to dead children by now,
but no. We've been sheltered here. I can't remember
the last time we had to kill one of the dead. It's
night now, the brief twilight of a Scottish Indian
summer, and many of the dead are still at the gate
and we've retreated to the pontoons around the
floating tanks of the fish farm.

Steve F and Daisy C talked about capturing the
King and finding out what makes him tick, but with
the crowd of dead around him — his subjects — it
would be a dangerous snatch, and Joe vetoed it.

Ralph should be back tomorrow. Meanwhile, dear
diary, let me explain where I am, and what I'm
doing. I always return to you in a crisis. To set
down a record just in case things go pear-shaped,
as my dear old dad would say.

We've been here two months, Ralph and I. Almost
three. Both of us working for the Human Resistance,
working on the natural history of the dead.

We're all, to use the hideous neologism Joe is
so fond of, zombiologists now. All of the living
must study the dead because they need to know how
to survive them. Where they lurk and where they
don't, how to trap and kill them, and so on. But a
few of us are trying to work out what makes them
what they've become, and how they're changing.

It used to be that the dead were dead and that
was that. Final as a full stop. But after the
plague began to spread and the dead began to walk,
death took on a new meaning, and that meaning
hasn't yet stabilised. And it's clear that the
dead are divided into castes and hierarchies as
complicated as the British class system. There are
the shamblers, who brainlessly stumble about,
driven by nothing more than ravening appetite —

most of the original zombies were shamblers, and most of those are no more than husks now, minds gone and bodies falling apart, walking skeletons with clattering jaws and keen hearing and an excellent sense of smell (they can scent blood from more than two kilometres away). There are the soldiers, two kinds. The first travel in packs and are united by a shared discipline, but otherwise aren't much brighter than the shamblers; the second are able to absorb and transmit new ideas, use weapons from clubs to rifles, and possess enough native cunning to avoid simple traps and break into buildings. Then there are the aristocrats, who can marshal the shamblers and soldiers and communicate with each other, and at the head of all of them is the King. Not C— W—, who waited all his life to become King and died in the getting of the throne, but the self-declared King of the Dead, Thomas Moreby, who died in the early 19th century and rose again in ours, the Patient Zero of the plague.

I met him once — Moreby. Ralph brought him to the Displaced Persons Refuge where I was working. That was almost three months ago. I hardly think of him at all now. No more than three or four times a day. His dry voice and odd accent. His mocking and mordant wit. His effortless assumption of superiority. He told me that he was the King of the Dead and I could be his queen, but he escaped before he made good his promise. Or I escaped him — but not his works, which continue to ruin and darken the world.

We're trying to drive back the dark with light of reason, as Joe likes to say. A handful of scientists and my own action man. Who's out there now, searching for the chemicals I need for my sequencers and gels. We're camped out in what used to be a small research station owned by a company that raised GM salmon and sea trout. A couple of lab huts on the shore, tanks floating in the shallows of the little sea loch. A little island at the loch's crooked mouth.

The island is where Joe and his post docs do their behavioural work; the labs are my fiefdom, where I isolate and type variants of a strain of HRV, the virus which transmits the zombie plague. When Thomas Moreby was disinterred in All Hallows Church in London, his cargo of fleas was quickened. The fleas carry bacteria; the bacteria carry the virus that kills people and brings them back from death. The bacteria also form highly organised colonies inside the dead, a kind of pseudonervous system, and the mt strain of HRV interacts with this, transmitting memories and skills between the dead. The bacteria are the hardware; the mt strain of HRV is the software. That's our working assumption, at any rate.

So far I've isolated more than a hundred strains, each one conveying a different skill set, each injecting a payload of DNA that, apart from a single highly conserved sequence, is different in every strain. And the sequence, dear diary, is deeply weird.

As-you-know-Bob, DNA encodes information about the amino acid sequences of proteins in triplet codons made up from four bases, AGCT. Before the plague, scientists would do fun things like encoding *The Complete Works of Shakespeare* in DNA strands and making a million copies that could fit in a drop of water. Some codes imitate the genetic code — the codon AGA, for arginine, representing the letter A, and so on. Others were binary. The bases A and C might indicate zero; G and T one. And once you're into binary, you can code anything. Texts, pictures, memories, the ability to drive a car or use a gun . . .

Ralph and I were talking about conspiracy theories one day. He likes to collect them. The ideal hobby for a spy. We were making up a list of conspiracy theories about the plague, came up with more than fifty without straining ourselves. A good number involved some sinister organisation of mad scientists cooking up the HRV virus from scratch, or tweaking it to do other things. Like transfer skills and memories.

Later, in one of those idle moments that incubate inspiration, I wondered if the highly conserved sequence I'd discovered might contain a hidden text. A signature. It was the kind of thing scientists liked to do, in the good old days. Computer programmers hid Easter eggs in code; geneticists wrote their names into artificial genes. All of which is a long way of saying that one evening the Spook and I took a look at the sequence, and pretty soon had cracked it. Not that it was hard. People who like to sign their work usually do so in plain sight.

With A and C coding for zero, and G and T for 1, and applying the simplest substitution code, three names dropped out of that sequence. G H Benson. M R Michaels. B R R Swenson.

Someone had signed the mt virus, all right. But who were they, and what had they done? And why had they done it?

[**REDACTED**: printout of *A 412 Base Sequence Common to All MT Viral Strains*]

Our little gang argued about it for a couple of days, but all we could agree on was that 1) the payloads mt virus strains were genetically engineered and 2) we didn't have enough data to know why it had been done.

Military, Ralph said. Only the military would be crazy enough to think there'd be some kind of practical application for educating zombies. A rogue state, according to Joe, who had impeccable liberal credentials. Big business, according to

Chris L, who liked to read Gramsci and Wolff in his spare time. An endless supply of undead workers. Fleshbots. A prank that had gone badly wrong, Daisy C suggested. Which I rather liked, because it was just crazy enough to be true. Someone had played around with the virus, given it a new property, and it had spread and diversified through Darwinian selection out in the wild. Why not?

But we didn't know. Not then. And because we had other things to do, we committed the finding to one of our carrier pigeons and sent it off and forgot about it.

That was a month ago. We're still waiting for a reply. Maybe the return message was eaten by a hawk. Or maybe our comrades have already cracked the code. It wouldn't surprise me. It isn't hard to do.

Meanwhile, I have been churning out sequences of mt-strain virus, and Joe and his team have been testing the ability of their pet zombies to learn new tasks, run mazes, and pass on new skills. Because the more we know about our enemy the better. Because if Moreby was telling the truth, if there truly is a hierarchy of the dead, one King to rule them all, one King to bind them etc etc, then perhaps we can learn how to use the mt strain and behavioural conditioning to control them. To defeat death, and restore the normal order of things.

But there's no work today because there are too many dead at the gates, and we've quit our little toehold on land for the spurious safety of the floating tanks.

Damn. I wish Ralph was here. He'd organise us. He'd drive the pesky dead back into the dark under the trees. Meanwhile I can hear them, the lowing and groaning of them, floating out in the still blue night, and I think of the King, my King, watching as his subjects test and probe our fences and trenches and razor-wire barricades.

Dr Alison McReady's journal, 18/09:
OK. The Spook is now Officially Late. Off gallivanting somewhere no doubt, slaying dragons and saving wenches etc. But damn it, we need him here. I need him.

Sixty-five at the gates today. More or less. We each counted them three times and pooled our numbers and derived an average. And that's all the science we did today, because the dead are inside the fence, roaming amongst the labs and the generator hut. So far they haven't worked out how to pick padlocks or batter down doors. Suppose they do? Suppose some dead genius works out how to use a *boat*?

Dr Alison McReady's journal, 19/09:
Still no Spook. I could kill him. And then I
picture him dead and feel cold and small. He takes
too many risks. It's his nature and he'd good at
what he does and I love him for it, but he's
playing against the averages in a house where one
mistake, one little love bite or infected scratch,
takes everything from you.

Eighty-six at the gates and in the compound.
Maybe more. The King sits on the dock, watching
the farm. His subjects approach at intervals,
cringing and subdued, and the King bites them on
the arm or neck, or allows them to kiss him.
Strange to see some shambling corpse sidle up and
plant a smacker on his mouth. Joe said that
there's definitely a hierarchy of who-bites-who,
who-kisses-who. "You kiss up and bite down," he
said, grinning at his own joke.

Later:
We've had a meeting, agreed that we should move to
the island. Steve F suggested that we capture the
King and vivisect him: we could learn a lot, he
said, from examining the structure of his
bacterial "nervous system" and cargo of mt virus.
Chris L and Daisy C supported him, but Joe vetoed
it, said it would be too dangerous. We'll watch
and learn, he said.

Afterwards, I thanked Joe, said that for all we
knew the King was preventing the others from
swarming all over us.

"You think he's studying us?" Joe smiled.
"Watching, waiting, gathering an army . . ."

"I once talked to someone who thought the dead
were becoming posthuman. The next stage in human
evolution."

"Ah yes. Your old friend Moreby."

"He hadn't forgotten who he had once been," I said.

"And you think the old King across the water may
remember who he was, once upon a time."

"He spent all his life being groomed to become King. Some of that may remain. His subjects certainly seem to think so."

"He's their alpha male right now, but sooner or later a rival will come along and they'll fight, and the victor will drink the loser's blood and absorb his skills and — who knows? — perhaps something of his thoughts too. Who knows what your King has absorbed, how many he's killed . . ." Joe looked sombre for a moment, then smiled again. "The dead exchange skills, but they don't create anything new. And that's why we'll find a way of defeating them."

And now, dear diary, we're on the island. Shaken, but safe and sound. It's late in the evening, the sun is dipping down over the hills for its brief disappearance, gulls are circling the rocky fangs seaward, and something in one of the cages is crying out, a raw sound like a crow's death squawk, and from the hut Joe and his post docs use as an office there's the lovely sound of a cello sonata . . .

Dr Alison McReady's journal, 22/09:
I haven't spent much time on the island before. I admit a certain squeamishness. Using the dead as lab rats in behavioural experiments was a bit too close to Nazi-style vivisection for my taste, even though I knew it was necessary.

Now, I've walked all the way around it. It didn't take very long. It's small and steeply tilted and roughly triangular, with sea cliffs along its western edge where sea birds nest. No trees, only a few ruined stone walls and a roofless bothy where hardy shepherds once lived.

We're camped at the point of the triangle, near the old jetty. A little beyond are the cages where Joe keeps his zombie Einsteins and Newtons. Small square enclosures with double fences of wire mesh topped with razor-wire, razor-wire rolls sandwiched between. The dead have kennels to sleep in and straw to sleep on, and various toys scattered about, like gruesome kindergartens. One even has an iPad; she likes watching cartoons, and making a strange atonal music with a keyboard app. She's also covered in a shaggy pelt, so it's easy to think of her as a wise ape — until she looks up, and you see her drooling mouth, her red gaze. Joe and his post docs are trying to teach them to communicate using a symbolic language they have devised. They've had some success with simple concepts like food or water, bad (shock) and good (rabbit jerky), but so far abstract concepts like time or emotion have eluded the dead.

Theirs is a different kind of intelligence. Apparently, Moreby was an exception, the bridge between us and them. Between, he'd no doubt say, the past and the future. The other subjects, in the big enclosures, are tested with different strains of mt virus to see how the virus expresses as behaviour.

The rest of the island is untouched. Stony overgrown fields, steep slopes clad in heather and

bracken, hollows cupping little bogs of bright
green mosses and cotton grass and sundews, the
windy clifftop. I went up there the first day and
didn't come down for a long time. Scanning the sea
to the south-west for any sign of Ralph's boat.
He's way overdue now. I feel sick about it.

Later:
One hundred and thirty-eight plus or minus sixteen
in and around the compound we abandoned. Some come
and go, bringing food. Two were seen dragging a
sheep, caught who-knows-where. There have been
several instances of the weakest shamblers being
overwhelmed and ripped open and devoured. The King
watches all, his calm poached-egg gaze serene and
untroubled.

He is back! My spook is back!

Later:
Calmer but a bit less sober (we broached the
second-last bottle of Bowmore — delicious!). We
made love and it was good and sweet and tender,
and now Ralph is sleeping in the narrow bed inside
our tent and I'm awake and sitting just outside in
the blue dusk and writing this in the light of a
little torch strapped to my forehead.

He came back late in the afternoon, without
warning. Steve F spotted the little motor cruiser
as it came around the headland, and raised the
alarm. We were all waiting on the stone jetty as
the cruiser sidled in. There was a long scratch
down its port flank and two windows in its cabin
were starred with bullet holes, but Ralph was hale
and hearty, and so was his passenger.

Dr Eva Hipfl, Austrian, small and stocky and in
her mid-fifties, with a halo of curly blonde hair
and an abrupt manner. She shook hands with Joe,
took in the rest of us like a new headmistress
surveying her pupils and finding them wanting.
Ralph says that we should be easy on her because
she had a hard time.

The facility in which she was working — a former
agricultural research station, controlled by what
was left of the Scottish Government — was overrun.
Eva escaped because she happened to be working in
the allotments where she and her colleagues grew
fresh vegetables. She saw the zombies swarm along
the track to the place, heard shots and screams.
Saw two jeeps and a covered truck come in, saw
armed men round up the zombies, drive them like
cattle into the truck, saw them take away two
prisoners. She doesn't know where they were taken,
or who the attackers were.

Everyone else was killed — either torn apart by
the zombies or shot. The labs were smashed and set

on fire, but Eva knew where copies of the records were cached and buried her dead and headed towards Glasgow, which was where Ralph ran into her.

He'd been searching for chemicals, and after failing to find any in the Naval base in the Clyde (burnt out and overrun by the dead), he'd headed into the city, to check out Glasgow University, which turned out to be occupied by a gang of crazed survivalists who took him prisoner. They didn't do much more than threaten him, Ralph said. "Pathetic, really. Middle-aged men living out a fantasy in the wreckage of civilization." He managed to escape after five days, and when he was driving back to the boat in a stolen Range Rover Eva Hipfl had run into the road.

And here she was, with the records of her research and of her colleagues. It's mind-blowing stuff. Actually, I don't think that "mind-blowing" begins to cover it. We need better superlatives in this brave new world.

Eva and her colleagues had been working on the fleas, the red fleas which had infested Moreby's body. Most research had been carried out on the bacteria the fleas carried, and the HRV carried by the bacteria. The fleas had been dismissed, overlooked. Bad mistake, it turns out. Because while the fleas seemed no more than a tough variant of the common human flea, *Pulex irritans*, they were in fact nothing of the sort.

This is where it gets deeply weird. As if the world was not weird enough already.

It's common knowledge that the red fleas are hard to kill. They survived a couple of centuries entombed with Moreby's body, they can survive complete desiccation or exposure to vacuum, they're resistant to insecticides, poisons, high doses of alpha or gamma radiation and X-rays. Drop them in liquid nitrogen, thaw them out, and they're as perky as ever. Temperatures above 400 degrees Centigrade will kill them, as will prolonged exposure to ultraviolet light. Smash them with a hammer, grind them under the heel of your shoe, they're done. They aren't immortal. But they aren't fleas, either. They aren't even living organisms, in the ordinary sense.

"They are machines," Eva Hipfl told us. "Or rather, they are colonies of many tiny machines, each imitating a cell. To the casual observer they look exactly like fleas. But section them thinly and look at the stained sections with an electron microscope, and you see the hooks that rivet the 'cells' together, and the circuitry they contain, see that the muscles are not cellular at all but some kind of polymer, and so on. In short, they are robots constructed using nanotechnology far superior to anything we know."

She had images to back her up, and data on the composition and operation of what she called the mechanocytes, the machine cells. A ton of plausible detail, wonderful and mindcroggling. No, she did not know who had made them. No, she could not speculate on why they had been found on the body of a man who had died in the 19th century. Perhaps they had been planted, she said, just before the body had been disinterred. But by who, and why? Eva did not know and did not care to make a guess.

The bacteria were bacteria. The viruses, as I well knew, were viruses. Strange viruses, possibly manufactured or tweaked, but within the spectrum of the known. But this stuff about the fleas was off the charts. It overturned everything we thought we knew about Moreby, and the plague. Not only were they intricately crafted machines created by some kind of superior technology ("Martians", Joe said, and not one of us laughed), they were also a delivery system for a catastrophic plague. Someone had made them. Someone had loaded them with virus-carrying bacteria. Someone had set them loose in the world.

We talked late into the night, Ralph leaning on my shoulder. The warmth of him, the smell of him, the weight of him. All so reassuringly familiar, the one real point in a world completely and utterly changed.

I'd once read an article about SETI. The search for extraterrestrial intelligence. According to the author of the article, finding alien beings from a distant planet as intelligent as ourselves or more so would change everything. The simple fact of their existence would mean that we were not alone, that we were not freak accidents in an otherwise lifeless, uncaring universe. I had thought it portentous at the time, but now I know what he was getting at.

Everything has changed.

Dr Alison McReady's journal, 25/09:
We still have to feed and water the experimental
subjects, and make our own breakfasts. The zombies
are still milling around the compound and the King
is in his counting house, counting up his
subjects. More than three hundred now. Maybe three
hundred and fifty.

Eva did not like that at all. We should deal with
it or move, she said, because there would be more
and more of them, and we should not think our
little island was any protection.

"If they cut the floating platforms free, or
smash them up and cling to the wreckage, the tide
will bring them past the island. And it only takes
one to infiltrate. And then there is the screaming
and the running and the biting. I have seen this
too many times."

Also, we had actual zombies, some of them very
smart, for zombies, right here with us. What, she
wanted to know, were we thinking? Joe's work was
like training rats to do pointless tasks. Mine was
mere taxonomy.

"It is not time to play such games," she said.
"It is time to find and exploit an obvious
weakness. Now we know the fleas are nanotech life
forms, we can discover their vulnerabilities. And
we should also be trying to find out who made them.
No doubt the same people who fiddled with the mt
virus, and left their signature. Such arrogance
should not go unpunished. But we cannot do it here.
We must regroup."

And so on.

Ralph didn't help. He said that the revelation
about the fleas was too important to entrust to
pigeon post. It should be hand-delivered to our HQ
in the Lake District. And if one or two of us
went, the rest might as well come along. Safety in
numbers, and all that.

"We haven't finished our work here," Joe said.
"And we can't take the experimental subjects with
us."

"Zombies are hardly in short supply," Ralph said.

Cue outrage from just about everyone. Even I got cross with his flippant remark. Afterwards — after Eva had looked around and declared that she saw no discipline here, and stalked off, and after the meeting had broken up — I told Ralph that he even if he was right he should be more diplomatic.

He smiled. "Oho. So you think I'm right."

"The way things are going, I don't think we can stay here much longer. But it took Joe a long time to create those smart zombies. They are essential to his research. If he can't take them with him, he'll have to start from scratch."

"I don't mean to denigrate Joe's work. Or yours. But surely Eva's discovery has priority. Don't tell me you don't think it's interesting. I saw how all of you behaved when she passed those photos around. Like cats fighting over catnip."

"So you are taking her side."

"Alison . . . I'm trying to take everyone's side."

Ralph was exhausted by his expedition; I was angry with Eva, and struggling to understand the implications of her research. And, yes, scared too.

I went for a walk, up the slope to the cliffs at the seaward edge of the island, to let the wind blow through me and watch the uncaring seabirds skim the breakers at the foot of the cliff. Something was floating down there, amongst the black rocks. A body, tattered and naked. Some drowned zombie. It washed to and fro, arms and legs limp in the tide, and then a current caught it and whirled it away.

After a while, Ralph came up with some lunch — two random MREs and a wrinkled apple to share. We were running low on supplies. We had left a lot behind during our hasty evacuation.

"Five hundred and eighty now," he said. "A whole

new batch just arrived. Half of them are standing in the water. I was in India once. Saw the people bathing in the Ganges. Reminds me of that, a little."

He'd brought some of Eva's documents with him, suggested that we look through them together. A peace offering I gratefully accepted. But first we made up in our own way, in the grassy hollow above the void. Sea, sky, wind on bare skin, Ralph. Afterwards, I skim-read half-burnt documents, ash staining my hands, while he stretched out in the sun like a cat and fell asleep.

An hour later, I was shaking him awake. He woke all at once, asked me what was wrong.

"Nothing. Everything. Look at this."

I thrust the page I'd found into his face.

"You're trembling," he said, with a strange look.

"Read," I said.

He glanced at the page and said, "You'll have to explain. This science stuff is so much alphabet soup to me."

It was the last page of a technical discussion document on synthetic bacteria. I pointed to the important bit. The list of authors at the end. There were fifteen names. Amongst them were G.H. Benson, M.R. Michaels and B.R.R. Swenson, the names in the DNA cypher.

"This is an internal report," I said. "Which means everyone who wrote it worked for New World Pharmaceuticals."

We shared a look.

Ralph said, "They did it. New World Pharmaceuticals."

I said, "At least three of their scientists modified the virus. And they *signed* it."

Well of course we had another meeting. And this time it was Ralph and me against Eva Hipfl. We wanted to take the documents to the Lake District HQ; she wanted to take it to what was left of the

Scottish Government. They were closer, she said. They had better resources. It was her research, and the NWP document, that was hers too. And so on.

Joe, ever the diplomat, suggested a compromise.

"It's simple," he said. "Alison and Ralph will go to the Lake District. Alison, don't object. You can't work here and you need to promote your discovery. Dr Hipfl can go with you, or if she so chooses she can take the dinghy and attempt to find her way back to her people."

Eva objected at once. Joe waited until she had spluttered to a stop, and said that it was her choice to go where she wanted, and ours to go where we wanted. Very polite and very firm.

"The news is too important to entrust to any single person or organisation. So we'll spread it in two directions. Meanwhile, I will stay here and continue my work for as long as possible."

And that was that. I burned a copy of my research on a memory stick and gave it to Eva, and gave her samples of mt virus strains, so that her people could duplicate my work. We made hand-written copies of relevant documents from her cache, and she reluctantly surrendered several micrographs of the flea "cells".

It's well after midnight now. Ralph is asleep. I've reviewed everything I need to take, and now I'm finishing this entry. Maybe the last, until we reach the Lake District. I'm apprehensive and excited and angry. Excited by what I've found; appalled by its implications.

Brrr. Everything has changed.

[**REDACTED**: Handwritten copy of NWP confidential report 017110/036]

Dr Alison McReady's journal, 26/09:
Writing this in haste. Resting up before moving on.
  Everything has changed.
  We were woken around midnight by a clanging handbell. Ralph was up and out at once. I was still wondering what was going on when I heard the first shots.
  That got me out of there fast.
  The dead were halfway across the island by then. Blue shadows in the blue twilight. Some shambling or lurching, some moving fast, zig-zagging through the broad grassy passages between the cages and enclosures, colliding with each other, stumbling over rocks, bouncing off wire mesh fences. Some dressed in the white pyjamas worn by Joe's brights: the invaders had opened the cages. And all of them were coming down the slope towards our little camp while people shouted to each other and Chris L, who'd first spotted the invaders, swung the handbell up and down.
  No time to wonder how they'd reached the island, no time to do anything but grab my go bag and research files — but the files weren't where they should be, and I was still looking for them when Ralph grabbed me and hauled me out of the tent. Something loomed at us in the half-dark and Ralph's pistol went off with a sharp bang and the dead woman collapsed. Then we were running helter-skelter for the little stone jetty and the boats, leaping over the ditch, dodging through the chicane of barbed wire coils, out of breath, hearts hammering.
  One of the boats, the tough Zodiac inflatable, was already heading out to sea, making a long curve as it rounded the island. And when we did a quick head-count we came up one short. Eva was gone too. And I knew then where my files were.

I told Joe what had happened; he told me that his files were gone too, and shoved a thin sheaf of papers into my hands.

"She left the material on the fleas," he said. "You know what to do with it."

"You're coming with us."

"You and Ralph will make better speed without us. Don't worry. We'll catch up."

There was no time to argue. Ralph was kicking cans of petrol into the ditch. Coolly lighting one of his cigarillos, waiting as the dead pressed towards him, stepping back and tossing the cigarillo into the ditch.

The petrol exploded with a thump and a wall of blue flame boiled up. The dead screamed with one voice. Some were shoved into the flames by the press of those behind, and staggered forward, catching on barbed wire and thrashing as they burned.

As Ralph jogged towards us, someone yelled, there was a shotgun blast, and I saw something down and thrashing amongst waves breaking over the rocks by the jetty. Two more figures were clambering up out of the water. Ralph took aim and shot a skull-faced man draped in a shawl of seaweed; Steve F shotgunned the second.

We hustled for the boats. Burning zombies trying to crawl through the wire behind us, zombies rising from the waves to either side. I caught Ralph's arm, told him about Eva.

"We'll find her," he said with the calm certainty I've come to trust. Man says he's going to do something, he does it.

Joe and his post docs took to the motor cruiser, Ralph and I tipped into the dinghy. I yanked on the cord of the outboard as Ralph dispatched two more zombies, and then we were off, bouncing through the low swell, leaving the island and everything on it behind, heading towards the mouth of the loch.

I flashed on the body I'd seen floating in the surf, and shouted over the roar of the outboard. "They walked up out of the sea!"

"I know!"

"Maybe they walked all the way out here along the sea bed! Like that stupid pirate movie!"

"I know!"

"They can think! Make plans!"

"You can slow down now," Ralph said. "I don't think they can swim after us."

It took an effort to ease up on the trigger of the outboard's throttle. I was shaking with adrenaline.

We were motoring up the middle of the loch. Dark water, dark trees rising on either side.

"She could have made a run out to sea," he said. "I wonder why she came here."

"I'm wondering why she took my stuff, and Joe's, but left her papers behind."

"She's up to something, all right. Are you okay?"

"Nothing that a long session with Doctor Whisky won't fix."

"You'll do fine," he said, and spoke briefly into his walkie-talkie. I heard Joe's voice, felt a wash of relief: he and his postdocs were standing off the island. The dead were all over it and more were coming up out of the sea.

"We're going after the woman," Ralph told him. "See you in the Lakes."

We motored on, trawling along until Ralph pointed, told me to turn towards the shore. I saw a black shape on a white crescent of sand, the Zodiac, brought the dinghy in, and Ralph jumped out into the water and pulled it onto the little beach.

"I'll just check along the road," he said. "You can wait here."

"No way, mister. I've seen too many horror movies. We'll stick together."

We climbed up through pine trees and rocks, struck the forestry road that ran along a contour line at the edge of the steep slope up to the crest of the ridge.

We found the jeep almost at once. Two bodies splayed beside it, clawed and bitten, blood black in the moonlight.

"She had friends," Ralph said. "I thought so."

I understood. Maybe the adrenalin made my thoughts move more quickly. "She was an agent. She infiltrated us."

"I'm afraid so. She ran out into the road, asking for help, and I brought her back like the idiot I am," Ralph said.

"You thought you were doing the right thing."

"It wouldn't surprise me if she's involved with the nutcases who took me prisoner. I did think, when I made my escape, that it was ridiculously easy. One thing's certain: she wanted to know what we were doing. She stole your research, probably set the dead on us too."

"I think the dead have their own agenda. She was still learning about what we were doing. Maybe she hoped we'd take her to the Lake District, but then they attacked and she bailed." I paused, then said, "That story about the fleas. Maybe it was made up. Maybe all the documents and photos were made up . . ."

"Some of it was genuine," Ralph said. "The paper with the code that cracked your little DNA cypher, for instance. It could all be genuine, but perhaps it isn't her work. She found it somewhere, used it as part of her cover."

He had been searching the bodies. Now he rubbed his hands on the ground to wipe off the blood and straightened. "No ID on these chaps. If we want to find out who she's working for we'll have to catch up with her."

We didn't have to go far.

Eva Hipfl lay on her back at the edge of the road, in a splash of moonlight. Ripped from throat to navel, her face mostly gone. I took one look and turned away; Ralph stooped, picked up the document case and handed it to me.

At that moment, a figure moved out of the shadows under the trees.

It was the King. Shadows shifted behind him.

Chills snarled my spine. Ralph stepped in front of me, raised his pistol.

"Wait," I said. My mouth was so dry it was barely a moth-squeak.

The King was studying us. His face a pale blue in the moonlight. His eyes red sparks.

After a moment he turned his back on us and drifted away into the darkness under the trees. His retinue of shadows faded with him.

Ralph and I looked at each other, and ran for our boat.

It's days later now, and we're elsewhere. Forgive the vagueness. It's what Ralph would call security protocol.

We're resting up on a little island where the living have gone and the long-dead lie untouched in their graves. A bothy someone tarted up, mostly tastefully, into a holiday home. A cast iron stove, a good bed, rabbits to catch, potatoes to unearth in a garden gone wild, and shellfish and fish, of course, to take from the sea. There's a few other houses which might have canned goods in them, and a hamlet by the harbour to explore, but we won't be here that long, I think. Just long enough to make copies of this last little diary piece, and roll them inside bottles and cast them into the sea.

And then we'll be on our way to join our friends. To spread the news about what we've learned, and find a way of using it to end the spread of this fucking plague.

PS. I cannot prove it but like to think that the King remembered us. Remembered that we had let him go free. Perhaps even remembered (although he was unconscious the entire time) that I had tried to cure him of his death.

PPS. One thing is certain. The dead know more than we think.

This is the sixth copy of AM's diary entries found, this one a typewritten *samizdat* (Olivetti portable, Courier face, red ribbon much faded). Despite termination with extreme prejudice and records purge, deniability of the work of Benson, Michaels and Swenson is no longer assured. Suggest a programme of grey propaganda is implemented at once to undermine the reputation of AM. Also respectfully suggest more active searches for location of AM and her associate, and all other Human Resistance cells. The current belief that they are a minor inconvenience is, in my opinion, far too complacent. We will survive this only by taking immediate and extreme measures.

Eli E. Edwards, Chief Officer, External Security Operations (UK), New World Pharmaceuticals Group.

The thing about county roads, even way out in the back of beyond, is you can always find a strip-mall, and the thing about strip-malls is you can always find a Radio Shack, and the thing about strip-mall Radio Shacks is that what you can always find *there* is shit that everybody else stopped selling at least a decade ago.

Like the cute little fossil into which I'm currently speaking. It's a Digital Dictaphone. Says so right there on the box, along with the boast "Completely Tape-Free!" as if that was still a big selling point in the second decade of the twenty-first century.

The Digital Dictaphone is a pretty good example of the kind of crap nobody wanted even before there was an app that made it obsolete, but I guess it gets the last laugh now: It runs on batteries and doesn't need an Internet server to function. It's still what it always was but, like the only blonde left at the bar when they call Last Orders, all of a sudden it ain't so ugly.

The other thing about strip-mall Radio Shacks, or at least strip-mall Radio Shacks during the end of the world, is that the clerks have all either gone home, gone to Jesus, or gone to Hell. Nobody's minding the store. Nobody wants your money. You can help yourself to as many Digital Dictaphones as you want.

Oh, and–whether it's the end of the world or not the end of the world–the thing about strip-mall Radio Shacks in the *south* is you can pretty much count on there being a Guns 'n' Ammo Outlet right next door.

Time-Code Imprint: 08:34:54

Okay, I stopped and played that back to make sure
it's working—I mean, you know, Radio Shack—but it
seems to be fine.

I'm leaving this record of what happened not
because I think anybody else will care, and not
because I care what anybody else will think. I'm
just leaving it for you, Jess.

I'm going to see you at least one more time
before you get to hear this, but I can't be sure
what condition I'll be in by then so—while I can
still think clearly and talk straight, while I'm
still *me*—I want you to know that I love you and
that I spent this day coming to get you back.

I'm shutting this thing off again for a while.
Gotta go steal a faster car.

Time-Code Imprint: 10:11:37

Here's what's happened before I hit the road and
found the Radio Shack:

I woke up about four, four-and-a-half, hours ago
and had no idea where I was.

Well, that's stupid. I knew where I *was*. I could
see where I was. I was in some back alley
somewhere. What I mean is I had no memory of why I
was there or what had happened. That was a bad
feeling.

And then the memories flooded in.

And that was so much fucking worse.

Because I remembered that you were gone, Jess. I
remembered that they'd taken you and that I hadn't
been able to stop them. I don't know if they'd
been stalking us, targeting us specifically, or if
we just won the worst place worst time lottery,
but either way we didn't see them coming. *We*.
Jesus Christ, what's wrong with me? You're fifteen

years old. It's not your job to see anything coming. *I* didn't see them coming. Not until it was too late and I was on my back with a monster's teeth buried in my arm and you were being dragged into the shadows . . .

Yeah. Those were the morning headlines, Denny O'Brian edition.

My daughter was gone.

And I had less than twenty-four hours before I turned into a zombie.

So I figured it was probably best to skip breakfast.

Time-Code Imprint: 10:47:15

A lot of people who'd never seen a gun, let alone used one, had to get familiar with them real quick once this shit started going down.

And the thing is, people didn't just need to get used to shooting guns, they needed to get used to shooting them accurately. Zombies don't share the finer feelings of muggers, stalkers, or burglars. They don't have a fight or flight response. You're not going to scare them with a near miss or a warning shot and you're not going to stop them even if you blow a hole in their chest. With zombies, you have to pay a little attention. You have to shoot them in the head.

So, if you were one of those people who didn't previously know how to point a gun so that the bullet went where you wanted it to go, then you had to develop a certain degree of skill and had to develop it fast. The ones who didn't develop it fast were soon finding themselves getting shot in the head by the ones who did.

Now, as it happens, I'm not one of those people who needed to learn how to shoot straight but, ironically enough, putting the bullet exactly where you want it isn't going to be that big of an issue when it comes to today's little adventure.

Zombies, you have to shoot in the head. Humans are easier. You can shoot *them* anywhere the fuck you want.

Time-Code: 11:32:43

You're going to hear this, Jess. After whatever goes down goes down, I'm going to make sure somebody gets it to you.

Here's what I want you to know, what I hope you already know:

Your father loves you. Always has. Always will.

But you'll have to accept that by the time you hear this, I'm not going to be around anymore. There's going to be a thing shambling around tomorrow that's going to *look* like me. But it won't be me, Jess. I'll already be gone. So if it ever crosses your path and if—or, please God, *when*—somebody shoots it in the head, you are not going to be upset. You, Jessica Judith O'Brian, are going to be cool. Because you're my girl. You're gonna shrug at whoever's with you and say, "Dude, that last zombie kinda looked like my old man. Weird." And then you're going to raise your own gun and you're going to keep shooting.

So that's what you know.

Here's what *they* know, those lunatic survivalist motherfuckers who took you from me:

One: They've captured themselves a beautiful piece of breeding stock. That's you, sweetheart, in case your new friends are trying to put a prettier face on the situation and not tell you how things really are.

Two: Nobody's going to do a goddam thing about it, because the last person left in the world who gave a shit about you was your dumb asshole of a father and . . .

Three: They left your dumb asshole of a father in the dust after they'd sucker-punched him in that alley and banged the dinner gong for a zombie the size of LeBron fucking James to come finish him off.

Yeah. That's what they know. Here's what they *don't* know:

One: LeBron might've gotten a pretty good chunk out of my left arm but, before I passed out, LeBron also got a railroad spike through his forehead.

Two: Tomorrow morning won't be the first time I'm going to wake up as a different person.

Honey, I probably should have mentioned this before, but your Dad hasn't always been an insurance salesman.

You always knew me and your Mom only moved to the south a year or so before you were born, Jess—I mean, how could you not, with the accent and everything?—but I guess we never made it clear to you that the move was . . . how shall I put it? . . . government assisted. And it wasn't your Mom—God rest her soul, six years now, can you believe it?—who was in need of relocation.

Look, there's a bunch of stuff I did back in my former life that I'm not proud of, sweetheart, but at least it means that today isn't the first time I've had to track people down in order to take an unfinished conversation to the next level.

And with these guys, it's not like tracking them is going to be difficult.

First of all, they think I'm dead.

Second, they ain't fucking hiding. Not from me or anybody.

So about two hours ago I'm in another abandoned convenience store, this one a KWIK-SHOP. Didn't even realize the franchise was state-wide, thought it was strictly local.

Remember it, Jess? The name, I mean. Remember how even *before* the world went to hell I used to find that name really depressing? A mash-up—no, not a mash-up, that would imply artistic intent—a lazy rip-off of two of its rivals, KWIK-PIK and STOP'N'SHOP. Which, Christ knows, were bad enough, but look: KWIK-PIK; okay, it's stupid and cutesy and apparently proud of its inability to spell but at least it fucking rhymes. STOP'N'SHOP, the same.

But KWIK-SHOP. Jesus. Such a lack of effort. Like it's not even worth pretending to try. The franchise name equivalent of going out for lunch in your pajama bottoms and Crocs. So yeah, depressing enough then. But *now*. Now it looks like the kind of precursor we all should've been paying attention to. *Check it out*, it says in its gleeful brain-dead way. *We were zombies already*.

Anyway, I'm in there, I've already thrown some batteries in my pockets, and I'm chewing on some string cheese, trying to persuade my body to pretend it still gets hungry, when I hear the shotgun cock behind me.

I put both my hands out to the side slowly, fingers spread. "Can I turn around?" I say.

"It's *may* I," a voice says.

Female, and just free enough of spin that I really can't tell where she was coming from with that schoolmarm correction. Like, is she being funny or is it truly her first concern when she's got the drop on someone that they watch their fucking grammar?

"I'm sorry," I say. "May I turn around?"

"Long as it's slow and easy."

So I make sure it was and, once I'm facing her, I risk an apologetic smile.

"I really thought there was no one here," I say. "If money's still any use to you, I've still got money." I've also still got my hands up, but I waggle a finger to point down at my pants pocket.

She's somewhere in her forties, running to fat, but she gives great deadpan and she's holding that shotgun like she and it are far from strangers.

"What else you got in that pocket?" she says.

"I'm not gonna lie to you," I say. "I have three handguns on me right now, two in back of my belt, one in a sock-holster. But that pocket, just a billfold, I promise."

She nods toward the front window, at the car I parked outside, but her eyes stay on me.

"Just handguns?" she says.

"No, Ma'am," I say. "Shotguns and semi-automatics in the trunk."

"Huh," she says. "Loaded for bear."

"Something like that," I say, and then, off her silence, "It's my daughter. She's in trouble."

She nods her head at me, still no expression. "You don't look so good yourself," she says.

Making no fast moves, I roll back my left sleeve and show her my arm, no point in pretending. The infection is radiating out eagerly from the wound now, got the run of the whole forearm and half the bicep. The bite itself, by this stage, doesn't look so bad. Which is, of course, very very bad. The necrosis is complete, ready for its mutation and its next life.

She's like, "How long?" and I tell her the truth, probably got fifteen, sixteen hours left.

She nods. "Come back here after those sixteen hours, and I won't waste time asking how you're doing," she says, and then she cocks the shotgun in case the sympathetic delicacy of her phrasing caused me to miss her point.

I nod, letting her know I understand. Can't hold it against her. It's just the way the world is now.

"So you say your daughter's in trouble," she says. "She bit too?"

"No," I say. "Taken."

"Taken?"

"Survivalists, I guess."

"Preppers, they been calling themselves the last few years," she says. "You know, from 'prepared'? Didn't want to be caught with their pants down at the end of the world. Always thought they were mental cases. Pisses me off that it turns out they were right. Wasn't quite the apocalypse they were expecting, of course, but I guess they'll settle."

"These particular guys had a whole Christian thing going on, too," I say, remembering their stupid flag and the painted sign on their truck. "Called themselves the Children of the New Jerusalem."

She doesn't actually bite her tongue—like anybody actually bites their tongue, ridiculous fucking expression—but I can tell from the tiny flicker of sympathy in her eyes that what she's stopping herself from saying is that it might have been better for you if you *had* been bitten.

"You know them," I say.

"Not socially," she says, and I still can't tell if what she's got is a nice line in very dry delivery or a simple case of tone-deaf and stupid.

"But you know where they are."

"I can point you in their direction," she says. "But I wouldn't advise you go there."

"They have my daughter."

"Uh-huh," she says, like that information's not new so why am I repeating it.

"You got any kids?" I say.

"Two boys," she says. "Both gone now."

And I'm like, "Zombies? Or with *them*?" I found a gentler way to say it, actually, but I can't remember what it was.

She shrugs, says, "What's the difference between a zombie and a Child of New Jerusalem?"

"Seriously?" I say. She's like telling a *joke* here? Man, she had that stay-detached thing down pat. We could've used this lady back in Brooklyn.

"One's a mindless shell that used to be a human being," she says, "And the other one's a zombie."

Not a good joke, but I give her a nod and a half-smile. She gives it a beat, and then half-lowers the shotgun.

"Help yourself to anything you need," she says, "and then be on your way."

Time-Code: 18:28:47

This'll be the last update before I see you, Jess. I'm inside the Compound right now, less than a half-mile from the main house.

Like I'd thought, Brother Zebulon—the KWIK-SHOP lady gave me his name—isn't much on hiding. Isn't much on fortification, either, though I guess he and his Children of the New Jerusalem figure that unless and until the zombies learn to use tools the razor wire and log-buttress perimeter fence is going to keep their party private.

Now I, of course, *do* know how to use tools, so the fence didn't bother me. It wasn't meant to bother me. What was meant to bother me, or any other inquisitive human, was the *Duck Dynasty* wannabes patrolling the inside of the perimeter. But the thing about armed guards—particularly the amateur type, and particularly the *God is on our side so He'll pick up the slack* type—is that, with a little patience, you'll eventually locate the jack-off ones.

I got here about a half-hour ago and it took me twenty minutes to find my jack-offs. There were two of them, and they'd paused in their patrol duties long enough to indulge in what must pass for sport for these sons of the Confederacy when it's Off Season for Deer.

Somehow, they'd lured a dozen or so zombies to the razor-wire and got them nicely tangled in it. And now they were taking their sweet time shooting chunks off them.

One of them, the one with a rifle, was lying on his belly like he'd seen real soldiers do in basic training in the movies, and the other was just sitting up by a tree, back against the trunk, and blasting away with a handgun.

"Hardly seems sporting, fellas," I said.

Yeah, I'd got close enough to them to talk at a conversational level without them hearing or sensing me beforehand. This did not say good things about their life expectancy in this changed world.

For one of them, the handgun one, bluster, as usual, was the way out of embarrassed surprise. He's all, "What the hell's it to *you*?" pretending he hadn't half-jumped out his skin at the sound of my voice.

The other one didn't flinch, didn't jump, and doesn't crack wise. He just looks at me. More significantly, he looks past and around me, taking measure, making sure. Okay, I think, him I might have to keep an eye on.

"It's nothing to me," I say in answer to Handgun's question. "Nothing at all."

"What do you want?" says the other one. Smarter. Focused.

"I want you to tell me how to get into the main house," I say.

"You think there's some kinda *password*?" says Handgun. "Like what?"

"I wouldn't know," I say, giving him a shrug like I've no idea but I'm willing to take a shot at it. "*Praise the Lord and Pass the Ammunition*?

Or some other stupid shit that mashes up Jesus and guns?"

"Is he trying to insult us, Garrett?" says Handgun. "You think he's trying to insult us?"

Garrett doesn't say anything. Keeps his eye on me, still not sure where this is going.

Handgun's on a roll, though. "I think he's goddam insulting us," he says, and then, directly to me, "You looking to get killed, brother?"

"Already dead, brother," I say, and hold my left forearm forward to let him and Garrett see the splendors of its blue and transmutating flesh.

"Holy shit!" Handgun shouts, "He's one of them!"

He starts to raise his gun. Garrett's quicker, of course, but neither of them are fast enough. The two from the back of my belt are already head-height, one pointed straight at each of them.

Hashtag, never got rusty.

"Whoa," I say, off their stunned expressions. "It's like *magic*." Bragging is unseemly, Jess, and you should try not to develop the habit. But sometimes—especially when dealing with douchebags—you just have to rub it in.

I look at Handgun. "I'm not one of them," I say. "Not yet. Don't you even know how this shit *works*?"

"I know it's the Lord's judgment on a sinful world," he says.

"Yeah?" I say. "That what Zebulon tells you?"

"*Brother* Zebulon," says Garrett, and the sour tone of his correction makes me kind of sad because I realize Garrett is a True Believer too and I'd been hoping he was a little smarter than that. A smart soldier knows when to stand down. A True Believer will die for his leader. I can't take the risk of that happening when his willingness to die might matter so I cut to the chase and shoot him. One. Two. Head. Heart.

It was quick and he didn't suffer, and Handgun sees that that's all I got in the way of mercy.

"Christ almighty!" he shouts, and drops his gun without even being asked.

"Let me ask you something," I say. "You think the Lord protects His own?"

He doesn't want to answer, thinks it's a trick question, but eventually gives a guarded and frightened nod.

"Let's find out," I say. "Go cut the fence."

"*There?*" he says, pointing to the zombies he's recently been having fun with and looking at me like I'm fucking crazy.

"There," I say.

"You want me to let them in?"

"I want you to let them in."

"What am I supposed to do then?" he says.

"You're supposed to run, asshole," I say. "You're supposed to run."

Thing is, *he* runs—like he needed telling twice—but I don't. I stand there, letting those things shuffle up toward me and hoping to Christ that I've figured this right.

My smell confuses them. I'm getting pale enough that I sort of look like them, but I don't *smell* like them. Not quite. Not yet. Fortunately for me, I don't smell like food anymore either.

One of them growls at me and shakes its head aggressively, but it's nothing. An animal thing. Territorial. Alpha-male jostling.

Other than that, it's pretty clear pretty quickly that they'd be prepared to leave me alone. But that's not what I want.

Time-Code Imprint: 04:22:17

The thing about Witness Protection is, before they give you the new Drivers' License, Social Security, and everything, before they drive you to your new house in your new state and tell you your new name, you do have to go through the embarrassment of actually sitting in court and presenting the testimony for which they're giving you that shiny new identity.

Which means all the defense attorneys of all your former colleagues get to call you all kinds of names.

One of them, for example, in an attempt to persuade a jury that they should perhaps take everything I had to say with a pinch of salt, pointed out that I was "a merciless killing machine, with no feelings, no remorse, and no humanity," which was not only way melodramatic but a bit fucking rich given the murderous scumbag of a client he was representing. But the point is this: Couple of short hours from now, I'm finally going to be what that little drama queen said I was.

So if I believed in karma, or poetic justice, or anything, I'd be able to draw a moral lesson here for us. But I'm not going to do that. I'm just going to give tomorrow's me a name. Like The Wrath of God. Or He Who Lays Waste.

Or Harry.

I've always liked the name Harry. Well out of fashion now, of course. But I have a feeling Harry's not gonna give two shits about fashion. Gonna be too fucking busy Laying Waste, isn't he?

I'd wondered if I'd catch Brother Zebulon mid-sermon or something, but by the time I walk right into the Great Room of the main house, he and all his Dukes and Duchesses of Hazzard are just hanging around drinking cold ones, like it was any other redneck jamboree.

Couple of his boys, drunk or not, have their guns up fast, so I'll have to give them that. Zebulon himself, though, waves them down, like he's actually kind of interested that I've managed to show up.

"Do I have some sentries to chastise?" he asks me, in a slow and frankly over-stylized drawl, but at least it jumps us past all that *how'd you get in here* shit.

"They're in no position to notice," I say.

"Then, sir, you have not only my gratitude for thinning my flock of those clearly unworthy to be in it—"

"Amen!" comes a knee-jerk interruption from some Gomer Pyle dickhead, which Brother Z doesn't even acknowledge.

"—but also my admiration for the courage it must have taken for you to come here on your own."

"Oh, I wasn't on my own," I say.

I whip out the guns, take out the two or three who look like they could do anything about it and then grab a moment to watch and enjoy.

Because that's when the doors and windows give way and Harry's future tribe-members join the party and all those Jeds, Jethros, and Ellie fucking Maes realize their God has abandoned them.

Hashtag, worst posse ever.

Here's what happened, Jess. When I found you in that back room and realized you were alive and that I was going to get you out of there, I felt the last good feeling of my life, an overwhelming rush of love, the thing I'm going to choose to remember when I close my eyes for the last time a few moments from now.

You're not with me now, of course. I left you with the people inside the safety zone the KWIK-SHOP lady told me about. They seem like decent people. So decent they were prepared to let me stay, too. Provided I let them chain me up so that I could die in peace among my own kind and they'd have a sharpshooter ready to end it once I woke up. But I said no. Partly because I don't want you seeing any of those last moments.

And partly because I owe Harry. The imminence of his arrival is what allowed me to walk among his

kind and save you. So I'm choosing to wake up
somewhere back where Harry can have whatever
passes for a life.

There's a third reason, too. But I'll get to
that in a moment . . .

I'm pretty much done now, Sweetheart. Next time I
close my eyes, it'll be the last time. So I'm
going to say goodbye and tell you again that I
love you and that that's all I want you to
remember. Then I'm going to turn this thing off
and hide it somewhere to keep it safe until
someone finds it and gets it to you.

Then I'm going to take a moment, not a long one,
to remind myself that my last day on Earth wasn't
entirely a bad one, that the parts that *were* bad—you
getting taken, me getting bitten—weren't my fault,
and that I managed to put right what I could.

Then I'm going to settle back down and not fight
it anymore. My limbs are going to numb up, my
tongue's going to stop working, I'm going to lose
consciousness, and I'm going to die.

I'm so glad you're not here to see it.

I'm so glad Brother Zebulon is.

You've probably been noticing those annoying
noises in the background, right? Scrabbling feet?
Whimpering? You weren't the only one I brought out
of the Zombie Jamboree with me, Jess.

Brother Zebulon is here in the barn with me,
just the two of us. He's tied up pretty good, and
probably more than a little scared right now. It
has, after all, become clear to him in the last
few hours that your dad's got quite a fucking
temper on him. But he shouldn't feel too bad. I'm
not going to lay a finger on him.

I'm just going to lie down here and die.

And then Harry's going to wake up.

And then Harry and Brother Zebulon are going to
investigate the possibilities of breakfast.

VERSION HISTORY
1.0 — First NZO release

AppEtizers

Formerly "WethaCrowd"/"WethaZ"
Copyright © New World Techology Group,
a wholly-owned subsidiary of New World
Pharmaceuticals Group

APP DESCRIPTION

Okay so fucking sue me. I re-used someone else's code again. They're dead. Who cares.

And also, I did the math. The survival math, which is the only kind that adds up to shit in these dark days. Do I spend the rest of my life starving to the point where when some Z finally gets me I'm no more than a fucking *snack*, or do I get with the program? Zeke's mom, god rest her soul, raised no fools.

Program? Meet Zeke.

You don't like it? Screw you. You're probably dead.

I'm not.

I just found a new client base. Follow the emerging markets, right? Ha ha.

So I repurposed the app one more time, and now there are read-outs for:

• Single human sighted
• Human group sighted
• Fortified human group

Enjoy the eats, my new friends. Clicks are uploaded and collated, and updates to the map in the app happen in real time.

And I have access to reliable servers now, so this baby's going to run and run. Like you assholes out there. *You* can run, too.

But you can't hide any more

Zeke @ New Zombie Order

[Vlog Entry 001: Sergeant Rochelle "Rocky" LaFortune]

[Excerpt A from US Army Informational Video "Project Warrior":]

Video of very active ants, all together, then traveling through rainforest

Female Voiceover:
"'Army ant' is in fact an umbrella term covering more than two hundred species of *Formicidae* known for what entomologists call 'legionnaire behavior'—that is, particularly aggressive predation. Army ant colonies do not construct permanent nests. They are stationary only for as long as it takes the eggs laid by the queen to hatch—two to three weeks. Then they're on the move again.

"Army ants are diurnal. The few nocturnal species haven't been studied—"

[Sharp cut to:]
Video: several ants running frantically about in a large round-covered glass dish

Voiceover (cont.):
"—workers you see here, sterile females, are blind, although in some other species the workers have very simple eyes with one lens—"

[Sharp cut to:]
Video: ants swarming along the floor of a rainforest; it's like a river of living ant bodies; they swarm over a small frog and kill it

Voiceover (cont.):
"—hunt in a single group that, while lacking anything like a leader, is totally cooperative. Together, they locate the prey and then simply overwhelm it."

Voice 01 [male, far from microphone but still audible]:
"Damn, sterile females are freakin' dangerous!"

[Laughter, male and female voices tell him to shut up, screw himself, etc.]

Voice 01 (cont.):
"Hey, it's not me, it's *Mother Nature!*"

Voice 02 [female]:
"That's *Ms* Mother Nature to you, asshat!"

[Louder laughter; even Voiceover is trying not to laugh]

Voiceover (cont.):
"All right, if we could please get back to—"

> *[Sharp cut to:]*
> Video: split screen; on the left, people watch behind glass as ants scurry about in a brightly lit area. On the right side of the screen is a room divided into three areas by two unbreakable transparent partitions that allow air-flow. In the center part, a zombie tries to get at a live human being on the left side, but ignores the figure in the space on the right. The third figure looks like another zombie but is then revealed as a living person covered in zombie parts.

Voiceover (cont.):
"—ants recognize each other by the profile of cuticular hydrocarbons, or CHCs in their pheromones—"

Voiceover (cont.):
"—purpose of existence is to attack other animals—"

> *[Sharp cut to:]*
> Video: split screen again; on the left, army ants are traveling through a rainforest; on the right, a montage of zombie behavior, all recorded from a helicopter—some shambling, some running fast, all pursuing people running from them; the last segment of the montage shows the helicopter circling a tall radio tower while zombies climb it, desperate to get at the live people; the zombies use their bodies to make the tower higher; they keep climbing on top of each other; at one point the top becomes unstable and comes apart, with zombies falling to the ground, but not all of them; zombies keep climbing. We see that even more zombies are climbing up on all sides of the tower, making it wider as well as taller, so it's more stable; if the helicopter continued to circle at the same level, the zombie tower would eventually reach it. People in the helicopter start shooting at the zombies; someone fires a rocket at the tower, destroying it. Bodies and parts of bodies, some on fire, fly in every direction but zombies are still climbing up from below, or trying to, as if completely oblivious to what has happened above them.

Voiceover (cont.) [but her tone is less professional and a bit more hesitant, as if she doesn't really want to talk about this]:
"—wide and over a hundred meters long. One colony can consume anywhere up to half a million prey animals per day. Although even the

most voracious species do not eat *every* animal, any small vertebrates caught in their raids *will* be killed. Of the species that hunt above ground, only a few are tree-climbers that attack birds—"

[Sharp cut to:]
Video: montage of zombies, all aerial POV; the last and longest sequence shows zombies climbing piles of zombie bodies on the outside of a building to get at the live people on the roof who are frantically signaling for help. The helicopter drops down for a landing. All the people get on just as the zombies reach the roof and run toward them. One zombie actually boosts itself up on the other zombies, jumping off their shoulders almost high enough to grab onto the helicopter. The helicopter veers off quickly.

Voiceover (cont.) [sounds even unhappier]:
"—column raid, where the members branch off on either side to forage, and the swarm attack, which is . . . uh, just what it sounds like.
"Because they're voracious nomads, it's impossible to keep army ants in the limited, controlled environment of a terrarium. Within a few days, the colony dies. It dies and that's all.
"Unlike our species."

[Vlog Entry 002: Sergeant Rochelle "Rocky" LaFortune]

Sgt. LaFortune:
"End of the first day. I did one hundred miles on a single charge but I'm ten miles short of a charging station. I hate to leave the Yamaha but I don't see myself walking it that far and I don't have the right tools to remove the battery even if I wanted to make a twenty-mile round-trip. So either I continue on foot or appropriate civilian transport. Seeing as how I'm UA, that would be theft under normal circumstances. Under martial law, it's looting and I could be shot, even if I'm unarmed. Even if I surrender.
"I *hate* the fucking Army.
"Things in my favor: no one knows where I'm going and I've disabled the GPS on the bike, and any location utilities in my electronics, including my iPad. *[pause]* It's not the Army's, it's *my* iPad. Mine. *[pause]* Another thing in my favor: I'm a crisis recruit—I was granted safe harbor in return for military service according to my ability and aptitudes, blah, blah, blah. After the failed attempt to take back the White House, the desertion rate

for CRs is a lot higher than for regular recruits. Army policy is not to actively pursue CRs, unless they're in possession of classified intelligence or materials. *[pause]* Or if you steal heavy artillery, like a rocket launcher or a tank. Then you better believe they'll come after you. "I'm pretty sure they'll write me off as just one more CR who got tired of saluting as soon as she got a full belly and decided to look around for a nice shopping mall to hide out in till the world comes back."

Jag attorney Lieutenant Franklin Kwame Agbesi, defense counsel:
"But they didn't just write you off, did they, Sergeant LaFortune?"

Sgt. LaFortune [softly]:
"No."

Judge Javeria Kashiray-O'Toole:
"You need to speak up for the record, sergeant."

Sgt. LaFortune [clears throat, speaks louder]:
"No. They didn't."

Prosecuting Attorney Lt. Ailicia Soledad Sposito:
"Does defense counsel *really* have to go over testimony already in the record? I suggest that if he needs to refresh his memory, he should review court transcripts—"

Lt. Agbesi:
"Your Honor, I'm only verifying—"

Judge [sighing a little]:
"Let's just move it along, counselors, time is not on our side. *[more to herself]* Time is *never* on our side."

Lt. Agbesi:
"But it turned out your CO had a very good idea where you would be going, isn't that so, sergeant? Why was that?"

Sgt. LaFortune:
"Marsh told her. Corporal Marshall Jackson, I mean. He told Captain Sotomayor I was going north to Fathom Five Marine Park in Canada. To Flowerpot Island."

Lt. Agbesi:
"Why? What were you hoping to find there?"
Sgt. LaFortune:
"Not what—*who*. My wife. Private Jolene Amanda Lindbloom."

Lt. Agbesi:

"Your wife, whose last known location was Manhattan. But Manhattan was nuked. As the spouse of a soldier on active duty, you yourself were evacuated beforehand by the military. Later, you discovered material uploaded to the Cloud by Private Lindbloom and time-stamped just before the bombing—a time that would indicate there was no chance that Private Lindbloom could have escaped alive. Isn't that so?"

Sgt. LaFortune:

"Manhattan has—uh, *had*—an extensive subterranean transit system. It's not impossible that Jolene—Private Lindbloom—could have been far enough underground to escape the worst of the blast."

Lt. Agbesi:

"Scans performed after the bombing indicate a lot of the tunnel system was destroyed. Wouldn't any people in them be buried under tons of rubble?"

Sgt. LaFortune:

"Those scans aren't all that reliable—they were done from the air, not at ground level."

Lt. Agbesi:

"Whether Private Lindbloom survived or not, she would most likely be in or near Manhattan, wouldn't she? What in the world made you think she was on Flowerpot Island?"

Sgt. LaFortune:

"I saw her. In a video."

[Vlog Entry 003: Sergeant Rochelle "Rocky" LaFortune]

Sgt. LaFortune:

"Dumb luck blessed me today. I spotted a reefer north-bound with an escort. Both truck and escort were designated as medical supplies and personnel. My ass. If that tractor-trailer wasn't full of corpsicles, it soon will be. It's not like there's a shortage."

[Cut to:]
Video: pan of abandoned suburban area in total ruins. Houses have burned or been partially destroyed by explosions, cars wrecked in the streets. Lawns and yards have been torn up by explosives and military tanks, fences knocked down. Here and there, kids' toys and bicycles lie where they were dropped; some are crushed. Likewise gardening tools; a lot of these are crusted with dried flesh, blood, guts.

Sgt. LaFortune:
"Here we are in *Leave It To Beaver*-ville, the day *after* the day after the apocalypse. No coming back from *that* block party. I shot this with my OTR cam. I couldn't knock out the GPS so I fiddled with the latitude and longitude settings and now my little On the Record (OTR) camera thinks it's in western Kansas. I shoulda just thrown it away or stomped it into pieces but . . . I dunno, I just couldn't. I don't consider myself on duty, I don't even consider myself a soldier any more—I'm not sure I ever really did. But I'm a witness, and this is what I saw. I'm encrypting copies and stashing them here and there in the Cloud. Maybe enough copies will survive so that someday in the future, if whoever's in charge tries to whitewash or airbrush or re-write history, one of these files will always pop up with the truth. I'm a witness. This is what I saw. *[silence, then burst of laughter]* Shit, am I a cock-eyed optimist or what? History is written by the winners—history's always written by the winners. But this time, there aren't any."

[Cut to:]
Video: what was once a military roadblock on a four-lane divided highway. Abandoned vehicles were used to block the road but something big and powerful burst through each side from opposite directions—perhaps the bus lying on its side a hundred feet or so away. Trash is strewn all over from garbage bags clawed open by wild animals. POV moves forward and walks along the barrier; the camera is apparently clipped to the front of LaFortune's shirt.

Sgt. LaFortune:
"It might look like somebody ran this roadblock—well, they did. But probably because there was nobody here to let them through or turn them back. There aren't any bullet-holes or shells—there was no firefight, no struggle. Nothing happened here. The soldiers just . . . left.
"Okay, it's possible they were deployed elsewhere and there just wasn't anyone to take their place. But I don't think so. If there weren't enough soldiers to man—or woman, ha, ha—all the roadblocks, Command would have re-arranged personnel to cover the most crucial routes. But we'd have heard about that at HQ before I left—hell, I'd probably have drawn

one of those assignments. But in the last week or so before I left, we weren't getting much news even about troop movements. Maybe because after the first counterattack on the White House people were just taking off and that's not something they'd want getting out. Desertion could be as contagious as zombie flu."

Video: LaFortune's hand rises to cover her mouth briefly, as if suppressing laughter, or possibly tears.

Sgt. LaFortune:
"Zombie flu. Jesus wept. *[pauses; clears throat]* I haven't heard a lot of chatter on the radio, at least not on the frequencies I can get. A few coded messages every so often, and I don't think most of it's military—official military, that is. I think survivors are banding together and hunkering down. That's what I'd do. Except I've got a hot date on Flowerpot Island and I'm running late.
"Anyway, this is the third roadblock like this I've seen in as many days. Where did they go? Probably found some survivors to band together with. I guess they got real good at camouflage because I haven't seen anyone since I left Washington HQ.
"But then, I was trying to keep out of sight myself at the start. I only came across some old campsites, all days old, whoever'd been there long gone. A couple of times I got to the outskirts of a town and saw smoke rising from a chimney. That's what we in the military call 'zombie bait'. I gave those places a real wide berth, miles and miles of berth.
"Now, you'd think zombies would want to stay away from fire, seeing as how they burn like friggin' candles. Instead, it's like a dinner bell. Living people make fire, they eat living people, so where there's smoke, there's food.
"Not that I'm saying that all of them actually reason. It's like a zombie instinct or something."

 [Vlog Entry 004: Sergeant Rochelle "Rocky" LaFortune]

[Cut to:]
Video: outdoors in a wooded area. Seven or eight zombies are stumbling around the trees, falling over underbrush; the scene is almost comical.

Male Voiceover:
"At a distance of one mile, there is no response." *[pause]*

> *[Cut to:]*
> *Video: the zombies continue to stumble around in no particular direction, although none of them wanders out of sight of the group.*

Voiceover (con't):
"At half a mile—"

> *[Cut to:]*
> Video: abruptly, all the zombies perk up, look to the left side of the screen and then start running in that direction. The POV switches to an aerial view twenty feet overhead; it tracks the zombies as they fight their way through the forest; some tear through thorn-bushes, leaving chunks of rotting flesh behind, others bump into trees, bounce off, keep going. Somehow they manage to travel together.

Voiceover (cont.):
"This was their response to one of our technicians lighting a cigarette half a mile away."

> *[Cut to:]*
> Video: the group changes direction slightly, veering off on a diagonal.

Voiceover (cont.):
"Mr. Jackson has put out the cigarette and is now moving rapidly away from the original location, yet the group are still able to detect him."

> *[Cut to:]*
> Video: the zombies become even more frenzied but at the same time, they seem to be arranging themselves in a formation—they start to fan out, as if in preparation to surround and overwhelm their prey. They erupt into a small, empty clearing and suddenly the assault is over. The zombies go from frenzied to milling around. They are obviously in search of something they expected to find and they continue to move around the clearing, some pushing into the surrounding brush and trees but always returning to the clearing. They move more quickly than when we first saw them but gradually they start to slow, as if losing some kind of momentum. Eventually, they return to their former state of near-comic shambling and stumbling. They linger a long time in the clearing before beginning to move on into the woods.

Voiceover (cont.):
"Mr. Jackson exited the clearing via a camouflaged entrance to the tunnels. I would also like to commend Ms. Gamache for building a soundless drone that really *is* soundless—stand up, Jeri. Jeri Gamache, ladies and gentlemen, a truly gifted engineer—" *[scattered applause; woman's voice too faint to be intelligible]*
"I know how you feel, Jeri. *[Voiceover laughs nervously]* I'd prefer to sit out the zombie apocalypse in Cancun drinking margaritas—"

Voice 01 [male]:
"Dr. Vachon, that word is unacceptable—"

Voiceover (cont.):
"What's the matter, don't you like tequila?"

Voice 02 [female]:
"You know very well the Colonel is not referring to margaritas. Please don't be disingenuous, Dr. Vachon. It doesn't become you."

Voiceover (cont.):
"God forbid I should be in any way unbecoming. Consider me thoroughly chastened."

Voice 01 [warningly]:
"Dr. Vachon, we've talked to you about these little episodes of insubordination."

Voiceover (cont.):
"Yes, I so enjoy our little chats. If you're not busy afterwards, let's have coffee—"

[Several voices talking at once in background]

Voice 02 [angrily]:
"Dr. Vachon—!"

Voiceover (cont.):
"That's my name, don't wear it out."

[Background voices become louder; Voice 01 keeps trying to shout over people]

Voice 03 [female; cuts through chaos]:
"That's enough!"

[Everyone shuts up; we can hear Dr. Vachon weeping]

Voice 03:
"I'm adjourning this presentation for the rest of the day."

[Voice 01 tries to argue, something about having orders]

Voice 03:
"I know all about your orders and who they're from, but I'm in charge of this facility now. I don't care how my predecessor ran things, but considering he decorated his office by blowing his brains out all over it, I'd say he sucked at management. Dr. Vachon is suffering from exhaustion and PTSD. So shut up."

[Voice 01 starts to argue again. There is a gunshot, the sound of a body falling. Total silence; even Dr. Vachon has stopped weeping]

Voice 03:
"Anybody else want to argue with me? I've got a few exhaustion and PTSD issues myself. *[very long silence]* Oh, for God's sake, it's just a tranquilizer dart. Pick him up and put him to bed. He'll sleep for six hours and wake up with a hell of a hangover."

Voice 02 [unhappily]:
"I have to report this."

Voice 03:
"Go ahead. I dare you."

 [Vlog Entry 007: Sergeant Rochelle "Rocky" LaFortune]

[Cut to:]
Video: the image is grainy, taken in low light with her OTR camera. For the first time, she is indoors, in an underground garage.

Sgt. LaFortune:
"That video's my favorite and I wouldn't have seen it if I hadn't met the Good Guys. Say hello, Good Guys."

[Cut to:]
Video: POV pans toward a group of people who hide their faces and wave at her not to film them.

Sgt. LaFortune:
"Hey, don't worry, I'm going to pixilate your faces and distort your voices, I promise. I swear on a stack of Bibles or any other books you like."

[Cut to:]
Video: the group stop trying to hide. We see and hear them all clearly. Small pixilated areas show up briefly on some of the faces; someone undid the pixilation. There's also the occasional glitch in the sound, indicating voices were also restored.

Sgt. LaFortune:
"This is Smiley."

Video: Twenty-something man grins at the camera; he has perfect teeth.

Sgt. LaFortune:
"And here's Eagle-Eye."

Video: slightly older male, with very thick glasses.

Sgt. LaFortune:
"Devil-Woman and DW, Jr."

Video: forty-ish black woman shakes her head, then covers the face of the twelve-year-old girl beside her.

Devil-Woman:
"You don't film her *at all*, that's the deal."

Video: camera moves quickly to a gray-haired man sitting cross-legged on the cement, eyes closed.

Sgt. LaFortune:
"This is Doc."

Video: POV pans to a teenaged Vietnamese girl sitting in a director's-style folding chair, eating a tin of cold spaghetti with a plastic fork.

Sgt. LaFortune:
"Miss Manners—"

▌ Video: the girl looks up sharply.

Sgt. LaFortune:
"No disrespect! They told us at Annapolis that the amenities are what distinguish us from brute animals."

Older female voice [quietly]:
"My son went to Annapolis."

▌ Video: Camera pans to a woman sitting on the floor beside Miss Manners. Her hair is short and very curly: a wig.

Sgt. LaFortune [speaking gently]:
"And this Shirley."

Shirley:
"Back when it was still the Naval Academy."

Sgt. LaFortune:
"Shirley, do you remember saying you'd testif—uh, let me interview you?"

▌ Video: Shirley looking troubled.

Shirley:
"You still want to do that, huh? Right now?"

Devil-Woman:
"You mind taking it somewhere else? It's movie night and I hate it when people talk in movies."

▌ *[Cut to:]*
  Video: interior of a Humvee—the civilian variety, not a military vehicle. Camera is on the dashboard, on the driver's side. LaFortune is closest to it, slightly out of focus; Shirley sits in the passenger seat, perfectly in focus.

Sgt. LaFortune:
"Shirley, I'd like to thank you again for charging my iPad and showing me how to access those files in the Cloud. I knew there had to be some way to—"

▌ Video: Shirley waves one hand dismissively.

Shirley:
"Yeah, sure. I'd like to get this over with, okay?"

Sgt. LaFortune:
"Of course, yes. I'm sorry. Go ahead. Whenever you're ready."

Shirley:
"Like anyone was ready for this. *[deep breath]* As immediate family of someone on active duty, I was evacuated early. What they thought was early. In fact, it was already too late, but even I didn't know that yet. But it was early enough that I was able to continue chemo at a field hospital. Not in a field, of course.

"I don't know what happened to the soldier who brought us to Fort Meade. They took him away, said he would be disciplined for unauthorized entry into a classified area with unauthorized civilian personnel. That makes it sound so clean and neat, like it wasn't this freaked-out Marine barely out of Boot Camp and four terrified civilians, one of them still hysterical. We were all that was left. Out of an entire friggin' *platoon* of Marines—that's a little over a hundred jarheads—and fifty-two civilians, only us five got away.

"They knew that at Meade. They knew what had happened, they knew everything that happened and everything that *was* happening. I didn't know that at the time, I was pretty clueless. But if I *had* known, oh, man, *if I had known*, I don't know what I would have done. *[long silence]* Really. I don't know what I would have done. Honest to God, I don't. I wouldn't have left—where was there to go? I had some rather specialized needs last year. I was only halfway through chemo when the world went to hell.

"When we got to the underground facility at Meade, I thought the best I could hope for was they could keep me comfortable and I'd be able to die with dignity—cremation, the end. No shambling around binge-eating." *[short humorless laugh]*

"But they told me they had the right drugs and I could finish my chemo. I said maybe they wanted to save them but they said no, if they didn't use them on me, they'd go to waste. And, well, I hate waste." *[the pause turns into a lengthy silence]*

Sgt. LaFortune [speaking gently]:
"Shirley, I'm sorry to make you relive this. But it's important."

Shirley:
"Yeah, I know. Just don't forget to upload it to the Cloud using the encryption they showed you. Otherwise, this'll all be for nothing and I just told you how I feel about waste." *[deep breath]*

"It turned out I wasn't the only person getting chemo. There was something like a dozen of us. But I only found out the truth when two died on the same day, practically within an hour of each other.

"They were both in the Navy, off the same aircraft carrier—one was a pilot, the other an air-traffic controller. My heart went out to the pilot because she was so young and even in this day-and-age, it's still hard for women to make it into that particular boys' club. After all that hard work, someone with her whole career ahead of her, and *bam!* She gets a visit from the cancer fairy. Talk about unfair.

"The ATC was older but I couldn't say how much. He was the sickest, from the chemo I mean. He was having such a bad time with it, I wondered why he went on with it. If it had been me, I don't think I would have. Oh, I don't know, maybe I would have. You can't know how far you'll go till you're on the way.

"Anyway, he was having such a bad time. He'd cry silently, then he'd dry-heave, then he'd start talking to his OTR cam. I wasn't sure if he was having flashbacks or hallucinations and even when I could understand what he was saying, it was all mixed up.

"He was in the middle of babbling about the aircraft carrier. The pilot, Julie, told me a little about what had happened to them—they were putting out to sea for some kind of rescue mission when they discovered everyone on board wasn't as healthy as they'd thought. They had a lot of civilians, volunteers from Médecins Sans Frontières and refugees. She didn't know how many got away. People thought their best chance was in the water, figuring zombies can't swim. I guess none of them saw the 'Miracle on the Hudson' video—zombies'll just keep trying to move toward where the people are. It's not what you'd call great swimming form but they don't have to worry about coming up for air.

"I told her she didn't have to talk about it if she didn't want to, but she said it wasn't as hard to talk about that as it was about anything else. I knew what she meant—I felt the same. Talking about the life you'd never have again hurt like anything. But just talking at all could be exhausting. I'd tell her to save her strength, but she didn't want to. She said she wanted to keep talking as long as she could.

"She never improved. Some days she wasn't going downhill as fast as other days but that was as good as it got for her. I talked to one of the nurses, asking why they hadn't switched her to palliative care. He said she was participating in a drug trial and she insisted on seeing it through to the bitter end.

"Now *that* shoulda tipped me off. It's the zombie fucking apocalypse and they're doing drug trials with cancer patients? But chemo makes you a little foggy. Or a lot foggy. And they were generous with the painkillers, which kept me fogged in.

"Anyway, she was in the middle of a treatment and she says to me, 'I think I'll take a little nap now,' and that was it. Her head fell to one side and I knew she was dead. The nurses got her outa there *fast*. And I look over at the ATC and he looks like he just saw the Grim Reaper. I can't take it so I think *I'll* take a little nap—what the hell, I'll wake up or I won't and if I don't, my troubles are over. But I do wake up and he's gone and there's someone else in his place. And in *hers*.

"So I ask the orderly who takes me back to my room, 'Jeez, how many cancer patients are there around here?' and he says, 'You're the only one.'

"And *bam!* Like that, I realize: these people are all infected guinea pigs. I didn't know whether to raise hell or go blind. They've all gotta know they're infected—it's not a mosquito bite, you can't miss it. So I ask them about how they came to volunteer. They're all like, 'Well, what have I got to lose? Maybe they can find a cure.' Very noble. Except Meade wasn't destroying the dead bodies.

"For a while, they were tagging them and releasing them so they could track their movements and activity with other zombies. But then they start freezing them and sending them north, to Canada, for different kinds of experiments. And not just them—they're rounding up anything newly dead and/or in relatively good condition.

"So I know what's gonna happen to me and I got my ass outa there, even though it meant missing my last round of chemo. What the hell. Either it worked or it didn't but I'm not gonna let them ship my dead ass up north. I'm stickin' with the Good Guys. They chop your head off and burn your body."

[Vlog Entry 010: Sergeant Rochelle "Rocky" LaFortune]

Sgt. LaFortune [voiceover]:
"I found this in the Cloud. Supposedly it's a hoax."

[Cut to:]
Video: an operating theatre. The medical staff are all wearing heavy-duty hazard suits and the zombie on the table is physically immobilized with all kinds of straps and bands, but is still trying to move. The left leg has been amputated below the knee and a team is attaching a replacement, which obviously came from a different body.

[Cut to:]
Video: another procedure in which a team is attempting to replace a thigh-bone with a metal rod. The muscles are flexing madly.

[Cut to:]
Video: the zombie that had its leg replaced limp-shuffles around an empty room, dragging the new limb.

[Cut to:]
Video: the same zombie shuffling around in a pen outdoors with very high walls, its gait slightly better. Abruptly it stops, looks to its right then runs, but very clumsily, occasionally falling down.

[Cut to:]
Video: another zombie in the same outdoor pen with two replacement legs, one above the knee, one below; this one has no trouble running. When it reaches the wall, it tries to climb.

[Cut to:]
 Video: a different high-walled pen with about thirty zombies. They all have some kind of damage—broken limbs, dislocations, torn flesh, badly disfigured faces. But they all try to move, even those that can barely crawl. The video freezes; a circle is drawn around a zombie that has appeared on the left side of the screen. This image remains on the screen during the audio sequence.

Lt. Sposito:
"Now, Sgt. LaFortune, you claim *this* is your late wife, Private Jolene Lindbloom?"

Sgt. LaFortune:
"I *know* it is."

Lt. Sposito:
"Really. Would it surprise you to learn that records show Private Lindbloom's remains left Flowerpot Island weeks ago?"

Sgt. LaFortune:
"I'd know her anywhere."

Lt. Sposito:
"None of these creatures is in what you'd call . . . mint condition. I don't know how you can be so confident."

Sgt. LaFortune:
"We were *married*—"

Lt. Sposito:
"Ah, but isn't it true that, as a military wife, you had to endure long periods of separation?"

Sgt. LaFortune:
"Yes. So?"

Lt. Sposito:
"Private Lindbloom's appearance is not so distinctive as to make her instantly identifiable. Which is to say, she's not exceptionally tall or muscular or in any way more eye-catching than any soldiers around her? This is not to cast aspersions on her personal appearance. I'm simply saying that Private Lindbloom does not immediately draw attention."

Sgt. LaFortune:
"Maybe not *your* attention, but I can pick her out."

Lt. Sposito:
"Let's test that, shall we?"

Video: photo of a platoon of soldiers, men and women in fatigues, standing at attention at a military base.

Lt. Sposito (cont.):
"Which one is Private Lindbloom?"

Sgt. LaFortune:
"She isn't in that picture."

Lt. Sposito:
"Are you sure?"

Sgt. LaFortune:
"Positive. I happen to know that Jolene *took* that photo."

Lt. Sposito:
"Hmm . . . you're sure you don't see her? Because—"

Video: zooms in on a soldier standing in the second row.

Lt. Sposito (cont.):
"—I 'shopped her into it myself. With a little help from someone more experienced than—"

Jag attorney Lieutenant Franklin Kwame Agbesi, defense counsel:
"Objection! This trickery is absolutely unacceptable!"

Lt. Sposito:
"On the contrary, your honor, this simply rebuts Sergeant LaFortune's claim that she can pick her spouse out of any photo. If Sergeant LaFortune were as keenly attuned to her spouse's appearance as she claims, she would have—"

Judge Javeria Kashiray-O'Toole:
"Save it. The defense's objection is sustained."

Lt. Sposito [stunned]:
"But your honor—"

Judge Kashiray-O'Toole:
"*Sustained.* You know what 'sustained' means, don't you?"

Lt. Sposito:
"Yes, but—"

Judge Kashiray-O'Toole:
"Did I stutter, counselor?"

Lt. Sposito [quieter]:
"Your honor, I respectfully submit that as someone relatively new to military law and the court-martial process—"

Judge Kashiray-O'Toole:
"Stop right there before I cite you for contempt, lieutenant. I'll admit to my inexperience but I'll also remind you—and anyone else in this room who might feel inclined to be critical—that you people came to *me*, I didn't go looking for *you*. I was drafted into your JAG Corps because of my fifteen years as a criminal court judge. I got a crash course in military law and I'm gonna tell you right now, the law's the law no matter what you're wearing. You don't wanna tell me I don't know what I'm doing because I'm a newbie. You people're Boy Scouts next to the sharks that've stood before me. Any of them would have you for lunch and crap you out before you even knew you'd been eaten."

Lt. Sposito [pointedly]:
"*Boy* Scouts, your honor? What about Girl Scouts?"

Judge Kashiray-O'Toole [grim chuckle]:
"Those cookie-pushers aren't as naïve."

Lt. Sposito [matter-of-fact but firm]:
"Objection."

Judge Kashiray-O'Toole:
"Over-ruled. When was the last time you got away without buying any? *[pause]* All right, that's it for today. Second shift on guard duty starts in a little over an hour. Those of us on the roster should grab chow and maybe a power nap."

[Video Archive of Lieutenant Franklin Kwame Agbesi, LaFortune Court-Martial]

Video: the camera is set up beside a table in a bare room where Agbesi and LaFortune are eating lunch together: sub sandwiches that don't seem to have much in the way of filling.

Sgt. LaFortune:
"At least the bread is good. I haven't had bread like this since I left Washington."

Lt. Agbesi:
"You want another one? I think I can scare one up for you, with more chicken or whatever you want. You're gonna need your strength. You're on duty this afternoon and tomorrow morning, you're back on the stand again. Sposito's got something up her sleeve. She put in some kind of requisition. I've been trying to find out what it is but so far, no luck. All I know it's something from Canada. Maybe more video. Or worse."

Sgt. LaFortune [shrugs]:
"I'm okay. Anything you can do about the water pitchers?"

Lt. Agbesi [puzzled]:
"Like what?"

Sgt. LaFortune:
"Like filling them with gin instead of water."

Lt. Agbesi:
"The gin went ages ago. The best I can do is some bad potato 'vodka'."

Video: he makes air quotes.

Lt. Agbesi (cont.):
"I've also got a source for beet wine and carrot wine."

Sgt. LaFortune:
"Yeah? What's that like?"

Lt. Agbesi:
"Cures alcoholism."

Sgt. LaFortune:
"Never been one of my problems. How's my request for fluoxetine?"

Lt. Agbesi:
"It might speed things up if you were on suicide watch."

▌ Video: LaFortune shakes head emphatically.

Sgt. LaFortune:
"It's not myself I want to kill."

Lt. Agbesi:
"I hear you."

Sgt. LaFortune:
"How do you think we're doing with the judge? I was kinda surprised at her ruling."

Lt. Agbesi:
"A different judge mighta seen it their way."

Sgt. LaFortune:
"And the jury?"

Lt. Agbesi:
"I wouldn't want to play poker with any of them. If things don't turn out how we'd like, I think not having any Crisis Recruits on the jury gives us grounds for appeal."

Sgt. LaFortune:
"And then there's the death penalty."

Lt. Agbesi:
"Appealing the death penalty's automatic. *[quickly adds]* You're not gonna get the death penalty. No one's been officially executed since 1961."

Sgt. LaFortune:
"Don't they give deserters the firing squad?"

Lt. Agbesi:
"They executed one war-time deserter in 1945. First one since the Civil War and, so far, the last. They're not gonna kill you. Especially not after what you did in Washington, the first time they tried to take back the White House. We need all the living people we can get and we sure don't need one more dead one."

Sgt. LaFortune:
"No? It seems to me the US military has finally found a way to really get

their money's worth out of every single body under their command, from the lowest grunts all the way up to full-bird colonels. Service no longer ends at death. *[pause]* And just because you're dead doesn't mean they can't draft you." *[another pause]*

Lt. Agbesi *[gently]*:
"You do realize that if the jury decides that isn't germane, that puts our case in the toilet."

Sgt. LaFortune:
"I can't imagine they'll feel that way. I really can't. Not after seeing that video—"

Lt. Agbesi:
"Which is a violation of classified information and therefore illegal. Our only defense is that someone else hacked in and spread it around, nullifying any secrecy. I think the judge would agree. The jury—I dunno. I told you, a court-martial jury isn't like a civilian one."

Sgt. LaFortune:
"I can see that. I really wish there were twelve, not six."

Lt. Agbesi:
"Even if we could round up more, I'm not sure it would work to our advantage, unless they were Crisis Recruits."

Sgt. LaFortune:
"The more people, the more points of view. They might deadlock."

Lt. Agbesi *[shaking head]*:
"There are no more hung juries. The judge would go with the majority verdict and if they split evenly, she'd decide it herself. Which *wouldn't* give us grounds for appeal. Mistrials and technicalities—you only get that kind of legal fucking-around in a civilization that *hasn't* collapsed."

Video: he looks at watch.

Lt. Agbesi (cont.):
"Our shift on guard duty starts in fifteen minutes."

Video: He takes small container from pocket, passes it to LaFortune.

Lt. Agbesi (cont.):
"Take three of the little round ones and three oblongs."

Sgt. LaFortune [reluctantly]:
"I won't come down for *hours*."

Lt. Agbesi:
"Remind me, I've got some pre-Z chlordiazepoxide."

▌ Video: LaFortune looks shocked.

Lt. Agbesi:
"It's only five mikes—a ramp down so you relax and go to sleep."

Sgt. LaFortune:
"What if they test me for drugs?"

Lt. Agbesi:
"That's a joke, right?"

 [Vlog Entry 012: Sergeant Rochelle "Rocky" LaFortune]

LaFortune's video: late afternoon/early evening, outdoors, POV facing a very tall wire fence. Zombies approach the fence intending to push through it or clamber over it but the fence is electrified. The bodies convulse. Some are thrown back; as soon as they are able to move again, they go at the fence again. Other zombies are unable to let go of the fence and continue to convulse until parts of their fingers burn through. Living people in protective hazmat suits move among them; they work in pairs. When they find a zombie in relatively good condition—recently dead, with less damage—one person takes a collar out of a bag carried by the second person and clamps it around the zombie's neck. The zombie immediately stiffens and falls to the ground immobilized.

They are followed by a slow-moving truck towing a large cage on wheels. Another team in the same protective gear pick up the immobilized zombies and toss them into the cage. Occasionally the truck rolls over more damaged zombies that are unable to walk but are still trying to get to the fence.

Sgt. LaFortune:
"I never thought I was going to have a distinguished military career. But I never imagined I was going to end up as zombie bait, either."

Video: camera pans across to Lt. Agbesi, beside her.

Lt. Agbesi:
"Everybody takes a turn in the shark cage. Even the CO."

Sgt. LaFortune:
"I keep seeing them taking Jolene apart, transplanting—"

Lt. Agbesi:
"That's not what happened to her. *[hesitates]* I know. I've seen the video."

Sgt. LaFortune:
"Oh my God, it's worse. Isn't it? That's why you won't even tell me about it."

Lt. Agbesi [hesitates again]:
"What you've already seen is bad enough. You don't need that in your head."

Sgt. LaFortune:
"And it's classified."

Video: Agbesi nods.

Lt. Agbesi:
"And it's classified."

Sgt. LaFortune:
"Inevitable discovery."

Video: Agbesi looks puzzled.

Sgt. LaFortune:
"It's all out in the Cloud. If I hadn't been caught, I'd have found it eventually."

Lt. Agbesi:
"You used to watch a lot of *Law & Order* re-runs, didn't you?"

Sgt. LaFortune:
"Jolene's favorite. I was more partial to *Ally McBeal*, myself."

Lt. Agbesi [surprised]:
"You're shitting me."

> Video: abruptly, the electricity in the fence fails. Alarms goes off. POV turns and runs toward a building where a squad of soldiers in protective gear carrying cattle prods are rushing out of a pair of heavily-fortified doors. POV rushes in past them.

Voice 01 [loudest]:
"*This is not a drill! All personnel to assigned stations! All tasers on max!*"

Voice 02:
"Did we recover the bait?"

Voice 03:
"Who the fuck turned the juice off?"

Voice 04:
"Breach! They're in the yard!"

> *[Cut to:]*
> Video: POV pans around very quiet room filled with men and women some in uniform, some not, a few in bathrobes, all sitting on the floor except for two soldiers at the door, who have chairs. They are armed with rifles, bayonets affixed. There is a large bag next to the soldier on the left, filled with weapons; some rifle barrels protrude from the opening.

Sgt. LaFortune [whispering]:
"I think this is the room I'm gonna die in. Forgive me, Jolene. I tried."

Voice (off-camera):
"Hey, we're not dead *yet*."

> Video: POV swings around; it's the Judge.

Judge Kashiray-O'Toole:
"Well, we're not."

> *[Cut to:]*
> Video: LaFortune POV running through a building among other people, carrying an automatic weapon; lots of yelling and screaming.

> *[Sharp cut to:]*
> Video: POV from the roof of a three-storey building, looking down on a bizarre scene: zombies are trying to reach the people on the roof

while other zombies in combat fatigues and wearing combat helmets are attacking them. But the attacking zombies' movements are very bizarre—they seem like marionettes ontrolled by invisible strings. Their arms and legs move independently of them while they look around trying to get a fix on something else entirely—viz., the humans on the roof.

Sgt. LaFortune [muffled, off-camera]:
"—don't care if they're saving our lives, it's hideous!"

Video: POV swings to three soldiers, two men, one woman, each using mini-tablets. They could be playing a video game, but they are somehow actually controlling the uniformed zombies that are attacking other zombies.

First soldier:
"Bullshit. If they were tearing you apart right now, you'd care a lot."

Video: Female soldier looks up briefly.

Female soldier:
"Where the *fuck* is that fucking chopper?"

Video: the zombies below are piling up so that other zombies can climb on top of them. The zombies in fatigues chase them and when they catch one, they tear them to pieces. Occasionally, they start to reach for each other but each time, they freeze briefly, then twitch as if an electric current runs through them before they turn away to look for a different zombie. But they keep looking up at the roof, as if the people up there are their real target.

[Off-camera: we hear the sound of a chopper overhead]

Video: lines drop down from the helicopter.

[Sharp cut to:]
Video: interior of helicopter; dazed-looking soldiers rescued from the roof sit while other soldiers at the open door help two more people inside and lower the lines again. One of the latter touches her ear.

Soldier [shouts]:
"Three more, then we're outa here! *[pause]* I'm not leaving them! You just hold this thing steady, I'll worry about who comes up!"

[Cut to:]
Video: two people come up on the last line and sprawl on the helicopter floor, one on top of the other. When one soldier gets up, we see the one underneath is a zombie in uniform.

[The sound of many weapons cocking]

First Soldier from rooftop:
"Stop, *stop!* It's one of ours, it won't hurt you!"

Video: the zombie in fatigues tries to stand, then falls over as the helicopter banks steeply and speeds away. Eventually, it levels off. The uniformed zombie struggles to its feet, looks around. It loosens the chinstrap of its combat helmet and tries to take the helmet off, but it seems to be stuck.

Female Soldier from rooftop:
"Hicks! Make it stop that!"

First Soldier from rooftop:
"I can't find the frequency! Tooley?"

Video: third soldier from rooftop simply holds up his mini-tablet; the screen is smashed.

Female Soldier from rooftop:
"Somebody stop that thing while I search—"

[There is the sound of ripping flesh; too late]

Video: POV swings around to show the zombie's scalp and portions of its skull have come away when it removed the helmet. It throws the helmet directly at LaFortune's camera.

[LaFortune doesn't make a sound]

Video: LaFortune raises her pistol and fires and the zombie's head explodes. For a moment, everyone just stares at her without moving. Then someone pulls her down to the floor.

Lt. Agbesi:
"Let me take that—"

Sgt. LaFortune [quietly lethal]:
"No."

Lt. Agbesi:
"Rocky, it couldn't have been her. It *couldn't* have been."

> Video: LaFortune holds up the helmet. Scratched into the outside are the words WE BELONG DEAD.

Sgt. LaFortune:
"It's what the monster says in *Frankenstein*. In the book. Jo loved that book."

Lt. Agbesi:
"That doesn't mean—"

Sgt. LaFortune:
"There's a dragonfly tattoo high up on her left arm."

> Video: Agbesi actually goes over to the body to check. He pulls down the sleeve but his position blocks the POV from seeing anything.

Sgt. LaFortune (cont.):
"Well?"

[Agbesi says nothing]

> Video: he looks at someone off to his left.

[We hear people shifting and a woman appears briefly]

Woman:
"I've got something to take the edge off."

Sgt. LaFortune [more urgently]:
"Well? It's there, isn't it? It was her, right? Right?"

> Video: Agbesi shakes his head sadly. As he moves to cover the dead zombie's arm, there is a brief glimpse of something that could either be a tattoo or just dirt or bloodless cuts in the flesh.

Sgt. LaFortune (cont.):
"It was her, I *know* it!"

> Video: Her POV begins to sink down onto the floor of the chopper.

Sgt. LaFortune (cont.) [her voice slurred]:
"'We belong dead.' Only Jo would think of that . . . only Jo . . . 'We belong dead.' Yeah, Jo, my Jo, my, my Jo . . . maybe . . . we all . . . b'long . . . dead . . ."

It's 3:00 am and I can't sleep. I keep thinking about this girl. She's the most beautiful thing I've ever seen in my life and I can't get her out of my head. Do you know who I'm talking about? If you do, even if you just THINK you do, send me a message. If you leave a note under your mattress I can get it when they take you to the lab. You know who I am. I'm the guy with his heart pinned to his sleeve. But you can call me Peter.

I hate this place. They took your note away from me before I could even finish reading it. Dr Jernigan told me it's against the rules to have personal contact with "the subjects". As if I didn't know that. I said yeah, OK, I wouldn't do it again and I think he believed me. He's got his own stuff to worry about so I don't think he's that bothered, really.

At least I know your name now. Elaine. And I wish I COULD send you a picture. Or a text. God, I miss my phone. My computer. My car. I miss so many things about the world before. Mostly I just miss living in a world that wasn't us-or-them. What do you miss the most?

I'll say your name until I fall asleep tonight. Elaine. Elaine. Elaine.

Elaine,

I'm glad you could hear me last night. I wasn't sure. You looked so peaceful, like you were dreaming of happier times. And I saw you on the way to the lab this afternoon. They took you through the garden. Is it nice for you to go outside? Or is everything just a reminder that you're here against your will? Do you have memories of your life before?

I can't believe you miss swimming the most! In this country? Are you crazy??? LOL I don't even know how to swim. Hey, maybe if we ever get out of here you can teach me.

To answer YOUR question, no, I'm not here because I want to be. I was just a lowly medical student before all this happened and they gave me a very clear choice: come in or get out. And "out there" was the Death. I mean the Death before — well, before the ones like you.

I don't like what they do in this place and of course I probably don't even know the half of it. But what I do know is enough to make me angry. They call themselves doctors and scientists but they're a bunch of bloody Nazis. I wish I could take you out of here and away from all this. They can see you're not dangerous. I just don't understand why your kind (I refuse to use the Z-word) have to be kept prisoner here. You deserve better.

I want to ask you something. But I don't want to freak you out or stir up bad memories. But this is the only way we can talk so I have no choice. Were you dead before you came here?

Your friend,

Peter

Peter,

I would love to teach you how to swim. And I'd give anything to see the ocean again. To hear the waves. To feel alive. Really alive. Sometimes I think I can hear it. We must be near the sea.

Do I have memories? Oh yes. They're all I have. Some are so bad I wish I could erase them. My whole family is dead. My parents. My sister. Even my dog. I wish I could scratch that whole day from my mind. And most of the ones since. But I have happy memories too. I try to think of those the most.

It's nice to have a friend. It's comforting to know someone here cares about me. Thank you for that.

Elaine

My dear Elaine (I love writing your name), I'm so sorry about everything, especially what happened to your family. It's terrible you remember all the bad things. And I understand if you don't want to tell me the details. I mean, you don't know me at all. I have no idea where my own family are or if they got away when the world went crazy.

Dr Jernigan says things are getting even crazier. I can't remember the last time I saw a news report or read a paper but I gather there's a war going on outside. I'm sure they'd like to keep us all in the dark here but I wonder if you know anything? They say you can sense things.

I'll try to come by your room tonight. Stay awake if you can and maybe this time you'll see me!

Your friend,

Peter

Dear Peter,

I saw you last night at my window. It was wonderful to see someone smile for once. And at me! I recognized you too. You were there the day they first brought me here. Do you remember? You looked very sad that day, like you'd been crying. I certainly had. I'd just been told my whole family was dead, killed by zombies. They said I'd be dead too, very soon. Because I'd been bitten. I tried to tell them it wasn't a bite. But they knew that, really. I guess they thought it would be easier for me (or them) if they could just pretend I'd turned naturally.

They wanted healthy human subjects and there weren't many of us left. They said we'd be doing a great service to mankind. And what they did changed me. I'm no longer human. It's weird to see that in writing. I'm not human. I have scars on my body from the things they did to me. Someone else's heart beats inside my chest. Some thing's heart. Some thing's blood flows in my veins. The dead Other gives me life so I can't really bring myself to hate it. (Him? Her?) And I'm one of the lucky ones. I've heard stories about other kinds of experiments, things I can't even bear to think about.

But you know all this. And it gives me hope to know that you don't agree with what goes on here. I remember thinking when I first saw you that you had a kind face, that you didn't belong here. The day I arrived — was it your first day too?

I wish I had happier things to tell you but maybe it will help to write the bad ones down. I have no one to talk to and it's so lonely here, especially at night. I like the thought of you watching over me while I sleep.

And I dreamed last night! I haven't dreamed in so long. You were in it. You made me feel human again.

You asked if I could sense things. I probably shouldn't write this since you said they took my first note away but there might not be much time left. They think they're keeping us in the dark too but we have secrets they'll never find. So many secrets.

Yes, there is a war out there. Between humans and zombies. (I don't mind the term. There is no other word for what I am now.) They weren't expecting us to change like we did. In our minds. They thought we'd stay brainless shambling monsters until we rotted away but that wasn't what happened. Now that they know we can think and reason just like them they're even more afraid. They should be.

I can't read thoughts. It's not like that. I can smell fear. Like an animal, I guess. And I can sense moods. I know who it's safe to trust, which is why I know I can trust you. And it's why I want to warn you. A revolution is coming. The others here — the other infected — are going to fight back. They can communicate with the ones outside and they're going to destroy the facility and free us. But I don't want to go with them. I don't want any part of their stupid war, not on either side. I just want to be with you. You're the only person who's seen me for who I am — who I was — since the whole nightmare began.

Is it too soon to say I think I love you? Maybe it's not soon enough.

       Elaine xx

My dearest Elaine,

I should probably destroy your last note like I did most of the others but I just can't. Not when you said what you did at the end.

Oh Elaine, I think I love you too.

I went by your room again last night. (I know it's a cell but I can't stand to think of it that way.) You were asleep. I tapped on the window but you didn't see me. Did you dream again? I never remember my dreams, not even good ones. I guess I envy you that.

What an ugly place the world has become. Only a few months before, I might have been smiling at you in a coffee shop on the high street as we both studied for exams. I might have even got up the courage to ask you out. Now here I am like a character in some old Victorian melodrama, pouring my heart out on the page to you every night. You're the only light in the darkness.

I promise I will keep all your secrets.

Dr Jernigan asked me yesterday what was wrong with me. He said I looked distracted. I wonder why! They've got me writing up their notes and doing other menial tasks, probably to keep me out of the way of their "important work". They know I don't approve, but I'm the low man on the totem pole so even if I objected I'd be no threat to them. So I'm going to keep my head down for now and at the first sign of trouble I'll come find you and we can go away together, find someplace safe. There must be places out there untouched by all this. I have to believe there are anyway.

Love,
    Peter

Peter,

I had the most wonderful dream last night. I dreamed you came to my room while I was sleeping and held me in your arms all night. I dreamed you talked to me and whispered that you loved me and said you wanted to be with me forever. I dreamed all this and when I woke up I had to remind myself that it wasn't a dream at all. You were really there!

Sometimes I think I must be going crazy, that you're too good to be true. How can a soul as beautiful as yours exist in such a terrible place?

I keep playing last night over and over in my head. Seeing your face in the window. Seeing you smile. Watching the doorknob turn and watching you come inside. You were so warm. I felt like I could just melt into you. I'm sorry I couldn't stop crying. I just couldn't believe you were real. Just hearing your voice, a loving voice, was almost more than I could handle. I'm glad my scars don't bother you. I think they're hideous. But you said they were beautiful because they were part of me. Now I'm crying again.

Like I told you, I have no idea how long I've been here but you are the only person to show me any kindness in all this time. Sometimes it's overwhelming.

I want to get out of here so much. I want to be with you. Please say you'll come again. I don't think I can cope with the rest of my life if you're not in it

Yours forever,

Elaine

My dearest Elaine,

I can only imagine what it must be like for you but let me reassure you that you are NOT CRAZY. Or if you are, then I am as well and so be it! Yes, your scars are beautiful because YOU are beautiful. Whatever they've done to you, however horrible, it hasn't changed who you are.

You have the bluest eyes I've ever seen. When I stare into them I lose myself. I can see strange and wonderful things reflected there. It's like you're from another world. In a way I guess you are.

We've seen too much horror. We're only young. Our whole lives are ahead of us. We should be out dancing in clubs or going to the cinema. It seems like a million years ago that I used to fight dragons on my computer. Now we might as well be fighting REAL dragons for all the control we have over our fate.

We don't belong in this world. And whatever happens, WE WILL BE TOGETHER. I promise you that.

I love you.
          P

(Hopefully I can tell you that in person tonight!)

My love, forgive me. I wasn't able to write again until now. They suspect something, I know it. They killed one of us the other day. You probably know about it. His name was David but to them he was just "ZS Z79". They told us he had some dangerous infection and they had to isolate him for treatment but we all heard the scream in his mind when they killed him. He was the strongest of us and I'm sure they just wanted to put down a threat. I cried for hours and I re-read all your notes to remind me there is hope.

It won't be long now. The others are furious but we all have to pretend we're unaware. We're going to act as though our brains are slowing. (It wouldn't surprise me if they are with all the drugs they give us!)

I've told the others not to hurt you. I said you're safe and they can trust you. I'm not sure if they all believe me but some of them do at least. I won't be able to send you warning but whatever happens, whenever it happens, just know that I love you.

E xx

My dearest Elaine,

I never thought it would be like this. I had such wild romantic fantasies of rescuing you, of taking you away from everything, taking you somewhere we could live in peace together, away from the rest of the whole rotten world.

The night we spent in the ruins of that old house was the happiest night of my whole life. It was cold and rank and the air still reeked of chemical fires from the facility but because you were finally with me none of it mattered. I saw a picture once of a tiny flower sprouting from the rubble of a bombing, one tiny speck of life in a dead landscape. I think that's how we would have looked if anyone could have seen us. I don't believe in God but I believe in you. In us.

I thought we could get away, head into the countryside and find somewhere to hide. I pictured us living it up in some abandoned manor house or even a castle. I still can't believe the other infected took you away from me. I keep replaying that in my head, that one moment over and over. I didn't want to fight I thought I could reason with them. Why wouldn't they listen? If not to me, then to you? I keep hearing your voice calling my name as they dragged you away. They must have just knocked me out because I woke up later with a splitting headache. I guess I should be grateful that they didn't kill me but taking you away from me is unforgivable. I wish I HAD fought them — even killed them. I honestly thought they would listen to me. HOW could I be so naive?

But I refuse to lose hope. I won't give up. We'll think of a plan and I'll get you out of there. At least I know you're safe for now. I wasn't even sure it was you at first when I saw you through the fence. You looked so thin and pale. So haunted. But then you smiled at me and your face was like an angel's.

I could write pages and pages but I'll keep this short in case someone else finds it before you do. I'm staying with a family not far away. They think I'm a shell-shocked freedom fighter. There's two blokes, Chris and Gareth, and Gareth's wife Alice, plus five kids of various ages from assorted broken homes. They collect them like lost pets and the whole group is like something out of an action movie. They're armed to the teeth and barricaded in their farmhouse waiting for an invasion any minute. I guess it's the same for you in there. How ironic that we're both prisoners of our own kind now.

I do have one funny story I can tell you. We were all sitting downstairs by the fire and one of the little girls, Emma, asked if the Queen was a zombie. We all looked at each other, not sure what to say. Alan, who's "eight and a half", said of course not because kings and queens always got their heads chopped off and everyone knows zombies can't live without their heads.

What about princes and princesses, I asked. Emma told me she was pretty sure Snow White was a zombie because she had black hair (!) and Cinderella was too because there's no way she had that many sisters without someone getting bitten. "My sisters bit everyone," she said gleefully. "They had to shoot my teacher in the head after."

From there she launched into an argument with Rosie (one of the other little girls) about which Disney princesses were zombies and which were not. They were both positive that Ariel was safe because there was no such thing as a zombie mermaid. I had to hide my smile and it was all I could do not to tell them they were wrong.

Well, I said I would keep it short but I just can't. You're all I can think about. I'll try to come to the fence every day at the same time — just before dark. I don't think the guards are all that vigilant because I stood there for almost an hour last night and they didn't even notice me. They must just assume the fence will keep us out. (Me! The ENEMY!) So until you can get free at least we can communicate like this.

I miss you so much. I feel like I've known you my whole life. My zombie mermaid, I'd brave the coldest and deepest ocean to be with you.

With all my love,
     Peter

Dear Peter,

Oh, your letter made me smile! And I really needed it too. It's so grim in here. I can't understand why the others bothered to escape at all if it was just to come here. I swear it was more fun being a guinea pig in the medical torture lab. At least there I had you.

All they talk about is war and death. Revolution, uprising, death, rebirth. New Society, New Religion, New Era, New People, New World. On and on. I'm so sick of their endless preaching and propaganda. I feel like I'm trapped in some psychotic undead cult.

I tried to tell one of the leaders about you when they first brought me to the compound. I said I didn't want to go with them, that I wanted to stay outside and take my chances. But he said they needed all of us to stick together, to stay strong. I told him surely it was my choice whether or not I stayed and that I didn't want to be part of anyone's war. He just smiled and said we were all "disciples" and that's what really creeped me out. His eyes had that look, that glazed, not-quite-there look of a religious fanatic. He didn't use the word traitor but I could see it in his eyes. I kind of even heard it in his mind. So I kept quiet after that. I thought I'd be able to sneak out but they watch us all the time. I guess I missed my chance to pretend I'm not right in the head and therefore no use to them. But who knows? They might have just put me down like a lame horse.

Your new "family" sounds deranged in a happier way. I wish they could meet your zombie mermaid.

Love forever,

Elaine

My beautiful Elaine,

Gareth and Alice told me about the so-called "New Religion". And they know about the compound, of course. They call it the Temple of the New Era. It sounds awful. Gareth has some kind of home-made radio and he uses it to talk to other people all over the country, which is how they found out about it. Apparently something happened in Wales that changed everything. That's when some of the undead started becoming aware. No one's really sure what happened but somehow that chain of events led to some kind of religious madness.

Whatever you do, don't let them know you're not on their side. Close your mind and don't let them in.

I broke down and confided in Alice. I said there was someone in the Temple I had to rescue. She looked at me like I was crazy but at least she didn't shoot me in the head! She said she understood how I felt but they couldn't afford to take any chances themselves, that it was hard enough defending the farmhouse against attacks.

The other night we saw a group of the dead on the road. There must have been about twenty or so and they were heading for the Temple. You've probably seen them by now. I think they're being summoned. Your captors are sending word somehow and they're all massing there. I don't know why. If you can find out what they're planning maybe I can convince Chris and Gareth that we need to do something before it gets out of control. They're already talking about moving further north. Right now they're on my side but I'm worried that will change if they think I'm too useful to let go. I didn't dare even tell them I was a medical student in case they decided to promote me to field doctor.

Anyway, something's up. Don't drop your guard for a second. Stay strong and know that you're always in my thoughts, even if you should try to keep me out of yours for now.

Always always yours,

P

It's worse than I ever could have imagined. This place is like something from my worst nightmares. You're right: the others are being called here. And I think I know now why they won't let me go. The doctors must have been giving us drugs in the facility to dampen our telepathic abilities because now that I'm no longer being dosed every day my mind is like a receiver for all their thoughts. I'm not the only female here against my will. I know you can guess what that means. I don't know how much time I have before they decide to make use of me.

I have to get out of here.

E

Oh my dearest Elaine, I wish I had good news or at least some words of comfort.

Emma is dead. It's the usual story. Bitten. Shot. Buried. Alice is off her head with grief like she was her own daughter. She glared at me like it was my fault and said something I won't repeat. I don't belong here. I don't want to be here. I can't stand these people much longer.

I told them all about you. I had to. I was desperate. I told them the danger you were in but they said they couldn't help. They mean they WOULDN'T.

I have one idea. It's crazy but so is the whole world and maybe I am too. If I were to get bitten . . .

I know, I know. I can guess what you'll say. But it would mean no more being on opposite sides. Your side would HAVE to take me in then. We could be together, even if it's in some stupid end-of-days cult compound.

Don't worry. I won't do anything rash. But I wanted to let you know what I was thinking. Your last note really scared me.

Please write soon. I check our spot by the fence every night and my heart sinks when I don't find a note from you and I start to worry that something's happened.

I miss you so much.
I love you,
P

eter,

don't have any good news either, I'm afraid. What they did to
e at the medical facility was terrible but I never realized they
ere also keeping me alive. Now that I'm away from there I feel
fferent. When I was in the facility I felt strange all the time
t now I feel ill. Really ill. My vision is blurry and my skin is
tarting to itch. It's coming off in flakes and my nails are
urning black. I think I know what it means but I daren't write
down in case that makes it true. I hope it isn't what I think.
Whatever you do, don't let yourself get bitten! The doctors
ade me the way I am. The dead don't all become aware. Some
, but there are many more that are nothing but walking
orpses. I can't even bear to think about you becoming like that.
u have to take care of yourself. And whatever's happening to
e, time is running out. I see the way they look at me now.
ey're wondering if they have enough time. They mumble
omething like prayers and talk about me as if I can't hear
hem. Or am I just picking up their awful thoughts?
You have to get me out. We have to go back to the facility.
My love, I'm so afraid.

    E

My love,

I made a hole in the fence. I got some bolt cutters and I circled the entire compound three times to find a safe place that wouldn't be noticed. I could only cut one wire at a time and I had to wait until the guard moved on again every time before I could cut another link but you should be able to crawl through now. It's a few hundred yards to the right of where we hide our notes. I didn't dare leave any kind of marker. Just follow the line of the fence. There's a white birch tree nearby that glows in the moonlight. Look for that.

I wish I could wait there for you but someone saw me outside last night and I'm afraid they'll be looking for me. I think they can smell me.

Go there as soon as it gets dark. Or whenever you can, whenever it's safe. Head straight into the woods. I'll find you there.

I love you.

P

Elaine,

I waited for you all night and when you didn't come I went back to the fence. My note was gone so all I can think is that you couldn't get away last night. It's OK. I'll wait for you again tonight. And the night after if I have to. I'm trying so hard not to fear the worst.

Please be OK.

All my love and hope,

Peter

Peter,

I'm so sorry. I didn't want you to worry. The guards were there all night. Probably still looking for you. So I couldn't get near the spot you mentioned. I'm going to try again tonight.

It's getting hard for me to see. Everything is fuzzy. And I hurt. My bones ache so horribly. I don't know how to tell you this so I'll just say it. I think I'm starting to rot.

Whatever happens, know that I love you. You are the only good thing left in the world and if I can't be with you I don't want to be here at all.

Yours forever,

Elaine

Oh Elaine, I hope you get this note.
We're almost there. We're so close.
I'm going back to the facility tonight to
see what I can find. If you can get out,
make your way there. Follow the moon
and listen for the sound of the sea.
You said you could hear it from where
you were kept. It's not far.
 Love,
 P

I don't know if you'll see this or not. So if you do, stay where you are.

I had no choice. I will be with you soon, my love. The facility was destroyed, everything burned, smashed. Only a few things were left intact. Enough to do the job. You said they made you in the lab and that's why you weren't like the others, the ones who were bitten. I hope you're right.

I can feel things now. And voices. I hear them in my head. They want me there. At the Temple. It's strange to walk among them. They look at me now and there's a kind of recognition. I'm one of them.

I'm weak. And I'm so hungry. But I know what I need, what we both need. It's not a drug. It's something else.

They will let me in. I'll find you. And I'll take you somewhere and make you better. Remember Alice and the others? How they wouldn't help me? I still have a key to the farmhouse. Why should they be allowed to choose who lives or dies? We have as much right to live as they do. We can go there and we'll be well again. I promise.

My Elaine. My beloved. Not even two deaths can spoil your beauty. You are still as lovely as the day I first saw you. Others may have made you but only I will ever know you. I am strong for now, strong enough to carry you. I'll take you to the sea. Would you like that, my love? You said you would teach me how to swim. I wonder if I can drown? I hope someone remembers us. I hope we have more than just the waves for our tombstone. I hope we don't wake up again.

Interviewer: "Bernie, good to have you on the show."

Bernie Maughmstein: "Good to be here."

Interviewer: "How you feeling?"

BM: "Hungry, you know what I'm saying here."

Interviewer: "Bernie, you going to be a good boy tonight?"

BM: "I'm always good."

Interviewer: "I mean the language."

BM: "Language?"

Interviewer: "Are you going to keep it clean?"

BM: "Fuck, yeah!"

Interviewer: "Very good. I asked for that, I guess. Bernie, you know what we are discussing, yes? About the needs and feelings of . . ."

BM: "Of zombies?"

Interviewer: "Well, yes."

BM: "Yeah. I know."

Interviewer: "So, Bernie, just for a moment . . ."

BM: "Hey, no rush, man. I got all the time in the world. It's a no-rush situation . . . you know what I'm saying? It's like, the whole world is divided into two, right? The eaters and the *eatees*."

Interviewer: "Or those with feelings and those without."

BM: "Look, I have feelings, man. I feel . . . I feel sadness, you know? I feel—"

Interviewer: "Do you feel pain, Bernie?"

BM: "I tell you what I do feel: I feel dreams."

Interviewer: "Don't you *dream* dreams, Bernie?

BM: "You don't know shit, man."

Interviewer: "I just meant—"

BM: "I know what you meant, man. The subject of this show is dead folks, am I right? Zombies, man! Wooo ooooh! Of course I'm right. It's a hot topic, man because, you know . . . there's more of us than there is of you folks right now."

Interviewer: "That has not been verifi—"

BM: "Fuck verifying, man. We all know the score. We da man, man. And now you need to figure us out. Well, listen up gang—and alla youse folks at home, busy battoning the doors and the windows. We do have feelings, man. And the best way for me to *verify* that—and I'm using your fucking word here, man—the best way to verify that is that I dream. Right? Didja know that?

"We sleep and we dream, man. It's like, 'Do Zombies Dream of Decayed Sheep?' You like that?

"Yeah, you like that, man. You fucking like that."

Archive AB/74457398 – E.Hem/Southern quadrant

Item no. 3234/entry date 18.12.13 – diary belonging to Valdez, Chucho Hector (fishing boat *Invierno* **impounded**); Item no. 3235/entry date 18.12.13 – log of the rented yacht *Moiragetes*; Item no. 3236/entry date 18.12.13 – journal belonging to Laura Hurling; Item no. 3237/entry date 18.12.13 – glass "moonshine" jug, no identifying marks [mould samples sent for forensic ERMI testing]; Item no. 3238/entry date 18.12.13 – note written by Laura Hurling to Victor Hurling

[All documents signed off by Michael Timmerman, Potential Hazards dept.]

Items Status: GREEN

Origination Area Status: RED

Item no. 3232/entry date 18.12.13 – blood-stained handkerchief

Item status: RED [Biosafety Level 4] – samples sent to following institutes for analysis: Friedrich Loeffler Institute, Isle of Riems, Germany (contact Professor Viktor Uhls, Virology Dept.); Health Protection Agency, Porton Down, UK (contact Professor Max Earnshaw, Special Pathogens Reference Unit)

Locations under threat/requiring investigation: Waters off Finisterre; Tonga, neighbouring islands; Ha'apai, neighbouring islands; Mora Tau, neighbouring islands; Vava'u, neighbouring islands

NB. These items are classified RESTRICTED and must not be removed from the archive without security clearance from Prof. William Coates, Director of Operation Outpost

* Stu . . . obv. check cross-indexed links with the ship s log and the journal used by Vic and Laura Hurling . . . make sure all Pacific islands tally . . . something not right here . . . the co-ordinates Vic Hurling listed in the ship s log dunk us right in the middle of the blue. Could be an error but I doubt it this guy was ten years in the Royal Navy. Talk to Bill about a recce? We need to get out there asap. Max.

Diary entry, Chucho Hector Valdez[1], fisherman from Baiona[2], northern Spain [trns by Emily Foy, Fragments Officer, 2 Quadrant] 11 December, 2013

We were fishing for turbot in the waters off Finisterre, hauling the nets for the final time that day. My good friend, our captain, Abilio Solo[3], had cut his hand and was unable to help. All our attention was on the nets, so it was he who saw something on the surface of the water, glinting in an unusual way. We know our ocean. It has its own particular movements. We understand its swells and its twists and turns. We are aware of the way the sunlight mixes with the crests of the waves. And this light was . . . different. It was harder. It did not ride easy on those green-grey combers. Once the net was stowed he **[illegible]** recover whatever it was. We are conscientious fishermen. We do not choke our water, our livelihood, with litter. Wherever possible, we will clean up the water if we see anything fouling it. We take from our seas but not too greedily, and we always give back.

I was first to hook the thing out of the water. It was a jar of some kind, large, with small, ringed handles on the neck. The kind of thing you might use to pickle onions, perhaps. There was a cork stoppering it, and this had been wrapped well with lots of twine. My brother, Fito[4], handed me his pocket knife. I sliced the twine, feeling **[illegible]** I was a boy on Christmas Day. Inside was something dark and leathery, coiled. I couldn't see properly because there was condensation inside the glass, and **[illegible]** of black mould. Once the cork was out – there

---

1   b. Baiona, SP, 02.04.61; married, two sons
    Status: GREEN
2   Baiona is a municipality in Galicia, Spain, in the province of Pontevedra.
    Predominantly a tourist town although its economy also relies upon fishing.
    Founded in 140 BC. Pre. Invasion pop. ±11,000 (rising to a tourist bias of
    ±45,000 during summer). Status: BLACK/DEADZONE
3   b. Portecelo, SP, 31.05.53; divorced, one son, one daughter (deceased).
    Status: GREEN
4   b. Baiona, SP, 18.12.66; married, no children.
    Status: AMBER (pending blood test, JL)

was a terrible stink that came with it, as if something evil had escape[d] that glass prison, along with what had been stuffed inside – I manage[d] to use a hook to drag the thing to the neck. It took a while, but v[e] managed it. There was the temptation to just smash the thing ope[n] but I didn't do it and nobody suggested it. Broken glass on a ship[']s bad luck.

So. I was relieved once I'd dragged it out of the jar. For a horrib[le] moment I thought the thing inside was a bat. But no. It was the th[in] oiled leather cover of a ship's log[5]. And a diary or a journal rolled [up] within it. Also a handkerchief, stained with dried blood[6]. Many of th[e] pages from the ship's log had been torn out. I imagine the only reas[on] this was done was to make sure the rest of it could fit inside the ja[r.] We huddled on the deck around this strange treasure, all thoughts [of] the fish we had caught, and the showers and dinners awaiting us [at] the harbour forgotten. Nobody touched the handkerchief. And none [of] us could read English, but we studied the pages anyway, and everyo[ne] grew quieter but more distraught, as we leafed through th[e] documents. The handwriting towards the end. My God. My God.

Abilio went to the radio and called the police.

---

5   Confirmed as the log from the Moiragetes. The Moiragetes is a luxury sailing
     yacht designed by the renowned Kerner/Dubois Naval Architects and built by
     Sunbeam Yachts, New Zealand, in 2007. Moiragetes is classed as a high-
     performance luxury ketch and has been available for charter in the South Pacif[ic]
     since 2009.
     In 2011 the yacht underwent a three-month full refit.
     Length: 175 feet
     High speed: 18 knots
     Compliment: 9 max.
     The yacht was chartered by Vic Hurling from Beachcomber Moorings, 273b
     Livermore St., Freemans Bay, Auckland NZ, on 07.07.13 and picked up from
     Port of Refuge Harbour, Neiafu, Vava'u, Tonga, three days later on 10.07.13.
     Current location: unknown, suspected shipwrecked/lost.
6   Confirmed infected blood. No traces of Laura Hurling (type O+) or Victor Hurlin[g]
     (A+) assuming no post-mutation.

Log entry by Vic Hurling[7], *Moiragetes*
10 June, 2013

18°38'S, 173°50'W
Heading SSE
Winds (light) SW

Noon. Two hours out of harbour. We can no longer see the coast of
Vava'u. There is just the boat with its fat sails, Loz, me and endless
sea and sky. I was going to start out using this log as a formal record
of our six weeks noodling around the south pac. But you know what?
Nuts to that. Nobody cares any more. The way this world is going . . .
anyway, it's important to concentrate on the right thing to do. We are
the future, if we can stay safe, stay clean and hope for swift
intervention by the authorities. We need to carry on as if nothing is
happening. Life _must_ find a way. Happiness _must_ be pursued. I won't
allow . . . the bad things happening in the world to spoil the freedom
and the hope that I have worked so hard for. I spent half my life filling
in dry-as-a-nun's-knickers logbooks. So this is no longer a ship's log.
This is a marriage log. The early days of nuptial jolliment. Us in the pink
on the blue under the yellow. But I'm not expecting to collect a tan for
the first few days, if you catch my drift, wink-wink . . . And oh, Mrs
Hurling. You look mouth-watering in that bikini . . .

---

7   HURLING, Victor "Hugo" Charles b. Leatherhead, Surrey, UK, 29.03.69; married
    (see HURLING (née Locke), Laura Yvonne, no children.
    Mr Hurling works as a military consultant for the Royal Navy and as a
    motivational speaker under the aegis of his company, Sea Change Ltd.
    Status: UNKNOWN

Diary entry by Laura Hurling[8]
11 June, 2013

Silly me . . . buying this diary at Christmas last year and failing – big surprise . . . I usually do at everything – to keep it up to date. Well. Don't we have other things to worry about these days, other than the pages of a diary that nobody will read? But that's the defeatist way of thinking. So. New leaves and all that. I'm determined to write something in my diary every day until the end of the year. How's that for a promise too easy to break? So yesterday we were married in Auckland and this morning we arrived in Tonga and just a couple of hours ago we began our honeymoon in a beautiful yacht. A big surprise. How Hugo kept that from me is astonishing. He's rubbish at keeping secrets. It must have involved a lot of planning. But what a sweetie! He led me to the harbour and we had breakfast and then he said, let's go look at some boats. And then he said, let's go on board one of them. And I was pulling back, thinking we were going to be arrested, and suddenly he pulls out a bottle of champagne and the keys and says, step aboard, my handsome bride! Heart melt! I'm such a lucky girl. And what a beautiful yacht. How the other half lives, huh? Yeah. How the other half lives. Jesus.

---

8   HURLING (née Locke), Laura Yvonne b. Hoole, Chester, UK, 09.06.74; married (see HURLING, Victor "Hugo" Charles), no children.
    Mrs Hurling works as a laboratory assistant at a pharmaceutical company based in Runcorn, Merseyside.
    Status: UNKNOWN (believed dead)

Log entry by Vic Hurling, *Moiragetes*
12 June, 2013

18°41'S, 173°12'W
Heading E
Winds (light) SW

Early morning massage for la wife, then on deck to soak up some rays before it gets too hot. We had a funny discussion over coffee and the last of the croissants we bought at the harbour. All the while we were engaged we never had such a morbid discussion, and I was a little irked, to be honest, that it should come now, when we're supposed to be rutting like possessed rabbits. Now is not the time. This is not the place. But Loz, for some reason, decided to ask me what we would do if one of us was to die suddenly. "What plans have we made?" she asked. And then: "I don't mean to sound ungrateful, but is this right, what we're doing? Swanning around on a big boat guzzling champagne, eating omelettes with shaved truffles, and meanwhile in places like London . . . Berlin . . . Paris . . . there are . . . people who aren't people who are . . . who are . . ."

She couldn't even come out with it, this thing she's so concerned with. I bit my lip. Who wants to have an argument two days into a marriage? I tried to defuse the problem, told her that what was going on in the world was only occurring in isolated pockets, and that most of it was contained. I said it had been the same panic over SARS in the early 2000s, bird flu, foot and mouth, rabies in the '70s . . . fuss about nothing. People gossip and fret and panic-buy bottles of water and fuel and then they don't die and before you know it we're back to bumbling onwards with our lives and not giving it another thought. I told her that I had inside sources who were telling me there was nothing to worry about and she seemed reassured by that. A white lie, I admit, but necessary in the circumstances. Probably the first in many fibs us marrieds will trade in a lifetime!

Haha! So shoot me. I failed immediately to keep to my own promise. Still, five days later is better than six months, which I've been guilty of in the past. Truth be told, nothing much has happened. We sleep in late, we make a lot of love, we eat a leisurely breakfast. We swim. We make a lot of love. We read. We eat a leisurely dinner. We listen to music, drink wine, stare at the impossible stars . . . did I say we make a lot of love? It's blissful. Hugo scribbles away in his log like the frustrated novelist he's always been. But . . .

God I hate that word. "But". Doesn't it just put a brake on everything? Doesn't it just make me sound like a spoilt, ungrateful bitch? I can't help it. If there's a but, there's a but. We're having all this fun, indulging, being decadent, living out our dreams, but I can't just block out what is going on in the real world. At some point we'll have to return to it, and deal directly with the threat. It's stupid to believe that we might just avoid it, that our little pocket of bliss will remain trouble-free for the rest of our lives. This is a major event in our lives, in our times, like the Great War, or famine, or plague. We need to be prepared for it. Smoked salmon and champagne is great, but all it does is highlight the possibility that it might be gruel and water for years to come. I tried to talk to Hugo about this a couple of days ago and he dismissed it. I think he's pissed off with me, and with good reason I suppose. At the back of my mind I'm thinking . . . unforgiveable, really . . . what was the point of even getting married? God, he'd better not read this . . .

Log entry by Vic Hurling, *Moiragetes*
23 June, 2013

20°56'S, 173°14'W
Heading SE
Winds (growing) SSW

The weather is changing. I'll be mightily cheesed off if we have to curtail this trip because of bad weather. No squalls of any kind in this neck of the woods for six months and now we're getting radio warnings that a belt of low pressure is on the way. Lovely. There's a chance we might just be out of its reach, but there's no point in taking risks. I'll talk to the guys at the RCCNZ[9], see what they advise.

Log entry by Vic Hurling, *Moiragetes*
25 June, 2013

26°47'S, 175°39'W
Heading S
Winds (hard) SE

Not good. Advised to get a wiggle on and head for NZ as planned. Strong wind warning for all Tonga coastal waters: E to NE 20-25 knots. Rough seas. Heavy E to SE swell. And then got this through from the TMO[10] in their 1pm bulletin:

Forecast for Nomuka, Tongatapu, Eua and Southern Tonga: north to northeast winds around 70 kph gusting to 115 kph. Overcast with rain, heavy at times, flooding of low-lying areas and rough to very rough seas.

9 Rescue Coordination Centre New Zealand
10 Tongan Meteorological Office

JTWC[11] at Honolulu suggest maximum significant wave height around 5.1 metres. Bad juju.

Australia, the Solomon Islands, Vanuatu, New Caledonia and parts Fiji are on alert.

. . . which is just great. Suggested we keep on to NZ as planned. A least we're going at a fair old clip . . .

Diary entry by Laura Hurling
26 June, 2013

Too busy to be scared. Arms burning with all the pulling and **[illegible** and winding and steering. I have never seen skies like this. Black clouc that rise like walls. Or seas. The waves look like **[illegible]** flexir muscles. And us in this tiny boat. I feel so small. Hugo says we're the edge of the cyclone. I can't bear to imagine what it might be like we're swallowed by it. Sorry for the handwriting. H reckons we cou be out of the worst of it in another six hours. God I hope so. I dor want **[entry ends]**

Log entry by Vic Hurling
27 June, 2013

I don't know where we are.

We should be dead, I know that. The storm hit us hard late last nigh We capsized. Both of us thrown clear. Thank God I managed to get Loz and grab hold of her in the dark. The yacht hit rocks or somethin

---

maybe even another ship – I don't know. Truth is, we were in waters deeper than Everest is high. No land anywhere to be seen. Nothing on the charts. Nearest spike of earth to us was maybe the Star of Bengal Bank at a depth of what, 50 metres? There was nothing wrong with my nav. I knew where we were and where we were headed. Even so. We washed up on a beach maybe three hours later, the two of us clinging to flotation devices. No first aid. No food. No potable water. But get this – Laura had her diary and a pencil in her sou'wester and the ship's log was where I always put it, zipped up in my cargo trousers. We didn't have any waxed matches to light a fire, but Christ, we could write a haiku about it.

We're on an island. It's not on any charts. Some way between Tonga and New Zealand. There's no way it could be anything other than a missed speck on the map. Maybe a relatively recent volcanic surge, a tiny belch of hardened magma teetering on top of a fragile lava tube. But there are trees here. Quite a dense-looking forest that must be centuries old. So bang goes that theory. It's quite sobering to think that there could still be some blank spaces on the map. And if that is the case then should we get back to civilisation, maybe we'll have fame and fortune to look forward to.

But that's the least of our troubles. Laura is pretty badly shook up. She injured her leg – a bad cut on her thigh, pretty deep. I've cleaned it as best I can, but it's quite humid here. I'm worried it won't heal in a hurry. If she gets an infection . . . well, best not to think about that just yet.

We've set up camp on the beach. When Laura has calmed down and gone to sleep I'll go off and try to find food. Some honeymoon.

Diary entry by Laura Hurling
28?? June, 2013

I have no idea how I was going to end that last diary entry. I hope it wasn't anything as melodramatic as <u>I don't want to die out here</u>. That's not like me. I'm tougher than that. My parents always remarked upon it, when I was a child. Tears did not come easily to me. When I was three a wasp found its way under my clothes and stung me four times on the shoulder. My mother panicked and was going to take me to hospital, mistaking my lack of reaction for anaphylaxis. The doctor suggested it was that I had a high pain threshold. Well, that theory is being severely tested now. My leg looks as though someone has been at it with a hatchet. Hugo cleaned it and dressed it with rags torn from his shirt. I feel a little woozy from the pain. Wish we had some analgesics, or even a bottle of booze. I've not tried walking on it yet. Hopefully help will come soon. Hubby managed to find some fruit and water from a stream. Things could be a lot worse.

Log entry by Vic Hurling
28 June, 2013

Worried about Loz. She seems a little squiffy either from the pain in her leg or maybe some infection. The colour of her skin has drained away. She looks grey. She's listless. Her sleep is shallow. Last night, while we rested (I've managed to construct a canopy from branches and some large leaves I found, the size of canoes!), I heard sounds coming to us from the forest. I was worried because we didn't have any weapons, and I thought an animal – a bear, perhaps, or wolves – were being attracted by the smell coming from Loz's injured leg. I kept the fire going, big and fierce, and we were not disturbed. Somehow I fell asleep. I woke just before dawn, roused by a loud noise. I thought it might be a rifle shot. Will investigate further. We might be lucky and discover that there are people living here.

Diary entry by Laura Hurling
282930 Junember my darling

thats not your face hugo

Log entry by Vic Hurling
29 June, 2013

A nightmare of a day. Laura talking in her sleep, her temperature off the chart. Her leg is infected. The sweat is lashing off her. She's raving. I don't know what to do. I'm worried she might die. Stoked the fire until it was raging and then walked for half an hour in a bid to find help but no signs of humanity. Couldn't go too far because I didn't want Laura to panic if she revived and found me gone. Also . . . there is something here. Some animal. I've heard it rustling in the undergrowth outside the ring of light cast by the fire. I'm sure I've heard its breathing too. Wet and constricted. Maybe some sort of warthog. Meat, perhaps, if I can trap it. Spent the rest of the day trying to prevent Laura from lapsing into a sleep she might never return from. Exhausted myself. And hungry. I found some berries, but I don't want to risk eating them. If I get sick too, Laura is done for. We subsist on the dry, rather unappetising kind of oranges from a tree at the edge of the beach. Dreaming of roast pork . . . I might have to amputate. . . Christ.

Log entry by Vic Hurling
2 July, 2013

Unbelievable luck! We are saved! As I write this I am seated on an armchair upholstered in soft, burgundy leather. A glass of wine is at my elbow. My belly is straining from its fill of what we were told was venison haunch though I've yet to see any deer. Delicious it was though, never mind its provenance. Loz is in a large bed, and has been given antibiotics. Her leg is on the mend, the swelling and discolouration in retreat. She also managed to eat a little. She's strong, that one.

We are in a house. A large house that stands on a promontory of rock at the north-east point of this island. We've been here for three days. It is a brutal setting. The seas thrash and boil at the foot of cliffs two hundred feet high. To the south, like thick black clouds rolling in, is a dense forest. The beach where we washed up must be ten miles away. I was worried we were at the end. The noises in the undergrowth were increasing, as if whatever lurked there was gathering courage in order to pounce. I was ready to fight it, be it lion, bear or giant snake. I could have taken on Kong.

I have seen the person who saved us – a giant of a man, perhaps six-feet five – on a number of occasions, and he looks driven, as if the devil were on his heels. Tarr[12], his name is, apparently. When he isn't fixing structural problems with the house he's in the kitchens preparing meals, or keeping the fire going in the drawing room's enormous hearth. I've seen him with a wrench dealing with plumbing problems in one of the bathrooms. I've seen him cleaning, greasing and assembling rifles in a grand room decorated with muskets and cutlasses. He's a jack of all trades, a dervish. But he always has time

---

12 Possibly TAROVICH, Marik b. Hrodna, Belarus, 25.12.53. Career criminal, spent many years in prison, specifically SIZO No. 1 (Minsk) for crimes including GBH, money laundering and arson. Has worked as a bodyguard for organised crime elements originating in the former Soviet Union, including the Yuri Ilovich organisation in Budapest, where it is likely he came into contact with József Kálmán. See following note.

for a smile, and asks after Laura in a voice thick with an accent I can't identify. I must ask him where he is from. He tells us only that the Master of the house, a man known as Doctor Josef[13], or Kálmán, is currently away, on a hunting expedition to the south of the island, but that he will see us soon. He loves visitors, apparently.

One thing about this place that gives me pause . . . there is a corridor in what appears to be an unused basement. It leads to a door that is not only padlocked, but also guarded by two large dogs. Rottweilers, I believe they might be, though crossed with something else. Wolves, maybe. Hellhounds, haha. Anyway, they're large bastards. I ducked my head down to have a look and they started growling, a sound so low and loud that I felt it in my ribcage.

What do they keep in that room?

Diary entry by Laura Hurling
3 July? 4?

I feel better. My leg is tender to touch but now I can feel some pain, which I know is a good thing. Before, it was just this swollen, numb grey balloon attached to me. Scary times. I've been pretty much out of it for the last four or five days. Reading back through this diary, I think I've had enough adventures to last me a lifetime! I've no idea how I could even hold a pen, let alone write the gibberish that went down on that page. "Thats not your face hugo"? I must have been completely out of it. And yet . . . something about that face I saw. Was it in a dream? Did I really see it? The face with its sloped features, as if every

---

13 Nothing on our database. Nearest match is a KÁLMÁN, József Dr. b. Sopron, Hungary, 01.11.58. Austro-Hungarian descent. Independently wealthy. Unmarried. He was arrested for murder in 2005 but escaped and fled the country before he could be tried. His whereabouts since then have been unknown. See following note.

muscle underneath it had given up the ghost? The blood on its skin, only it was dark and tacky, like treacle. But not dried blood. Fresh, coming from cracks in the flesh that looked as if it had been whitewashed. A smell of something so bad it stung the nostrils and stopped you, almost immediately, from smelling any more. It must be a dream, perhaps one brought on by fever, and if that's the case then I hope I never get another infection like it. It seemed so real. The eyes turned back in their sockets so I could see the whites, discoloured slightly, like eggs cooked for too long in their shells. Ugh.

I've been able to get some soup down me (I won't eat much if I keep thinking of that horrible face . . .), and I'm drinking plenty of water. Hugo says I must be dangerously dehydrated. This reminds me a little bit of my hen night, though I know I shouldn't be so glib. But getting falling-down drunk and walking London back alleys in the teeming rain and waking up in a beautiful bed in a hotel on Park Lane . . . it's the closest I can get to describing what this is like. We're immensely fortunate. This could easily have been an uninhabited Pacific island, treacherous, filled with God only knows what kind of venomous or carnivorous creatures.

Hugo seems unsettled by something. I've seen him like this before. He can't relax when he's in a place he doesn't like. And by that I mean the house, not the island. Something here does not agree with him, but he won't tell me what it is. I think he's trying to protect me.

Log entry by Victor Hurling
4 July, 2013

At last, we meet our host. He's a tall man, with a slight limp. He has a full beard, very lush, and small but brilliant green eyes. We shook hands and it felt as if my arm was about to be engulfed. The man's fingers were the size of bread rolls. He was with men I assumed were not

regulars on the island. They were pale, and struggling with the
They had dressed unwisely for the weather. I got the impression
had only recently arrived, perhaps from far-off lands. One of t
struggled with a large holdall that was unfastened; it bulged with
looked like a variety of weapons. Semi-automatics. Sniper r
Shotguns. There was another holdall, but this was securely zippe
There were clear plastic bags sheathing it, filled with ice. Ne
Doctor Kálmán nor his companions made any attempt to explain
it contained. The man carrying that holdall went straight downs
to the basement. I heard keys in the padlock I had seen. I too
opportunity to ask the doctor why his basement was off limits . .

Please excuse the way the following is written. I thought long and
about it and felt I had to nest it within a prose structure. I
distancing technique, I suppose. Christ, I wish. I wish I was still i
briny, miles and miles away, floating, clinging to Loz and the remr
of our boat.

"Mr Hurling, isn't it? A drink, perhaps, before we talk in earnest?

I nodded and agreed to a small Scotch, which he poured from a cr
decanter once we'd entered a large room containing a snooker
and several high-backed leather chairs. The coals of a dying
shimmered in the grate. We took our glasses to the chairs ar
stoked the embers to a fierce cherry red before arranging a ha
of kindling over the heart of the fire. Once that had caught, he se
a large piece of wood over the top. Soon the fire was crackling
and he backed away from it, his eye on the flames, his whisky catc
and flashing reflections across the mantelpiece and the wall, whe
large sombre oil painting of a woman, fiercely beautiful, killed its

He said: "You question my decision to lock a room in my own h
where you have been allowed to stay, a well-kept guest, for the
week?"

"But the dogs," I protested, already feeling ashamed at my gambit . . . I hadn't even thanked the man for his hospitality, for providing essential first aid for my wife. "The padlock. What are you guarding?"

"Guarding? That really is my business, Mr Hurling," he said. His voice was rich and sonorous, every word containing a strange succulence about it, as if he were speaking through a mouthful of brandy-soaked fruits. His lips were tidy and quite small, almost feminine in their shape. That voice reminded me of a famous actor, but I couldn't recall his name. Joss something. Didn't he once do adverts for flour? The same kind of voice, albeit touched by eastern European tones. Anyway, it was entrancing to listen to and what with the whisky and the rising heat I found myself becoming more and more drowsy. "You have been given full rein of my house and it is not enough, it seems. What if I were to escort you back to your shelter on the beach? Would you prefer that?"

"No," I said. And I apologised. I thanked him for saving Laura's life, and for feeding and watering us.

His demeanour softened. He smiled and I saw that here was a charming person. Something about the swiftness of the change, though, the easy slip between coldness and warmth, niggled at me. There was something of the lizard in him. Something silent and still, and deadly.

"Where are we, anyway?" I asked, eager to change the subject. "This island wasn't on any of the charts I was using."

"Ah," he said. "Charts. Maps. Because it is cast on to paper it must be true, yes? We know so little about our own world. We are all too eager, too impatient to fly off in our rockets to visit the Moon, to send probes to Mars, and all the while our own planet is here, ignored, a well-packed secret parcel, waiting in vain to be unwrapped. That said, I'm impressed that you even made it here. We don't usually receive visitors. Anybody that comes to this island is usually transported. You are strong people. Your wife is a fast healer. Resourceful. What are you, ex-military?"

I told him I had served in the Royal Navy for seventeen years. That I still do some work for them, but I'm no longer "in the field". That I also have my own business.

"Ah, splendid," he said, "a sea-faring man. I have always been envious of the professionals in the armed forces. I myself tried to join the army[14] when I was a teenager but I was barred from doing so. Poor eyesight. The saying you have about cards . . . what is it? I was dealt a bad hand? What could I do, with a congenital defect like that? But I never wore glasses. I found a doctor in the north of my country, an excellent physician, and he helped me strengthen my eyes with a series of hard focusing exercises. I worked on my eye strength with the devotion an athlete has to sport. And now . . . well I'd wager my eyes are as sharp, if not sharper than your own and you a good ten years younger than me, at least, I'd have thought."

"My eyes are pretty keen," I said, and wished I'd kept my loose little trap of a mouth shut. The competitive streak is hot within me, to my detriment. And as soon as I'd said it, his mood switched again, though I had not slighted him, not directly at least. I'm a pretty good reader of character and I've seen what is in him before, usually during a door-stepping at the hands of one of my superiors. He was fighting to quell his anger. It was as if he was chewing on it, something sour and indigestible. Something he swallowed against, like hot bile. Out of the

---

14 The Hungarian Defence Force, the Magyar Honvédség, has supplied information stating that József Kálmán's eye condition was detected at a medical screening during recruitment in 1979. The information strongly supports the suspicion that the Josef Kálmán on this particular island is in fact József Kálmán, the fugitive. Further corroborating evidence comes from the records at the St. James Szemészeti Központ (eye clinic) in Budapest, suggesting that a József Kálmán was treated there regularly during the 1980s for ocular Myasthenia Gravis.

scramble of my thoughts came one very clean, very clear message: <u>this man is dangerous</u>.

He bested whatever resentment he had against me and poured us both another drink.

"When can we expect to leave?" I asked him. "Do you have a supply ship that makes regular visits? Do you have your own vessel? Perhaps we could charter . . ."

"I do have my own vessel, but I'm afraid it is not for hire."

"If you can't spare the men, I would be glad to pilot her myself and reward you handsomely for it. I could have funds wired to your account by this evening if you'll show me where your telephone . . ."

"There is no telephone on the island, Mr Hurling. No phone. No Internet. No carrier pigeon or smoke signals."

"But how do you communicate with the outside world?"

"I have no need to, Mr Hurling. I am one of those few people who no longer need to interact with the outside world. Politics, business, war . . . all of it is irrelevant to me here. On this island, I exist in a state of splendid isolation. I have no need to work. I have no need for love – I never married, I never wanted children – and money came easily to me. You could say I was born to it. You might call me lucky, or insane. Maybe, maybe. The fact is that I am happy here. The fact is, I need for nothing and nobody."

I thought of Loz on that beach, sick, feverish, skating so close to death. I thought of how bereft I would be if she had been snatched from me. "No need for love," I said. "Love isn't something you can beckon or deflect at any time. Love happens to you. It's like an attack of something. Flu, or the measles."

"We agree to differ," was all he said.

"So who is the woman in the painting on your wall?"

Again, the lizard in the eyes, the disdain, the coldness. "My mother, Mr Hurling, dead many years now."

"I'm sorry," I said.

Our drinks finished, he made it quite plain to me that he expected me to leave the room. He bid me good night at the foot of the stairs and I ascended, feeling his eyes on me, watching me as I went. I felt as if he were, I don't know . . . weighing me up. And then, just as I was about to round the corner of that sweeping staircase, he called to me.

"I'm sorry, Mr Hurling?"

"Victor," I said: a slim bid for détente.

"Victor. You'll forgive my pursuit of this. I suspect I'm much like you in this respect. You see, I can't turn my back on a challenge. Even an implicit one, like yours."

I began to protest, but he held his hands up to silence me.

"Tomorrow, after breakfast, I'd like to show you something. And perhaps make concrete the challenge you alluded to when you suggested your eyesight was keener than my own."

"Dr Kálmán, please, I meant no such—"

"Nevertheless," he went on, "you will indulge me." And then he smiled, and I stepped back, almost tripping on one of the low, carpeted risers. It was as if his head had split open across the axis of his mouth. It was less a smile, I felt, and more a visual threat. A warning. His tongue was the colour of sliced beetroot, and his teeth were the largest I'd seen outside an animal's mouth. The smile never went near his eyes. I felt myself shiver. I felt my <u>insides</u> shiver. I nodded curtly and hurried to bed.

Diary entry by Laura Hurling
Early July. Shit. Who cares any more?

What a mess. What. A. Fucking. Mess.

I miss the diaries I used to write when I was younger. I remember how . . . anodyne they were. Every day I began each entry with the same words: Got up, had breakfast, got dressed . . . They were like chloroform, those words, a way to desensitise me to what was going on at the time. And not an awful lot was. Everything I did, I described as being "in". I was in a dead-end job; I was in a dead-end relationship. I lived in a bad room in a rented house with three other wage slaves. I didn't have much money and most nights I stayed in. And when we did go out, we just swapped one roof for another that was only slightly more imaginatively lit. The sadness followed me around like an unwanted dog on a leash. What I was describing was prison, without ever actually using the word. The diary was a way out. And then, suddenly, I was free thanks to Hugo. The chance meetings we experience in life . . . I would never be here if it wasn't for that one night I decided, sod it, I would go out after all, and spend some time in an art gallery, a place I hadn't been for years. But there had been a Turner exhibition on, and I do so love Turner. The only time I have ever seen a dawn like something from a Turner painting: misty and fluid and uncertain and gorgeous . . . it was when I was on a boat with Hugo.

And now we are out. And we are alive. But maybe not for much longer. I'm tired, I'm hungry, my leg is hurting, and this is the first rest Hugo has allowed me since we left the house what . . . six hours ago? We won't stop again until we are out of sight of the house, at least, he says. Not while there is still a shred of sunlight in the sky. I'm still in a daze about what happened yesterday. I remember waking up to find Hugo wasn't in bed. He'd left a note saying that he had a breakfast meeting with Dr Kálmán. So I bathed, replaced the dressing on my leg, and went for breakfast. But the door was locked. I knocked on it, shouted

hello, but nobody came to help me. I waited until breakfast bec
brunch became lunch, but Hugo didn't return. I was getting wo
and I had actually gone to the window to see if there was any
could climb out, but we were maybe sixty feet from the ground
directly below us was a yard where Kálmán's dogs – a dozen of
– moped around waiting to be fed. There were bones in that yar
and when I opened the window I could hear the dogs' jaws workin
ends of them, the wet, muffled crack of them as they gnawed. Be
them, the forest and beyond that the cliffs and the sea. No ship
the horizon.

I'd escaped the misery of my youth only to end up inside again. Lc
up, this time. So I sat and waited. I thought I heard raised voic
some point, and the engines of one of the 4x4s that the staff us
drive around the island. And then – it must have been late after
because the sun's light was softening – I heard two gunshots, sp
about thirty seconds apart. About an hour later, I heard a key tu
the lock and Hugo came into the room. He was holding a bunch of
in his hand. His arms and face were horribly scratched. He had
looked like a bite on his hand that was bleeding badly. He tore a s
off the pillowcase and bandaged it.

I went to him and we embraced. I could smell the outdoors on h
mix of fresh air and salt spray and pine. There was also some
else, a bitter smell – gunpowder, maybe – and also a more ar
stink that was very faint, but there nonetheless. Where have you b
I asked him. Why was I locked up? Did a dog attack you?

For a while he wouldn't answer. He was shaking. I've never seen
scared before and it's the worst thing in the world, seeing som
who appears so unflappable being reduced before your eyes t
small boy that he left behind years ago. Eventually he turned to me
placed his hands on my shoulders. His eyes were damp and re
looked as if he had not slept for days. And despite the presence o

scared child, he also looked old. He was grinding his teeth, a habit he's always had whenever he's had to deal with a difficult decision. I've seen him clench and unclench his jaw for hours while he works out how best to let a member of his staff go. Finally, he said that we had to leave and we had to leave now. I asked him if there was a boat coming to take us home and he shook his head. Nobody knew where we were. Kálmán did not own any kind of broadcasting equipment. There was no way to send any kind of signal of distress.

Then where are we going? I asked.

I don't know, he said. We take our chances. Maybe we can find a boat.

I asked him again. What's going on?

He couldn't say it. His eyes were fierce, they were intent on my own as if he was trying to pass on what he wanted to communicate via their heat alone.

What, Hugo? What is it?

Kálmán is a hunter, he said. His words came out in a rush, then, as if his name had been some kind of stopper: I offended him in some small way . . . I implied that my eyes were better than his, or he inferred it at least . . .

Hugo, what? But he was gabbling now, squeezing my shoulders so hard they began to hurt.

. . . and so he challenged me to a duel, really, he's quite mad. We'd have been better off on the beach, taking our chances, just you and me. Better off in the sea, truth be told, drifting with the rest of the flotsam. I got away. I came back here and overpowered the guard. I got the dogs, you know those hounds in the cellar . . . One of them bit me, but I brained it with a candlestick. I got the other one to chase me and I doubled back and locked it in the dining room. I went to the room they were guarding. I went to the cellar. Loz. <u>I went to the cellar</u>.

He was scaring me. I told him so.

He choked on his words. His eyes cleared and he let go of my shoulders.

What's in the cellar? I asked him.

But he had clammed up. He just kept urging me to leave with him.

We left the house and there was nobody to stop us. I wondered if Hugo might have killed somebody but I was afraid to ask. I've never seen him like this before. The dog was barking from the dining room. We got to the main entrance and opened it and there was Kálmán and his henchman, that giant, striding towards the house from across the fields, perhaps half a mile away.

"Run!" Hugo shouted, and did not wait for me. He started off in the opposite direction, so he did not see Kálmán raising his hand to wave, and to blow me an extravagant kiss.

Log entry by Victor Hurling
5 July, 2013

I haven't told her everything. How could I? How could I possibly? I'm not even sure I believe it myself. So many things stacked up before me in the space of a few hours and any one of them would send the most grounded, reasonable person out of his mind. I've tried to persuade myself that I did not see what I saw, that it was a construct of a brain that has been undernourished these past few days, or bruised senseless in the fall from the yacht. Too much of Kálmán's strong red wine . . . But no, it was true. I know it. And it goes down here on the page but I will never allow the words to pass my teeth. I'll take those images to the grave with me.

I don't even know how to describe . . . or what to mention first . . . Oh, Christ . . . just get it down, get it down fast, it doesn't matter how. We are dead. If we are lucky. We are finished, no matter which way you cut it. But for someone out there. Someone who might find this document . . .

it wasn't a cellar. It was a . . . trophy room
he took me out to the woods
there were . . . things . . . in that room . . . heads . . . mounted on plinths
. . .
and he was so very proud of what he wanted to show me
heads . . . my god . . .
in the deepest part, a clearing . . .
and not animal heads . . . and some of them . . .
where there was electrified razor wire
some of them were not even human heads . . .
and in that . . . pen . . . that prison . . .
and their mouths hung slack
there were people but not people hundreds of them I don't . . . I don't
. . . I can't . . .
and they were rotted but only freshly killed
and he told me they shipped them in from infect zones, hunted them
for sport
faces grey or green or black . . . he varnished them . . .
letting two or three out at a time
to keep them from spoiling too much . . .
and he and Tarr would track them
their eyes rolled back in their heads
and shoot them like fish in a barrel
their mouths filthy you could smell the stink of death and disease
coming off them like heat
and he showed me one he favoured
all over the walls

like it was his pet

and there were others

he called it . . . him dammit, him . . . these things were people once

just a few

he called him Lockjaw a little joke, a nothing joke

and these were not diseased

but he had no lower jaw at all

these were unspoilt apart from death

and Kálmán had a cool-bag filled with brains

normal people, men women

i didn't ask him what type . . . pig I hope . . . I hope they were pig brains

and there were children too

i couldn't ask him anything if I opened my mouth I'd have vomited

he hunted children

and he tossed Lockjaw a brain and the noise it . . . he made

he's insane

the noise

he's insane

it was like cows lowing, or dying . . . a desperation in it . . . a sadness

he's insane

Lockjaw tore at the brain and put chunks of it in its mouth but because there was no jaw, nothing to hold it still while he chewed, they just kept falling out

am I insane?

and Tarr and Kálmán laughed at him they kept laughing as he tried to feed, as the pathetic bastard tried to put these gobbets of brain in his mouth . . .

"Why?" I asked him, on the way back, not long before I escaped. "Why?" But I could barely shape the word.

"Why not?" he said. "Our planet is failing . . . Mankind is on the brink. Why not play? Why not fiddle while the world burns?"

"The children," I said . . . I didn't know how to go on.

"The children have no future. Consider these . . . mercy killings. Yo[u] know it to be true."

All of which answers my own question, repeated so often now it ha[s] become like a mantra. Why us? Why us?

The answer is, of course, why _not_ us? It wouldn't matter who we wer[e] or how we came to be on his island. Kálmán is a psychopath. He wa[s] always going to try to kill us. The fact he has turned it into a sport doesn[t] sugar the pill at all. Twenty-four hours he said, before he sets them fre[e]. I doubt he'll stick to his side of the bargain seeing as though I didn't stic[k] to mine. They're probably out of the pen by now. Don't think about [it]. Concentrate on the here and now. Concentrate on surviving, escapin[g].

If it comes down to . . . a choice between dying or . . . going on but n[ot] going on . . . of becoming something . . . unnatural . . . I will end it. F[or] both of us. I won't allow Laura to suffer.

Diary entry by Laura Hurling
[Undated]

There is nowhere to run. We must have criss-crossed the island thre[e] or four times in the past three days. I am exhausted. We have n[o] stayed still since that first night. No boats at the jetty. No visitors an[d] no knowledge of when the supply ship might come. My leg is r[e] infected, I think. It is numb, the lips of the wound white and puffy. [It] throbs like an outboard motor. I'm trying to keep it clean but the wate[r] on this island is probably crawling with microbes. If I survive this I[']ll become superhuman. What doesn't kill us, and all that.

There are impenetrable sections of this island. To the north there ar[e] sheer cliffs. The waters here are at their roughest. Impossible to ge[t] to, and even if you could, no boat would be able to reach you. To the south is the forest, but there are also swamplands carpeted with low mists. The stench coming off that place is like a piggery after feeding time. Hugo reckons it's decades, maybe centuries, of rotting vegetation. We thought of trying to traverse it, but he's worried about quicksands. And it would be all too easy to get lost in that eerie mist, and go walking off a two-hundred-foot drop. No. We stay safe. The western coast is a series of savage spikes of rock, the Needles I believe I heard Tarr call them, and these are interspersed with thickets of spiny vegetation, a woody kind of cactus, as if the plant life was aspiring to replicate the geology. Impassable, although we haven't explored that area completely yet. It's to the east that Hugo has pinned his hopes. The beaches are sandy (albeit black as coal dust) and the sea is calmer. Hugo reckons we should try to set up some kind of distress signal here, visible from the sea or from the air. He's also talking about building a raft, but I can't face the thought of setting out to sea without any food or water. It would be suicide.

Hugo spends any time during the rest he allows us cleaning and checking the gun. He found it in the cellar, he told me, but he doesn't say anything about what else he found down there. We have snatched some sleep, but only when the other person is keeping watch. When he's not cleaning the gun, he's holding the leather-bound ship's log, as if it was some kind of pacifier.

"He won't stop," he told me. "He wants to show how he is superior to the British soldier in strategy, stamina and strength. Typical under-achiever trying to make up for lost time. Lost opportunities. He's mad. But he won't stop. He'll kill us, or . . ." and then he paused, looking out over the forest, listening – "or something else will."

We've camped in the folds of rocks towards the south-east of the island, close to the border of the mists. Hugo thinks we could move a little way into that fog, if needs be, if things get desperate, just for a short while. Or there's the beach. He seems pretty adamant that whoever's after us won't be able to follow us into the surf. Something isn't right. Duh, of course not. But I mean with Hugo. I've never seen him like this. He looks . . . God this sounds stupid, because of course we are being hunted . . . but he looks . . . hunted. Haunted too. I can't break through to him. He's seen plenty of bad things in his career, the tours of duty, but I've never seen him look so . . . so scoured out. So shocked. Our hopes are pinned on the supply ship. I don't know how we can evade capture, or those bullets in Kálmán's rifle, for much longer.

Maybe we should try to reason with him. Go back to the house. Surrender. Beg for help.

Log entry by Victor Hurling
6 July, 2013

Christ. Close call. I saw Kálmán and Tarr just now, making a sweep of the coastline. They were carrying high velocity rifles – what looked to me like Ruger 44 Magnum Carbines. So they'll be using jacketed flat-nose bullets. Ideal for hunting. One of those gets inside you and your organs will be just so much pâté.

We kept low, and stayed in the scrub. I'd been out earlier creating false tracks and they seemed to confuse them, although, dammit, Kálmán kept pointing up the beach to where we were hiding. Tarr showed him his watch and they both looked at the sky. Evening rushing in. Kálmán made gestures with his hands. I don't know. Maybe containment gestures. I wondered what I would do if I was in his position. Try to flush us out someway, I guess. I couldn't see what kind of sights they were using but maybe they weren't infra-red. Maybe they were calling the hunt off for the night.

And then Kálmán brought his rifle up in a precise, economical movement and my mouth went dry. He could see me. He must be able to see me. He was aiming straight at me. I reached out and gripped Loz's hand and sent a silent farewell. This was it.

A shot – massive, apocalyptic – seemed to split the sky and I heard it echo and swirl and echo again in the air as if it never wanted to go away. I was alive. You hear the shot, you survive the shot. And I was thinking, this guy is not the bullseye bandit he reckons he is. But then I heard something slump into the scrub and Loz saw it too and I watched her stuff her knuckles into her mouth to prevent herself from screaming.

The shot had taken its leg off at the knee. The other leg was little more than a shred of denuded tissue and old bone, splintered and mashed and bruised as if it had been tamping the ground for years. It lay on the floor squirming like a cut worm. It might have made some noise if it possessed lungs. There was a gigantic hole in its chest ringed with moss where damp had encouraged vegetable growth. The edges of its exposed ribs were rimmed with bright green. I was more concerned by Loz's reaction than the way it bucked and heaved in the long grass, or whether Kálmán would come to confirm his kill. Because obviously it would not die, not unless he put one of those bullets through its head.

Loz was in shock, I could tell. She was opening and closing her mouth but she was making no sound. Drool spun from her lower lip; all the colour drained from her face as if in sympathy with the thing writhing in the grass. It reached for her with lobstered hands: all fingers rotted to stubs but for the thumb and pinky. Something black and shiny and multi-legged was preening in what was left of its right eye. It coughed – a single hard, harsh bark filled with blood-mist – and fell silent. Tarr and Kálmán were finally moving away, back up the coast. I reached for Loz and half-dragged her towards a line of rocks fringing the beach, keeping an eye out for any more of those . . . things. She saw what I was doing and she started swearing and shouting at me. I clamped a hand over her mouth and drew her into the shelter of the rocks, shooting glances back down the beach in case Kálmán had heard her protests. Thankfully not: the wind had torn her voice in the opposite direction. I calmed her down, which took many, many precious minutes, and tried to wipe that foetid blood from her face and arms and legs where it had landed. Strange freckles. Finally she punched me in the face, hard. It seemed to do the trick. The fight went from her immediately. I rubbed my jaw and waited for it.

"You knew," she said. "You knew about that thing. And you didn't tell me. We're married, Victor. We're fucking married. Married for what? Less than a month. And already you're lying to me."

I was more shocked by the fact she'd used my proper name – a sign I was in big trouble – than by the ferocity of her examination of me.

"I didn't lie," I said. "I didn't tell you because I didn't want you to worry. But I didn't lie."

"You withheld the truth. It's the same thing. How long did you think it would take for me to find out? You'd rather I was shocked half to death than be forearmed with a little knowledge? You thought you could shield me from that until we got off this island? And then what? Back to civilization? Whatever that means? Back to roads choked with bodies. Back to curfews and daily blood tests and the constant racket of helicopters and sirens and screams?"

I couldn't answer that. Her words had punched the air from me more effectively than her fist. We sat staring at each other for a while, until the dark came and turned the air between us into a shifting haze and her features swam within it and I reached for her and held her hand in fear that she might disappear altogether.

Diary entry by Laura Hurling
[Undated]

The moon just slipped out from a **[illegible]** of cloud and there's silver glints all across the sea. It could be beautiful. At least there's a little light by which to write these words. I'm not feeling too **[illegible]**. My leg has stopped aching. It feels numb, as if I've been sleeping on it **[illegible]**. The rest of my body is tingling, and hot as hell. Sweating like a pig. It's pouring off me. My breath stinks. Bad eggs. I'm sick. I say I'm writing this by moonlight but **[illegible]** I'm guessing. I can hardly see the page. So sorry if you can't read this. Sorry, Hugo. I didn't mean to hit you. I love you. You know that. For ever, Hugo. I love you Mum and Dad. I love you Si and Heather.

I don't have much time.

I'm tempted to wake Hugo and . . . persuade him to join me, but I know him. He'll say no. He'll hide the gun and try to save me. But I'm beyond that now. Then perhaps I should shoot him and then do for myself. What hope has he got of escaping? Frying pans and fires and all that. I should shoot him in his sleep and save him. That way, we can still be together.

My god. What am I thinking? What am I? I'm sorry, Hugo. I'm sorry. But I can't go on.

[Illegible] I mean it, Hugo. You must go on. You must find love again. But do not have children. You must wait. Do not bring children into this world, I beg you.

the moon   the first time we kissed o hugo

teribl pains hart   feel I want to vomit   blck thouts   jesis chrst

dalring you smell dlicous oh gd o no god

hngry

no

Log entry by Victor Hurling
7 July, 2013

My final entry. The gunshot woke me. ~~Loz~~ Laura shot herself throu~~gh~~ the eye. She was changing. There must have been some kind infection from the thing on the beach. Maybe transfer in the drople~~t~~ from its cough. Maybe it found a way into Laura's leg wound. The~~re~~ was the telltale opaqueness in her other eye. Her skin was spongy ~~to~~ touch, and she was very hot. She smelled bad too. My love. Sh~~e~~ remains undefiled. ~~She was~~

~~I was~~

I read her journal. I love you too. Rest now. There is nothing more ~~to~~ say. No more words.

I will seal these documents in a bottle I have found on the beac~~h.~~ Maybe that glass container found its way to these shores from a sa~~fe~~ haven many miles away. Here's hoping it can find a route back. May~~be~~ it won't. Or maybe, by the time it fetches up, there won't be anybo~~dy~~ left. But if somebody does find this, and decides to come looking f~~or~~ me, beware. This island is infected.

You will find my body back at the house on the bluff to the north. A~~nd~~ by God, I mean you to find at least one more.

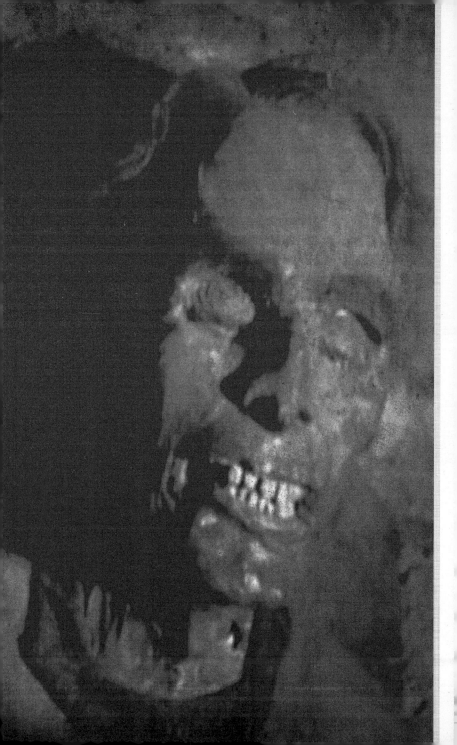

Scotty, I know you're probably not going to ever see this — hell, I know you're probably not even still alive — but just in case I'm wrong, please write back. I'd love to hear from you. Maybe you'll write back and I won't get it — I don't know what's working these days and what's not. If I don't answer, call me, text me, whatever.

Because here's the thing: I'm coming back to L.A.

I haven't written to you since the whole thing with Bobby, have I? You know I left L.A. to see him (god, how long ago was that? It seems like another lifetime, but I think it was really only about five months ago). Well, by the time I crossed the country and made it to Virginia, he was dead. Long story. I won't go into the (literally) gory details here. After that, I wound up in Washington D.C. Spent some time there, but . . . that place is dead (no pun intended). I mean, the new President is a good woman (I actually worked for her, can you believe it?), and I want to believe she can pull us back together, but . . . she can't. There's too much working against her, and I'm not talking about zombies. The Old Boys' Club is still alive and kicking in Washington, and they're killing us all.

I couldn't stand it there, so a few weeks back I left. Just got in a car one day, packed some supplies, and hit the road.

Except (hold onto your hat — or is that a tiara in your case, you little queen? ☺) I didn't leave alone. I've got a kid with me. Yep, an honest-to-goodness twelve year old. Yeah, I know — me, Kevin, the original "marriage is for the breeders" queer, with a kid now. But Maxi is not an ordinary kid. He's smart, and serious, and quiet, and somehow we just really bonded in Washington. It was as much Maxi's decision as mine to vamoose outta there. He's got a sister in L.A. he wants to see again, so that's why we're heading back.

But it's been a tough trip so far. That's why it's been a few weeks, and we're only in Kansas.

See, there's this little thing that happens on the East Coast that us native Angelenos don't know about: it's called "winter". And it piles up this white shit called "snow", and it's really hard to get around in. The storms have been really bad this year. Twice we've had to hole up somewhere for a few days and wait for the roads to clear. There are no snowplows working anymore, for one thing, and not much by way of traffic to melt it away quicker. There's just us . . . and zombies. Still lots of zombies. It's weird watching them in these blizzards — the cold doesn't kill them, but they literally freeze and can't move until they thaw again. I watched one snap an arm off at the shoulder. Fucking zombies.

We also have to stop once a day and find gas and food. We left Washington with what we thought was enough food, but we ate it all the first time we had to take shelter from a storm for several days. Fortunately, the weather's been a bit warmer for the last few days and we're in the Midwest now, so we hope it'll get better. I think we're going to have to head way south, though, since I can't see how we'd get over the Rockies right now.

Anyway, I'll say it again: if you get this, please answer. I hope I'll see you soon.

Love,
Kevin

From: Kevin Moon <moonykev@laex.com>
To: "HottyScotty" <hottyscotty@laex.com>
Sent: SAT, Dec 21, 4:43 PM
Subject: Me again

I didn't hear back from you, so I know you're probably dead. Or worse.

Whatever. The fact is, it helps me to keep track of shit to do this, and it makes me feel better. I guess a part of me still thinks you're alive and reading this.

Things have changed since I wrote you three days ago. We found this place . . .

Okay, let me back up. The day after I wrote you, we were driving along Interstate 40, and suddenly Maxi said, "Hey, stop — *stop!*"

I slammed on the brakes, and saw Maxi looking out the window to our right. I squinted in that direction, and there was smoke. Not a lot of smoke, like a forest fire or something, but a nice little plume, like maybe you'd get from a small factory.

We both watched it for a second — we couldn't see where it was coming from, but I guessed maybe a mile from the freeway. Maxi turned to me and said, "Let's check it out."

We needed food again anyway, so I nodded, and drove again.

In maybe a quarter mile we came to an exit ramp. The sign beside it read PEETERSVILLE — 1 MI.

"A town," Maxi said, "that could be where the smoke's coming from."

"Probably," I said. We exited and merged onto a two-lane county road. The area was a little hillier than a lot of the flat plains we'd already passed through, so we couldn't see what was coming.

We'd been maybe a half-mile when Maxi said, "That's weird."

"What?" I asked him.

"No zombies."

He was right — we hadn't seen one since we'd left the Interstate. Normally we'd spot a few ambling along these roads, going nowhere, just hungry . . . but we'd seen none. Nada.

"Possibly a good sign," I said. "Maybe Peetersville's got its act together."

We rounded another small hill, and the town appeared before us. It looked pretty much like every other small Midwestern town we'd passed — a main street meandering past a few stores and diners and gas stations, a little park, in the distance a church steeple, farmhouses and corn fields surrounding it all — except for one important thing: Peetersville was completely surrounded by a tall chain-link fence topped with razor wire.

But there were still no zombies.

The smoke column was closer now, coming from the far side of the town. It was fading as we watched, spreading on a slight breeze.

And there were people in Peetersville.

Scotty, I don't know what L.A.'s like these days, but here in the East and Midwest, you just don't see shit like people strolling on sidewalks anymore; it's a thing of the past. But the past must be alive in Peetersville, because that's *exactly* what we saw: people going in and out of shops and diners and nodding to each other and smiling like nothing was wrong, like the world hadn't ended and the dead risen.

"People," Maxi said. It was all either of us could manage.

I drove up to the fence, which turned into a big gate across the road. There was a little guard shack there, and we could see a man inside, but he didn't come out. Then we heard an amplified voice. I think Maxi and I both jumped before we saw the speakers mounted on top of the guard shack. I rolled down my window and heard the announcement repeated: "Welcome to Peetersville. Please exit your vehicle, hands up, and walk slowly toward the fence."

Maxi and I looked at each other. I told you he's a really bright kid, right? So we knew what we were both wondering: *Go along with it, or turn around and go back the way we came?*

"I'm hungry," was all Maxi said.

"Me, too."

We got out of the car and put our hands up.

As we walked toward the fence, the voice came again: "Is there anyone else in your vehicle?"

"No," I shouted, shaking my head in case he didn't hear me.

"What's your business in Peetersville?"

"We just need food," I called out. I thought quick, then added, "We've got things we can trade."

"We could use antibiotics. Clothing. Batteries—"

"We've got batteries!" It was true; we'd found a hardware store three days ago that had miraculously gone unlooted, and Maxi had been smart enough to suggest we take all the batteries.

"Okay. Hang on."

We saw the man in the guard booth pick up a phone and speak into it.

A few minutes later a man and a woman came walking toward us. They smiled and looked happy and healthy. When the woman saw Maxi, she waved. He tentatively raised a hand, but didn't really wave back.

They nodded to the guard, who stepped out of the booth with a key. He unlocked the heavy-duty padlock securing a length of chain that kept the gate sealed, and he pushed it back on its wheels. The man who waited with the woman called to us, "You're welcome to drive your vehicle in. You can park anywhere."

We got back in our SUV and drove through. I pulled into a space in front of a store called simply LUCY'S. Behind us, they rolled the gate shut again and locked the chain tight. That made my gut clench — it meant nothing could get in, but we also couldn't get out.

But the smiling man and woman were already walking up to us, so I'd have to think about that shit later. We got out of the car as they reached it, hands thrust out. "Welcome to Peetersville," said the man. "I'm Nate Arlington, and this here's Stacey Duncan."

We shook their hands. "Kevin Moon," I said, and nodded at Maxi, "and that's Maximiliano Robles, although we call him Maxi for short."

The woman — Stacey — had too much curly hair but a pleasant face, mid-thirties. She did that stupid thing a lot of adults do when they talk to kids: she leaned forward, put her hands on her knees and seriously invaded Maxi's personal space. "Well," she said, with way too much cheerfulness, "with that last name, Maxi, you must be Mexican."

Something about the way she said it made my stomach churn, and I had to remind myself that Peetersville might have been pretty isolated even before HRV. But Maxi turned it right back on her when he said, "No. I'm from Los Angeles."

Her smile flickered only slightly. "And is that where you're headed now?"

I put a protective hand on Maxi's shoulder (I know, Scotty, but it's true!), and said, "Yep. We've been working in Washington, but we had to get out. Things weren't going so well there."

Nate said, "I'm not surprised," but didn't elaborate.

"Moon," Stacey said, peering at me as if I were some alien creature, "is that Oriental?"

Oriental! I swear to God, Scotty, that's what she said. "Korean," I answered, trying not to laugh. I was sorely tempted to add, "Oh, and I'm also a homosexual."

I realized that I'd smelled something for the last few seconds: some kind of disinfectant, that sort of greasy stuff you put on cuts and blisters. It was coming from Nate and Stacey, but I couldn't see anything wrong with them, other than a hint of bandage peeking out from under the cuff of Nate's jacket.

"Where are all the zombies?" Maxi asked. He can be blunt like that; I actually think this kid's probably a genius.

Nate made a big show of looking around and grinning. "Well, you're right, Maxi — I don't see any zombies. You're completely safe as long as you're inside Peetersville's fences."

"But I don't see any outside, either. There are always at least a few walking around."

Nate exchanged a quick look with Stacey, and she answered for him. "Oh, you'll see some soon enough, I reckon. Now, how about lunch? If you're here looking for food, I'll bet you're hungry, and we've got fried chicken."

Maxi's eyes widened. "*Real* fried chicken?"

Stacey laughed at his expression. "Yep, not frozen or anything. We've got our own livestock here in town. Now, c'mon."

They led us two blocks down the street, nodding at people we passed, until we came to a storefront labeled MASON'S CAFÉ. We went inside and the smells were enough to make me weak — frying chicken and fresh coffee brewing. We sat down in a booth, and a guy in an apron came over, carrying a little pad. He saw us with the other two, and asked, "Well, Nate, Stacey — who've we got here?"

While they introduced us, I was staring at the chef's arms: unlike Nate and Stacey's, they were uncovered, and were crisscrossed with scars and bandages. I must have been staring, because at one point he got self-conscious and cleared his throat as he tried to pull his elbows in tight.

Everybody ordered chicken and mashed potatoes with coffee (and a coke for Maxi), and then we answered lots of questions about our trip, what the rest of the country was like, what was going on in Washington. Nate and Stacey listened carefully and nodded frequently, as if it was all news they'd expected.

Finally we got around to Peetersville. They told us about the barter system they'd put in place, and the factory that still made tools at the other end of town (that'd been the source of the smoke we'd seen), and how trucks still came with food and medicine to trade for the tools, but they figured the trucks would stop coming soon, so they were managing their own food production, growing grains and vegetables, harvesting milk and meat and eggs, and they'd even learned how to make their own goat's cheese.

"Wow, sounds like you've really got it together here," I said.

They kind of shrugged and looked proud. Nate said, "Well, we've done our part, but we really have the Lord to thank for our salvation."

"And Pastor Winn," Stacey added.

Now, Scotty, you know I've never been much of a church guy. I mean, it doesn't help that half the Christian community sees you and I as Satanic sodomites bent on corrupting their sons. I remember us getting drunk one night after work and ending up with a series of jokes about that book *Are You There, God? It's Me, Margaret*. I'm like Margaret — just kind of wonder if He's there.

So when Stacey mentioned Pastor Winn, I wasn't sure what she meant. Is a Pastor the same as a Father? A Minister? A Reverend? To be nice, I said, "So has Pastor Winn been in Peetersville for a while?"

"No," Nate said, "not even a year, but . . . well, we're not kidding when we say he really showed us the way. He directed us on building the fence, he set up our barter system and our agriculture, he told us to keep the factory running when we didn't see any point to it . . . we owe our survival to him."

"You can meet him, if you like," added Stacey.

I was glad the food arrived then. I have to say, that might have been the best goddamn chicken I've ever had. Or maybe that's just because I hadn't had much of anything fresh in months; even in Washington we'd lived mainly off reconstituted shit. Y'know, you mix water in the little foil pouch and get scrambled eggs or whatever.

After lunch, they walked us another block down to a sort of grocery store. There was one person working behind the counter — Janelle, Nate called her — but she didn't use a cash register. Instead she had a little Excel spreadsheet open on a laptop computer, and whenever somebody came in and took something, she tapped it out on the keyboard.

Maxi and I picked out a week's worth of cans, and asked them what they thought would be a fair trade. "I've got a better idea," Nate said, "how about you spend the night here in town, and tomorrow we can finish our trade. Oh, and since today's Saturday, tomorrow will be church — you're welcome to stay and meet Pastor Winn then. How does that sound? A nice, soft bed, in a safe place?"

"You could stay with me," Stacey said. "I've got two spare bedrooms since . . ." She broke off and looked away, and I thought it was the first real display of human feeling I'd seen since I'd been here. At least they weren't all Stepford Wives.

"Stacey lost her husband and her own boy to HRV," Nate explained. "He was about Maxi's age, so I know she'd love to have you stay with her."

I looked to Maxi, who shrugged. That was his version of "yes".

"Well, if it's not any trouble . . ."

Stacey smiled, genuinely pleased. "It's not. I just live down this way. If you want to load up your car with the cans first, we can head on over."

At least they weren't going to try to gyp us on the food.

From: Kevin Moon <moonykev@laex.com>
To: "HottyScotty" <hottyscotty@laex.com>
Sent: SAT, Dec 21, 9:13 PM
Subject: Update

I'm writing this from Stacey's house, where we're spending the night. She's actually a sweet lady, and she's obviously smitten by Maxi — she fawns on him like he's her own flesh-and-blood. She made us cheese omelets for dinner, and afterward we had canned fruit salad for dessert. After we ate, we played Monopoly (Maxi won).

The only weird part of the evening was when she took off the jacket and we saw her arm was covered with cuts and Band-Aids, just like Mason the café owner's had been. "Stacey, I noticed that Mason had all those cuts, too . . ."

When I said that, she looked a little nervous and ran her fingers up and down her arms. "Oh, everybody here in Peetersville has them. I know how it must look, and . . . well, it was strange to us when Pastor Winn first brought it up, but it's part of what's kept us safe. If you join us for services in the morning, you'll see."

Maxi was none too happy about that prospect, from the way he eyed her arms. "Will I have to get cut, too?"

"Oh, no, honey, not if you aren't going to stay."

"Uhhh, Stacey — we're *not* going to stay," I said. "Remember: we give you some batteries in the morning, and then we're gone."

She tried to smile, but it didn't go well. "Of course. After services."

More later . . . Maxi's calling from his room. BRB.

From: Kevin Moon <moonykev@laex.com>
To: "HottyScotty" <hottyscotty@laex.com>
Sent: SAT, Dec 21, 9:27 PM
Subject: Shit's gettin' weird(er)

I just went over to Maxi's room (I think it used to belong to Stacey's son; mine's more like storage than a real bedroom, but Maxi's has *Transformers* posters and shelves of books and toys). Maxi had the window open and his ear pressed up to the screen. I asked him what he was doing.

"Listen."

I moved up next to him and cocked my head. Sure enough, there was a weird sound wafting in on the night breeze — some kind of distant low thrum, almost like a moan, but too steady. "What *is* that?"

Maxi shook his head. "I don't know. It's creepy."

Scotty, it is SRSLY creepy. I shut the window and pulled the drapes closed, then told Maxi to get some shuteye so we could get the hell out early in the a.m.

"I like that plan," Maxi said.

I'll let you know if we find out anything else.

From: Kevin Moon <moonykev@laex.com>
To: "HottyScotty" <hottyscotty@laex.com>
Sent: SUN, Dec 22, 3:13 PM
Subject: Holy shit

Oh holy shit, Scotty. Holy shit. Literally. I really don't know any other way to say it. Well, except to tell you whappen . . .

When we woke up in the morning, Stacey was already up and wearing a nice respectable dress, with a short jacket over it. She offered us both a hot shower (Peetersville has its own water, electricity, and propane), and by the time we finished she was standing in the living room anxiously clutching her purse. "Well, don't you two look better. Now, c'mon — we're going to be late!"

"Late . . .?" Maxi said.

"For services." She moved to the front door, opened it, and paused in the doorway, looking back at us.

I almost said, "No." I almost said, "Look, you can have all of the fucking batteries, and we'll be on our way, thank you." But . . . well, dammit, she'd been nice to us and I didn't want to be ungrateful, and I was sort of curious anyway.

So was Maxi, because he shrugged.

"Let's go," I said. We followed her out.

The church was three blocks from her house. We walked. Lots of other people were walking, too; seemed like every single person in Peetersville went to church.

The church itself was pretty typical — white clapboard, steeple, crucifix out front — but I noticed there was no sign indicating the name of the church or the denomination. I did see a couple of post-holes in the front lawn where a sign might have stood once.

There was a line of people waiting to enter the church, all dressed up in their Sunday best — men in suits and blazers, women in skirts and dresses. I actually felt self-conscious in my jeans and leather jacket. But I wasn't thinking about that — I was listening to that moaning sound, the same one Maxi and I had heard last night, but louder and clearer now.

It was zombies. A lot of them. But even given that, there was something else in that moaning, something I hadn't heard before.

"Stacey, why am I hearing zombies coming from behind the church?"

"Oh, well, you didn't think we had *no* zombies, did you? We've got them, like everywhere else."

That was all she said — no other explanation. I didn't push it, even though my skin was starting to crawl.

The line was about greeting the pastor, who stood on the front steps of the church, smiling and nodding at his flock. He wore a black robe over a shirt and tie, and even from fifty feet away I knew there was something wrong with him — he seemed stiff, his skin an odd color . . .

But it wasn't until we got near him and I smelled the rot and saw the congealed blood turning his eyes red that I was certain:

Pastor Winn was a zombie.

Have you met one of the intelligent ones yet, Scotty? I had to work with one in Washington (and please, no jokes about our Congressmen all fitting that description, except maybe for the "intelligent" part), and they're just as terrifying — but in a different way — as the standard garden variety dumb-as-a-stump ones.

As we neared him, I sensed Maxi beside me getting ready to run, and I put a hand on his shoulder, mainly because I had images of all these nice churchgoing folk turning on us like the mob in that old movie *Invasion of the Body Snatchers* if we tried to run. Instead, we reached the Pastor, and he turned those red eyes on us, and the stench of death (which he'd at least tried to cover with some cheap cologne) nearly gagged me.

"Well," he said, and his smile was rotting, too, "these must be our two visitors. Now, let's see: you'd be Kevin, and this is Maxi."

Thankfully he didn't extend a hand. I felt Maxi draw closer to me (and this is a tough little kid), and I had to work hard to manufacture a smile. "Wow, I guess word travels fast in a small town, huh?"

"Actually, we have an online forum, and not much else to talk about." His voice was still deep and smooth, and I thought this guy had probably been a pretty dynamic speaker when he'd been alive. But most of the intelligent zombies out there aren't nice; they still look at us first and foremost as food, and they're smart enough to grab the knife and fork and before we even know it they're cutting chunks out of us. We're kind of like Big Macs that are dimly related to them, I guess.

But this Pastor Winn had been in town for a while and hadn't eaten the population, obviously, so there was something else going on. Were they feeding him from their livestock? I'd heard of the zombies eating non-human animals, too, although they didn't enjoy it.

"Well, we're running a little late, so if you'll excuse me . . . I hope we can chat more after the services, Mr. Moon." He smiled and went into the church.

"He's amazing," Stacey whispered next to us.

Maxi and I followed her into the church, which was packed to capacity; they'd obviously added benches along the walls and we had to squeeze into the last spots available. That bench wasn't comfortable and neither was I, but the attitude in the room was pleasant, even kind of excited, as if it was a concert or something that was about to start.

It looked like a pretty ordinary church, for the most part: pews and benches taking up the floor, a little raised area at the front, some pretty stained glass windows showing angels behind it, a big metal and wood cross behind the pastor. The only weird thing I noticed was something mounted diagonally against the cross — it looked like a spear, about ten feet long with a pointed and stained metal end. I knew there was a legend about Christ being jabbed with a spear, so I guessed it was related to that somehow.

The pastor took to the stage (or whatever they call it — is it a stage in a church?) and started. The first few minutes were more town meeting than sermon, with shout-outs to some of those present ("Happy Birthday to MaryEllen Johnston — how many years have you been 39, MaryEllen?" or "I understand that Bill Arnheim harvested our first hothouse tomato this week — well done, Bill!"). Then came the religious stuff; the theme of the preaching was hard work, and it was all the pretty standard mix of Bible quotes and self-affirmation suggestions. I was practically nodding out when he said something that made my head jerk right back up. He was talking about Jesus and he referred to "that seed of resurrection He planted in so many of our brothers and sisters."

Huh? Now, like I said, you know I wasn't exactly a Theology major in college, but that sure as shit didn't sound like any religion I knew of.

Then the bomb dropped.

This is what I think he said; I've probably missed a word or two, but overall this kind of seared itself into my brain. "In 2 Thessalonians," he said, behind his podium, "we read, 'if anyone is not willing to work, let him not eat'. And I know some of you might hear that and wonder about our resurrected kin wandering the wasteland out there — the 'infected', as they are called. They don't work, and yet they demand to eat, so how can they be the holiest of holies? Because, my friends, they are beyond work. We know that each of them carries that little piece of Christ's resurrection, and so they are sacred. 'Then Jesus said to them, *Most assuredly, I say to you, unless you eat the flesh of the Son of Man and drink His blood, you have no life in you.*' They are each a walking embodiment of our Savior. You must toil to serve God, but they have given of themselves and moved beyond that, to a state of risen grace."

Do you get it, Scotty? *They think every zombie is a little part of Jesus Christ.*

Jesus Christ.

But that was nothing compared to what came next. He finished the sermon, said, "And now it's time for collection," and stepped down from the stage.

Two boys came up beside him. One had a big huge platter, like the kind you'd put a turkey on. The other had a basket full of something I couldn't see from the back of the church.

I expected everyone to take out their wallets (which, of course, is stupid now that I type that — who'd have wallets in a barter system?). But the good citizens of Peetersville all took off their jackets. Their arms were bare underneath, and I saw that all of them were layered in red stripes and first aid.

The pastor, moving between the two boys, approached the nearest aisle of parishioners and he held out a knife. The first man in the aisle was tall and middle-aged, with the lined face of a farmer, someone who'd spent a lifetime outdoors. He took the knife, extended his other arm, and cut out a spoonful-sized piece of flesh. He dropped his flesh offering onto the plate, and took one of the paper-wrapped packages from the other boy's basket.

Of course — they were Band-Aids.

"What the fuck . . ." I said, probably more loudly than I intended.

Stacey whispered, "Kevin, *please* don't use that kind of language here."

"You're all cutters!"

Stacey squirmed. "It's not like that — we're not teenagers. It's the offering for Pastor Winn."

I looked back at the zombie handing his flock a knife, and I understood why he hadn't eaten the local population. Because he *had*. He'd just figured out a way to do it so that he'd have a never-ending food source, offered up in reverence to him every Sunday.

"We're going now." I grabbed Maxi, who was too freaked out to say anything or resist. There was a side door near us. I took it. I heard some whispers behind us, and Stacey cried out, "*Kevin—*!"

The side door opened onto a walkway that went to other buildings, probably meeting rooms or offices for the church. I was so pissed off I got turned around and stormed off toward the back of the church, dragging Maxi along with me. We passed a parking lot and a cluster of trees, we turned left at the last building . . .

And we froze as we saw the source of that moaning sound.

The area behind the church was bordered with a neat little white post fence. Beyond the fence was a meadow, with low yellow grass and trees sprinkled around the edge.

In the meadow were dozens of crucifixes, big massive wooden things standing straight up. Nailed by hand and foot to the crucifixes were zombies. Mostly naked, just wearing filthy rags around their midsections. All moaning.

There was a light breeze, the direction shifted, and the stink of all that decaying flesh and agony hit us, and I doubled over and rolfed up all that good food they'd served us yesterday.

When it was over, I looked up and saw that Maxi had found a gate in the fence and was walking up to the nearest crucifix. "*Maxi*—!" I cried out, even though the thing hanging there couldn't hurt him. I ran through the gate and up to the boy, who'd stopped and was standing still, staring up.

The zombie hadn't just been nailed to the wood; sturdy cable had been used to bind its arms to the crossbeam. I guess zombies don't think twice about ripping a nail through their own hand to escape.

But they couldn't move this way; they could only hang there and suffer.

Now, I've heard lots of zombies moan in my time, Scotty; they moan when they're hungry (which is pretty much all the time), and when they're frustrated . . . but I'd never heard any of them moan like this.

These things were in terrible pain.

Yes, even zombies can feel excruciating pain, despite what you might have heard in media hype. Dozens of them, scattered around that meadow, hanging from those crosses . . . who knew how long they'd been there . . .

"Christmas," said Maxi.

"What?" Like I've said before, the kid's a genius. He's way ahead of me most of the time.

"Christmas. It's in a few days' time. That's why they did this, I'll bet."

I almost said, "It makes sense" . . . and then realized how that sounded. Sure, crucifying zombies to celebrate Christmas because your undead preacher told you they each carried some tiny spark of the birth and resurrection of the Christ-child made perfect sense.

Maxi kept staring, and I realized that he and I had never really discussed religion. Heck, his parents might have been practicing Catholics. This shit might have meant something more to him.

"And they stabbed each one in the side, probably with that spear in the church."

I looked where he was looking, and sure enough — the zombie that hung above us had a ragged gash in his torso, just below the rib cage. They all did, all — what, forty? Fifty? *He who eats My flesh and drinks My blood abides in Me, and I in him* . . .

I grabbed Maxi's hand. "C'mon. We're going." I started to turn to lead him out of there . . .

Stacey and the pastor stood at the gate. Most of the congregation was milling around behind them, watching us. There was no way around them or through them, so I'd have to talk our way out.

"Look, we just want to leave in peace."

Pastor Winn tilted his peeling head toward Maxi. "'We'? Are you sure you speak for both of you?"

Stacey took a step forward. "Maxi, you could have a home here with us. We can care for you better."

My blood froze. I saw in that instant that they intended to keep Maxi. I didn't know whether they'd let me go or not, but they sure weren't turning Maxi loose.

He didn't say anything, but he looked up at me and squeezed my hand.

It was enough.

"He's not staying. He's coming with me."

Pastor Winn fixed his bloody eyes on me and said, "The likes of you have no place in caring for a boy."

Ahh, there it was. I should have known.

I considered the situation. We couldn't fight or run or negotiate. That left only surrender . . . or deception.

I let my shoulders sag, then I knelt down before Maxi, hoping that he'd clue in to what was going on. "They're right, Maxi. You should stay here. This isn't the place for me, but . . ."

I saw tears starting in his eyes, and realized he didn't get it. There had to be something I could say, something that he would get but they wouldn't.

"Remember that promise I made you when we left Washington, about how I'd find you the right home someday?" I'd made no such promise. I saw confusion cross his face for a second, then — hallelujah, he got it. He nodded, gulping.

"Well, I think maybe this is it."

The kid was good, Scotty — he suddenly threw his arms around my neck in a perfect mimicry of a teary goodbye. I returned the gesture.

When we finished the hug, I stood up, pretended to wipe tears away, and walked toward Stacey. "He doesn't have much, but there are a few things of his still in the car . . ."

The look on her face was so joyful that I felt bad about what we were doing . . . but not *that* bad. "Of course," she said. I walked toward her and past her, apparently heading for the car. The congregation separated. Were they really going to let me go?

A hand clamped down on my shoulder. I turned, and there was Pastor Winn right behind me. "You're doing the right thing, son," he said. When he grinned, there were flecks of flesh in his chipped, yellowed teeth. "I pray that God will show you the way out of sin and you'll come to Him."

I tried to nod and not shiver.

Fortunately he didn't follow me to the car, but Stacey, Maxi, and Nate did. I opened it and dug out Maxi's little backpack. There was nothing in it but two shirts, another pair of jeans, a beat-up copy of his favorite book (*The Grapes of Wrath*), and a crinkled old photo of him with his sister, now a zombie somewhere in L.A. I handed the pack to him. "Here you go." I also pulled out a crate of batteries; it was more than I'd intended to offer, but given the circumstances I figured dickering was a bad idea. "And this is my end of our bargain."

Nate took the batteries. I saw his eyes move to the three other crates stacked in the back of my SUV, and my stomach shot into my throat. I really thought I was done.

Instead he thanked me for the batteries, and then added, "I'll see you to the gate so I can lock it behind you."

The rest of my exit from Peetersville was uneventful
. . . provided you can call being so tense you can
barely move "uneventful". But they did let me go,
and I didn't exhale until my foot was on the
accelerator and I saw Nate rolling that gate shut in
my rearview mirror.

I drove until I passed that little rise that hid the
town from view of oncoming traffic, then I took the
first turn I came to. It was a right. I drove a mile
or so and turned right at another street, this one
little more than an unpaved track running between
abandoned fields.

I drove until I could just make out the Peetersville
fence in the distance. I was far away from the
entrance, and hoped no one would spot me here. I
turned off the engine and settled in to wait.

And that's where I am now, Scotty. Typing this to
pass the time until the sun sets. Once night is
here, I'll walk the half-mile or so to the fence
with the bolt-cutters I've got in the back, clip a
nice hole in the chain link, sneak in, get Maxi out
of that house, and hit the road. With any luck, they
won't find out until morning.

'Course my luck hasn't been great lately, has it?

I'll fill you in tomorrow, Scotty. I like to imagine
you're holed up in L.A. somewhere, dressing the tree
for Christmas, reading these messages and just
hanging on my every word . . . instead of long dead
or beyond caring what happens to me.

Okay, it's now sixteen hours after my last message, and here's how it went down:

I waited until about three hours after sundown; my experience the night before had told me that the good folks of Peetersville all hit the sack pretty early. I was hoping they'd all be snoozing away by the time I arrived with my trusty bolt-cutters.

I made it through the field (although I did it in darkness and tripped a few times), and reached the fence. It wasn't easy to snip through, but I only had to cut a few of the links until I had a sizable enough flap I was able to pull back enough to crawl through. I even wrestled it back into place from the other side, in case anyone happened to come along (which was pretty unlikely, but better safe than sorry).

I was in somebody's backyard. I jogged across an overgrown lawn and came to a wooden gate. I opened it carefully, wincing once at a squeaky hinge, then stepped through and walked quickly down one of Peetersville's residential streets. I thought I was about two blocks from Stacey's.

Nobody saw me, and I made it to her place. I ran up to the window of the room where Maxi had stayed the night before, hoping that my instincts were right and she'd given her new son her old son's room. I pulled the screen away and wrapped softly on the glass; then I waited, holding my breath.

A few seconds later the window slid up, and there was Maxi, with his little backpack. He didn't say a word to me; we didn't need to talk. We just needed to go.

Except we didn't go. I started back the way I'd come, but Maxi tugged me in the opposite direction. "No, this way."

"Maxi," I whispered, "the car is *that* way."

"I know, but . . ." He didn't finish, but instead inclined his head toward the sound.

That fucking sound. Those poor tortured animals in that meadow behind the church. You know how when you live in a city, there's always a low level of sound, even in the middle of the night — the constant hum of traffic, of life? This was the constant hum of misery and death.

I looked at Maxi, and I knew what he wanted, because I wanted it, too. No, not wanted — *had to do.*

"I don't know how . . ."

Maxi got my meaning. "I've been thinking about it — use that spear in the church. It's long enough."

I remembered; that spear that was up against the cross on the dais. It had to be the same one they'd used to pierce each of the poor bastards' sides. "Yeah, that'll work. Okay."

We ran silently through the night, to the church. I tried the main door, and it was unlocked. Of course it was; there was no crime in the good church-going community of Peetersville.

We used our flashlight to pick our way past the empty pews; I tried not to shudder when the beam picked out dark stains on the wood. We reached the front, and I handed the flashlight and the bolt-cutters to Maxi while I jumped up and grabbed the spear. I expected it to be either impossible to remove or a flimsy, useless prop, but it was solid and real, and held in place with no more than some guide-hooks. I slid it out and hefted it. "This'll work," I told Maxi.

I jumped down from the dais and we were heading for the side door when a voice stopped us. "That would be acting against the will of God, you know."

We turned and saw the good Pastor Winn approaching us from the rear of the church. His eyes glinted red in our light. I held the spear out defensively. I wasn't sure I could use it on an intelligent zombie, but if he made a move toward Maxi we'd find out.

I asked, "What are you talking about?"

Winn stopped maybe six feet away, just close enough that we could smell him. "The people of Peetersville are waiting for the crucified ones to die. When final death comes, the bodies will be carted off to achieve their real resurrection and ascend to Heaven. Since we don't have a cave, an abandoned grain silo will be used."

"And what were they going to do when the bodies just rot in that silo?"

"You're not a believer, Mr. Moon. You couldn't understand."

"You're right, I'm not a believer — if subjecting dumb animals to torture and mutilation is part of your belief."

"It's what the Christ-child endured."

"Yeah, well, I don't give a fuck what bullshit you've gotten these people to believe in order to get them to feed you parts of themselves. Those things out in that field aren't Christ, and they're in pain, and this is over now."

"I taught these people how to *survive*."

"You mean you figured out a way to exploit them so *you* could survive."

The pastor took one step forward, said my name, started to reach out to Maxi . . .

And I jammed that spear right through one of his bloody eyes.

His mouth dropped open in surprise, and then he collapsed, pulling the spear down with him. I yanked it free, and paused just long enough to make sure he was dead. Maxi stared until I said, "Come on."

We went out into the meadow.

It took about an hour. Maxi held the light while I jabbed right up through the chin into the brain of each one of them. We were careful not to get splattered. We didn't bother to try and get them down once we were done; we just made sure they weren't suffering any longer.

Whoever eats My flesh and drinks My blood has eternal life, and I will raise him up at the last day.

There were 48 of them. When we were finished, I tossed the spear aside and looked down at Maxi. "What do you notice?"

He thought for a moment, and then said, "The night's so quiet."

"Yeah. Which means we probably need to get out of here before somebody else wakes up and realizes that."

We ran.

We made it back to the SUV before sunrise. By the time we reached it, we were both staggering with exhaustion, but I knew we couldn't stay. I gunned the engine, turned the car around, found the Interstate and headed west again.

We drove for two hours, until I couldn't hold my head up any longer. We pulled off the freeway and took shelter beneath an overpass; the area seemed deserted, and if they were coming after us they couldn't see us down there.

That's where we are now, Scotty. I wanted to type this out while it was still clear, before I fall asleep and awake to convince myself it was just all some terrible dream, with the memory already fading.

I know I'm typing this for me, not you. I'm putting it down because I feel bad about killing Winn, who really had saved the people of Peetersville; and I feel bad for Stacey, who may never have the love of a child again. Or maybe this is really for Maxi, so he'll have a record of it, if he starts to forget.

I know you're dead. I hope you're *really* dead, and not shambling along forever in search of food that never satisfies you . . . or worse, used as a pawn in some freak's power scheme. Mainly I just hope you're at peace.

I think we are now.

See you soon.

Love,
Kevin (and Maxi)

Moreby: ". . . So you made it. I'll check out the record on the camera. I imagine you think you're safe now?"

2nd Moreby: "Well - since you are evidently myself, and you are apparently in command in this . . . this fortress of the future—"

Moreby: "Indeed, but it took much planning to get this far. And it finished with this . . ."

[The image moves to reveal a corpse lying on the bloodstained carpet of the Oval Office. "President" Moreby turns it over with his foot. What remains of the head rolls back and reveals the face. It is the same as that of the two men in the room.]

2nd Moreby: "He is you. And me . . ."

Moreby: "He claimed to be our descendent in these Colonies. Or maybe a Moreby from another timeline. The original, perhaps. If there is such a thing."

2nd Moreby: "How did he perish?"

Moreby: "If you must know, I cracked his skull like a chicken's egg and ate his brain. I *became* him. Will I become twice as intelligent, twice me? It is worth the experiment. But that is a treat for later.

Now listen to me. Once I was you. Once I emerged from the tomb in London, all but naked as you are, and flew through time to this place. Where I was met by him. And was thrown back in time. He sent me back because there was a great deal to be done in the past, a kind of rebuilding, before this glorious triumph could come to pass.

"Well, I did as he asked, and I waited out the centuries - it was *me* who met you at the crypt, Moreby - and then when the time was right I came here - for him. I knew where to find him after all. And I killed him because he did to me then what I must do to you now.

"Which is where you come in . . . But before you can get to be me, I need you to go build this great enterprise."

⟦He holds up a business card. Clearly legible is: T.J. MOERBITZ, NEW WORLD PHARMACEUTICALS GROUP.⟧

2nd Moreby: "Build it? But where, how?"

Moreby: "Where? Back, of course. Back in time, back into history. How? Worlds within worlds, Moreby. Think of time like a continuous strip of paper with a single twist in it - a two-dimensional surface with only one side, thanks to a twist in the third dimension. Now think about the past and future travelling around and around the surface of that paper in one continuous line, seeking an end, but with no border to separate the two sides.

"I have already done what you are to do. And who knows how many before *me*. It took me centuries to replicate - and *improve* upon -

Leonardo's *Macchina*, but in the end I succeeded. I had it installed in that conceited woman's mausoleum at Brompton Cemetery, ready for your arrival, with the co-ordinates pre-set to bring you to this very place at this precise time.

"That is how I knew that you would be able to solve the puzzle – the cemetery, the code, Bonomi's grave. I knew, because I had done it all already. And you will have plenty of time to work it all out. Oh, but first I will take this . . ."

⟦He grabs the back of the other Moreby's neck, forks his fingers into the left eye socket, and plucks out the eye. As the newcomer screams, blood pouring from the socket, we see at the edge of frame that the "President" has lifted his eye patch and is pushing the eye into the hole in his own face.⟧

Moreby: "Back you go. The clock will be re-set, and you will create yet another new timeline – where once again our New Zombie Order shall rise up to conquer the world and reach out to the stars beyond . . . Oh, and do not forget the card."

⟦He shoves the NWP business card edgeways into the empty eye socket of the other Moreby, then spins him around, pushes him against the stone pillar, and forces his hands onto the handles of the monolith . . . There is an explosion of light, and the surveillance feed abruptly cuts out.⟧

⟦*Video clip ends.*⟧

Hello Mum,

It feels strange to be e-mailing you,
not least because I realise now that
it's something I should have done far
more often in the past. The phone's all
very well but I always finish a call
feeling I've got side-tracked and missed
the chance to say anything in particular;
and also that words, when they've been
said aloud, have a way of falling apart
and dissolving afterwards, becoming lost
and left behind in ways that thoughts
set down on paper never do.
Perhaps that's just the lawyer in me
talking. Get it down, make it binding,
make it *real* (and then bill by the hour,
naturally). But I don't believe so. I
think this is why we started to paint
and write in the first place, why we
treasure old letters and notes, why the
idea of a person's signature still means
something even now so much has become
virtual and digital. We trust in the
things we can reach out and touch. We
try to make our ideas and emotions as
concrete as things are in real life, to
stop the past breaking apart like a
flock of birds. Maybe that's what I'm
actually missing, if I'm honest. When
you and dad told us you'd decided to
retire to Florida, Karen burst into
tears but I was all, "Yes, what the
hell, go where it's warm, play golf,
drink margaritas, you've earned
it . . ." — because I felt that's what
you needed to hear — and maybe I didn't
think hard enough about what *I'd* be
losing, looking back. Yes, we talked

every week, of course, and I've been out to Sarasota many times, but it's not the same, is it? I'm old enough now to understand that the house in Dulwich was just one of several to you and dad, not the forge of life and crucible of childhood it was for me and Karen. However, I also now realise that we can Skype all we like but it's never going to be the same as turning up at that house, chucking my coat on a chair and strolling straight into the kitchen to find you already warming the pot — ready for us to start up the same old conversations in the same old places, drinking tea from the same old mugs. Perhaps by the age of forty-one I should have moved beyond the need for those kind of physical comforts, but I haven't. Maybe no one ever does, and it's just that we all grow-up and move and die and there comes a point where you can't do those things any more — and so you pretend it doesn't matter because no one wants to start every day in tears.

But . . . anyway. I'm writing to you now.

This whole farrago is supposed to honour the past, of course, as well as treasuring the present and looking forward to the future. That was the sell, the spin. But I remember dad explaining to me a long time ago (during the slog toward O-Level History, I assume) what the expression "bread and circuses" meant, and that's all the HS4 rail link actually is, or has ever been: smoke and mirrors, a cynical attempt to pretend the country wasn't sinking into the swamp, that the recession + the sodding government hadn't effectively bounced us back to the 1950s. I'm not even sure *who* they are trying to kid. The Americans? Europe? People on Mars? If you're living in the UK there's no way you can miss what's been happening — from the pushing through of the Police Special Powers Act to the subsequent massacre in Leicester Square. That is unless, of course, you're really, really stupid — which sadly, a lot of people are. The papers have been full of it since the day HS4 was announced. Some days it's the only story in town (which, of course, was the point of it in the first place). Furrow-browed analysis of how much celebration there'll be when the two countries are linked by high-speed rail, in newspapers pandering to middle-Englanders whose minds and horizons are too small to be seen by the naked eye. In-depth exposés in the "qualities", pontificating about who's taking back-handers and creaming profits off the top (politicians and building contractors, you'll not be surprised to hear) and whether sufficient attention will be paid to off-setting the carbon debt . . . Posturing to their demographic, in other words, while making no real difference to anything at all. And, of course, endless breathless speculation *everywhere* over which "celebs" might deign to travel on it — not to mention a special "reality talent show" to pick who sings the national anthem at the opening ceremony (for God's sake!).

Bread and circuses, smoke and mirrors. An endless "silly season", an attempt to generate enough white noise to mask the sound of the country crumbling around us. I once described it to Zoe as fiddling while England burned. It was funny then. I can see the skyline through my window as I type this letter, and it's not funny now.

I was making a concerted effort to tune the whole bloody thing out until about three weeks ago, when Zoe came stomping into the kitchen one lunchtime ranting about something she'd just caught on Radio 4 — a breezy mention that pre-construction work was starting on one of the HS4 sites — which basically boiled down to cheerfully destroying the grounds and graveyard of St. Botolph's in the City. I suppose I must already have been missing you and dad more than I'd realised, because — even though I'd totally forgotten the church existed, if I'm honest — suddenly it all came back. I remembered how you used to drive us up to take us on walks across Greenwich Park on day trips to mooch around the Royal Observatory, and then north in a cab over the river, with lunch always in that Garfunkel's near Carnaby Street and a toy from Hamleys if we were good.

It all seems like a very long time ago now — but when I heard about the destruction of the graveyard it came crashing back, along with another memory (one which I'd revisited more recently, in fact): that of dad explaining to me about death one morning on one of these walks, standing looking through the railings at St. Botolph's, at the

graveyard with its old and tilted stones.
I think it was pretty soon after Nana had
died, and I'd always got on really well
with her, and so dad explained (as best
you can, to an eight-year-old child) why I
would never see Nana again except in my
mind, and how sometimes that just had to
be enough. He crouched down next to me to
explain this and he was calm and measured
and (I realise now) very, very strong,
given we were talking about *his mother*,
and she was only about two weeks dead.
Even Karen seemed to absorb the ideas in a
positive way, when (as you know) my
darling sister had a tendency to stomp on
the melodrama pedal even back then. I
recall glancing up to see you standing
behind him, your hand gentle on his
shoulder as he spoke.

And standing there in the kitchen with Zoe I
remembered, too, what it had felt like years
later when I went away to college. Being away
from home, finally having to lift my head
from the meadows of childhood to take a look
at the adult world with its long roads and
dark alleys and mountains and broken bridges
and rainbows and big skies. Alone for the
first time in my life — with no one standing
behind me, hand on my shoulder, letting me
know I was being looked after. And yet . . .
I knew that you *were* still there, both of
you, and that I need never look through any
of life's fences alone.

Anyway. I found myself suddenly furious. I
couldn't believe that the government and
their familiars were allowed to just start
digging up a churchyard — *our* churchyard,
as I now thought of it, (ridiculously, I

know) — and I decided Zoe and I had to do something, and do it right away. That's something else I got from you and dad, I suppose, for better or worse — from the CND marches you hauled us on, the anti-apartheid protests, all that. The belief that everyone *can* do something about *everything*. Not anything big, perhaps — but *something*. A conviction that although it's easy to think the world has become too big and complex to affect, turned into an unstoppable train travelling too hard and fast through the night for any individual to stand a chance of making a difference . . . actually we still can.

So we got our coats on and went over there. We found nothing in the way of organised protest when we arrived: just a few old codgers hanging about in a vaguely indignant way — the kind of people you'd *expect* to see protesting at the digging up of the grounds of an old, forgotten church in the middle of London. (Sorry, no offence meant, I realise you technically reached "codger" status some years ago, but you know the kind of oldsters I mean. The dusty kind.)

I got talking to a middle-aged academic type. Some kind of professor. She had a bee in her bonnet about something to do with the history of the St. Botolph's site, and got very excited when I let slip that I was a lawyer. She seemed to have more indignation at her disposal than actual evidence, however, and warning bells went off for me when she started banging on about plague pits and some disciple of Nicholas Hawksmoor (you remember, the 18th century architect, a pupil of Christopher Wren). People have got it into their heads that Hawksmoor was one step away from a black magician (the Ackroyd novel is partly to blame, and the admittedly odd architectural style of Hawksmoor's churches, but it can't just be that) — and as soon as you hear someone conjure the guy's name — or that of one of his followers — it's a fair chance you're dealing with a nutter, or at the very least someone who's put two-and-two together to make five. That's what I thought, anyway, and so I made my excuses and backed away, and she pretty quickly understood I was going to be no help and shook her head and hurried off. Just before she turned the corner I saw her glance back, and in her face I thought I saw the look of someone who was on the verge of becoming very gently unhinged.

I was wrong. I realise now that it was *fear*. I think back and wish I'd read the woman's face better at the time. The past is not some idyll where everything was simpler and better and blessed with the soft sunlight of childhood afternoons — creatures with big, sharp teeth live back there, too. I had a brief affair a few years back, for example. (I know this is *way* too much information in a mother-son email, but I'm putting it down anyway.) It didn't last long and I ended it myself, before I'd even had to admit to Zoe what was happening. Why? Because though the "now" of it was fun, I knew it would never stack up against all the yesterdays — and tomorrows — of the relationship I already had, and which I wanted to keep.

For one night and a few afternoons I forgot myself, that's all. I forgot myself, got lost in time.

I *got something wrong*, is what it boiled down
to, but on that occasion at least I had the
chance to put it right. Zoe and I had our
problems at the time (it happened soon after
our fifth failed IVF, when the curtain came
down on all that and neither of us were sure
what the hell we were going to do with our
lives); but "now" is not the only game in
town, just like the "truth" is not always the
thing that must be told. What's gone before is
still here. The past hangs around us, inside
us: like our clothes; like our lies; like our
bones. The past is what holds you up to face
the future, too, but when you find you can't
have children — what do you do? Where's your
road to what's coming up? How do you keep
being part of *something*? You do it through
trying to keep staying part of the flow, I
suppose, though trying *not* to be one of those
middle-aged buffoons who stop understanding
anything or liking anything new; who step off
the moving walkway of the now and retire to
yesteryear, to carp and moan about all the
things they don't understand.

Anyway. Zoe and I hung around the church for a
while, looking disapproving, but it didn't
seem like much was actually happening, and
there was no one to give a piece of our mind
too, so in the end . . . Well, we left, and
went and had a nice ploughman's lunch at a pub
on the Thames. Not exactly a protest to be
celebrated in legend and song, I'll admit,
hardly the '68 Paris riots or Greenham Common
II . . . but there just didn't seem much else
we could actually *do* — on that day, anyway.
And it got us out of the house and having
lunch together, at least, which was nice.
Remember the first time you met Zoe? I'm sure

you do. That was a pub lunch too, up in
Highgate. Dad took to her immediately, but I
could tell from your face or body language
when we left that you didn't quite approve,
or weren't convinced . . . Yet. But you'd
been that way with girlfriends before (admit
it), and I was never sure whether it was a
genuine take on the girl in question or
merely you being generically protective. You
came round to Zoe pretty quickly in the end.
How could you not?

Ten days have passed. More crapulent
newspaper coverage of HS4, and amidst the
fluff and nonsense, I spotted a tiny piece
about a patch of Hampstead Heath (which has
been protected ground for centuries, of
course, the biggest patch of wild countryside
in any city in the world) that had somehow
been co-opted to the project and was about to
have a huge tunnel built underneath it. I
realised then that St. Botolph's was *not* a
one-off, that the government truly was
prepared to stomp all over London's history
for their overpriced high-speed rail link to
the North, and it infuriated me to realise
how people just don't understand the past any
more. Attention spans have shrunk to nothing
— but not just in the obvious way, the kind
of thing dad and I have happily moaned about
since I became old enough to realise the
Younger Generation isn't just a phrase but a
fact. I don't mean all the usual guff about
MTV and video games and information being cut
up into tiny chunks for tiny minds. I've
watched the children of our friends playing
video games, for hours upon end, and I know
they *can* focus on something when they choose

to. It's more that history, *time itself*, has become truncated, advert-breaked, atomised. People simply can't understand the continuum of experience any more. Anything before the 1950s is black and white and I-don't-know and I-don't-care unless it has to do with Hitler or the Pharaohs. So why would they care about some old church, and the bodies buried there? Or get worked up about some patch of countryside that people just, like, walk around? Dead, dusty words blown away in the wind. People don't honour the past because they don't understand how *real* it was, how *written down in acts*, that it was as genuine and rich and dangerous as today. That the people in that shadowy dream we call the past ate and drank as we do, that they slept with each other and loved and murdered and lied, and that they did other things whose echo still sounds, hundreds of years after they've died.

And that made me angry, and galvanised us both. The funny thing is that maybe, if we *had* been able to have kids, we wouldn't be going back there now. Maybe little Ethan or Madeline (the names we'd chosen, but didn't get to use) would need to be picked up from school or driving to some after-class activity and we wouldn't have to be there when they start digging up the bodies. Wouldn't have to see the shards of ancient coffins, or the skeletal shapes in tatters of shrouds yanked unceremoniously from the ground.

But we *are* going back there now to join people like us — people with banners and placards who, despite the huge numbers of police who will be there (many carrying automatic weapons), are seriously unhappy about what is happening and what it represents. Unhappy . . . And maybe even disturbed.

We know from the TV news that there are also a lot more police and army, forming a defensive cordon around the excavations. Many of them are armed, despite looking little more than teenagers. I noticed they appeared nervous, as if something has already happened that had them seriously spooked.

I don't know what will happen, what the future holds for us, but I *do* know that we have to make a stand now or else see our history erased forever. And we simply can't allow that. So as soon as I send you this email, Zoe and I are heading out to join the other protestors at St. Botolph's. I'm sure that everything will be okay, and we will be back in a few hours and I will send you another quick email to let you know that we are home safely.

But just in case something *does* go wrong, if something unexpected occurs and, for whatever reason, we get caught up in it, then I just wanted you to know I'll always have you in my mind, and

I love you.

HS4 UNEARTHS "4,000 CORPSES"

High-Speed Rail Project Reveals Burial Ground Mystery

NATHANIAL GRAINGER-SMITH
EVENING STANDARD TRANSPORT
EDITOR

THOUSANDS of bodies buried under the City of London are being unearthed by HS4 rail tunnelling work.

The remains have been discovered a few feet beneath the Liverpool Street station site by workers building a utility tunnel.

Museum of London archaeologist Charles Bainbridge, who is helping to oversee excavations, said: "Thousands of commuters head to work every day from Liverpool Street station, unaware that they've been walking around on bodies from one of the densest burial grounds in the country. It is a veritable city of the dead down there."

Prime Minister Boris Johnson's controversial HS4 project was given the go-ahead despite objections from environmental campaigners and after the Supreme Court dismissed claims that the UKIP government was cutting corners to rush the "unnecessary" project through parliament. Protesters claim that the cash for HS4 would be better spent on improving existing railways and crumbling infrastructure.

The £150 billion high-speed rail link will eventually link Penzance in Cornwall with Inverness in the Republic of Scotland, resulting in huge economic benefits for both countries the government claims. First-stage tunnelling is taking place beneath some of London's oldest and most densely populated sections.

The many hundreds of skeletons were found in a two-acre pit that is originally believed to have been dug in the mid-17th century by order of the mayor after parish graveyards became greatly overfilled.

The remains – many of them preserved in remarkable condition – were uncovered in the sediment of the historic channel of the River Walbrook, which flowed beneath the burial ground for Bedlam, the notorious lunatic asylum run in the early 19th century by the infamous Jacob Sims.

HS4 archaeologist Jason Carver estimated that more than 4,000 bodies could be revealed and appealed for public help in identifying them, as the names are scattered in parish records across London.

"This is a fascinating and unexpected discovery," he said. "It is one of the most diverse burial grounds in London, a real cross-section of its people across hundreds of years, and you don't get to dig that up normally."

Over two centuries plague victims would often be buried next to the rich, poor, young, old, mental health patients and other citizens whose corpses were never claimed by their families. In many cases, the skeletons were thought to have been prisoners, with evidence of starvation and beatings.

However, preliminary forensic examinations of some of the shattered skulls and bone fragments found in the pit not only failed to determine an exact dating of the remains, but also seems to indicate the presence of human tooth marks. This has given rise to the possibility that some of the people whose bodies were buried there may have exhibited cannibalistic tendencies.

Local historian Professor Margaret Winn has her own theories about the bite marks: "There are numerous legends surrounding this area of the City of London," she explained. "An architect named Thomas Moreby, who was denounced for Satanic practises back in the early 19th century, was responsible for constructing the tunnels and catacombs that run beneath St. Botolph-without-Bishopsgate church, and there have been recorded sightings of Roman soldiers appearing and disappearing through walls there dating back centuries.

"As you know, building of the Liverpool Street station started in the mid-1800s on the site of the Bethlem Royal Hospital, which is better known today under its popular nickname of Bedlam, which has long been synonymous with madness and lunacy. It is not unreasonable to suppose that many of the poor wretches who were incarcerated within its bleak and hopeless walls were eventually forced to consume human flesh to survive."

Archaeologists also admit to being baffled by the discovery of a recent model mobile phone, which was reportedly excavated from the mud at the same level as the human remains were discovered.

Although the Museum of London will now analyse the finds, the phone itself will be sent away for testing.

"It is more than likely that the smart phone we discovered in the same area as the bones was probably dropped there accidentally by one of the workers on the site," said Jason Carver. "It's no great mystery, but we are going to have the SIM card examined to see if we can trace the original owner."

CGHQ

From: Historic Retrieval Group, GCHQ Cheltenham
To: All departments (BCC)
Subject: Sony ZA Phone
Status: Restricted
Date: October 31, 2014

Further to our earlier report, we can now confirm that the smartphone found at the Liverpool Street site is of a recent style and make.

However, that does not explain why our radiocarbon dating tests have so far failed to give us any information as to how old the object is or where it came from. The appearance and condition of the phone would seem to indicate that it has been in the ground for a very long time, which is obviously impossible given the fact that the manufacturer has confirmed that this particular model has only been in production for the past year or so.

Attempts to extract any information from the phone have also been extremely difficult, given the fragile nature of the casing and the fact that the SIM card was badly corroded, no doubt due to the strata of ancient river sediment that the device was reportedly discovered in.

After extensive tests, we managed to recover a single text message from the memory card before it disintegrated, but we are no nearer to explaining whom it belongs to or how it came to end up where it did. The message reads as follows:

LISTEN TO ME. WE'RE ALL IN DANGER. CAN'T YOU SEE? THEY'RE AFTER YOU. THEY'RE AFTER ALL OF US. OUR WIVES, OUR CHILDREN, EVERYONE. THEY'RE HERE ALREADY. YOU'RE NEXT. WHATEVER YOU DO, DON'T DIG DOWN BELOW

The message ends there.

We will continue to carry out tests on the apparatus, but at this stage I doubt that it will reveal anything more.

Marcus Layne
Head of Historic Retrieval (South East England)

Zombie Apocalypse! Theme Song
(Sung to the music of "Champion, the Wonder Horse")

Zombie Apocalypse!
Zombie Apocalypse!

When the rotten corpses lay siege to your town
When the running undead disembowel your friends

When a fiery holocaust is raining down
You'll hear the people screaming it's the end
The time will come when everyone will know that it's a Zombie
Apocalypse!
Zombie Apocalypse!

If you feel your skull a-splittin'
And you're doubled up in pain
Then you know it must be Them Zombies
Eatin' out all of your brains

If your guts are on the table
And you're spurtin' from all veins
Then you know it must be Them Zombies
Eatin' out Eatin' out
Eatin' out all of your brains

Zombie Apocalypse!
Zombie Apocalypse!

When the rotten corpses lay siege to your town
When the running undead disembowel your friends

When a fiery holocaust is raining down
You'll hear the people screaming it's the end
The time will come when everyone will know that it's a Zombie
Apocalypse!
Zombie Apocalypse!

ACKNOWLEDGEMENTS

Many thanks to Duncan Proudfoot, Dorothy Lumley, Nicola Chalton, Pascal Thivillon, Joe Roberts, Max Burnell, Clive Hebard, Michael Marshall Smith, Les Edwards, Christopher Fowler, Robert Hood, Reggie Oliver, Sarah Pinborough and all the contributors who found the, er . . . *time* to take us through the Zombie Apocalypse! Special thanks to Robert Bloch, Richard Connell, Philip K. Dick, Hampton Fancher & David Webb Peoples, Jack Finney, Stefan Jaworzyn, Frankie Laine, L.A. Lewis, H.P. Lovecraft, Daniel Mainwaring & Richard Collins, Richard Matheson, Russell Rouse & Clarence Greene, and David A. Sutton, for those who know . . .